Praise for *The Silent Room*

"The explosive opening of *The Silent Room* introduces a gripping thriller with a very human face. Nobody understands the many faces of cops better than Mari Hannah."　—Val McDermid

"A tense and compelling stand-alone thriller from one of our foremost crime writers. This book gripped me from the opening pages and never let go."　—David Jackson

"An author taking a break from a series should revel in the opportunities this offers. With *The Silent Room*, Mari Hannah certainly has. Totally enjoyable on all levels. Great book, great characters, and superb pacing."　—Yrsa Sigurdardóttir

"Mari Hannah has always had two key specialities: a gift for genuinely ingenious plotting matched by a skill at choreographing suspense sequences that is the equal of more stellar names in the genre. Both characteristics are at full stretch in *The Silent Room*, with everyone involved leaping off the page."
—*The Independent* (UK)

"Curiously gripping and enjoyable."　—*Literary Review* (UK)

"Taut storytelling and razor-sharp dialogue . . . make this a novel not to be missed."　—*Daily Mail* (UK)

"[Full of] delicious twists and turns."　—*Sunday Express* (UK)

"A hard-as-nails stand-alone thriller."
—*Peterborough Telegraph* (UK)

"Very creepy. Read it on your commute and you'll be looking over your shoulder all the way home."　—*Marie Claire* (UK)

MARI HANNAH

The Silent Room

Minotaur Books

A Thomas Dunne Book
New York

This is a work of fiction. All of the characters, organizations, and events portrayed in this novel are either products of the author's imagination or are used fictitiously.

A THOMAS DUNNE BOOK FOR MINOTAUR BOOKS. An imprint of St. Martin's Press.

www.thomasdunnebooks.com
www.minotaurbooks.com

Library of Congress Cataloging-in-Publication Data

Names: Hannah, Mari, author.
Title: The silent room : a thriller / Mari Hannah.
Description: First U.S. edition. | New York : Minotaur Books, 2018. | "A Thomas Dunne Book."
Identifiers: LCCN 2017041305 | ISBN 9781250115669 (hardcover) | ISBN 9781250115676 (ebook)
Subjects: | GSAFD: Suspense fiction.
Classification: LCC PR6108.A56 S55 2018 | DDC 823/.92—dc23
LC record available at https://lccn.loc.gov/2017041305

Our books may be purchased in bulk for promotional, educational, or business use. Please contact your local bookseller or the Macmillan Corporate and Premium Sales Department at 1-800-221-7945, extension 5442, or by email at MacmillanSpecialMarkets@macmillan.com.

First published in Great Britain by Macmillan, an imprint of Pan Macmillan

First U.S. Edition: January 2018

10 9 8 7 6 5 4 3 2 1

For Rob and Marit

1

Jason Irwin locked his prison van. No armed escort today. The only copper he'd see for the rest of his shift was securely handcuffed in the back, a disgrace to his profession according to the grapevine, suspended from Special Branch on allegations of misconduct, something to do with illegal firearms. His name was Jack Fenwick.

Flicking away his cigarette, Irwin climbed aboard and fastened his seat belt. Waiting for the thumbs up from security, he rammed the vehicle in gear and pulled away, keen to get rid of his last delivery.

As he cleared the exit gate, he head-checked the road, turning left towards Newcastle Quayside, his eyes scanning the front steps of the Crown Court as he passed by. Outside the sandstone building, a gang of scruffy youths gave him the one-finger salute as he stopped at traffic lights, their eyes full of hatred. Not long ago, Irwin had transported one of the group into the care of Her Majesty – exactly where he belonged, in his opinion.

Loser.

He turned right and immediately put his foot down, watching the group get smaller in his rear-view. Crossing the River Tyne via the Swing Bridge, he drove up a steady incline, following the signs to the south and on through

Gateshead as the autumn drizzle worsened. Not perfect conditions for driving, but hey: he couldn't have everything. It was Friday. Tomorrow he'd be Cyprus bound, spending half-term with his family, a pocketful of euros and nothing to do for two whole weeks.

Irwin made good time. Somewhere close to the border between Tyneside and Durham, the sky darkened and the wind got up. The rain increased in intensity until it was almost impossible to see through the windscreen, even with the wipers on full pelt. Their inability to do the job they were designed for was not lost on his new colleague, Philip Storey.

Storey was a posh boy, a graduate in Roman Archaeology from Durham University. Even with an impressive degree, he'd struggled to find work in his field of expertise. He'd been forced to seek other employment to pay for his flat. The alternative was to go home and live with his parents, a fate worse than death, apparently. They, and he for that matter, thought security work was beneath him. Taken on by the company less than three weeks ago with minimal training, the lad had found fault with everything: the pay and conditions, the early mornings, and currently the state of the wipers, a thin strip of which had broken away and was flapping across the windscreen like a small black eel.

'Welcome to the private sector,' Irwin said.

'You should complain,' Storey grumbled.

'On what grounds?'

'We have a right to health and safety. It's illegal not to

be able to see through the glass.' Storey's tone was flat. Disinterested. 'How long have you been doing this poxy job anyhow?'

'Twelve years, give or take.'

'On fifteen grand?'

'You're doing it.'

'Only as a stop-gap.'

'Don't knock it, son. It puts food on the table.'

As Irwin turned his attention back to the road, a red light forced him to depress the brake pedal. Stopping the van, he glanced at his watch. Right on schedule. He'd make Durham prison by four. He waited for amber, impatient for his shift to end, to be rid of the jumped-up kid sitting by his side. Storey had riled him once too often this week. What was so special about scratching around in the dirt anyhow?

At least his was a proper job.

A dark blue Clio pulled up behind, the volume on its radio turned up so high it could be heard in the next county. The driver was singing along to Coldplay's 'Yellow', his body swaying to the drumbeat. He was wearing a peaked cap and sunglasses. Optimistic, Irwin thought, unless . . .

Too late.

The soundtrack stopped as an Audi A6 overtook at speed, screeching to a halt in front of the prison van, boxing him in. Pressing his alarm, Irwin floored the accelerator, ramming the car. It hardly budged. Selecting reverse gear, he did the same to the Clio behind. He was about to repeat the action when two men emerged from the Audi pointing sawn-off shotguns at his windscreen, gesturing for him to vacate his vehicle.

'Open up!' one yelled.

A foreign voice.

Irwin froze as a young woman moved into his eyeline beyond the man holding the gun, the sound of crunching metal having drawn her attention. Time stood still as she stopped to gawp at the spectacle. When the armed man looked over his shoulder, she sprinted for cover. Irwin couldn't hear himself think due to the racket his cargo was making. Fenwick was banging on the inside of the cab, demanding the low-down on what was going on, begging him to take evasive action. This was serious shit.

Really? Like he didn't know.

In the distance, the running girl stopped. She turned, took out her phone and held it up. What was the mad cow doing? Willing her to get the hell out of there, Irwin yelled at Fenwick to quieten down.

He wasn't helping.

Praying that the Clio would back up, offering him an escape route, Irwin's hopes died as the driver exited his vehicle, leaving the door wide open. Keeping his head beneath the window line, he crawled to the rear of his car on his hands and knees and legged it across the road into woods that ran along the west side of the carriageway. Irwin didn't blame him – given the choice, he'd have done the same.

Realizing they were trapped, Storey began to weep.

Irwin urged him to get a grip. They were going to be fine. He'd get them out of there. Somehow. The words had hardly left his lips when the gun was raised. Both security guards ducked as the windscreen shattered, a large gaping hole appearing at its centre where the shot had pierced the glass. No longer could either guard see their attackers, but they could hear the shooter's instructions to climb down and open up the back, his voice muffled through a balaclava.

'Do it!' Storey yelled. 'It's not worth losing your life for peanuts – or that piece of shit in the back.'

Irwin told him to shut it. 'Do I look stupid to you?'

'No!' Fenwick bawled. 'They'll kill us all.'

'That's helpful, pal,' Irwin yelled back. 'Got any bright ideas? Because, if you do, now's the time to spit 'em out.'

The Special Branch officer's opinion was valid – and probably correct – but then *he* wasn't the one with the gun pointing at his head. His reply was lost in the general mayhem as the passenger door was yanked open. Whimpering in fear, crying for the mother he couldn't stand the sight of, Storey was pulled from the vehicle, the butt end of a gun rammed into his stomach. He dropped to the ground like a stone. With the gun now in his back, he was told to lie face down.

Seconds later, Irwin joined him, thrown with such force, two of his fingers snapped as he hit the deck. Out the corner of his eye, he saw keys dangling from the Clio's ignition. For a split second – no more – he wondered if he could make the car without getting shot in the back. He decided against. He couldn't leave Storey to the mercy of these two. Besides, this was no time to play the hero.

Sucking in a breath, Irwin tried to lower his heart rate.

His chest felt like it might explode. If he were a gambler – which he wasn't – he'd have taken bets that the men in the masks weren't going to kill him. Why bother dragging him out of the van otherwise? Why not shoot him dead in his seat? Still, he decided not to test his theory.

Storey had gone into shock. He was shaking so much his safety helmet was knocking a tune on the road. Irwin wanted to comfort him but didn't dare move. The lad had shut his eyes tightly, expecting to get his head blown off at any second. It unsettled the older man, who had a flash-back of his wife and kids packing suitcases at home, his eldest daughter singing along to 'Yellow' – a bizarre co-incidence.

For a moment, nothing happened. Then Irwin heard the familiar squeak of the van's back door as it was pulled open. With sound but no sight of what was going on, he counted the seconds, his nerve gone completely. No longer sure it wouldn't end there on that wet and deserted stretch of road, he shut his eyes, wondered if he'd hear the shot that killed him.

Idling engines purred . . .

Rain hit the tarmac . . .

Storey vomited.

Flinching as a pair of heavy-duty boots arrived by his side, Irwin exhaled as they moved away again, his stom-ach heaving in relief. A door slammed, then another and another. Expensive. *The Audi.* As it took off at speed, he lifted his head. His prisoner was gone.

2

The events of the past month had caused Detective Sergeant Matthew Ryan a lot of anguish, none of it of his own making. The arrest and detention of his senior officer, Detective Inspector Jack Fenwick, had shaken him to the core. It had come without warning, with no reason given. The first Ryan knew of it was when he received a flying visit from the rubber heelers shortly after five the next morning, the nickname for Professional Standards hardly apt on that occasion. There was no creeping around. No softly-softly approach. In fact, the opposite was true. Their rap on the door of his seaside cottage was so loud it woke half the tiny coastal village of Dunstan Steads.

Ryan asked himself if he'd ever doubted Jack. The truthful answer was yes – but only because he was half asleep when his Northumbria colleagues took *him* in for questioning. After three hours of intense and often hostile interrogation, common sense kicked in. Now he was as convinced as he could be of his DI's innocence.

In the course of his interview, Ryan had learned one or two significant details. Firstly, the allegation that Jack had firearms concealed in his garage had been delivered to the Chief Constable's aide. More importantly, it was acted upon immediately, despite the fact that the intelligence was anonymous and rubbished by those close to the Special Branch officer, an action guaranteed to raise suspicions among those in the know. A warrant was obtained, Jack's home searched – on whose say-so Ryan wasn't sure – but even he had to concede that the evidence was compelling. Guns had been found wrapped in an old army blanket Jack denied owning, and yet fibres from it had been lifted from the boot of his car. His subsequent remand in custody had put him out of reach. What little information Ryan had managed to cobble together since had come from Jack's wife, Hilary, who'd been grilled by police, the experience leaving her distraught and angry, unable to comprehend what was going on.

Hauled in for the same treatment, Ryan had told Professional Standards to back off, refusing to give the allegations houseroom. With no knowledge of the cache of arms in question, he had nothing to say on the matter. It was a fit-up, surely. Any detective worth their salt could see that. But those dealing with the case had Jack in their sights and they weren't letting go.

Ryan checked his watch. It was almost five.

It would be dark in an hour.

Time he wasn't there.

'That was a big sigh.' Caroline's cool hands began to massage his neck and shoulders, taking away the tension. He hadn't heard her approach or noticed her set a mug of tea by his side. 'Are you going to tell me what's up?' she asked.

'Up?' Even in his head, his response sounded lame.

'I don't need eyesight to see how worried you are,' she said. 'It's obvious you have something on your mind. If it's the house, just say and I'll put it on the market. It's not a problem.'

'It's not the house.' Reaching up, Ryan laid a hand on hers, stroking it gently. 'You live here because it makes your life easier. Mine too, knowing you're secure. I want you to stay for as long as you like.'

He meant it.

They had been born upstairs in the same bedroom where their mother had died peacefully in her sleep, with Caroline sitting in a chair beside her. After the funeral, Ryan had offered to move back in, but she wouldn't hear of it, insisting that she was doing fine all by herself.

The massaging stopped.

Caroline sat down under the scrutiny of her twin. Immediately, her guide dog shuffled forward, sinking his nose into the folds of her faded skirt. His sister was slim and very beautiful, with a dress sense most sighted women would die for. It pained Ryan to think that she'd never seen colour. Never seen him. He felt guilty about that.

It could so easily have been him.

Being blind from birth had never stopped her living. Ryan was immensely proud of her many achievements. She had first-class honours in criminal law, was a gifted musician with, it seemed, the ability to do anything she put her mind to. She was looking directly at him, dark curly hair like a shawl around her shoulders, bright eyes so normal an outsider would never guess that she lived in perpetual darkness.

'I want you to be happy, Matt.'

He smiled. Now they were parentless, she was the only one in the world who called him that. Everyone else called him Ryan.

The lie on the tip of his tongue came easy. 'I am happy.'

'You don't sound it.' His twin was a walking, talking lie detector.

He apologized. 'I've not been very good company, have I?'

She'd misread him. 'Roz has a point, doesn't she? This house is your inheritance too. You love each other. It's only natural she wants to live with you.'

That was never going to happen.

Ryan allowed the conversation to stay on his ex. Coming on the back of their mother's death, his twin had been upset by the arrest and detention of his boss, her friend, Jack Fenwick. He didn't want to add to her distress by telling her that his relationship with DC Roz Cornell was also over. A different type of blindness had hidden differences between them until a couple of weeks ago. He didn't have it in him to forgive her for what she had in mind for Caroline. Recognizing the value of a Grade II listed property in Alnwick – prime Northumberland real estate in a market town once voted the best in the UK – Roz was prepared to turf her out on her ear in order to release his newfound wealth. He hadn't spoken to her for weeks and that suited him fine.

It was an amicable parting – *almost*.

If his twin had known about the separation – more importantly the reason for it – she'd have felt guilty about holding him back. Ryan couldn't cope with that. He'd tell her when the time was right.

Suspicious of his silence, she was trying her best to make him see reason and put the house up for sale. 'It would enable you to buy a place in town,' she said.

'I don't want a place in town. I live by the sea because I love it. It's good for me—'

'Then explain what it means to you. I'm sure Roz will understand.'

'No, she won't. She detests it up there.' He listed all the reasons she'd given: too cold, too windy, nothing to do. 'How she can view the Northumberland coast as boring is beyond me,' he said. 'She thinks landscape is a page orientation.'

Caroline laughed.

'Where is she anyway?' She didn't wait for an answer. 'Working, I suppose. Why anyone would join the police force . . .' Stalling, she reached out her hand and found his, a pained look on her face. 'I'm sorry, Matt. You know what I meant. You both work too hard, that's all. Why don't you take a break, a long weekend, go somewhere hot? Roz loves the sun, even if you don't. It would be good for you.'

Ryan didn't comment. He'd never seen the point of taking a fortnight off to lie on his back and fry when there was so much more out there to explore: the countryside, the coast, the rich heritage of their own country – stuff he'd rather be doing on his days off – a lot of it on his doorstep, none of which Roz appreciated.

'She'll come round about the house,' Caroline was saying. 'Maybe if you had a bigger one at the coast?'

It was typical of her to play peacemaker. During spats between their parents – even when too young to fully understand what they were about – she'd say something silly or ask a question that would make them collapse with laughter, kiss and make up.

'Can we talk about this later?' Ryan saw off his cold tea and stood up before she had time to put forward a fix for his broken love life. He ruffled Bob's shiny coat, receiving a tail wag in return. 'I have to go. And don't give the house another thought. I'll pop by on my way home.'

'There's no need—'

'I'll be here.' He kissed the top of her head.

His mobile rang: *Hilary Fenwick.*

Ryan considered leaving it to voicemail and then changed his mind. Hilary had been in court earlier, a specially convened bail hearing choreographed by her husband's solicitor. Instinctively, he knew the result wasn't going to be good. If he'd been released, Jack would've called the minute he was out. Still, the least Ryan could do was play along.

'Hilary, hi!' He tried to sound upbeat. 'How did it go?'

The woman was hysterical, words tumbling out of her mouth – not fast, not slow, but jumbled and incoherent. On the chair opposite, Caroline had dropped her head on one side, her super-human hearing picking up every word, alarm flashing across her face. She adored Jack, almost as much as he did.

'Rewind, Hilary.' Ryan sat down. 'Tell me exactly what happened.'

'Jack didn't get bail. I've had Professional Standards here. It sounds crazy, but they say his mates have helped him escape. The prison van never made it to Durham. It was attacked by armed men.' Her voice broke and she began to cry again. 'He's gone, Ryan. Jack's gone. He hasn't been sprung . . . he's been abducted. Oh God . . .' She choked back her tears. 'The police are looking for you.'

'Well, they're not looking very hard. I'm on the other end of this mobile. You found me, didn't you?' Ryan placed the phone in the crook of his neck and picked up a pen. 'Where did this happen? Was anyone hurt?'

'I don't know,' Hilary sobbed. 'They wouldn't tell me.'

'I'll be right over.'

'No! That's not a good idea. They've stationed a car outside.'

'So? I'm not in hiding—'

'You're not at work either. Your office said you were at headquarters. Complaints say they can prove your car hasn't been there all day. They're viewing that as suspicious. They think you're involved. They practically accused me of tipping you off as to the time Jack left court. Be careful. They're gunning for you.'

As Hilary rang off, Caroline's head went down. When she looked up, she was sheet-white. This was bad – very bad – they both knew it. For once in his life, Ryan was pleased she couldn't see his face.

3

Six p.m. In the two and a half hours since the hijack, investigators had pulled together an extensive file. A countdown of events leading up to Jack Fenwick's flight from custody: witness statements, times, actions, several diagrams of the scene – all necessary for an incident that would dominate the coming weeks. Detective Superintendent Eloise O'Neil had questioned his wife, telling her to make contact if she heard from her husband. *Unlikely. And where the hell was DS Matthew Ryan?* He was to have been her next port of call. All attempts to find him had failed.

Far from happy, O'Neil scanned his picture. Ryan had dark hair, brown eyes and enough grey-flecked designer stubble to hide a small scar on his chin from being thrown over the handlebars of a pushbike when he was a kid. He was a dead ringer for Henry Cavill. Unmarried, she noticed. Probably best. Few relationships survived the rigors of a job that demanded your devotion 24/7. She detected hidden depths, as if he had a story to tell.

She bloody hoped so.

Throwing the photograph on her desk, she pulled out her phone and scanned her emails. As usual, her superiors were screaming for a result, but piecing together an exact sequence of events was proving difficult. One vital witness – the driver of a Renault Clio abandoned at the scene – hadn't yet been traced. According to prison escorts, corroborated by one other witness, the guy had fled the scene and hadn't reappeared after the hijacking.

O'Neil's internal phone rang.

Frustrated, she picked up the handset. 'I said I wasn't to be disturbed.'

'It's the front desk, guv. DS Ryan is in the building.'

'Where exactly?'

'Fenwick's office.'

'Tell him to wait there.'

Ryan stood up as they entered. Eloise O'Neil was Northumbria's most revered Professional Standards officer. With a reputation for impartiality, she'd clocked up years of experience, an impressive track record. Unlike some in her department – namely the male by her side, DS John Maguire – she could punch above her weight. These two were not the same officers who'd interviewed Ryan when the case broke.

These were the big guns.

'Guv.' Ryan extended his hand, receiving a firm shake from her, a glare from Maguire. 'How can I help you?'

'It's good to meet you . . . finally.' It was a dig. O'Neil was looking directly at him. Judging him. In her hand was his personnel file, a white label on the front displaying his name, rank and number. She nodded to her cohort, a man Ryan couldn't stand. 'DS Maguire has been trying to find you.'

'Did he not think to call me on this?' Ryan held up his phone.

O'Neil glanced at her DS, a question in her eyes. He shrugged, his colour rising. The Detective Super let it go. Cautioning Ryan, she asked if he required representation from a solicitor or a Police Federation official. He declined, telling her he'd done nothing to warrant one. She asked him to think again. When his answer was the same, she got stuck in, levelling her gaze at him, her expression inscrutable. 'On Saturday the twenty-first of September you were interviewed in connection with firearms found in DI Fenwick's house. Is that correct?'

'Yes, guv.'

'Well, take a seat, I have a few more questions for you.'

Ryan got a whiff of expensive scent as she moved closer. It was hot in Jack's office. Before sitting down, he loosened his collar and left his desk to open the window. He didn't care that his action might be misconstrued as nervousness on his part. Still, he was glad she couldn't see the trickle of sweat running down his spine.

'Have you heard the news?' O'Neil took the seat opposite.

'About the hijack? Yeah, I heard.'

'Who told you?'

'My DI's wife.'

'Oh?' Maguire interrupted. 'Thick as thieves, are you?'

'We're friends. She's frantic with worry and wanted my help. By your presence here, I'd say she has good reason. I told her I was as much in the dark as she was.'

Placing a couple of stills on Ryan's desk, O'Neil turned

them round to face him. The images showed the hijack taking place. He looked at them for a few moments, memorizing the time and date at the bottom of both, information that might come in handy later. The incident had been over in less than two minutes.

'Now tell us DI Fenwick isn't guilty,' O'Neil said pointedly.

Ryan eyeballed her. 'He's not.'

The Detective Superintendent shook her head. Clearly, she didn't share his faith. She pointed at the photographs, her voice calm, measured. 'He was getting into the car with them – as cool as you like – I have the whole thing on videotape and eyewitnesses to back it up. You need to understand, Ryan. He wasn't running or being dragged. He was walking of his own free will.'

'You've had the benefit of the footage, guv. I haven't.'

'Then you'll have to take my word for it.'

'What can I say? No offence, but I think you're wrong.'

Ryan's eyes flitted from one officer to the other. They were a perfect fit for the job they were doing. In contrast to O'Neil's fair-mindedness, Maguire was a nasty piece of work. The good cop/bad cop routine was alive and well in Northumbria force. No one liked bent coppers, least of all Ryan, but Maguire enjoyed his job too much. Often boasted about how many colleagues he'd locked up. It wasn't as if he had anything to be proud of either. Despite his overinflated ego, his arrest–conviction ratio was crap. He represented everything Ryan hated in a policeman.

All the gear – no idea.

'Fenwick clearly had assistance,' Maguire said. 'A co-conspirator, if you will. We're here to investigate where it might have come from.'

Ryan locked eyes with him. ''Fraid I can't help you.'

'Where have you been all afternoon?' O'Neil asked.

'I had a personal errand to run—'

'I *bet* you did.' Maguire pulled up a chair and sat down. 'Care to enlighten us?'

'I was visiting my sister.'

'The blind one?'

Ignoring the moron like he wasn't in the room, Ryan directed his answers to the senior officer. 'I'm sure DS Maguire is well aware that I only have one sister, guv. Our mother died recently. My twin has taken it very badly. I popped up to Alnwick to make sure she was OK.'

O'Neil bristled, not on account of him, if Ryan was any judge. Maguire's heavy-handedness had angered her. 'I'm sorry for your loss,' she said. 'But you can appreciate the position I'm in. Because you were not where you should've been at the time someone was helping Fenwick escape, you're on dodgy ground. Whether you like it or not, I have to assume that your twin would say anything to save your skin. It's a weak alibi. In fact, it's no alibi.'

'Fair comment,' Ryan said. 'It doesn't change my answer.'

'Can anyone verify what you say?' Maguire again.

'My sister can.'

Dissatisfied with his answer, his attitude or both, O'Neil attacked. 'We're investigating a criminal conspiracy involving illegal firearms, DS Ryan. You may be involved. You may not. Either way, we need your full cooperation.'

She opened his file, telling him how impressed she was with his record. 'You've not put a foot wrong, have you? Apart from a couple of unsubstantiated complaints from members of the public – I've picked up one or two myself over the years – you've been a force poster boy.' She looked up. 'You're acting DI in your boss's absence. You stand to lose a lot if you're lying to me.'

'I'm not, guv. And I have nothing to add to the statement I already gave.'

'You deny any wrongdoing?'

'Yes. So, unless you have proof that I aided an escape, I have work to do.' Ryan climbed down. It would be unwise to put her back up. 'Listen, I don't want to be a pain in the arse. I realize yours is a difficult job but, throughout his interrogation, Jack Fenwick protested his innocence. Ever considered the notion that he might be telling the truth?'

'Not for a millisecond,' Maguire answered for her. 'We have forensic evidence.'

'A plant maybe?'

Maguire wasn't finished. 'Maybe we'll catch you out too.'

'That would be difficult, given that I'm squeaky clean.'

'Don't smart-mouth me.'

'Or what?'

'Oi, you two, cut it out!' O'Neil's eyes flashed a warning to them both, eventually coming to rest on Ryan. 'I'll ask you again, Detective. Do you know anything about those firearms, Fenwick's involvement in concealing them, or who might be responsible for helping him escape from custody?'

'No, guv. My DI plays by the rulebook.'

'Shame you don't.' Maguire couldn't help himself.

Ryan repeated that he didn't believe Jack Fenwick had done anything wrong. 'As far as I'm concerned, he's as straight as they come.'

Maguire gestured for him to stand.

Ryan got to his feet. Instinctively, he knew what was coming. Maguire had waited a long time for this moment. He'd want to make the most of it, not let it pass without a fanfare. More worried about the safety of his friend and colleague than the trouble he was in personally, Ryan wondered if he might convince O'Neil to take him on. Allow him to aid her investigation. With his knowledge of Jack and his close contacts, he might be of use to her. Putting it to her in as few words as he could, he told her she'd have more success working with him than without.

'Believe me,' he said. 'I want to get to the bottom of this and find my DI as much as you do.'

'No chance,' Maguire said. 'In fact, you know what? You weren't where you should've been this afternoon. You'd buggered off for some spurious personal reason. Now you'll have to face the consequences. You're suspended.'

'On what grounds?'

'I just gave you the grounds.' Victorious, Maguire began to count on his fingers. 'Neglect of duty; inappropriate use of a police vehicle—'

'You forgot theft of diesel,' Ryan mimicked his tone.

'You're quite the comedian.' Maguire was almost smirking. 'We'll get round to that too . . . eventually.'

Ryan stared him down. 'That's the best you can do? It's bollocks, Maguire. You know it and so do I. I covered the expenses. Check the logbook.'

'I will, except it might take a while. Right now I'm busy.'

'What is this? Payback for being passed over for Special Branch, or something more personal perhaps?' Ryan enjoyed taking him down a peg. 'I won't spell it out with your guv'nor here. That wouldn't be fair. Unless . . . yeah, that must be it: you're afraid I might get to the truth before you do. I guarantee it.'

'No.' O'Neil was all over him. 'You'll do no such thing. From this point on you are suspended. You will not involve yourself in this matter in any way. Failure to comply will only land you in more bother. If you have *anything* to say to me, say it. We don't need you on duty in order to follow it up. Do I make myself clear?'

'Crystal,' Ryan said.

Maguire stuck his hand out. 'Warrant card.'

Ryan wanted to punch his lights out. His eyes found the floor instead. He took a moment to regain his composure. The outcome of the interview was even worse than he'd imagined. When he raised his head, O'Neil looked decidedly uncomfortable. Unlike the goon sitting beside her, she took no pleasure in seeing an officer of his calibre hand over his most prized possession. Taking his warrant card from his breast pocket, he presented, or rather threw it down. It landed with a solid thump on the desk. Skidding over the polished surface, it tipped over the edge into Maguire's lap, wiping the sneer off his face.

'Close the door on your way out,' he said.

Grabbing his jacket from the back of his chair, Ryan told O'Neil that he had every confidence in her ability, and Maguire that he was making a big mistake. With his head held high, he walked out, leaving his office door wide open in his wake. Without access to the station, he was screwed.

4

Grace Ellis turned on the TV. She was bored. She'd been bored since 20 December 2010, the day she retired. A succession of displacement activities, some paid, some voluntary, had kept her interest for a while, the pick of which was Foreign Office courier, a job that had taken her all over the world. Even with the perks of diplomatic status, within a year the novelty had worn off, so exhausting was the travelling. To get over it, she'd spent the past month chilling with a mate in Sainte-Maxime, a few kilometres from St Tropez, enjoying glorious weather, fine wine and brilliant company, with a view to moving there. But she'd returned to the UK, unsettled, with little appetite for life in the slow lane.

Emigration simply didn't appeal.

Although undeniably at a loose end, she was nowhere near ready to sit on her arse and get fat. With no firm plans for her evening, beyond shoving on the washing machine and necking a bottle of red, she flicked through the TV channels until she happened upon the theme tune for the local news. On camera, the ITV News presenter, Ian Payne, gave the headlines, listing them in order of priority.

Thinking she'd misheard, Grace turned up the volume.

The news anchor's expression darkened as he returned to the day's top story. 'And in news just in, a disgraced Northumbria detective has escaped from a prison van in a daring hijack in broad daylight. The police officer was arrested and suspended from duty in September following allegations of possession of firearms without a licence and misconduct in public office. We're going live to the scene, where our correspondent Helen Ford has the details. Helen, what can you tell us?'

On screen, the image switched to an outside location where Ford was standing by in the dark. 'The former Special Branch officer was en route from Newcastle Crown Court to Durham prison following an unsuccessful bail hearing. The security van was hijacked on the main road you see behind me, an audacious attack that has shocked this rural community.' She gestured over her shoulder, telling viewers that the road had been cordoned off and would remain so for some time. 'Prior to his arrest, DI Jack Fenwick was a decorated policeman, trusted by his superiors and assigned to highly sensitive cases, including counter terrorism. As recently as three years ago he'd been tasked with monitoring subversive organizations operating within our force area.'

Lighter fuel ignited with a mini-explosion. Grace pulled the flame towards her, lit a cigarette and threw the pack on the coffee table, eyes glued to the TV as the report cut back to the studio, the focus of her attention an image of Jack Fenwick that had just uploaded on the left-hand side of the screen. His face seemed to get larger the more she looked at it.

'Do we know what the detective had been working on?' Payne asked.

Ford glanced at her notes. 'We have no specific details on that. According to his solicitor, Paul Godfrey, the officer has always protested his innocence and denied all charges. Today's events, however, seem to support the contention that he may be involved with some pretty heavy people.'

Bullshit.

Adrenalin rushed through Grace's veins, transporting her back in time. Her living room walls seemed to expand and disappear until all that was left was her armchair and the TV. In her mind, she'd just pulled on a uniform. Whatever had happened during her holiday in France, she was certain of one thing: wherever ITV were getting their information, it was wrong. Working with Jack in the Serious Incident Squad had been a blast, every shift exciting, every tour of duty better than the one before. He was her protégé, his promotion to Special Branch after she'd left the force well deserved. A more decent guy you couldn't wish to meet. The press had a duty to report the facts, of course, but they had no right to imply any more than that, or sully a fine officer's reputation.

Taking another hit of nicotine, Grace checked her watch. Six-forty. She picked up the phone, dialling a number she'd committed to memory years ago. It was answered on the fourth ring, no greeting given, just a patient and weighty silence from the man on the other end.

Same ol' Newman.

'Fancy coming out to play?' she asked. 'I need your help, Frank.'

'Hello, Grace.'

'Listen to this.' Putting the phone on speaker, she turned up the TV.

In the studio, Payne continued, 'What do we know of the hijackers?'

Ford reappeared on screen. 'I've spoken to one witness who confirms that there were two men, both armed. They drove away at high speed in a silver Audi – registration NB59 HFT. Police are keen to trace the getaway vehicle as well as the detective who fled the scene . . .'

Grace pulled the phone towards her. 'Did you get that?'

'Yeah,' Newman said. 'Sounds serious.'

'It is.' A number plate flashed up on screen. 'Hold on a second.'

Grace scribbled down the registration as the presenter carried on, placing great emphasis on the distress caused to two security guards who were helping police with their enquiries. Not for the first time was she regretting her decision to retire. She'd enjoyed every minute of her job, but then the organization changed beyond all recognition. It became so diluted she couldn't stomach it any more.

Until today.

Now she had a burning desire to take positive action. She'd do anything – *anything* – to throw her life into reverse and carry on working. 'The guy that was sprung used to be one of mine,' she said, back on the phone, heart beating too fast, imagination in overdrive. 'What you heard just now is crap.'

'Sounds like you rate him.'

'I do. You going to help me out or not?'

'Not. I'm otherwise engaged.'

'Doing what?'

'That's my business.'

'Sorry I troubled you.'

Stubbing her fag in the ashtray, sending a chimney of smoke upwards, Grace was kicking herself for having pried. Frank was a man of few words. She'd not seen him for almost four years. He could be doing anything – with anyone – a fact that was as heartbreaking as it was annoying. In other circumstances, things could've been so different between them but, for now, their conversation was over. Hanging up, she screamed at the TV in frustration. She could've played that better. Should have. She sat back in her armchair, piles of unwashed clothes on the utility room floor forgotten, her French vacation a distant memory. Jack Fenwick desperately needed help. If Newman wouldn't lend a hand, another of her former devotees, DS Matthew Ryan, would.

5

Ryan drove home to Embleton Bay through the arse-end of the rush hour with the intention of calling on Caroline, a plan that quickly faded as he passed the signpost for Alnwick on the way to the coast. If he couldn't share his split with Roz with his sister, he sure as hell couldn't face the prospect of telling her he'd been suspended from Special Branch. She'd blame herself for getting him into trouble when it wasn't her fault.

Best not go there.

Since the death of their mother at the end of June, Ryan had worked out an arrangement with his boss; in exchange for working out of hours, without claiming overtime, he could piss off during the day to sort Caroline out. Now he came to think of it, the idea had come from Jack. That was the kind of compassionate guy he was. He didn't seem to care that it would leave him short-handed.

Quite the opposite: anyone would think he wanted rid of him.

Ryan hadn't bothered mentioning this private pact to O'Neil. What was the point? He didn't have it in writing and it would merely act as another black mark against his DI. A spirit of cooperation didn't exist when complaints were on the table.

The miles flew by and he was home in no time. He drove past his house and round the back to the courtyard parking area. Not another car in sight. Most of the properties in Dunstan Steads were holiday lets. Second homes converted from old farm buildings. The tranquillity of the place was the perfect antidote to a hectic life as a serving police officer. A short stroll across the golf course and he was on the beach.

Bliss.

Through force of habit, not need, he locked the car.

Opening the gate, he crossed the yard and let himself into a hallway that doubled as a dining room, anger over his suspension boiling in his gut, an emotion he had no time to indulge. If he was going to help Jack, he needed to focus. He may be locked out of the station – *any* police station – but Maguire couldn't take away his ability to investigate a crime or keep his promise to Hilary. With or without the power his warrant card afforded him, Ryan was determined to find out what was going on.

But where to start?

Stripping off, he took a shower, purging himself of O'Neil's warning that he should stay the hell away from the case or face the consequences. He dressed in jeans, an old sweater and leather jacket – his dad's; a throwback from his drug squad days. It was falling to bits, but Ryan didn't care. He'd worn it since he'd grown into it twenty years ago. The image of his old man with it on was the only one he had.

Leaving the house, he returned to his Land Rover Discovery and got in. The interior of the British four-wheel-drive utility vehicle smelled permanently of Caroline's dog. The car was old and rusting but it suited his personality and lifestyle perfectly. He was an off-road kind of guy – another thing Roz hated about him.

South of Stannington village, Ryan took the slip road – signposted Blagdon – then turned right over the bypass on to the Berwick Hill Road. The radio was full of the hijack, the weather doing its utmost to persuade him to put off 'til morning. He ploughed on regardless. It was too risky to be seen near the crime scene and too late in the day to talk to Jack's solicitor. *Hilary* – he'd begin with her.

The house was in a quiet road in Ponteland, half a mile or so from force headquarters. Ryan arrived at nine. He'd been there so often, he could've driven it blindfold. She was washing the dishes when he was shown into the kitchen by her eldest, Robbie. The eighteen-year-old had his father's good looks, the same rugged features and deep-blue eyes.

Lifting her hands from the sink, Hilary dried them on a tea towel. As she walked towards him for a hug Ryan couldn't work out if she looked tired, ill or lost – probably a combination of all three. He remembered the first time they had met – here in this house – a surprise birthday party thrown by Jack. They had danced in the garden, got steaming drunk on tequila and ended up challenging each other to an arm-wrestling match that, bizarrely, she won. While she'd never once embarrassed him by mentioning it, Jack had never let him forget it.

Good times.

As she withdrew, Ryan forced a reassuring smile for her three children, who were standing in the doorway waiting for him to say something. Robbie in the middle, his sisters Jess and Lucy holding his hand on either side, dressed in pyjamas and ready for bed. Ryan had held Lucy the day she was born, five years ago. Once an ugly duckling, she'd grown into a gorgeous little girl. As her godfather, he'd accompanied her to reception class on her first day at school a month ago in place of her dad. No substitute – he would never be that – but better than nothing on one of the most important days of her life.

She ran and buried her face in his lap.

Ryan cleared his throat. 'I'll find your daddy if it's the last thing I do. I promise you, my lovely girl.' Getting down to her level, he brushed away her tears with the back of his index finger, catching Robbie's concerned eye. 'Can you put the kids to bed while I talk to your mum?' Then to the girls: 'I'll come and tuck you in if you're good.'

As the lad led the youngsters from the room, Ryan fetched himself a glass and sat down at the kitchen table, pushing the remains of the children's supper to one side. He refilled Hilary's glass with a generous measure of white wine from a half-empty bottle and poured one for himself. He was off duty. Permanently. Besides, he needed a drink after his head-to-head with Maguire. The prick had him bang to rights. There was no wriggle room.

They both knew that.

For a while, Hilary sat in silence, her long fringe obscuring puffy eyes. She was trying hard not to lose her composure. Police officers' partners soon learned to be tough. That didn't mean she needed less support. On the mantel above the old-fashioned kitchen range there were cards Ryan recognized, a spray of flowers too, the product of an office whip-round, a gesture of consideration for the family until the madness stopped.

Following his gaze, Hilary managed a smile. 'Please thank the team for those. Jack would appreciate it too.' The smile vanished. 'He was so certain he'd be home today. I'd taken a bag to court with a change of clothes. Godfrey told him it was a foregone conclusion. Have you met him?' She was talking about Jack's brief.

'Many times. He's well respected, the best there is.'

'Not today he wasn't.'

'Did Jack say anything to you during his appearance?'

She shook her head. 'They wouldn't let me in.'

'Why not?'

'The hearing was held "in camera" at the request of the CPS.'

'Figures. Despite their best efforts, Jack is still a serving officer.'

'Not for much longer, if they get their way.'

Ryan's eyes fell on a third glass on the kitchen table. 'You've had company?'

'Grace popped in.'

'She's back from France?'

Hilary nodded. 'Saw the news on TV. She's in a worse state than I am, although she's pretending she's not. You know what they were like. There was a time she saw more of him than I did. You too, come to think of it. She just wanted to make sure me and the kids were OK. That's why they're still up . . .'

Her voice was drowned out by thoughts Ryan kept to himself. Grace Ellis would want a damned sight more than that. She'd have been fishing for information. Fine. He rated her. Everyone who ever worked with her did. They had kept in close touch since she retired. He knew she'd be ready to kill someone over the day's events. No wonder it hadn't taken her long to make an appearance.

Glancing over her shoulder, Hilary made sure the door was closed. It was. Even so, she dropped her voice to a whisper. 'You've had a lot on your plate, Ryan. You may not have noticed that Jack hadn't been himself.' She took in a raised eyebrow. 'Don't misunderstand me, I'm not blaming you for not looking out for him and I'm not saying he's done anything wrong.'

'So what are you saying?'

'Underneath the surface he was a worried man.'

'Worried how? Why?'

'You know as much as I do.' Her left eye twitched nervously.

There was more. Ryan sensed it. 'Is there stuff you're not telling me?'

'Yes, no . . . I don't know. Something has been niggling at the back of my mind. You know what a scribbler he was, a pen and paper man, even when he was at home?' She caught Ryan's nod. 'Then why can't I find his most recent notebooks?'

It was a good question.

'Maybe the police took them,' he suggested.

'No. They didn't.'

'Tell me again how it went down when he was first arrested.'

'It was like a scene off the TV. Terrifying. For the kids especially. A SWAT team of armed officers stormed the house. No warning. They searched everywhere: house, sheds, garage.'

'You were with them the whole time they were searching?'

'Yes. They found the guns immediately.'

'Not surprising, is it? They knew exactly where to look.'

'That's what Jack said. You should've seen his face when they discovered the weapons.' Covering her mouth with her hand, she held on to her distress. 'I know him, Ryan. He wasn't faking it. He didn't have a clue they were there. He was gutted.'

Ryan laid a hand on hers as she took a breather. 'You OK to go on?'

She nodded. 'They led us into the house to continue the search. Jack kept asking what they were looking for. They wouldn't answer. After turning the place upside down, they marched him out in cuffs, in the clothes he stood up in. He had nothing with him and no time to hide anything. They put the firearms in the boot of a panda and drove off.'

'So where are his notes?' Ryan asked.

'I don't know, but I have feeling they were important.'

'Maybe he transcribed them—'

'On to what? Apart from Robbie's iPad, we don't own

any technology. You know that. He didn't want it in the house. Said it was bad for kids.'

'Did you ask him about them?'

'No, it only just occurred to me.' She misted up. 'Even if I'd thought of it earlier, I'm not sure I'd have asked. His head went down after his remand in custody. He was so depressed in there.' Hilary paused, staring at him.

'What about after his arrest? Was anyone in touch with you?'

'"In touch" might be stretching it. Two detectives arrived to carry out a second search immediately after the first lot. They weren't interested in talking, Ryan. They went through the house like a dose of salts, even tipped the kids' cornflakes out of their box. It was as if they were looking for drugs, not firearms. Jack told me it was routine, that they were probably after ammunition.'

'That makes sense.'

'Does it . . . really?' She held his gaze. 'I could tell he didn't believe that any more than you do. Be honest, Ryan.'

Ryan sidestepped the comment with a question. 'Did the detectives ask if Jack had a lock-up, if he was a member of a gym, a shooting club, anywhere he might stash stuff?'

'Yes.'

'There's just the golf club, right?'

Hilary answered with a nod.

'OK, leave it with me.' Ryan stood up. What he could achieve on his own, he didn't know. He couldn't tell Hilary he'd been suspended. Not now. She'd hear about it soon enough from one of the other policemen's wives. 'I'll make some enquiries. Get some rest.'

As he reached the door she called out to him.

Her eyes were full when he turned around. 'I'm scared,' she said.

Ryan was too, but didn't verbalize it. A thought occurred. 'Do you have Jack's locker key?'

'From the golf club? No. He'd already volunteered it to the uniforms.'

Ryan just looked at her. If that was the case, then whatever his DI was hiding, he knew the police wouldn't find it there. *One less place for him to look.* 'Did you tell Professional Standards this?' He took in her surprise. 'I know O'Neil and Maguire were here earlier.'

'You've seen them? What did they say?'

'That's not important. Did you?'

Hilary shook her head. 'I assumed they knew.'

Ryan stopped talking. If the search team had found the guns and kept on searching they must have thought there were more. Or there was another explanation. Was Jack trying to tell him, through Hilary, that there was something else he should be looking for? The word ammunition had two connotations: bullets or supporting facts. *The notebooks.*

6

Eloise O'Neil ran a tight ship. She understood the implications of having a rogue Special Branch officer on the run, especially one as clued up as Jack Fenwick appeared to be. There was no telling what intelligence he could pass on. She had to find him – fast. According to the court stenographer, it was two thirty when his bail application ended. Fenwick was held back in the cells for a while, waiting to see his brief, then placed in the security van for transfer to Durham.

'Was Ryan in court?' Maguire was scanning the crime-scene diagram.

'No, he wasn't.' Viewing the same document, O'Neil noted that the prison van had commenced its journey at 15.04, crossing the High Level Bridge two minutes later. Traffic was slow leaving the city on a Friday afternoon. Consequently, they had an ETA of 16.00 at HMP Durham. No incidents had been reported prior to the hijack. She'd requested CCTV along the route. Number plate recognition would tell her if the Audi or Ryan's car were shadowing the security transport for all or part of the way. She glanced at Maguire. 'They didn't deviate?'

He shook his head.

'Any cameras on board?'

'Inside and out.'

'What was Fenwick doing?'

'Just sitting there until the van came to a stop—'

'He didn't look agitated?' the Detective Super asked.

'No more than any copper heading to the pokey.'

O'Neil's eyes were back on the diagram. The hijack had taken place at 15.44, a fact verified by witnesses. 'The strike must've taken some planning,' she said. 'There weren't that many locations en route where they could hit it. The hijackers were thorough and highly organized.'

Maguire nodded in agreement.

'The driver – Irwin?' O'Neil asked. 'Is he on the level?'

'Seems to be. He's worked for the company for over a decade and never put a foot wrong. He pressed the emergency call button at the first sign of trouble. On the other hand, Storey, the co-driver, is just out of short trousers.'

O'Neil gave him a questioning look.

'He's only worked for the company for three weeks.'

'Has he?' She sat back, placing her hands behind her head. 'Worth another look?'

'I'd say for sure. Something he said might be worthy of further investigation.' Maguire flicked through his notes. 'When all hell broke loose, he lost his bottle completely. According to Irwin, he started yelling at him to open up. To quote Irwin, his exact words were, "Do it . . . there's no point losing your life for peanuts – or that piece of shit in the back." Unquote. Odd that he said *your life*, not *our lives*, don't you think?'

O'Neil chewed over this for a while. 'I want a word with them both. Set it up, soon as we're done here.'

'You'll have to be quick, guv. Irwin's booked on a flight to Cyprus tomorrow afternoon. He's been dreaming of Ayia Napa and said to tell you it'll take a court order to keep him here.'

'That could be arranged.' O'Neil wasn't joking. 'Hopefully, it won't be necessary. Make the arrangements, John. But tell him there are no ifs or buts. I don't give a damn how many statements he's given already. He sees me tomorrow or he doesn't travel. This is a serious matter and he's our star witness. You sure there were only four others?'

Maguire nodded. 'A female pedestrian who thought she was witnessing an RTA until the hijackers got out brandishing firearms.'

'She didn't stick around?'

'Would you?' Maguire made a face. 'She legged it PDQ, a fact corroborated by both security guards. She's a teenager, guv. Her parents rang in as soon as our number went up on the six o'clock news. We have two witnesses who live close to the junction where the incident took place, and one other – the Clio driver who still hasn't come forward to reclaim his car.'

'Guv?' a voice said from behind.

O'Neil and Maguire both turned round. A worried-looking female civilian was standing in the doorway. She'd overheard them talking and held up her phone. 'I got a message from Control. The Clio was reported stolen from Byker at around midday by an eighty-year-old who'd refuelled at the garage at the top of Shields Road and left the key in the ignition while she went to pay for petrol. When she came out, the car was gone.'

'Damn!' O'Neil glanced at Maguire. 'So, is Clio Man a probable suspect or a thief who dumped a stolen vehicle when his luck ran out?'

'The former, I'd lay odds on it—'

'Because the car was stolen not far from the Crown Court?'

'There is that.'

'You know something I don't?'

'In Irwin's statement, he said the driver of the Clio was wearing sunglasses even though it was pissing down. He thought it was odd at the time, but then lots of people wear them for driving, including me.'

'Why? Does it make you look cool?'

'Just an observation.' Maguire was blushing.

'They could equally have been a way to hide his iden-tity.'

'Yes they could. Oh, and he likes Coldplay.'

'Come again?' O'Neil said.

'He had the radio on. Volume turned up high, Irwin says. The music stopped as the Audi arrived. I reckon it was at full blast to mask the sound of the hijackers arriving at speed.'

'Works for me.' O'Neil called out to the civilian: 'What's the tale with the Audi, Cath?'

Cath was back at her desk. She got up and walked towards them, a sheet of paper in her hand. 'The owner is Nicholas Wardle. Resides on the outskirts of Sunderland. There's no answer at his address, according to area com-mand. The place is locked and secure. His neighbour claims he's working away in Nigeria. That could explain why he hasn't reported the vehicle stolen.'

'Or that's the story he's put out and he's involved,' Maguire suggested.

'Did they say who he worked for?' O'Neil asked.

'No,' Cath said. 'They were very vague. Apparently, he plays his cards close to his chest. Something to do with the oil industry they think, but aren't sure. He didn't like it, though – working in Nigeria, I mean.'

'Can't say I blame him. Keep on it, Cath. We need to trace him.'

As the civilian went back to her desk, O'Neil received a text from one of her team:

Crime scene traffic lights tampered with and those either side. Clever eh? Ensures no vehicles approaching hijack from either direction – and no witnesses.

Swearing under her breath, O'Neil dropped her mobile into her pocket and turned her attention back to Maguire. 'They had help,' she said, sharing the development.

'They'll have paid a couple of kids to do the business.'

'Yeah, well, we need to find them. You sure there were no other eyewitnesses?'

He shook his head. 'That's it, guv. Squad cars were dispatched as soon as the SOS came in. By the time they got there, the hijackers were long gone, Fenwick along with them. We've put a marker on the PNC to trace the Audi, with a warning that it may contain armed offenders and/

or firearms and needs to be preserved for Forensics. No one was seriously hurt. I suppose that's something.'

O'Neil was thankful for that. The situation could've been so much worse. Her job was made more difficult because on-board communication devices had been rendered useless when the two guards were pulled from the prison van. Cameras in the vehicle's lock-up bay were smashed by the hijackers the second the rear doors were opened. The last visual relayed to Control was the butt of a gun as it was rammed towards the monitor, another fact she shared with Maguire. 'Which means we have no footage of Fenwick getting out of the van or what happened next. What was he doing when the hijack was going down?'

'He was going crackers, yelling at the driver to put his foot through the floor. Deserves a BAFTA, no?'

She held his gaze. 'Why don't we view the evidence before we give out any nominations?'

'He had nothing to lose, guv. And everything to gain.'

'So you said. He has a family, a wife and three kids he adores. If someone threatened them, he'd do anything he was told, wouldn't he? Even if it made him look as guilty as sin.'

Maguire was almost sulking.

O'Neil wished she could knock that malicious streak out of him. In his head, he had the cuffs on the Special Branch DI and was marching him towards a ten-year prison term. There was a difference between investigating and prosecuting complaints against police officers and revelling in their downfall. A good detective Maguire may once have been. Shame he also had to be such a dick.

7

Ryan was waiting outside Godfrey, Smart & Co solicitors when it opened for business first thing on Saturday morning. He looked on as Paul Godfrey, senior partner, parked his silver Jaguar on the office forecourt. Checking his watch as he got out of the car, the brief strode towards his office with a sense of urgency, a heavy briefcase weighing him down, a sheaf of papers under his arm.

Ryan stepped from the shadow of an overhanging tree. 'Sir, may I have a word?'

Godfrey pulled up sharp, appearing more riled than startled. It wasn't the first time he'd been doorstepped. Even so, he seemed visibly relieved to see a decent human being and not a thug standing there. If it didn't pay so well, he'd bin his criminal cases in favour of divorce. The clientele weren't any better but, instead of fighting him, they tended to fight with each other – a healthier scenario all round.

A flicker of recognition crossed his face.

'DS Ryan, isn't it?' His accent was regional but cultured. Public school, Ryan guessed. Put it this way, he'd not struggled to learn to read and write in a classroom of thirty-odd.

'Yes, sir, Matthew Ryan, Special Branch.'

'Then I can't talk to you.' Godfrey walked – keen to end their exchange before it had even begun – disappearing through an impressive front door.

Ryan followed.

The office smelled of polish. It was spacious, contemporary, furnished in shades of grey, with cool black-and-white images adorning the walls. A young couple were waiting to be seen, nicely turned out, neither of them paying attention to who had just walked in. Not shite, Ryan was certain. If he was any judge, these were hard-working folks, probably buying a house or making a will. Ignoring them, Godfrey greeted his receptionist. Scooping up his mail, he turned, almost bumping into Ryan – a resigned look on his face.

The detective wasn't budging.

'You have two minutes,' Godfrey said. 'Follow me.'

Dumping newspapers and correspondence on his desk, the solicitor opened his office blinds to allow the sun in and took a seat. Ryan remained standing, hands behind his back. Detectives never sat down until invited to do so.

'OK,' Godfrey said. 'Let's start again shall we?'

'I appreciate your time,' Ryan stalled, unsure of exactly how to play his hand. Experience told him that the best way was straight with men like Godfrey. If it didn't go well he could always change tack. 'I should tell you I'm currently suspended, sir.'

'I see. Then that makes things rather difficult.'

'Depends which side of the fence you're on.' Ryan kept his focus on the lawyer. 'Do I have to engage your services before you talk to me? If so, where do I sign? My North-umbria colleagues have tarred me with the same brush as someone we both know. If they can, you can.' When God-frey said nothing, Ryan carried on: 'I realize it's unethical for you to discuss a case with someone other than a client, but Jack Fenwick has rights too. I happen to believe he didn't escape but was abducted by an organized gang. I'm convinced his life is in danger. Now it's your turn.'

Godfrey was teetering, weighing up in his mind how to respond, whether or not he could trust Ryan who, by his own admission, was under suspicion for conspiracy. And still he kept quiet, staring across his expansive desk, con-sidering his position, taking his time. Time Ryan didn't have.

'Please,' he said. 'I need your help. Time is running out. You went to see Jack in the cells after his bail hearing. What was your take on his demeanour? What was he doing, saying? In short, I have to get my head around what was going through his. Are you going to help me or not? Because I'm all he's got.'

Godfrey cleared his throat. 'Off the record?'

'What record? I'm persona non grata as far as the police are concerned.'

'Take a seat.' The brief waited for Ryan to make himself comfortable. 'Despite forensic evidence, your colleague was adamant he was being fitted up. He said the guns were planted to frame him – to discredit him and sully his good reputation. Ditto the blanket fibres found in the boot of his car—'

'Tell me something I don't know.' Meeting Godfrey's

intense stare, Ryan apologized for being flippant. 'Jack has a point though, doesn't he? Anyone could've put them there.'

'Quite so. For what it's worth, I was inclined to believe him. The problem is, despite several hours in consultation, he gave me nothing to work with. That weakened my position, making it virtually impossible to refute the allegations. You're not the only one trying to operate in difficult circumstances, DS Ryan.'

'Fitted up by who?'

'He never said.'

'He must've said something.'

Godfrey shook his head. 'Only that it had far-reaching implications.'

Ryan's brow creased. 'I was working with him until his arrest. Mostly routine stuff, nothing heavy.'

'My understanding is that it had been going on a while. He never mentioned what it was. Only that he didn't have enough evidence to make a case. He wouldn't divulge any details until he was sure of his facts.'

'Even though, potentially, he was facing seven years?'

'He hinted at corruption. He said scores of innocent people would be affected if he went about it in the wrong way. He'd obviously been putting a case together under the radar. He was worried that if he was rumbled they, whoever they were, might eliminate witnesses and destroy evidence. He didn't know how far the conspiracy extended or who could be trusted. Don't ask me what he meant by it. He was planning to tell *you* though—'

'Makes you say that?'

'He seemed to think you were the only one who could get him out of the trouble he was in. Clearly he had more time for you than he did me.'

There was more. Ryan sensed it. 'And . . . ?'

The brief let out a loud sigh, a regretful expression on his face. 'He asked me to make contact with you. That's the only reason I'm talking to you. Had events not over-taken us, I would've done so. I had other cases yesterday. By the time I made it to the office, the hijack was breaking news. I know one thing though: he was desperate to see you. I gather he wanted you to arrange a VO.'

Ryan never flinched. Never showed the guilt that was eating him up. 'Save the black looks,' he said. 'I feel bad enough without you making it worse. I couldn't make contact with him while he was banged up. I was warned off. Told it would be unwise to seek a visiting order. The officers dealing with the matter were at pains to point out that Jack was being prosecuted for possession of firearms without lawful authority, that I should choose which side of the law I was on. In case you're in any doubt, that's code for "back off or else".'

'You misunderstand,' Godfrey said. 'I meant yesterday.'

'He didn't ask for me until *yesterday*?'

'After the bail hearing.'

'You sure it wasn't before then?' Ryan queried.

The brief stared him down. 'I may be long in the tooth but I'm not completely gaga, Detective. That's the first thing he said when I entered the cells. He was shattered that he wasn't getting out.' Godfrey's jaw bunched. 'I'm afraid I led him to believe that bail was a distinct possibility. They changed the sitting judge at the eleventh hour.'

'Is that right? I don't suppose they gave a reason?'

'You know how these things work, Ryan.'

'So what you're saying is—'

'I'm saying nothing.'

'But you're not disputing that he'd have fared better with the listing judge?'

'You are correct in that assumption.'

Ryan's heart began to beat faster. If Jack wanted him to visit, he must've been under the impression he was going straight to jail. He wasn't expecting to be sprung. *He wasn't.* Taking a pen from his pocket, Ryan reached forward, helping himself to a yellow Post-it note from a pad on Godfrey's desk. Writing down a name – *Det. Supt. Eloise O'Neil* – he scribbled a number beside it and handed the note to the solicitor.

'I'm not here to put words in your mouth or tell you what to do, sir. If you believe Jack was innocent, I'm sure you'll follow your conscience.' Ryan pointed at the note. 'O'Neil is the SIO. Jack's gone up in the world. He still needs your help and she needs to know what you just told me.'

Godfrey read the note and then stuck it to his computer screen. 'Won't it put you in an even worse position with Professional Standards if I talk to them?'

'I don't give a monkey's what position it puts me in. Neither am I asking you to lie on my account. However, if you could find a way to have that conversation without mentioning my name or the fact that we've spoken, I'd be grateful. All I'm interested in is the truth and finding Jack. There's something terribly wrong here. His wife thinks so. I think so. You've had years of interviewing prigs. What do you think?'

It was a rhetorical question.

Godfrey's face was enough to convince Ryan that his DI was being well and truly shafted – and not only by persons unknown. His own force had abandoned him. They were hunting him down like a common criminal. It needed sorting. Ryan happened to think that he was the man to do it.

8

Jack Fenwick opened one eye, incapable of opening both. He swallowed hard, felt the pain of broken ribs, the effects of dehydration. He tasted a mixture of blood and chloroform, the latter forced over his mouth and nose in the car, ensuring his compliance. He hadn't been able to time the journey or second-guess in which direction the hijackers had taken him. They were done with him for now, but they'd be back.

Jack listened.

No hum of traffic. Not a whisper. This place must be buried deep within a building, possibly underground or in a rural location. Shutting his eyes, he held the image of an arm around his neck, a sleeve pulled taut, a wide wrist, a Swedish flag tattoo depicted in three slivers, confirmation that he'd been pursuing the correct lines of enquiry. Jack understood national pride. He'd spent his life defending Queen and country.

Patriotism was overrated.

The place he was in was windowless. Pitch-black. He thought of Caroline, wishing he had her sensitivity to the dark – her inbuilt radar. Unable to tell if there were solid objects around him or not, he worked gingerly from left to right, in a zigzag pattern, a fingertip search. He estimated the area was no bigger than eight by twelve. It was rough underfoot, earthy rather than dusty, damp and cold. A stifling claustrophobic space, not a breath of air, empty of furniture – on the ground at least.

Hauling himself off his knees, he faced the wall, feeling his way around the room. Brick built. Solid. Standing on tiptoes – his shoes and socks had been removed – he reached up, hoping for shelving, a weapon, anything he could use to make good his escape. The roof was rounded, like a tunnel, perhaps an air-raid shelter or part of a church. At six three, his head was hunched into his chest, the curvature of the wall making it impossible for him to stand upright. He couldn't comprehend the space and found nothing of use in his search.

Unlucky, he was done for.

Abandoning his search, he turned his attention to the arched door. It was firm. Unyielding. No handles on the inside. No leverage. Jack stepped away. Tried a shoulder charge. He squealed in pain as he made contact: once, twice, three times. It was useless. Exhausted, he slumped to the floor. Beaten. There was nothing he could do except wait for the bastards to come again. They had hurt him but not enough to kill him. That meant only one thing. They thought he'd talk. A realization dawned: silence was his only currency. Anything less would sign his death warrant.

9

Godfrey's words floated in and out of Ryan's thoughts as he walked to his vehicle. The more he turned things over in his head, the more convinced he became that Jack was in serious trouble. He had to find him soon or face the possibility of telling three wonderful children that *their* father was never coming home.

Ryan flinched, an icy hand settling on his shoulder.

In a split second he was ten years old, sitting on the stairs, his knuckles turning white as he clung on to the banister, unbearable images scrolling before his eyes: his mother's world collapsing, a colleague of his father's breaking her fall as her legs gave way, easing her into a chair as the shock hit home, followed by a sound that Ryan's younger self felt sure could only have come from an animal in distress – a strangulated wail that seemed to last forever.

For years that sound had invaded his dreams.

Ryan couldn't bear the idea of turning into the death messenger. The bogeyman. He'd done it many times in the past – it was part of his job – but never to a family with whom he was personally involved. That was one task he wasn't ready to face. It would be like history repeating itself in the cruellest way possible.

That unsettling thought lingered in his head as he

crossed Gosforth High Street. On the other side of the road, he fell in step with half a dozen locals going about their business on a Saturday morning. Everything normal. Not a care in the world. The street used to be teeming with life but it had gone downhill. Now it was drab, all the best shops having moved elsewhere. He and Jack used to drink there when there was a police station around the corner, before it was moved to another part of the city, the building turned into an apartment block for those who could afford it.

Ryan remembered those days, a bundle of laughs and secrets shared over a pint of Workie Ticket in the Brandling Arms. So why hadn't Jack shared this particular confidence? A good copper, he'd worked hard to rid the streets of those who maim or kill. Were those shady characters now taking revenge? Wasters he didn't want to tip off to the fact that he was on to them?

Weaving his way round dawdling shoppers, Ryan sifted the possibilities, trying to figure out who hated Jack enough to fit him up, slating himself for missing clues Hilary said were there.

Jack hadn't been himself for months.

He'd hidden it well then. Ryan had no real inkling. Or did he? Somewhere deep down, Hilary's words resonated with him, which only served to make him feel more guilty. How could he have failed to notice the level of Jack's stress or tackle him about it? Replaying recent conversations, he realized that consideration had been a one-way street, Jack asking how he was, how Caroline was, not the other way round. Pressure of work was Ryan's only excuse.

Not good enough . . .

If he'd been more attentive, might Jack have told him?

Ryan didn't think so.

Jack was the kind of guy who wouldn't be pushed, preferring to keep his plans and opinions to himself until he was good and ready to share. If he was so worried, Ryan wondered, might he have confided in a counsellor at Durham prison: probation, chaplain or psychologist?

As quickly as the idea arrived, Ryan discounted it.

If Jack hadn't talked to him, his brief or his wife, he'd hardly blab to a stranger, even if incarceration did strange things to people. Hilary had mentioned remand prisoners giving him a hard time: par for the course if you were a serving copper – even one who had allegedly gone over to the dark side, ending up in prison.

Criminals had long memories.

But was Jack really at breaking point? Ryan didn't buy that either. It would take a damn sight more than a shove in the back from scum or a few weeks inside to unnerve Jack Fenwick. Maybe Hilary was seeing things that weren't actually there. She was, after all, under tremendous pressure.

As he rounded the corner, heading for the park, an old MGB drew up alongside. The window went down in jerky movements, a familiar female voice yelling his name from within.

'I wondered if you might surface,' he said, climbing in. 'How did you find me?'

'Retired doesn't mean stupid. I just got off the phone to Godfrey.'

Grace Ellis only had one speed – and it wasn't slow. She was as mad as hell, her black mood a reminder to buckle up. Adjusting the strap of his seat belt, Ryan got ready for a bumpy ride – in more ways than one. Without another word to him, Grace pulled hard on the steering wheel, completed a U-turn and sped off the way she'd come.

On the A1, heading south, she turned right at the Blue House roundabout. Ryan didn't have to fill her in on what had gone down while she was out of the country. She was following the evidence. In the last few hours she'd spoken to Hilary, watched extensive news coverage, read all the newspapers and spoken to Jack's brief. Discreet enquiries within the force had found solidarity. Never one to miss a trick, she was clued up and ready to go.

'The CPS wouldn't know the truth if it ran up and bit them on the arse,' she said, flooring the accelerator. 'I don't give a damn what they think Jack's done. You and I know different.' She chanced a glance in his direction. 'I'm sorry to hear you're in trouble too. Don't worry, we'll soon get you out of it.'

'What they have on me will never stick. It's Jack I'm worried about.'

'Did Godfrey tell you anything? He and I were never on the same page. He was less than forthcoming with me.'

'Only that Jack was working under the radar on something he omitted to share with me. He was planning on telling me, apparently. Shame he never got the chance. Some partner I turned out to be.'

'Drop the self-pity. It doesn't suit you.'

'Hilary said he was worried. I should've seen the signs.'

'You're not a mind reader, Ryan. If Jack didn't tell you,

he had a bloody good reason. Did Godfrey give you *any* inkling?'

'Major corruption case, by the sounds of it. Something he hadn't quite cracked when his circumstances changed. Godfrey implied a conspiracy with far-reaching consequences. Jack was convinced that people might be at risk if he didn't handle it correctly.'

'Deep. What the hell does it mean?'

'It means people might get hurt.'

'Well, he was right about that, wasn't he?'

'His notebooks are missing from home, Grace. We find them, we'll be halfway to finding him.'

Ryan held on as she took a bend at high speed, heading to her place in the leafy suburb of Fenham if his internal satnav wasn't up the creek. She told him she'd drop him at his car when they were done. He was happy with that. They needed a strategy, a plan of action to find their man and return him to his family. Ryan wanted nothing more. Coming under Jack's command was the best thing that had happened to him since he'd joined the force.

'What can we do, realistically?' he said. 'You're retired. I'm suspended. With no access to the station, we're out on a limb, wouldn't you say?'

'In what way?'

'In every way.'

'You're not up to the job?'

Her words stung.

Ryan swallowed his anger, an emotion he found hard to suppress and one that wasn't only directed at her. He was pissed at Jack for not trusting him enough to share intelligence. They were professional partners – well, he'd thought they were. Now he wasn't so sure.

'Get a grip,' Grace said. 'We're not taking the situation lying down. Not if I have anything to do with it.'

10

Ryan had dropped the defeatism by the time they reached her house, a detached property on Nuns Moor Road. Grace went off to find coffee, telling him to make himself at home in the living room. As people, they were polar opposites. He was peaceful. Considered. She was combative, argumentative, in a very different place to him – a situation she was well aware of. He had to be careful. As a retiree, her pension was already in the bank. As a serving officer, his was at risk.

He had a damn sight more to lose than she did.

The sound of cutlery and crockery being placed on a tray reached him from the kitchen. While he waited for Grace to reappear, Ryan walked to the window and looked out over a pretty garden. The sun had come out, turning autumn leaves gold. His thoughts were on Jack and how best to proceed. The smart answer would be to back off, let O'Neil do what she was paid for. She was an experienced officer. But with the best will in the world, although high on her priority list, Jack's case was one of many on her desk. The odds were not in his favour and Ryan wasn't taking chances.

In his head, he saw Jack's children lined up at home, their anxious faces turned in his direction, waiting for him to wave a magic wand and conjure up their daddy. He'd pledged to do that, a promise he intended to keep, if it was humanly possible. The responsibility was almost too hard to bear.

Grace entered, apologizing for the state of the place.

Ryan turned, her comment prompting him to scan the room for the first time. A suitcase lay dumped in the middle of the floor awaiting attention – a carton of two hundred smokes spilling out the side. Grace set a pot of coffee down, telling him to get stuck in. He was about to help himself when his phone rang: *Roz*. Ignoring the call drew a suspicious glance from his host. Well, tough. Ryan didn't want another post-mortem with his former girl-friend on how the perfect couple had gone so horribly wrong. Inevitably, any such conversation would warp into a full-blown argument. Roz would play the 'me' card all over again, making his relationship with Caroline sound unhealthy, incestuous almost, because they were so very close. And Ryan certainly didn't want to bare his soul in front of Grace.

The phone rang three more times – same caller. Only when it became obvious that Roz wasn't giving up did he take the call. He answered curtly, telling her that he was busy and couldn't talk, an action that drew a lengthy silence. His words had thrown her.

She'd *already heard.*

'Ryan, is it true?'

'Is what true?' he said.

'It's all round HQ that you've been suspended.' She spoke softly, as if someone on the other end might overhear. 'I can't believe Complaints. John is dishing the dirt, as always. Is he mad?'

John?

'The answer is in the question,' he said, and hung up.

Grace raised her head. 'You two been fighting again?'

He looked away, didn't admit or deny it. She was an astute and intuitive woman who knew him well enough to see through him if he tried to pull the wool. Best to keep shtum.

'I'm sorry to hear that,' she said. 'Roz might come in handy.'

Grace had a point. Potentially Roz was an important ally, a direct line to information. Without her, Ryan would soon run out of options. He'd lost a lot recently: his mother, his girlfriend, and was on the point of losing his job if Maguire got his way. Having his ID confiscated felt like someone had ripped his heart out. He couldn't bear the thought of losing Jack as well. Besides, he couldn't allow Maguire to get one over on him. What he'd done to Jack was just unforgivable. Ryan couldn't sit on his hands and do nothing. Uncovering the truth and finding his friend was a mission he couldn't contemplate turning down. He and Grace would stick together because it was the right thing to do. It was the only thing to do. If it involved asking Roz Cornell for help, then he'd bite the bullet and beg if necessary.

11

Ryan watched O'Neil drive out of headquarters, heading for the village of Ponteland. He followed, turning left on to the main road towards Newcastle. In stark contrast to Grace Ellis, the Superintendent drove like she worked, precisely and progressively, her aim to get from A to B in one piece. Maguire wasn't with her today – a stroke of luck – Ryan didn't need an extra pair of eyes that might spot a tail in a wing mirror.

As a Special Branch officer, he was highly trained in surveillance. Few were better at it. Most were a lot worse. To do the job properly he'd need at least five vehicles – all of them double-crewed. On his own, the job was more difficult.

That didn't mean impossible.

Despite O'Neil's conservative approach, he had his work cut out keeping up in his battered set of wheels. A Land Rover Discovery was hardly unobtrusive. Leaving two-car cover, he nearly lost her as she entered the roundabout with four possible exits: Bank Foot, A1 North, Newcastle, A1 South. Traffic lights changed. Fortunately for Ryan, the cars in front sneaked through on amber and he was able to follow suit.

He drove on, knowing he'd be in trouble if O'Neil

caught sight of him. She'd forced his hand. What other choice did he have? He was looking for a fellow officer in danger. She was looking for a wanted fugitive. Same task. Different perspective. With a life at stake, his priority outweighed hers.

O'Neil had the upper hand, including access to witnesses. Ryan's guts were telling him that's where she was going now. Twelve minutes later, his theory was upheld. She indicated, pulled slowly to the kerb outside a private address north of Gosforth. She got out as Ryan drove by, hoping she didn't notice him. Why should she? As far as he was aware, she'd never seen his car. Turning his head away as he overtook, he parked fifty metres further on, glancing in his rear-view mirror. She hadn't noticed him. She was knocking on a door. After a while, a middle-aged man answered, a sling on his right arm.

Ryan smiled. Pound to a penny this was one of the security guards from the prison van.

O'Neil was holding up ID.

They hadn't met before.

Half an hour later, she left the house. As soon as she'd driven away, Ryan was out of his car, moving like a bullet towards the door she'd just come out of, the prop of an empty manila folder under his arm. He pressed the doorbell then stood back, examining the peeling white paint on the wicket fence, the weeds in the garden.

No contender for Britain in Bloom.

Expletives reached his ears from the other side of the glass panel facing him. Kids were being yelled at. A woman's voice, extremely irate by the sounds of it. Ryan took a deep breath, intending to make up the truth as he went along.

The door was yanked open suddenly.

'Sorry, sir . . .' Ryan spoke before the occupant had time to. 'Detective Superintendent O'Neil has one or two further questions she'd like me to put to you. It'll only take a second. Apologies for the inconvenience – won't keep you long.'

The man on the threshold was clearly agitated. Three fingers on his left hand were taped together and there were beads of sweat on his forehead. He was quite well built, dressed in chinos, a tight T-shirt. 'Listen, pal, no offence, but your boss is pushing her luck. I have two weeks off. *Two*. In five hours I'm catching a flight from Manchester. Know what I'm saying? Why my daft cow of a wife couldn't find one out of Newcastle is beyond me. But my life won't be worth living if we're late and they refuse to let us board. So ask your questions, then be nice and piss off, because she's driving and I'm not keen.'

'Point taken,' Ryan said. 'May I come inside?'

'Do I have a choice?'

Ryan gave a grin.

'Nah, didn't think so.'

As the homeowner stepped inside, Ryan entered the house, his eyes everywhere. The place was a tip, the decor drab, in need of updating. The walls were roughly painted and damp had eaten away at the plaster in places. A security guard's uniform jacket was hanging on a peg in the hallway. The living room was equally grim, but he was in luck. Suitcases littered the floor. A handbag lay open on the coffee table, passports and a travel wallet sitting beside it. The owner's ID wasn't going to be a problem.

Ryan felt his tension drain away. If O'Neil had taken Maguire along, his plan would never have worked. 'May I take the number on your passport, sir?'

The man spread his hands. 'What for?'

'Routine. You're the star witness in a high-profile case. If you went walkabout we'd look pretty silly, wouldn't we? You're lucky I'm only asking to look at it, not keep it. My boss is a stickler for the rules. She likes things tidy.'

'Help yourself,' the man said.

Ryan sifted the documents until he found the one he was looking for. He skim-read the man's passport and put it back, committing his name and date of birth to memory. 'You're a lucky man, Mr Irwin. Exactly how long are you away for?'

'Two weeks, if I ever get there.'

'I take it you gave the Super your contact details in case we want to get in touch?'

'Of course . . . don't you people talk to each other? I told her everything. Everything.'

Ryan relaxed.

A teenager made an appearance and got short shrift from her dad. Then a woman Ryan assumed was Irwin's wife popped her head round the door looking daggers at her husband. Jabbing her wristwatch with her right forefinger, she told him she was leaving in fifteen minutes, with or without him.

A mismatched pair – there was a lot of it about.

'Sorry, mate.' Ryan winced as Irwin's missus disappeared, slamming the door behind her, chipping another bit of plaster off the wall. 'You want me to have a word? She doesn't look too chuffed.'

Irwin waved away the offer. 'She never looks chuffed. You wouldn't think I was nearly a goner yesterday, would you? All she's bothered about is humping her own clobber to the car and making my life hell because we're going to have to spend my hard-earned adding another driver to the insurance in Cyprus. You could fit what I'm taking in a plackie bag. She's given me earache all morning. Those thugs yesterday didn't scare me, your boss doesn't scare me, but my missus does.'

'It must've been a tough shift yesterday.'

'You could say that. It nearly finished my co-driver—'

'And you too, I imagine.'

'Not like Storey – the kid was bricking it.'

Storey? Ryan wanted to hug him.

'Want my honest opinion?' Either way, Irwin was hell-bent on giving it. 'That'll be his last shift as a security guard. It'll also teach the little shite not to look down his nose at the likes of me. Educated, know what I mean? So far up his own arse he can nearly see his tonsils. I'll be pleased to be rid of him.'

'My boss all over.' Ryan thumbed over his shoulder to his imaginary colleague. 'The Super might seem very nice to you, but mess with her . . .' He drew a hand across his throat. Taking a peek in his empty file, grateful that at six three he had several inches' height advantage over his witness, Ryan posed a question. 'Actually, do you have a mobile number for Storey? I think she forgot to write it down.' As Irwin read it out, Ryan scribbled it on the front of the file and then dropped his voice to a conspiratorial whisper. 'Between you and me, my guv'nor has your prisoner pegged for some heavy shit. I know the guy personally. Don't quote me, whatever you do, it's just that I happen to believe he's innocent.'

'I'm with you, pal.'

'Really? You have no idea how happy I am to hear it.'

'Fenwick didn't have the first idea he was going to be sprung,' Irwin said. 'Storey was bad enough, but your man was going ape-shit. He kept pounding on the cab, yelling at me to get the hell out of there. There's no way he wanted to go with those prigs. No way! And I'll tell you something else: I think your boss has her doubts too. What did you say your name was?'

'Maguire,' Ryan lied. He could see he'd made the wrong choice as soon as the word was out of his mouth. He stuck out a hand. Unflappable. 'As in Chris, not to be mistaken for DS John Maguire, another idiot with his head up his arse. Like you and Storey, we don't really see eye to eye.'

'You got that right!' Irwin huffed.

Ryan changed the subject. 'Can I give you a hand with these bags, mate?'

'Nah, leave 'em. It'll give her indoors something else to crow about.'

Ryan grinned at his newfound friend. Male bonding was a wonderful thing. Now they understood one another, it was time to ask a few pointed questions. Then he could relax with a fortnight's grace while Irwin was out of the country with his family. By the time he returned to the UK, one way or the other, it would all be over.

12

Jack woke suddenly as the key turned in the lock. Before he had time to look round, he was hauled on to his back, a flashlight trained on him. The bright light blinded him, forcing his eyelids closed. Pushing away the Swede's arm, he blinked them open. He could smell garlic on the guy's breath. This was the one who did all the talking, the one who took the most pleasure in inflicting pain.

'Give it up, Jack?' The balaclava-clad face looked ominous illuminated behind the torch.

'Go to hell!' Jack's voice was hoarse. He'd been yelling to attract attention, for all the good it had done. He cried out as the man struck him a blow to the side of the head with a fist that felt like a rock. The pain was excruciating. Nauseating. He almost lost consciousness. Wished he had.

The eyes behind the mask were smiling. The bastard was enjoying himself, unconcerned that Jack was a policeman or that the whole of Northumbria force – and possibly forces countrywide – were looking for him. Such blatant disregard was disturbing. It messed with Jack's head, clear indication of the trouble he was in. Trouble he might never get out of.

'Come on, Jack. This is so unnecessary. We know you've been gathering intelligence. Talking to people. Poking around in business that doesn't concern you. It really won't do. It makes people nervous. Angry even—'

'You know nothing, or I wouldn't be here.'

'Save yourself, Jack. Your contact had the chance to talk to us. He didn't. He's since been taken care of. But you already know that, don't you? Despite what you think, I'm a reasonable man, prepared to give you that same chance. Take it.' He paused. 'No?'

The Swede struck Jack with a hand as big as a shovel, a blow even harder than the one before.

'Okay,' he said, 'have it your own way. I'm a patient man. But know this: I will keep coming back until you cooperate, until that information is in my possession.'

'I have no idea what you're talking about.'

The Swede glanced over his shoulder, nodding to his cohort who was standing behind him, backlit by a shaft of light filtering in through the open door, midges dancing around his head. The man stepped forward, drew back his leg and gave Jack a good kicking, winding him, breaking more ribs.

The Swede again. 'Jack, don't be stubborn. I need to know what information you have, what you plan to do with it and who you've told. Was it Ryan or someone else? I know you passed it on, because it's not in your house.'

Jack tried not to react but his eyes gave him away.

'Oh, I didn't tell you I'd been through your house and met the family? My mistake. It must have slipped my mind. Your wife Hilary was *most* amenable, your children too, especially Lucy. Pretty thing, isn't she?'

Jack was dying inside. If either of these two had

touched one hair on Lucy's head he'd hunt them down and kill them both. The Swede was bluffing. He had to be. Ryan would be looking after Hilary and the kids, keeping them safe from harm. That much he knew. That much he hoped.

13

Ryan showed up half an hour early. Grace Ellis was waiting on a first-floor terrace of the Pitcher & Piano on Newcastle's Quayside with a pot of coffee and a pile of newspapers spread out on a corner table with headlines guaranteed to sell: *Audacious Hijack in Broad Daylight. Suspended Special Branch Officer Flees Justice. Prison Van Hijacked at Gunpoint.* As soon as she saw him, she started banging on about the press, her face twisted in anger.

'They love dishing the dirt, don't they?' She didn't stop for a response. 'Whatever happened to innocent until proven guilty? It bloody annoys me. You want coffee . . . something else?'

Waving away the offer, Ryan kept his thoughts to himself. Grace was spot on, though. Whenever coppers were involved, the media always had a field day. It bugged him that they could get it so wrong. More often than not they would report that officers had been charged with criminal offences when they weren't police at all but civilians who'd worked for five minutes on a front desk, in the Control Room or in an admin office at HQ.

Ryan sat down.

Picking up a newspaper, he scanned the print for information that might prove useful, anything she might have missed that they could possibly work with. Names of witnesses they didn't know about, people who might talk, given the right stimulus – which usually meant money.

And still Grace protested . . .

The copy was full of shit . . .

Jack had been hung out to dry.

Tuning her out, Ryan wondered how Hilary and the kids were coping in the media spotlight. Unscrupulous journalists would do anything to get their names above the fold. As if the family hadn't already been through enough.

The screech of seagulls made him look up.

Dozens of the birds had taken refuge on the arc of the Millennium Bridge and on the roof of the Baltic, a contemporary art centre on the south side of the Tyne. In the foreground, the river was as grey and choppy as the mood around the table and a dark sky threatened rain.

A mobile bleeped several times in quick succession.

Not his.

Lowering her newspaper, Grace pulled out her phone. 'Jesus, I've got a full house.' A number of text messages had arrived all at once, she told him. With a face like thunder she scrolled through them, then pocketed the device, dark eyes on Ryan. 'It seems I have less friends in high places than I thought. The rumour squad have shut up shop. No one's talking.'

'Which means they're nervous.'

'Yes it does. O'Neil has her enquiry locked down tight.'

'She'll be pissed,' Ryan said. 'I mean really pissed. Can't

say I blame her. Jack's case is not going according to plan. One of her witnesses went to the BBC with footage she didn't know they had. The hijack was on the news at one. I watched it just now in the police club.' Taking in her surprise, he prodded at the air with his forefinger. 'I still have the combination to get in. The lasses behind the bar were as good as gold. They not only served me beer, they gave me all the gossip they'd heard across the bar.'

'Which is . . . ?' Grace was never one to underestimate the police grapevine.

'The evidence is hard to argue with. The footage shows Jack climbing out of the van, an Audi A6 taking off at speed. I have to warn you, it's not good quality. Whoever took it was moving away. It's very shaky. O'Neil has something similar, she told me. No wonder she thinks Jack is guilty. That video needs a professional eye. Proper enhancement.'

'Oh yeah? And how do you propose we manage that?'

'I have my contacts.'

'Good luck,' Grace said flatly. 'A private job will cost thousands.'

'I'll cover it. My inheritance has to count for something. My mother liked Jack. Caroline adores him. He was very kind to both of them. Believe me, if they were here, they'd approve. There'd be no argument.'

'That's very generous.' Grace raised her voice above a crocodile of noisy schoolchildren making their way along the quayside, teachers front and back instructing them not to dawdle and to keep holding hands. 'Was Jack in the front seat of the Audi or the rear?'

'Can't tell. Only two figures are visible, the driver and someone in the rear. Assuming they're the hijackers, Jack was probably lying in the footwell out of sight. O'Neil was on the money. He was walking, not running to the car. No one shoving him around, no gun in his back – we need that analysis.'

'We need to talk to the witness who sold the video to the BBC,' Grace said.

'I've got feelers out. For what it's worth, I think Irwin's on the level. He was kissing the tarmac when the hijackers opened up the security van. He didn't look round so can't say what actually took place. He claims there was a loud smash as the comms were disabled. It was all over in a matter of minutes.'

'Did Jack say anything when they took him?'

Ryan shook his head. 'Not a whisper.'

'*No* words exchanged – you sure?'

'The co-driver told it the same way.'

Grace wasn't happy. Keen to see the footage for herself, she suggested reconvening at her place. The introduction of news programmes 24/7 ensured that the video taken at the scene would be replayed over and over, hyping up the intrigue, making Jack look like a dangerous fugitive. As she carried on talking, Ryan stopped listening. His thoughts were still on Irwin. The security guard had proved to be more intuitive than Ryan had given him credit for, specifically in his observations of Eloise O'Neil.

'Ryan?' Grace said. 'Are you even listening to me?'

He looked up. 'Sorry, I was miles away. What did you say?'

'Nothing. Where were you – if I'm allowed to ask?'

'According to Irwin, O'Neil has her doubts about Jack's guilt. I asked Godfrey to contact her and tell her what he told me. I was wondering if he'd done so. You think I should call her and repeat my offer to assist her enquiry? I know Jack better than anyone. I have a lot to give, expertise Maguire stupidly dismissed out of hand.'

Grace was shaking her head. 'That's a really dumb idea. Eloise is a fine officer. I respect her but she's not like you and I. She plays by the book or she doesn't play. We can't afford to tip her off that you're not on a golf course practising your putting. She'd lock you up as soon as look at you.'

'For . . . ?'

A raised eyebrow screamed: *Wanna list?* She proceeded to give him one. 'How about, disobeying a lawful order? Or maybe neglect of duty? Or, because you've been stripped of your warrant card, she might prefer impersonating a police officer.'

'Why should I be any different? Maguire's been doing it for years.'

Grace laughed. 'I'm not joking, Ryan. You've seen her. Any magistrate would melt if she asked for a remand in custody to keep you out of her hair. Besides, you said yourself it was a feeling Irwin had, nothing she actually said. She's very deep and therefore not easy to read. He could've picked her up wrong. I've done it myself on numerous occasions. No, we need more information before tackling her again.'

Ryan had only met O'Neil the once but she fascinated

him. In other circumstances he was sure they would get along. He didn't know her well enough to make a judgement call. Grace knew her better. If she was wary of pooling information, it was probably wise to hold back. They had the opportunity to work incognito, to do a 'rubber heeler' of their own with no one looking over their shoulder. It made sense to keep it that way. When they had positive intelligence to share, Grace would facilitate a meeting.

'Did Irwin say anything about the hijackers?' she asked.

'Big bastards. Foreign. That's it.'

'Foreign?'

'Well, one of them is. Irwin's no linguist. He told me that only one of them spoke, that he was probably Eastern European. Storey disagrees strongly. He thinks Scandinavian – definitely not European, Eastern or any other kind. His best guess was Icelandic or Norwegian. The voice was muffled through a balaclava. He couldn't be sure. There wasn't a lot of conversation going on. The hijackers let their weapons do the talking.'

Ryan checked his watch: two thirty.

Catching the eye of a waitress, he signed an imaginary bill on his hand. As she hurried off to sort it, he turned to Grace, rubbing his chin with the palm of his hand, a smile playing round his lips.

'Something amusing you?' she asked.

'Maybe.'

'Care to tell me what?'

'Maguire never asked Storey about accents, only Irwin.'

'You're kidding me!'

Ryan shook his head. 'I didn't push it in case the lad got suspicious.'

'And who do you believe?'

'My money's on the graduate, which means O'Neil and Maguire might be looking in the wrong direction.' He met her gaze across the table, the smile gone. 'Actually, it's not so funny. We should be sharing this with Professional Standards. They could be wasting precious resources on misinformation—'

'Tough. You offered your services. They weren't bloody interested. It suits us that their eyes will be elsewhere. Let's play that to our advantage. Make our own enquiries. If we uncover anything they have to be told about, I'll do it. Eloise knows I plan to write a book. I'll tell her I've decided on real-life cases, that interviewing witnesses is part of my research.' She grinned. 'There's no law against it.'

Ryan liked her style. It wasn't a bad ploy, either. It meant she could also talk to police. Not that the latter would be forthcoming. O'Neil was nobody's fool. She'd have gone through Jack's personnel file a million times. She'd know that he and Grace had once enjoyed a close working relationship and had probably kept in touch. It wouldn't take a genius to work out what was going on.

Then again, she'd have to prove it.

14

They left the Quayside in separate cars, Grace giving Ryan her key so he could let himself into her place. She had a quick errand to run and would swing by on her way home. The minute he opened her front door he sensed there was someone in the house, a feeling confirmed by the smell of a freshly lit cigarette.

Leaving the door ajar, he crept inside, looking for a weapon. On the hall table, a marble figurine stood out as the most weighty object with which to defend himself. Lifting it gently, keeping his back against the wall, he took one step closer to the living room, peering through the narrow gap between the door and the jamb.

A man stepped into view.

He was lean, not skinny. About five ten. Casually dressed, smoke drifting from the cigarette in his mouth. A small holdall lay at his feet with wires hanging out: mobiles, chargers and cameras.

Thieving bastard.

As the focus of his attention switched to the rear of the television, something snapped in Ryan's head, white noise taking away his power to concentrate, the association of the lean man and the TV bringing bile to his throat. Blood drained from his face as the intruder morphed into a killer, a druggie hiding his stash inside a TV shell, the internal workings having been removed.

Like a loose-leafed calendar being blown in the wind, his mind raced backwards – ten years, fifteen, twenty . . . and stopped in 1988. The eighteenth of July. The day his boyhood hero, twenty-one-year-old midfielder Paul Gascoigne, left Newcastle United and joined Spurs – and the last day of another hero's life: *his father's.*

Out of curiosity, and against Jack's advice, Ryan had read the case papers of the incident – and wished he hadn't, even before he'd closed the file. The photographic evidence alone gave him nightmares, woke him sweating and calling out to his dad in the middle of the night.

Told you, mate. But would you listen?

Ryan should have listened. Having lost a sibling in tragic circumstances, Jack had spoken from experience. Also prey to sleepless nights and bad dreams, he knew only too well that the younger detective would live to regret his actions – and so it proved. Despite his best efforts to bury the past, horrendous images Ryan would rather not know about were embedded in his memory, ready to loom up in his internal rear-view mirror at every opportunity. It was something that he and Jack had talked about often over a pint, the glue that bound the two men together. But it wasn't helping now . . .

Ryan's heart was kicking a hole in his chest from the inside. In his head, he saw his father and another drug squad officer enter a house on the say-so of a snout, an everyday drugs bust that went horribly wrong. Having discovered the cache of drugs hidden inside the TV, DS Ryan Senior had placed them in a pile on the coffee table, pointing out to the offender that it was too great a quantity to pass off for personal use. Realizing he was facing a long term of imprisonment, the dealer had charged like a bull at the arresting officers, a flick-knife leaving its casing as he took them on.

Pulling at the neck of his T-shirt, Ryan tried to calm down and deal with the here and now, but the documentation and crime scene photos were still with him: his father lying dead on the floor of a stinking fleapit in the city's East End, deep puncture wounds to his chest, his colleague calling for backup, trying to stem the flow of blood with his bare hands as his partner's life ebbed away.

Ryan's left hand felt the repair patch of leather on the jacket he was wearing. Despite several attempts to remove it, the silk lining was still stained with traces of his father's blood, the knife having gone straight through. Looking down at his right hand, Ryan saw that his knuckles had turned white from gripping the marble figurine so tightly. Lifting it in the air, he drew in a deep breath, flashes of his father continuing to scroll through his head: his lifeless body, the TV, the drugs, the knife.

The front door creaked as it was pushed open.

Fearing assault from behind, Ryan swung round. Grace was standing there, bewildered. Another noise . . . this one from over his shoulder. Ryan swung round again to find the lean man standing in the doorway, a wide grin on his face, his eyes on Grace. He studied her for a moment before turning his attention to Ryan, still poised to strike, beads of sweat on his forehead, his face drained of colour.

'Heard you arrive, pal. Figured you'd gone to make tea.' The lean man turned to Grace. 'You never told me you had a new toy boy.'

Ryan exhaled. 'Who the hell—?'

'An old friend.' Grace realized instantly why he was so spooked. 'It's okay, Ryan. Put the weapon down. I'm sorry, I didn't know he was here, I swear.'

Feeling stupid, Ryan did as she asked, eyes on the man he'd believed to be an intruder. 'You have a name, *pal*?'

'Frank . . . Newman.' He stuck a hand out. 'I hear you have a problem. I'm here to help.'

Newman was around fifty-five years old, give or take, in good shape, with ice-blue eyes that gave nothing away. He wore jeans and a black polo shirt. Good shoes. No wedding ring. He had straight shoulders and, despite the lack of bulk, an air of confidence that would scare those who got on the wrong side of him. Ryan took a punt at ex-military.

'Thanks . . .' He accepted the proffered hand. 'But no thanks. We don't need your help.'

'Suit yourself,' Newman said. 'Wouldn't want to butt in—'

'Guys, give it up.'

The two men conformed.

Grace moved through to the living room, giving Newman a black look as he stepped aside to let her pass. Ryan followed her in. She slung her bag on the sofa, picked up her cigarettes and lit one.

'I have a few house rules,' she said. 'One: this is a testosterone-free environment. Two: this is a testosterone-free environment. There's no room for egos here. Ryan, you want to find Jack? Frank is how we do it. Trust me. We need his help. There's no one better.'

15

O'Neil was as mad as hell. Her efforts to get a handle on the hijackers had come to nothing. She'd looked at CCTV along the route, checked house-to-house forms until her eyes bled, tried to find Clio Man without success. Organized Crime Command hadn't fared any better. And, to add to her woes, Maguire was getting on her tits.

He was a useless bagman.

Senior officers of her rank on the Serious Incident Squad or the Murder Investigation Team got to choose their own staff. She didn't have that luxury. Maguire had come to her under a cloud, forced upon her almost, a case of take it or leave it. She'd long since made up her mind that she'd be better off without him. Practically horizontal, with his size tens on her desk, he was bleating on about the case, bemoaning the fact that Fenwick had nothing to lose and everything to gain in making good his escape.

She sighed. 'You don't say.'

Taking in her glare, Maguire sat up straight. 'C'mon, guv! He was looking at a long stretch he couldn't face. Once bail was refused, he saw the writing on the wall, if you ask me. I'm not convinced Ryan isn't in on it either. He thinks he's so cool. We should get him in here. Pile on the pressure. Give the cocky git something more than a suspension to worry about. I don't buy his alibi—'

'Will you shut up and let me think!' O'Neil rubbed at her temples. Her head was bursting with competing actions. On top of that, Fenwick's solicitor had called. He'd told her that following an unsuccessful bail hearing his client had specifically asked him to make urgent contact with DS Ryan, news she shared with Maguire. 'Which begs the question of why he'd do that if he was involved in his own escape—'

'Don't doubt yourself, guv. That's what Fenwick wants you to do. I said he was dodgy. I never said he wasn't clever. Ryan's no slouch either when it comes to covering his back. Slimy bastard.'

'We have no evidence whatsoever on Ryan. We know it and so does he.'

'Doesn't mean there isn't any.'

'Doesn't mean there is.' Her second-in-command's tunnel vision was more than O'Neil could stomach most days. She was about to rein him in again when her phone rang. Picking up, she covered the speaker with her free hand, ordering Maguire to chase up Nicholas Wardle, the Audi owner.

'You're having a laugh,' he said. 'It's no easy task finding someone in Nigeria.'

'If you can't find someone when you have a copy of their passport, I can't see you being much use to me in detecting this offence, can you?' She glared at him. 'Shut the door on your way out.'

For once, Maguire did as he was asked without argument. He stomped off in a strop, rattling paper-thin walls as he shut the door behind him. O'Neil went back to the phone. A BBC newsroom editor was returning her call – and not before time. He sounded defensive when she said she wanted to see him. He had a 'window' in approximately half an hour, he told her. Well, bully for him. Hanging up, she set off to meet him alone. Maguire could bore someone else while she was out.

Broadcasting Centre was on Barrack Road in Fenham – an area west of Newcastle – a twenty-minute ride from headquarters. O'Neil pulled up at the secure car park ahead of schedule. Pressing a button on the control panel, she identified herself, giving the purpose of her visit. The barrier lifted slowly, allowing her entry. She turned right, finding a spot close to the revolving front door.

Inside the building, BBC Radio Newcastle was playing gently in the background, the *Simon Logan Show*. O'Neil knew the presenter through a mutual acquaintance. She signed in at reception, was given a visitor pass and invited to make herself comfortable on the sofa provided for studio guests.

A few moments later, a young woman approached. Smart and smiley, she asked O'Neil to follow her to the second floor. She was shown into the staff refectory, a light and airy room where she could get something to drink. It was a far cry from the one at HQ, or any other police canteen the Superintendent had ever seen. Before she'd even sat down, she was collected and shown into the news editor's office.

Nick Barratt rose from his chair, stuck out a hand. 'How nice to see you again, Eloise.'

'I very much doubt that.' Ignoring his greeting, O'Neil took off her coat, slung it on a chair and sat down. The coffee he offered was refused. She hadn't come to get cosy. She wanted answers, not caffeine. 'I'm investigating a very serious matter, Nick. It would have been nice to have seen your footage before it went live. We usually cooperate with one another. I fail to understand why you didn't think it necessary on this occasion.'

'It was a question of timing.' The editor cleared his throat. 'It's a serious case. I took the view that it was in the public interest to show it. I had a tough call to make: run with it or hand it over and wait for permission to broadcast. Somehow, I don't think you'd have been too happy with that.'

'I hope you're not suggesting I'd veto it because it involves a Northumbria detective, because I can assure you that is not the case.' O'Neil didn't try to hide her contempt. 'You know fine well it's not how things are done. It's important to control information in the public arena. I need the name of the person who brought it to you. That's not too hard a call to make, is it? I hope you paid them well.'

'I didn't pay them at all,' Barratt bit back.

O'Neil's expression was clear: *Do I look stupid to you?*

The editor's attention strayed to one of three desktops. News feed was continually being added. Like O'Neil, Nick Barratt was a very busy man. After a moment, he opened his drawer. Removing packaging that bore the label of Express Quest Courier Services, he pushed it across his desk and threw her a low-baller. 'The details of the sender are dodgy. I had them checked out.'

'You weren't in that much of a hurry to broadcast then?'

He held her gaze. 'I thought it was important.'

'And when you found the address was fictitious, you ran with it anyway. Like I said, I thought we had an agreement, you and I.'

Barratt sidestepped the dig with a question. 'What's going on, Eloise?'

O'Neil looked at him. She could understand those wanting to benefit financially by selling a vital piece of evidence to the press, young kids wanting cash, their names in print or an opportunity to appear on television, although, in her considered opinion, it would be very unwise in this instance. The hijackers were seriously dangerous men. But the absence of a request for payment worried her. An anonymous package was altogether more sinister. Who sent it and why were questions for which she had no answer . . . yet.

Taking an evidence bag from her handbag, she put the package inside and sealed it.

Barratt was asking if she'd be able to lift prints or DNA.

'That's the plan,' she told him. 'It'll take a few days. In the meantime, it would help if I knew who in your post room has handled it.'

'Of course. I've watched the footage several times. Have you?'

'Naturally.' O'Neil pulled at the neck of her sweater. 'How the hell do you work in this heat?'

'I could ask you the same question.' Master of the double entendre, he studied her closely. 'Someone wants Fenwick's head on a plate, in my opinion – unless it's your head they're after. I've always loved conspiracy theories. They're so . . . newsworthy.'

'Don't read too much into it. In my experience, things are rarely what they seem.'

'If you are in charge of the investigation I'd say they've achieved their objective. This could be a disaster for you if you get it wrong.'

'The same could be said of Fenwick if I get it right.'

'You be careful, Eloise.' Barratt crossed his arms, relaxing back in his chair. 'Did I mention that I'd met him once or twice? He seemed like a really good bloke. Trustworthy. Wouldn't you say so?' He paused for effect, enjoying himself at her expense. 'Ah, I see you haven't had the pleasure.'

They both fell silent.

Barratt's warning rattled around in O'Neil's head. Someone was trying very hard to make Fenwick look bad. It was the obvious conclusion to be drawn. One she might have made herself if the evidence against him hadn't been so compelling. Until she had the footage analysed, she wouldn't commit herself. Getting to her feet, she held up the evidence bag with two fingers.

'Thanks for your time.' She tapped the bag. 'Any more like this and I'd appreciate the heads up.'

Barratt stood up too, walked round his desk and said he'd shout her dinner – a peace offering.

After compromising her investigation? *It would be a cold day in hell.*

16

Late afternoon. Ryan drove slowly past the crime scene, Grace in the front passenger seat, Newman in the rear. The stretch of road was busy and more remote than any of them expected; three houses on one side, a parking lay-by for several cars, a set of traffic lights whose sole function was to aid safe journey into public woodland opposite.

'Two cars in the lay-by,' Newman said. 'No one inside. Go round again.'

Keeping tabs on all vehicles, stationary or otherwise, Ryan did as he asked, checking the route for Professional Standards. 'The road wasn't blocked off for long,' he said. 'O'Neil must be confident she has all the evidence she needs. We might just be in luck.' For now, he thought, but didn't say.

There was always the chance she might revisit.

They rode in silence, the atmosphere charged with electricity, their minds on the job they had gone there to do. They needed to be in and out, in sync with one another. Ryan hoped they could pull it off. On the fourth drive through, when he was fairly certain they weren't going to bump into anyone official, he stopped the car and checked his watch.

'Three forty-four – bang on time.' Ryan glanced to his left. 'You ready, Grace?'

'As I'll ever be.'

'We have a two-hour window and one chance to get it right,' Ryan said. 'Only one.'

'Let's do it,' Newman said.

They all got out, separating like an army detail. Sunset today was 5.58 p.m. In just over two hours it would be dark. With a camera each, Ryan and Newman moved to opposite sides of the street. From a fixed point – the traffic lights – they paced out the road, taking shot after shot from different angles while Grace covered the few properties along the highway, a quick house-to-house, asking a series of pre-planned questions she'd collate at her place later. An hour on, way ahead of schedule, they were out of there. It was a clean operation.

It was gone six when they arrived back at Grace's house, an accident on the northbound carriageway of the A1 delaying their journey. Within minutes, they were down to business, Grace and Ryan on notes harvested from her mini house-to-house, Newman uploading images on to her new computer, the latest iMac she'd bought with her commutation. Not much for thirty years' service, but perfect for what he had in mind.

'I'm impressed,' Ryan said, watching Newman.

Grace winked at him. 'Frank has his uses.'

Newman glanced up. 'Will you two naff off and give me some space. I prefer to work without an audience, if it's all the same to you.'

'C'mon,' Grace said. 'Leave the grumpy bugger to do his stuff.'

They retired to the kitchen to make a meal. Nothing fancy, just comfort food: a modest spaghetti bolognese with olive bread, a side salad to go with it. They needed it – they hadn't eaten all day.

Ryan slumped down at the kitchen table, his mind in overdrive. On the return journey from Durham they had discussed their findings, including the jemmied signal box at the traffic lights. With Irwin abroad, Ryan had called Storey the second they got in, asking if he'd noticed anyone standing at the lights as they changed to amber before turning red. He didn't think so, although he'd seen a motorcycle pull away, something Irwin had failed to mention when questioned.

'Perfect.' Ryan mumbled under his breath.

Grace lit the gas and placed a frying pan on the heat. 'What is?'

'Everything: the execution, the isolated location, the way they stopped the traffic to make it look like a sloppy job carried out by amateurs. Well, I don't buy it. The bastards thought of everything, pretty much. They were pros, not the type to leave anything to chance.'

Something was niggling at the back of his thoughts. Why hadn't they killed his DI? Whatever their reasoning, Jack's daring flight from custody added weight to the phoney firearms bust, deflecting attention from whatever it was he'd been investigating under the radar.

It had worked, too.

'What's up, Ryan?' Grace had picked up on his concern.

'I was just thinking . . .'

'I can see that.' She was stirring mince. 'What about?'

'O'Neil has taken the easiest course of action. Convinced that Jack is on the run, she and her team will be checking ports and airports, assuming he'll make a run for it. I would too, in her position, but my compass is pointing in a different direction altogether. I don't know why, but I don't think Jack is far away, geographically speaking.'

'Yeah, but where?'

'That I can't tell you.'

'Whatever is happening to him won't be good.'

'No. The guys who took him mean business. They've gone to a lot of trouble to grab him. Hitting prison transport in broad daylight is a high-risk strategy in anyone's book. If they didn't kill him, chances are they need something from him. This is pure guesswork, but I think the hijackers are under the impression that he passed on information to someone else and they need to discover that person's identity.'

'Let's hope they don't know about you, then.'

Ryan was thinking the very same thing, but his own safety wasn't a priority. 'You know Jack better than anyone, Grace. Assuming he's still alive, he won't roll over and cooperate; he'll be fighting, no matter how futile his efforts against armed men determined to get him to open up.'

She stopped what she was doing and sat down at the kitchen table. Dragging a whisky bottle towards her, she poured them each a shot and slid one across to him. Ryan stared at the amber liquid for a long time, trying hard not to let his head go down.

He failed miserably.

'What else?' Grace said. 'There's something you're not telling me.'

He glanced at his watch. 'It's been almost twenty-seven hours. I'm worried.'

Grace didn't deny she felt the same. 'Listen, I know you can't talk openly about what you were working on. I understand that. I also know that you'll have been over and over it in your head, but are you absolutely sure Jack wasn't nervous about anything currently involving foreign nationals or issues of that nature?'

Ryan shook his head, eyes on the whisky glass. 'There were no covert ops going on, certainly nothing that posed a threat to the wider public. We were intelligence gathering as always. We weren't involved in any extremist shit.'

'Close protection? Anything involving the CTU?'

Another shake. The Counter Terrorism Unit had been quiet for a while.

'So what were you doing,' Grace asked, 'generally?'

'Trying out a new ID system at the airport. Mundane stuff.'

'You sure it's not relevant?'

Ryan shrugged. 'Who knows?'

'Well, is it working or not?' Grace climbed down. 'Sorry for being arsey. I didn't mean to jump down your throat. What I meant was, are there no problems that haven't been sorted, anything that might threaten national security and let terrorists in? Does the new system do what it says on the tin?'

Her eyes were like lasers, looking for a reaction. Ryan didn't need to tell her that the e-Borders system wasn't happening. With more than two hundred million passengers crossing into the country every year, the idea was to check them before they began their journey, allowing the UK Border Agency to target those who shouldn't be allowed in. When he didn't answer, she let it go.

'OK,' she said. 'Let's see what Frank comes up with.'

'You seem to have a lot of faith in him.' Necking his drink in one go, Ryan set the glass on the table for a refill and chanced his arm. 'You guys have history?'

'Makes you say that?'

'Do you?'

'Way back.' Grace looked away. 'It's over.'

'Doesn't seem that way to me.'

'What? You think he still has the hots for me?' She rose from her seat, smiled. 'Do me a favour. I'm way past my sell-by date and, even if I wasn't, I wouldn't be telling you.'

Her attempt at cheerfulness was woefully inadequate. It was tough for her to talk about Newman in romantic terms. Any fool could see that. Ryan apologized for having stepped in something that was none of his business. He stood up and walked round the table. Extending his arm, he was about to lay a hand on her shoulder, but then thought better of it and took it away again.

'Sometimes life sucks,' he said.

'We were good together once.' She didn't look at him. 'You're curious about him. That's OK, everyone is. He has that effect on people. It's irresistible . . . to both sexes. We worked together a long time ago, a short secondment for me when I was riding high on the way to promotion. We were young and very much in love.' She looked sideways, eyes misting slightly, and managed a brave smile. 'We've kept in touch but seen each other infrequently the last twenty-five years, sometimes planned, the last time not – a chance meeting in a railway station in Prague.'

'That must've been difficult.'

'Not at all.' She was blushing. 'We spent the night together.'

'Let your guard down, eh?'

'No one was twisting my arm.'

'You're a real catch, Grace.'

'Ha! I'm the lucky one.' She sucked in a breath. When she spoke again, her tone was laced with sarcasm. 'It was much more difficult when he vanished five hours later.'

'He just took off?'

Her nod was almost imperceptible. 'He had no choice. I never saw him again until today.'

'He's MI5?'

'Not any more.' Grace turned her head away. Ryan caught sight of her reflection in the blackened window, pain etched on her face. She pulled down the blind as if she couldn't bear to think of herself as young and see herself now, even though she was in excellent shape for her age. She turned to face him. 'It's never been easy for us. We've always had to tiptoe around one another. A long time ago we had a choice to make: a stolen night here or there, or nothing.'

'That must've been difficult.'

'We did the best we could under the circumstances. I don't expect you to understand, but when you've found your soulmate, time is immaterial. Now you know why I never mentioned him.'

'Too risky, eh?'

'Something like that . . . I represented baggage, Ryan. That was a no-no in his game. Besides, he's not the forever type. It would never have worked out.'

'He's here now.'

Grace fell silent and Ryan left it there.

Pouring Newman a drink, he wandered into the living room, wishing he'd kept his big mouth shut. The former spook was still hard at it, the dining room table strewn with images and a diagram he'd printed off the computer, along with notes from their mini house-to-house which had thrown up no anomalies, no conflicting statements they could get their teeth into.

Setting the glass down, Ryan looked past him to a wall-mounted mirror, rubbing at the five o'clock shadow covering his jaw. He needed a shower, a shave, but there was more work to do. He withdrew to Grace's favourite arm-chair and called his sister. They had spoken every single day since he'd left home aged nineteen. Never missed. Not once.

'There's no news,' he told her. 'I'll swing by tomorrow if I have time.'

Caroline wouldn't hear of it. 'Keep looking for Jack. I miss him.'

Ryan's words caught in his throat. 'I miss him too.'

They said goodnight.

*

At eight-thirty, Grace called them through to the kitchen. She insisted they take a break for dinner, even though Newman had made it clear that he would much rather push on through. He ate in silence, leaving his whisky untouched in the living room. When they were finished, he excused himself from the table and went straight back to work.

'The man is a machine,' Ryan said as he and Grace began to wash and dry the dishes.

'You wouldn't think he'd been up since four a.m.'

'Doing what?'

'Sourcing the equipment he brought along, presumably. Getting his car ready for the long drive south.'

'From where?'

'He didn't say.'

'You don't even know where he lives?'

'Fisherman's cottage on the east coast of Scotland. I'm not sure exactly.'

'Must be an official secret,' Ryan said drily.

Grace gave a half-smile. 'I bet you'd love it all the same.'

'I'm sure I would. Not that I'll ever get an invitation.'

It was half past midnight when Newman finally knocked off. Sitting back in his chair, he stretched his arms above his head, rotating his aching neck. He yawned loudly. In total, it had taken him six hours. Using technology the police could only dream of, he'd created a three-dimensional image of the crime scene, in bad light, from several angles, superimposing the prison van, the Audi and the Clio with precise measurements. They were in business.

17

Jack woke suddenly, panicked by what the Swede had said about Hilary and Lucy, hoping it was just a ploy to get him to talk. He clung on to the notion that Ryan would die rather than allow anything to happen to his family. If they were at any risk, no matter how slight, he'd have them in a safe house, locked away, official or not. That thought – and a conviction that his DS would be doing his utmost to find him – was all that was keeping Jack's head up.

Something – he didn't know what – crawled up the side of his cheek across an open wound. He yelled out, flicking it off with swollen fingers that felt like rubber and didn't seem to belong to him, shuddering as it hit the wall and scuttled away. Apart from the Swede's voice and keys turning in the lock, the creature's bid for escape was the only sound he'd heard since he'd been thrown to the ground and held captive.

The vicious kicking he'd taken last night had left him lying in a pool of blood and vomit. Together with the stink of piss from the makeshift urinal in the corner of his hovel, the stench made him baulk. Overnight, the temperature had plummeted. His extremities were numb, his left eye completely closed, upper and lower lips split and swollen. Lying with his back to the floor, he stared into the darkness, listening for the slightest sound that might give his location away.

Still nothing: no hum of traffic, echoes or reverberations of machinery, no aircraft or railway noise. A silence made worse by the pitch darkness and a sense of loneliness unlike any he'd experienced. Closing his eyes, he imagined arguments at work, the chatter of police radios, the squabbles of his children at the breakfast table, his wife's harsh tone telling them to cut it out – all things he thought, until now, got on his nerves.

Thinking of his family again brought hot, salty tears to his eyes. Were they safe with Ryan looking out for them? Jack had to believe it. The alternative was unthinkable. Either way, they would be inconsolable, his wife especially. Hilary was tough on the outside, soft on the in. she'd fight the grief and pretend she was handling herself, but she'd be barely holding it together. With only three years until his retirement, she'd already planned a million things to do before they turned up their toes. Jack wasn't ready to go yet . . .

Not here . . .

Not now.

For her sake, and for the sake of his kids, he had to survive.

He pictured Hilary lying on her side in bed, propped up on one elbow, her beautiful eyes wide with excitement, discussing their bucket list: *We could go to Niagara Falls, and Table Mountain. I want to see the aurora borealis too – from anywhere on the planet. Jack, we must!* They had made love until they were both exhausted, Jack pointing out that they had the rest of their lives to do stuff like that. There was no rush.

Now he wasn't so sure.

Guilt ate away at his insides. He had to live long enough to take Hilary back to Norway. He'd taken her there in the summer under false pretences. When she'd discovered his hidden agenda, they had fallen out over it, the worst quarrel in the whole time they had been married. He had to make it up to her – somehow.

Jack felt for his watch, its luminous dial the only measure of how long he'd been kept prisoner. It was gone. Without it, he couldn't tell if it was night or day. Alone and disorientated, he wondered what steps were being taken to find him. The police would be looking, of course, if only to make an arrest. But how hard? They were stretched at the best of times and he was now just one more scumbag on the run, a fugitive from justice who'd be caught some day.

He coughed up blood and spat it out, his throat parched. He'd been given nothing to eat or drink since the hijack. His tongue felt like it was twice its normal size. Lying in the dirt in the dark, he rolled his head first one way, then the other, his neck crunching with every rotation. Stretching his arms out to either side was painful beyond belief. He could touch both walls.

He was in the centre of the room.

Hauling himself off the deck, he staggered to his feet. One hand clutching his ribcage, he began pacing to keep himself warm. If he stood against the far wall, it took four paces to reach the other end, lengthways, only three from side to side. When breathing became difficult, he slumped into a sitting position, propped up against the wall, his knees pulled towards his chest. His favourite movie came to mind: Steve McQueen enduring solitary confinement in *The Great Escape*. Only difference was, Jack didn't have a ball or anything else to keep his mind off his inevitable fate, no breakout plan.

The cooler.

Of course . . .

His cell was subterranean. Not the end of a bricked-up tunnel but an underground chamber, an icehouse like he'd seen in big country estates in the middle of nowhere. The question was, where – still in Durham, or somewhere else?

Wherever it was situated, its isolation scared him.

Think!

Only one of his captors had come the time before last. If that happened again, perhaps Jack could rush him. With great effort, he struggled to his feet and found the door. He fingered the edges. It opened inwardly. If he were to position himself behind it, and hit it hard enough, he could use its size and weight to crush someone hardly expecting him to put up a fight.

How many steps would it take to reach it?

Several times he measured it out. Timing would be crucial. A split second late or early and his plan would fail.

Who was he kidding? With broken ribs, he'd puncture a lung for sure. Then where would he be? In spite of the risks, he had to try. After the beating he'd taken last night, his abductors had come back to check on him, free of masks and fully tooled up; indication of intent. They weren't reckless in revealing their identities. It was no happy accident, in his opinion, but their way of unnerving him, relaying a message of such clarity it made him tremble. It was then he realized he wasn't going home to Hilary and his kids. Not now. Not ever. For the first time in his life, he was petrified. Unless he took drastic action, he wasn't going to make it out alive.

18

Sunday morning. Shortly before dawn. In Grace Ellis's living room, Ryan reached forward and turned up the radio: '. . . The hunt goes on for Northumbria Special Branch officer, Detective Inspector Jack Fenwick. Police have flooded the region in order to recapture him and apprehend the men who assisted his escape. A press official stressed that under no circumstances should members of the public attempt to approach these men. And in other news . . .'

Ryan tuned the presenter out in favour of three active computers on Grace's dining table, all of them switched on. On one monitor, an image rotated so it could be viewed from every angle, the result of Newman's efforts the previous evening. He'd worked with scrupulous attention to detail, creating what could only be described as a mini crime scene, with vehicles in situ. A conjuring trick, the result of which was spectacular.

The second screen was running footage of the scene as the hijack took place, sent by courier to the BBC. The third was similar footage; this one taken by the female witness whose video was in the hands of Detective Superintendent Eloise O'Neil. Every police officer in the force had been shown the latter. Ryan was grateful to Roz for downloading a copy on to a memory stick for him to use as a comparison, despite the danger of losing her job if caught. His ex was doing her best to get on his good side.

She was wasting her time.

'So . . .' Ryan slowed the footage down, comparing the videos frame by frame. 'It seems that the person who took the BBC video was not the girl running from the scene. Hers was much closer to the action. O'Neil will come to the same conclusion eventually.'

'She will,' Grace said. 'But she'll need a specialist to re-create what Frank's done here – and they don't come cheap. She'd have to be certain it's worth her while to jus-tify that kind of expense to headquarters. We have the jump on them.'

Ryan studied the screen. The degree of planning was obvious. The vehicles were on the southbound carriage-way. The woods to the west were significant, he was sure of it. There was no footpath on that side of the road. Was that why the prison van was hit at that particular point? he wondered.

In Newman's 3D diagram, based on meticulous calcu-lations, there were two crosses outlining the exact position each person was standing when the videos were taken, prompting Ryan to pose a question. 'You think the girl who took O'Neil's video saw the person who took the other?'

'Not unless she has eyes in the back of her head,' Newman said.

The spook didn't elaborate. He didn't need to. Ryan knew what he meant. The videos were almost identical, except that one was taken from much further away. Someone was standing several metres behind the female witness and off to one side. And there was something even more odd about the footage he couldn't quite put his finger on. Then it came to him, a faint light emerging through the fog.

Picking up a remote, Ryan rewound to the point where Jack jumped down from the security van. Flanked by the hijackers, he was led to the waiting Audi, the bonnet of which was protruding slightly in front of the stricken van, before disappearing from view. Ryan pointed at the screen, another question arriving in his head. 'So *why* did the hijackers take him round the east side of the security van? The west side is more direct and the safest option as it's away from the houses and therefore out of sight.'

His words hung in the air.

Ryan reminded the others of what Irwin had told him, moving his index finger over the monitor as he spoke. 'The Clio driver legged it across the northbound carriageway and into the woods here, the girl on the pavement this way towards the houses. Initially, I assumed that the couriered video was taken by one of the householders living nearby, but it couldn't have been. The angle is wrong. If that had been the case, it would have been taken from the girl's left, not her right. The photographer would hardly run into the middle of the road, exposing him or herself to risk. They would have taken it from the security of their locked front door. Pound to a penny, Monsieur Clio is involved.'

'Told you he was good.' Grace threw a smile at Newman

that wasn't returned. 'The Clio driver could have waited until Irwin and Storey were face down on the ground and crept out of the woods to take the second video.'

Newman remained silent, his expression unreadable.

Leaving them to cogitate, Ryan went off to use the bathroom. He was parched from inhaling their smoke, in dire need of a drink and some clean air. A run on the beach was on the menu later if he could possibly manage it. Halfway to the door, he paused. 'I'm going to grab a coffee. Anyone want one?'

Newman waved him away like an irritating fly.

Ryan couldn't get a handle on him. He was a man of many secrets and few words. That part he could understand. Being in Special Branch, he too had operated in a world of shadows and whispers, but the former spook's uncommunicative approach bugged him. It felt personal. Every time Ryan tried initiating conversation, the irritating shit either cut him off, or else made light of it.

On the way back down the stairs, Ryan decided to wait for his coffee. Instead, he went into the kitchen and got himself a glass of water before rejoining the others. He hadn't meant to eavesdrop but the sound of Newman's voice prompted him to stop short of the living room door, curious to know what words of wisdom the quiet man was about to impart on the other side of a partition wall while he was out of the room.

'What makes you so sure you can trust Fenwick?' he was asking.

'Gut instinct,' Grace said. 'I've known him years. I trust him.'

'Would you think the same about me?'

She didn't answer.

'Would you?' he pushed. 'You never know anyone a hundred per cent.'

'That's true . . . I thought I knew you once.'

Ryan was about to cough, to flag up his re-entry into the lounge, to avoid a potential and embarrassing 'elephant in the room' moment. But as he reached for the door, Newman suggested that Jack had gone dark, that selling firearms seized by the police and due for destruction was a lucrative business. That was very true, Ryan had to concede. They could be resold for anything between fifty quid for a handgun to three hundred for a double-barrelled shotgun, to scum stupid enough to buy one.

In the living room, Newman was getting short shrift from Grace. She was pointing out that there had never been any suggestion that the guns recovered from Jack's home were ever in the possession of the police.

Newman again: 'You don't know that any more than Ryan does. O'Neil may be keeping that one up her sleeve. Clever move, if you ask me.'

'I'm not asking you,' Grace snapped. 'I know Jack. Take my word for it, he's as straight as they come.'

'What about Ryan?'

'What about him?'

'Is he as straight as they come too?'

There was a long pause.

In the hallway, Ryan imagined the black look that might have passed between them. Grace was degree standard in that respect. She was confrontational at the best of times and fiercely loyal to her friends. He imagined her glowering at her former lover, the man she'd kept secret all the years he'd known her.

'Are you questioning my judgement?' she asked.

Yup. She was pissed.

'An observation is all.' Newman's tone was flat. 'O'Neil had nothing on Ryan first time he was interviewed. Ever ask yourself why she suspended him second time around?'

'A minor breach,' Ryan said as he walked through the door. 'They want me out of the way while they find Jack.'

'Unless *they* took him,' Newman said.

Ryan mocked him. 'This is not Russia, my friend.'

His comment drew a snigger from Newman. 'Oh, you don't think that's possible? Think again, pal.' He glanced at Grace. 'You sure you trust this guy?'

A knot formed in Ryan's stomach as his anger grew. At the same time, he was trying to be grown-up about Newman's scepticism. As ex-MI5, by definition he was trained to be suspicious of everything and everyone. Hell, they all were. That didn't mean it didn't hurt. Yesterday, he'd seemed like a team player. Today, he was anything but. What had passed through his mind during the night was anyone's guess. Whatever is was, it had cast doubt on *his* credentials.

There was only one way to go. Ryan walked out.

19

Pulling away from the house, Ryan took a left towards the city with Newman's accusations ringing in his ears. This early on a Sunday morning there were few cars on the road and fewer people; one or two locals walking their dogs, some heading to the local newsagent, no doubt waiting for the next instalment of the Jack Fenwick saga.

Leaving Fenham behind, he drove over the busy central motorway and on through a set of traffic lights. On his right, cows grazed lazily on the Town Moor, a thousand acres of common land – the green heart of the city – and in the distance, St James' Park football stadium dominated the skyline. The sight of Newcastle United's hallowed ground was usually uplifting. Today it reminded him that his boss had missed the last two home games on the trot. Unheard of. Ryan was losing faith that he'd get see another.

The thought of Jack's empty seat unsettled him, transporting him to the stadium, a game against Cardiff City. Everyone was yelling, supporting the team, no clue that the absent fan, his friend, was languishing in jail on a trumped-up firearms charge, stripped of all he held dear, separated from his wife, his kids and close colleagues. Surrounded by over forty thousand screaming fans, Ryan had never felt so lonely. Unable to bear the anguish any longer, even though his team were winning, he'd left the stadium before the game ended.

Another first.

Slowing for a cyclist crossing the road ahead, he turned left through Kenton, eventually joining Ponteland Road, where he picked up speed. As he approached the slip road near Black Callerton, a sign alerted him to lay-by parking. Had there been room, he'd have pulled off the road for a few moments of peace and quiet, to get his head straight before facing Hilary. As it turned out, the lay-by was full of cars, their owners unhappy about exorbitant parking charges at the city's airport half a mile further on. Ryan knew the score. One by one, mobile phones would ring as planes touched down, then drivers would move off in convoy to pick up loved ones.

Hilary was in her garden when he arrived, the kids still fast asleep in bed. She wished she could rest too, she told him, but he could see she'd done little of that in the last few hours. Torment oozed from every pore.

'I'd rather keep busy . . .' She put down her secateurs, swept a rogue hair from her pale face. 'It's the only way I can cope with this bloody nightmare.'

They sat down on a bench under a Japanese acer that overlooked an ornamental pond. Ryan and Jack had dug it out one hot weekend a couple of years back, a summer BBQ afterwards, a few beers, a lot of laughs following a hard day's graft. Fringed with reeds and well established, it looked like it had always been there. It was a welcome addition to a tranquil outside space, a good place to sit and contemplate.

Not today . . .

Jack's birthday.

Ryan didn't know whether to mention the occasion or leave it be. 'How are the children handling things?' he asked.

'As you'd expect.' Irritation crept into Hilary's voice. She looked him straight in the eye. 'I didn't ask you here for small talk, Ryan. When were you going to tell me?'

So that was why she'd texted him to come over so early.

'Who told you?'

'Steve's wife. She rang last night. It was bound to come out eventually. I'd much rather it had come from you.'

'I'm sorry. I didn't want to worry you.'

'Worry me?' she huffed. 'In the whole scheme of things, your suspension is low on my list of priorities. I don't mean to sound callous, but you and I both know it'll be temporary. No one will make such a puny allegation stick in a million years. Eventually, O'Neil will realize she's made a mistake. In the meantime, your unemployment might work to our advantage – or Jack's.'

'Hilary, without a warrant card I'm stuffed.'

'Don't you see? This is good news. You're now available to work full-time on finding him. I know you can do it, Ryan. I told Robbie as much last night. No wonder the poor bugger is still asleep. He's exhausted, and so relieved to hear that his father is finally coming home. Knowing that you're on the case has given him such a boost.'

Jesus! Ryan dropped his head.

What worried him most was her certainty that his availability would trigger a new impetus in the case. She was talking with confidence, as if the outcome was a foregone conclusion, one he didn't share. When he glanced up, her expression was strange. It didn't fit with the seriousness of the situation. He reached for her hand, managed a weak smile, and fought to keep his eyes from giving away his true feelings.

He looked down at the cloudy sky reflected in the water, her false high playing on his mind. She was almost euphoric, clearly not herself. Ryan was no doctor but even he could tell that she was on some heavy medication that was only now kicking in. He didn't have the heart to tell her that things were moving slowly. He couldn't mention that Grace had brought a spook in, let alone that there was some infighting going on, that Newman was suspicious, that *he'd* walked out.

He didn't tell her much . . .

An hour later, when the kids got up, he left.

20

Ryan decided to face the music at his sister's house in Alnwick. If Hilary knew of his suspension, then it stood to reason Caroline would too. Presently, he had something more serious to worry about, a sudden and overwhelming feeling that he was being watched. It began as a prickle at the base of his neck, a feeling so strong he wanted to look over his shoulder to check if he was alone in the car.

His eyes found the rear-view mirror instead.

Nothing untoward.

Telling himself not to give in to paranoia worked for a short while only. A few miles further on, he felt the same physical sensation that he was under surveillance. This time he made the tail. At least he thought it was a tail. He couldn't yet be sure. Yes, there it was again: a dark car, edging out from behind a trailing lorry, then pulling in again – an old BMW.

Approaching a major roundabout, he considered going round twice and then decided against. It would only serve to tip them off that he was wise to them; far better that they didn't know. Instead, he turned left on to the A1, heading north, driving in such a way as not to raise suspicion, continually checking behind. To be absolutely sure he wasn't imagining things, he doubled back, a detour. The village of Stannington was perfect for his needs.

One road in . . .

One out.

Bringing his car to a stop, he parked in the front row of the Ridley Arms car park, nearest the road. In his peripheral vision he saw the Beamer drive slowly by as he got out of the car. Pointing his key fob at his vehicle, he locked the door and went into the pub. A few minutes later, he left again, a bag of crisps and a bottle of water in his hand.

When he pulled away, the BMW appeared almost immediately. Parked a good way down the street, its occupants were doing their best to pretend they were waiting for someone. Ryan knew different. He also knew they were a lone surveillance team. Had they been anything else, a second car would have taken the eyeball.

O'Neil's men.

Immediately, he called her office. Considering the fact that he no longer had rank, he didn't bother giving it when the phone was answered. 'This is Matthew Ryan. Put me through to Professional Standards.'

The line clicked and he was put through. He requested O'Neil and was placed on hold. A few seconds later, she came on the line, that velvet voice, as cool as you like. She probably figured he'd had enough time off and was ready to cooperate with her investigation.

She was a mile wrong.

'Call your dogs off,' is all he said.

'Dogs? If you're suggesting you're under surveillance, I can assure you you're not.'

Ryan didn't expect her to admit it. There was no hesitation in her voice, though. Nothing that might indicate she was lying. If she was, she was good. *She was very good.* Fair enough. As a police officer, he too had been consistently economical with the truth in the course of his job. There was no point reacting with outrage. She was perfectly within her rights to follow him as she saw fit. So why was she so infuriated by the accusation?

'Ryan, if you're being followed, it isn't us—'

'Oh yeah?' He didn't let her finish. 'Maybe you forgot. Slate-grey BMW 3 Series. Double-crewed. Both male. Remember it now?'

'No, listen! I'm being straight with you. If you are being followed, you need to watch your back. You could be in danger. I swear it's not an official tail. If it was and we were rumbled, I'd tell you. Despite what you may think, I don't lie to fellow officers. I have enough grief without inviting more.'

It irked him that she thought him stupid; even more that she was entertaining the idea that he was also dishonest. Despite the fact that they were on opposite sides, he respected the way she handled herself. Always had. It took a special kind of person to do her job and keep their friends when it came to investigating her own kind.

The day he was suspended from duty wasn't the only time Ryan had seen her. The first time had been at a fund-raiser held at HQ. They'd not been formally introduced. He'd merely observed her from across the room, talking to a visiting chief constable who obviously didn't have the nous to realize who was interrogating who.

A wry smile crossed his face.

He admired O'Neil's strength and intellect. Unlike Roz, she appeared to be a woman of integrity. Everyone said so. Instinct told him she was on the level. So, if she wasn't responsible for the surveillance operation, who was? *Maguire*. He could have organized it without her knowledge or say-so. He'd made his feelings clear. There was bad blood between them. The moron would like nothing better than to hang a Special Branch colleague out to dry, another high-profile collar, another tick in the target box.

'Ryan, are you there?'

He cut the connection.

21

Ryan lost Maguire's surveillance team just to piss him off, arriving at Caroline's house shortly before midday. His concerns over the jungle telegraph were not unfounded. She knew of his suspension and was terribly upset, her face puffy and tear-stained. For her to be in her dressing gown so late in the day was unheard of. Sitting in her kitchen, nursing a mug of black coffee, she looked like she'd been up half the night.

Even her guide dog looked sad.

Ryan felt bad. 'You had enough on your plate. I never meant to add to your grief. I thought – wrongly as it turned out – that my troubles would all blow over and the suspension would be lifted before you got wind of it.'

'Well, you were wrong, weren't you?' she snapped.

He tried changing the subject. They talked for ages about Grace and, without being specific, another person helping him. They also discussed Hilary and the kids, O'Neil and Maguire, the incompetence of the officers who'd followed and lost him, the fact that he'd come up with nothing worth a damn. He told her everything and didn't stop until he was done. Eventually, she stopped crying.

'I'm to blame,' she said, wiping her eyes.

'No, you're not. My looking in on you during work time was sanctioned long before Jack's arrest. When I find him, he'll tell Maguire that. My absence was only a minor breach of the rules. It won't go anywhere, I promise you. It's not your fault that the moron decided to act on it. He did it for his own reasons—'

'To get rid of you?' Caroline asked.

'That's one way of putting it.'

'What other way is there?'

Ryan said nothing.

'Tell me you weren't rude to him.'

He didn't answer.

'Oh, Matt . . .' Her lips were a hard, thin line. 'I still can't believe you didn't tell me.'

'I was trying to protect you from more upsetting news. Bad move on my part, I accept that now, but I did it for all the right reasons. C'mon, this is no time to fall out with each—'

'Yeah, well, you should've thought about that before treating me like a child.'

'I'd never do that!'

'Wouldn't you?'

A further attempt to appease her failed. In fact, his words had the opposite effect. He'd never seen her so riled.

Conscious that her yelling was distressing Bob, she crouched down to give him a cuddle. When she looked up, her bottom lip was trembling. Slowly, she began to calm down. Still, her tone of voice had an edge to it that cut him dead. 'What's happened to you, Matt? Since when do we hide things from each other? It's not like you. Why has Jack's disappearance made you so secretive?'

'I said I'm sorry.'

'I'd like to know why you're giving up on him—'

'I'm not!' *Anything but.*

'Aren't you? He's your best friend. He's *my* best friend!'

Wrung out from the tongue-lashing, Ryan left her alone and climbed the stairs to the room he'd grown up in, where he stayed over often rather than drive to the coast late at night. He sat on the edge of the bed, images of his late father looking down at him from every wall. PC Ryan, as he was then, in full dress uniform, steely eyes shadowed by the peak of his cap. His cap badge, all shiny and new, shone out like a beacon from the photograph, reminding Ryan that he had one like it and that it might just come in handy.

His eyes flew to the bedside cabinet.

Fishing inside the drawer, he found what he was looking for: his old warrant card, replaced when he was promoted. He flipped it open, took in the issue number embossed in leather on the left-hand side. Running his thumb across the silver badge, a lump formed in his throat as he recalled his time as a detective constable. He was happy then – full of enthusiasm for a job that now seemed to be shafting him from every angle.

A tap on the door pulled him from his daydream.

'Matt? Can I come in?' His sister entered.

Ryan got to his feet, apologized again. Putting his arms around her, he held on tight, feeling her body relax into him as her anger faded away, his eyes on the warrant card still in his hand – *his ticket to information*. Caroline was correct. Whatever Newman thought of him personally, he couldn't abandon Jack. He promised to get his act together and look for him.

22

Ryan took a shower, changed his clothes, packed a bag and left the house immediately, telling Caroline he didn't know when he'd be back. It could be days. He'd keep in touch by phone. As he reversed off the driveway, he noticed her standing at the Georgian window of the living room. She waved. Instinctively he waved back, even though he knew she couldn't see him. It almost cracked him up.

The BMW showed up as soon as he met the open road. The surveillance detail was sitting in a lay-by waiting for him. Ryan had memorized the registration on the way up. Number plates were something that stuck in his mind. Years of training had fine-tuned his ability to recall them at will. Lifting his mobile off the passenger seat where he'd thrown it, he accessed the voice memos app and spoke the registration into it for future reference.

Maguire's goons were such amateurs.

As he drove on, Ryan considered his future in the force, questioning whether or not he wanted to remain a police officer in a culture that allowed the presumption of guilt even when a man was innocent. Jack might not be feeling the love, but then, come to think of it, neither was *he*. Fighting crime had defined his whole life in more ways than one. What else was he good for? He could think of no other job that would supply the same adrenalin rush.

His phone rang: *Grace.*

Before she had time to speak, he apologized for walking out in a strop. 'It was petulant. I'll make my peace with Newman when I get to town. A difference of opinion doesn't mean we can't work together. The important person here is Jack. I'll just have to prove to Newman that his suspicions are unfounded.'

'How very grown-up,' Grace said. 'It's a cliché, but actions really do speak louder than words. If it's any consolation, the situation is getting to me too. You need to understand that stress is not a word in Frank's vocabulary. He's used to it. I'm not defending him. I'm trying to make you aware of where he's coming from. Trusting no one has kept him alive, Ryan. What he said about you, about Jack – it's not personal. Anyway, believe me when I say that we've come to an agreement that you're one of the good guys. We need each other.'

'I know.'

'What's happening your end?'

'Caroline just gave me earache.' Ryan explained about the row with his twin. 'Other than that, life is hunky-dory.'

'Don't worry about it,' Grace replied. 'She'll calm down soon enough. In case you've forgotten, it's not in her psyche to be mean or resentful.' That much was true. Caroline was kind and caring, always saw the good in people, never the bad.

Despite the reassuring words, Ryan still felt like he'd let her down.

'Anything else I need to know?' Grace asked, an attempt at getting him back on track.

'Yeah, none of it good. O'Neil is having me followed – although she says she's not.'

'You talked to her?'

'Briefly. She denies it, of course.'

'Could be Maguire.'

'That would be my guess.'

Grace swore under her breath as if Newman might be listening. 'Don't tell me they have this address?'

Ryan felt her anxiety down the line. That would be the worst possible scenario.

'No,' he reassured her. 'I called in on Hilary after I left you. They tailed me from there. I'm certain I wasn't followed from your place.'

'Can you shake them off?'

Smiling, Ryan put his foot down.

23

He needed to get rid of his car. On a Sunday, with less traffic on the roads, there was only one way to do it. Travelling at speed on the A1 south, Ryan took a detour into Newcastle, entering the city centre at five past three. Dropping down on to St James' Boulevard to Times Square multi-storey car park, he drove up to the fourth floor, heading for a bay as close to the exit door as he could get.

Grabbing his bag, he locked the Discovery and legged it to the stairwell. As he pressed for the lift, he ventured a look through the narrow panel in the door in time to see the Beamer drive up the ramp, the men inside scanning in both directions looking for him. He couldn't believe their incompetence. There was one way out of the car park and there were two of them. Anyone with half a brain would've parked up on the street and sent their colleague in on foot.

He continued to watch as the BMW pulled up sharply.

The passenger jumped out and approached his car, a look of disdain on his face when he realized there was no ticket on the windscreen. It was a pay-on-return facility and he had no bloody idea how long Ryan intended to stay.

Time to put some distance between them.

Entering the lift, Ryan pressed for the ground floor.

Once outside, he sprinted up Railway Street, the wind

at his back. This was never a busy part of town and he needed the cover of others to blend in and disappear. The lights were on red, so he crossed the road and sped up Marlborough Crescent, passing the Centre for Life on his right. Cutting through Times Square was a good move. In seconds, he was lost in a crowd attending an art exhibition set up in the centre of the pedestrianized area. Only then did he chance a look over his shoulder. There was no one on foot following him.

Now was as good a time as any to make a move.

Mingling with drinkers making their way into the Blonde Barrel for a pint, he edged his way nearer to the Neville Street exit, then peeled off and broke into a run. Keeping an eye out for the BMW, he moved swiftly past a line of taxis waiting in the car park, dodging smokers getting their fix outside the entrance to Newcastle's recently modernized railway station.

He checked the clock on the portico.

Perfect timing.

One flash of his old warrant card at the barrier and the ticket inspector let him through in time to jump aboard the 15.48 Edinburgh train. So what if he didn't have a ticket? If challenged, he'd call the British Transport Police and invent some cock-and-bull story about trailing a serious offender. By the time they checked his ID – *if* they checked his ID – he'd be off the train at Alnmouth. In the end, that wasn't necessary. He was sweating so much, pressing his point that he was hunting someone on the run, the ticket inspector took little notice of his warrant card and let him through.

Thanking him, Ryan jumped aboard Coach M, a first-class carriage. He removed his jacket, took a seat. No point moving down the train if he could get away with a free upgrade. East Coast staff even offered to feed him. Much as he could've done with a shot of alcohol, he opted for coffee instead and a packet of shortbread biscuits, his favourite.

He called ahead.

A taxi was waiting for him when he disembarked at Alnmouth station at ten past four. It whisked him away and in no time he was back at his mother's house, calling out to Caroline as he closed the door behind him.

She appeared from nowhere. 'Did you forget something?'

'Sure did.' Pleased to see that she was up, dressed and looking a lot less agitated, he bent down and kissed her on the forehead. 'I need to borrow Mum's car. OK with you?'

'What if I want to use it?' she joked. 'What's up with yours?'

'Nothing. I just fancied a try of a Honda Jazz.'

Caroline laughed, even though she'd never seen one.

He made it to Grace's house surveillance-free at quarter to six, explaining his delay. Newman handed him a beer on the way in. That was all he was getting by way of apology.

They clinked bottles.

Nuff said.

Newman didn't like the sound of the tail on Ryan, suggesting it might not be the police. Maybe the Security Service was involved somewhere down the line. All options were on the table until they discovered what Jack had been investigating.

Grace threw Ryan a smile. 'Told you it wasn't personal.'

Newman's proposition sounded too far-fetched. Ryan wasn't buying it, although he had to concede that conspiracies weren't always theoretical. Maybe Jack had found his Watergate, a scandal so big that government departments were involved at the highest level. The only way to be sure if Newman was pissing in the wind was to go along with it.

The spook offered to drive around and check on police safe houses in case Jack had been taken there and held against his will. And, because Ryan was Special Branch, they had a starter for ten because he knew exactly where they were.

'For what it's worth,' Ryan said. 'I think we're wasting our time. The guys following me were useless.'

'We've got sod-all else,' Grace reminded him.

'I have the registration of the surveillance vehicle,' Ryan offered. 'There's one way to find out if it's the police on my tail and that's to clone a car myself. A mate of mine has the exact same model, arguably in better condition than the one following me, but not noticeably so. I'm sure he'll let me borrow it if I ask nicely.'

'Mind if I take care of the rest?' Grace asked.

The two men looked at her.

'O'Neil and her team aren't looking for me,' she added. The suggestion made sense. Besides, Grace had set her sights on going undercover, her favourite aspect of police work since joining up thirty-odd years ago. Having listened to her outline what she had in mind, the two men grinned. They liked her style. It was a plan that just might work.

24

While Newman went off to check safe houses, Grace went shopping. Not only for food – although she bought that too – along with enough office supplies, alcohol and fags to keep three going for the foreseeable future. The coming days would be frantic. Meals would be simple and easy to prepare, a case of take it or leave it. She'd selected a particular supermarket, one she was familiar with. When she was done, she dumped her purchases in the boot of her car and did a recce of the car park, thinking through her undercover strategy for the following day.

The southwest corner was ideal, assuming Ryan could persuade his pal to part with his beloved BMW. It had been windy the last couple of days. Some overhanging horse-chestnut trees had lost their leaves. Perfect for what she had in mind. She didn't risk picking any up in case she was seen acting suspiciously, but made a mental note to collect some on her way home.

On the way back to her car, she pulled out her mobile and called Ryan.

He picked up immediately.

'Any joy with that BMW?' she asked, getting in.

'Yup, we're good to go.'

'Did your mate ask why you needed it?'

'He's Job. He knows better.'

'I like him already.'

Grace rang off and made another call. The guy on the other end owed her a favour. It was time to call it in. Ordering a set of number plates, she told him she'd send someone to collect and pay for them first thing in the morning. No names were mentioned. No receipts required. Hanging up, she drove away.

Further on, she scanned the street. Spotting a horse-chestnut tree, she pulled up alongside and got out. Collecting a handful of fallen leaves from the ground, she shoved them surreptitiously in her bag, climbed into her car and continued on her journey, arriving home a few minutes later.

She packed away her shopping, satisfied that her idea had legs. While she was out, Ryan had cooked a simple shepherd's pie. When Newman got back, they all sat down to eat. The spook was none the wiser from his trip round the safe houses. He hadn't seen the BMW in any location visited. He'd returned hungry and weary, much like Grace. For the first time since they had met, Newman and Ryan seemed to hit it off over the meal. This was gratifying for Grace, given that she had to go out again. She had an urgent errand to run.

Leaving them deep in conversation, she left the house and made her way across the road, returning fifteen minutes later, armed with a couple of weighty plastic bags and a walking stick with a bone handle in the shape of a wolf's head. Not ideal for her needs, but not far from it. In the art of subterfuge, she'd been taught never to use a prop that might draw unwelcome attention or could easily be traced. But, on this occasion, she couldn't help herself.

She smiled at the irony.

All she needed was the sheep's clothing.

Mounting the stairs two at a time, she went off for a dress rehearsal. Setting the contents of the two bags out on her bed – clothing, wig, costume jewellery and stage makeup borrowed from a neighbour heavily into amateur dramatics – she took her time applying face powder and pink blusher, pencilling in overly arched eyebrows and slapping on lippy too dark for the pale complexion of the octogenarian she was trying to create.

Next, she changed clothes: thick tights, a grey skirt, a flowery blouse done up to the neck, a bulky cardigan, an overcoat, scarf and flat black heavy shoes with laces. The grey wig was a perfect fit. She added a hat, picked up her walking stick and looked in the mirror. She had to admit, the transformation was amazing. Even her mother wouldn't have recognized her. *She was her mother.*

25

First thing Monday morning they breakfasted together, Ryan and Grace opting for a full English to keep them going all day, Newman helping himself to muesli, the eating of which he managed to turn into an art form.

This guy did nothing in a hurry.

Afterwards, Grace sent him off to pick up her dodgy registration plates and Ryan to collect his friend's BMW while she got dressed for the performance of her life. By the time the two men returned, shortly after nine, she was cloaked in the invisibility of old age.

Ryan fitted the plates while Newman took the leaves she'd collected the night before and super-glued them under the windscreen wipers, enough to obscure the tax disc without raising suspicion.

'You ready?' he said.

'As I'll ever be,' Grace answered in an old lady's voice.

She drove to the supermarket, parking up in a spot she'd chosen on her previous visit, making sure the car was in full view of CCTV. With the aid of her walking stick, the handle taped over to hide the wolf's head, she hobbled into the store, bought a newspaper and made her way to the cafe, where she overstayed the three-hour parking limit, knowing it would trigger the issuing of a ticket, then she shuffled up to the information desk, apologizing profusely for having done so.

Although sympathetic, the tall, thin lad behind the counter couldn't do anything to assist her. He didn't brush her off. On the contrary, he took his time explaining that it wasn't up to him to police the car parking area. Although employed by his management, the security company responsible for that side of the business would most probably spit out a fine automatically if an offence had been committed.

Grace knew they were shit hot. A friend of hers had been caught more than once and had received fixed-penalty notifications in the post the very next day. Employing the most distressed face she could muster, Grace peered at the lad through a pair of bifocals, telling him she was only just managing on her small pension and had no money with which to pay a substantial fine.

'Someone told me it will be seventy pounds,' she said, her bottom lip quivering.

The lad tried for reassurance. 'Less if you settle within seven days.'

'But still . . .' Reaching for the counter, Grace feigned distress. 'I lost my husband. Please,' she begged. 'I can't pay.'

'I'm sorry.' The lad seemed genuinely upset by her predicament, his face the picture of understanding. He took a sheet of paper from under the counter and held it out to her. 'Here are details of the security company. Why don't you give them a ring?'

'Could you? I'm not good on the phone.'

There was a moment of hesitation. 'OK. What's the registration number?'

'Bless you.' Grace reeled off the number of her false plates.

The lad made the call, explaining her situation almost word for word. From the look on his face, he was getting the precise reaction she'd anticipated: indifference. Repeating the registration number, he paused, listening to the person on the other end, his expression one of regret. Asking them to wait on the line, he covered the speaker with his hand. 'I'm sorry,' he said. 'The ticket has already been issued.'

'Really?' Grace checked the clock behind his head. 'But it's only one thirty. I'm only an hour overdue.'

'He said that he needs a word.' The lad held out the phone. 'Apparently, the registration number has come up as a blocked vehicle. He's asking for your name and address.'

'Oh no!' *Oh yes!* Grace dropped her voice to a conspiratorial whisper. 'I haven't been truthful with you, young man. That's because I . . . I bought the vehicle from the police and now I'm concerned because I've not yet informed the DVLA. I've changed my mind about the ticket. Please tell him I want to pay.'

Taking the receiver, the lad did his best, then shook his head and handed her the phone.

This time she took it. 'Hello,' she said, her voice all of a quiver.

'I need your name and address, madam.'

'Can't I appeal?'

'No, sorry, pet.' He sounded nothing of the kind. 'I don't get the money myself, you understand. I just work here. I've heard every excuse in the book as to why people don't deserve a ticket.' He laughed. 'Take my advice: don't appeal it. Clear the debt and take more care next time. You'll save yourself a lot of grief.'

Patronizing bastard.

Grace gave him dodgy details, rang off and left the store.

Only when she'd cleared the car park did she call Ryan, letting him know that the surveillance vehicle was blocked. That meant that the car was definitely official. O'Neil, Maguire . . . or maybe not . . . it could be CID or, even worse, someone from the Security Service, as Newman had already hinted at. If so, they were operating independently of the police. That begged a worrying question. Was a department or organization other than Professional Standards after Jack?

26

Ryan put down the phone. The blocking of the BMW by the DVLA only told half the story. The vehicle might well be official, but there was an alternative to the teams Grace had suggested might be responsible for the surveillance operation.

'What's stopping clever offenders cloning a vehicle and making out they're someone they're not? If Grace can do it, anyone can.'

Newman was nodding. 'What do you want to do?'

'The important thing is finding out who exactly they are.'

'Agreed. Tell me who to track and I'm on it.'

They waited until Grace got back for a debrief. After a short discussion, they agreed to lay a trap. Grace had done her bit for the day, so Ryan asked Newman to drop him in town behind the Central Station, away from prying eyes. They couldn't afford for the wrong people to see Newman's car and track them to Grace's. The two men left the house immediately.

Newman parked in Forth Street. Ryan got out and walked to Times Square multistorey, where his own car was parked. He paid his dues, collected his Discovery from the fourth floor and drove out of the car park, turning right and right again, then along Forth Street, straight past Newman, who was poised to follow on behind.

A few seconds later, Newman called him. 'BMW behind you with two-car cover,' he said.

'Got him.' Ryan replied. 'OK to lose him?'

'Be my guest. I also have cover.'

'OK, good luck. Let me know what gives.'

Newman grinned as Ryan pulled away. The BMW followed suit and so did he. Trying to keep up with Ryan in the city would take all the concentration of any surveillance team, even more so if they were sloppy. These clowns in the Beamer were so incompetent, he was sure that while they were looking ahead, they wouldn't be taking any notice of what was going on behind. In twenty minutes, they had lost Ryan completely.

The BMW slowed and stopped.

Pulling up on the other side of the road, Newman saw the driver slam a hand on the dash in frustration, ranting at his co-driver. The surveillance team, such as it was, had fallen for their deception and been outclassed. Newman was impressed with Ryan. He'd made losing them look like child's play.

The guys in the BMW cruised around for almost two hours trying to pick up the scent, checking car parks, on and off-street. If they were official, Newman knew they would do anything rather than return to base and tell their supervision that they had failed once again in their mission to keep an eye on their target. As darkness fell, it became obvious that Ryan had vanished into the chaos of rush hour as many thousands poured into their cars trying to make it home.

Pressing a speed-dial button on his phone, Newman kept an eye on the BMW and gave Ryan a call, updating him on where he was and his direction of travel, giving a running commentary of his changing position through the hands-free as he drove. Eventually, the Beamer stopped outside a grotty pub in an unlit road on the edge of an industrial estate. Its two occupants got out and went inside, presumably to lick their wounds and get their story straight for when they returned to base. Newman waited a few minutes, making sure the coast was clear, then got out of his car as Ryan pulled up behind, killing his lights. *Game on.*

There was never any dispute which of them would attach the tracker. As a serving police officer it wasn't fair to ask Ryan to do it. And, with a history of covert operations in MI5, Newman was well placed to take on the task.

He moved quickly and got to the car unseen.

Attaching a comms transmitter to his lapel, Ryan looked on as the spook dropped to the ground, reaching under the rear end of the vehicle to attach the tracking device. Ryan guessed that Frank Newman wasn't his real name. It would be one he'd inherited in the service of Her Majesty, a handle that had arrived complete with legend. New background. New identity. Untraceable. A history that bore some truth, enough to convince anyone who looked into it – probably someone MI5 knew was already dead and buried.

The sound of a door opening made Ryan freeze.

A shaft of light lit up the street and then died as a well-built male came outside, allowing the door to swing shut behind him. If he hadn't sparked up, Ryan would've lost him in the darkness. The man moved forward, dragging heavily on his cigarette, the glowing ember pinpointing his position.

'They're on the move,' Ryan whispered, retreating into the shadows. 'Abort! Abort! Unidentified figure approaching at your three o'clock.'

Newman was quick to react. Rolling over, he clasped hold of the underside of the BMW and heaved himself underneath without making a sound. The smoker didn't move. He took another hit of nicotine, before the door opened again and a second male joined him.

Shit! The two men were heading straight for the car.

As they got in, Ryan's first thought was to step forward and speak to them. He hesitated. That moment of indecision meant he was too slow to intervene. Car doors slammed shut. The vehicle's engine started up. Lights came on and it drove away. Ryan held his breath and his position until the taillights disappeared from view, his heart beating rapidly, eyes straining to readjust to the darkness. Taking a mini-Maglite from his pocket, he shone it along the road to where the car had been parked. Newman was lying there motionless. Ryan listened, watched. There was no movement of any kind, no sound, not even a whisper of wind through the chain-link fence and surrounding vegetation.

'Newman? You OK?'

No answer.

'Newman?'

Moving closer, Ryan's stomach knotted. An image of Grace entered his head as she shared a private joke with Newman that *he* wasn't party to. At some point in the past, their relationship had been really special. Despite years apart, it was clear that their feelings for one another hadn't diminished. Ryan had observed the odd lingering look, the occasional supporting hand on her shoulder, a sexual tension as tender as lovers half their age.

They were still very much in love.

Ryan was trying to figure out what to say to her when Newman got up, rubbing his head where it had bounced off the tarmac when the guys got in and started up the car. 'That was a tight squeeze,' he said, brushing muck from his jumper. 'I'm glad there was only two of them. The suspension wasn't up to much.'

'You mad bastard. They could've driven over you!'

'Relax – they didn't.'

Ryan let out a long breath. He had no need to comfort Grace on the sudden death of a lost love. Somehow they had managed to get away with it. They had a tracker on the car. Job done.

27

Jack Fenwick knew how police officers' minds worked. Even mates he'd served with for years might think he'd gone dark. He couldn't bear the thought of being remembered as the arsehole who'd escaped out the back of a prison van helped by thugs carrying sawn-off shotguns. It had been stupid not to share his concerns with anyone, not to have told Ryan where he'd hidden his notebooks. He'd find them eventually – *a week, maybe two* – but it would take him even longer to decipher and make sense of them, a thought that hit Jack hard.

By then it would be too late . . .

For him, anyway.

Unless he could manage to escape, chances were he'd end his life in this tomb. It was probably so well hidden, no detective in the world would be able to find him. The sad truth was, the Swede would kill him eventually. He and his cohort were facing a long stretch for abduction, possession of firearms, false imprisonment and wounding with intent – and that was just for starters. Manslaughter would be added to the list if Jack could get the word out.

If was a very big word.

As hope died, the sound of heavy boots made his heart race. For a moment, Jack wasn't certain he'd heard correctly, or if fear had triggered a hallucination. He strained to listen. The footsteps were real, echoing as they connected with a hard surface. Definitely moving towards him. Only one pair, he was sure of it.

Adrenalin pumped through his body as a key turned in the lock.

Could this be his lucky day?

An arc of dim light flooded his cell as the door swung open. Jack was thankful for that. Any more and it would've blinded him after spending so long in pitch darkness. Like Bruce Lee on speed, he took a deep breath, raised his leg, snapping it forward rapidly, releasing a breath as he struck the door with such ferocity, the force of his weight behind it sent the hijacker sideways, smashing his head against the brick wall, his gun flying from his hand.

The kick was executed perfectly.

Jack was in luck . . .

It was the Swede's sidekick this time, not the man himself.

Down but not out, the hijacker scrambled for his gun. Jack got there first. Using the butt end of the firearm, he smashed the guy full in the face, breaking teeth. Whether in defiance or raw fear of retribution from the Swede, he came back at Jack, his neck muscles bulging with the amount of effort he was using to propel himself forward. Jack managed to duck, hit him again, felt a spray of blood as the weapon connected with his nose, knocking him out cold.

Staggering out, Jack locked the door behind him.

Barefoot, he inched his way along a narrow passageway and up a deep flight of stairs, bouncing off moss-covered walls on either side, expecting the Swede to appear at any moment.

No one came . . .

No sound either . . .

It was eerily quiet.

At the top of the stairs, Jack waited, allowing his eyes time to readjust. Bats were ducking and diving all around him, annoyed at the disturbance. He imagined his opponent regaining consciousness in the chamber below ground. Now he'd seen the terrain, the thought didn't worry him. No one would hear him scream from there. The jailer had become the prisoner. Until the Swede came looking, Jack was fairly sure he was safe.

He peered out from the entrance, the moon through tall trees casting long shadows on the ground. Good camouflage. In the distance, a walled garden, overgrown. Beyond it, a ruin of some sort, a romantic mansion Hilary would fall in love with and beg him to buy.

Which way?

Jack hesitated.

Closing his eyes, he listened, heart racing. An owl hooted nearby and Jack could hear the distant hum of traffic, a mile, maybe a mile and a half away. He didn't think he'd make it, but he had to try.

Panic set in when he heard the sound of a car approaching – *the Swede.* Jack had to get out of there, fast. Sharp stones beneath his feet made progress difficult as he set off, taking cover in hedges where the landscape allowed, then running for his life, arms like pistons, sweat leaking from every pore. He was weak, his breathing deteriorating with every step, slowing him down. He had to find a road . . .

A phone . . .

Ryan . . .

He had to.

The fall to the ground knocked the wind out of him. Jack looked up at the inky sky, forced to rest. He wanted to sleep but couldn't risk shutting his eyes, certain that he'd never wake again. His breathing was getting worse, what air he managed to inhale coming in shallow gasps. He knew he was in trouble when a sudden pain began in his shoulder and spread across his chest, like an elephant's foot pressing down on him, crushing him.

A heart attack?

No. Broken ribs. Like sharp, serrated knives inside his body, they were cutting and injuring him each time he took in oxygen, causing an incredible amount of pain. Convinced that his lung was punctured and might collapse at any second, Jack feared he might die within yards of the highway he was trying to reach as lorries thundered by in convoy, drivers listening to music or chatting with each other to kill the boredom of a long journey, oblivious to his plight.

Looking back the way he'd come, he saw a flashlight moving from side to side. At least one of the hijackers was hunting him. He urged himself on . . . he must get up . . .

make one last effort to escape. If he didn't tell his story, more people would die.

Rolling over on to his left side, a silent scream leaving him, he hauled himself to his feet, swaying like a Bigg Market drunk on a Saturday night, unable to stand still, walk a straight line or see the way ahead. Incapable. Insensible. Except drunks were numb from the effects of alcohol. He had no such anaesthetic to dull the pain. He could feel every inch travelled. Every last breath.

Another few yards and he'd be there . . .

Ten . . .

Five . . .

He wasn't going to make the road.

Hugging himself, trying to stem the agony and maintain consciousness, he stumbled around in the dark, painfully aware that he was running out of energy. Running out of time. If he didn't get help soon, he was a goner. He'd never again make love to Hilary or cuddle his kids, never tell Ryan what a great friend he'd been – the best a guy could hope for. Those thoughts drove him on, gave him a reason to live, an extra incentive to survive.

It took superhuman effort to propel his body forward, but he wasn't giving up. Not yet. Not ever. Just a few feet more and he'd be there. He was almost at the point of collapse by the time he reached the road, each step a little closer, but increasingly tortuous. He wept as he felt the smooth tarmac beneath bare and bloodied feet. Time stood still. There was a lull in the traffic. Then nothing. The road was empty. No noise whatsoever. No lights.

No!

Unsure whether or not he was hallucinating, Jack peered into the darkness. He listened. Silence. Then out of the gloom, a blob of light emerged on the horizon, faint and far away, but definitely travelling towards him. It multiplied before his eyes. Yes! Cars were coming . . . both ways now . . .

He had to flag one down . . .

He had to.

The first vehicle flew by although Jack was sure he'd been caught in the headlights. The second also failed to stop. Who could blame the drivers? In so rural an area, in their shoes, he might also think twice. Women would feel especially vulnerable, suspecting robbery or rape on such a lonely stretch.

The flashlight was getting closer and then it found him.

Staggering into the middle of the road, he raised his hands and prayed that he'd be seen.

The next car wasn't slowing . . .

Wasn't stopping . . .

Oh God!

Jack knew what he had to do.

Now!

As he'd been trained to do, he tried launching himself high in the air to lessen the impact on his legs, but he was so feeble after his terrifying run that he failed to get off the ground. The car was going at such speed he hardly felt the impact. He just flew over the bonnet and roof so fast it was like being sucked at high speed through a wind tunnel. He landed with a solid thump, skin ripping from his body as his weight carried him forward. He ended up facing the rear of the car that struck him.

Barely conscious, Jack turned his head as a vehicle on the other carriageway slowed and then took off without stopping. Fifty yards away the flashlight went out. Now all he could see, up ahead, were two fuzzy blobs of red.

Brake lights . . .

Stationary . . .

Forty metres ahead.

The driver of the four-by-four that hit him got out and moved quickly towards him, an indistinct silhouette in the moonlight. A tear left Jack's eye. At last, help was on its way. It seemed to take forever for a pair of work boots to arrive.

'Hello, Jack.'

The foreign voice chilled him to the core.

The Swede crouched down, leaned in closer. 'Now do you have anything to tell me?'

Jack's stomach heaved. If he gave in now, he was finished.

'As you wish.' The Swede took off.

As he got back in his vehicle, white reverse lights came on.

28

The tracker led Ryan straight to the Regional Organized Crime Unit office. It angered him to think that they were involved in Jack's situation somewhere along the line, a situation that ate away at him as he drove to Fenham to share the information with Grace.

Newman had beaten him in.

Grace convened a meeting at the kitchen table, clearing away notes she'd been working on while they were out, replacing them with a hastily prepared supper consisting of sandwiches, crisps and pickled onions. Newman's underwhelmed expression angered her so much she gave him what for.

'Don't screw up your face, Frank.'

'It's hardly nutritious—'

'It's food. Get it eaten. While you've been out playing dodgem cars, I've been doing all the mundane stuff, otherwise known as hard graft.'

Newman picked up a sandwich.

Ryan stifled a grin – they sounded like an old married couple.

'So,' Grace said. 'Which one of you is going to tell me where we go from here?'

'The Serious Crime Unit don't know we're on to them

. . . yet,' Ryan replied. 'I want to keep it that way for the time being. Whatever Jack was working on, you can safely assume those bastards knew about it. I want answers. Like why they didn't come clean before he was locked up and thrown in a cell to rot. If they had, the abduction would never have happened.'

'You think O'Neil knew?' Grace asked.

'I can hardly ring her up and ask,' Ryan said, 'Can I?'

Grace let it go. She could see he was pissed off and didn't want to rile him further. They finished their supper in silence, no one bothering to clear away afterwards. Ryan was deeply troubled. The weekend had flown by and he was no further forward in discovering his DI's where-abouts or what had brought about his spectacular fall from grace. What's more, he had the distinct impression that time was running out for Jack.

'There can only be one explanation for the Organized Crime Unit's involvement,' Newman said. 'They think Jack was into something heavy.' He lifted his hands in surren-der before the others could shoot him down. 'I didn't say I agreed with them. It's a logical conclusion, based on what we know.' His gaze shifted from Grace to Ryan. 'If they're following you, chances are they were trailing Jack long before his arrest.'

'And they think Ryan will lead them to him?' Grace asked.

'That's certainly what it looks like.' Newman was play-ing devil's advocate. 'Which means they are looking in the wrong place, wasting precious resources that could be utilized to find our man. I don't know how, or who, but someone has their wires crossed. The whole thing sucks.'

Ryan stood up, began pacing.

Newman was right – when was he anything else? – but that didn't make it any easier to swallow. Neither did it make sense, to him or to Grace. Defeated, she pushed her chair away from the table, dropped her elbows to her knees and put her head in her hands, devoid of ideas. Ryan was similarly stumped. Nothing added up. When Grace raised her head, a question in her eyes, his heart leapt. He'd seen that look before. A flash of inspiration as tangible as any he'd witnessed lately. So why did she look so worried?

Somehow, he knew he wasn't going to like it.

'Did Maguire confiscate your warrant card?' She knew the two men didn't get on.

'What do you think?' he said.

'Shame. I was hoping—'

'I have another.' Ryan produced his old ID from his breast pocket, a smug expression on his face. 'Got a new one when I was promoted. Forgot to hand this one in. Nothing's monitored nowadays. No one asked for it, so I didn't offer. I had a feeling it might come in handy one day – and it did.' He explained about using it on the train.

'Smart move,' Grace said mischievously. 'What would you say if I told you that my home was once a police house and that the wires to run a major incident room are still under the floorboards, ready to be resurrected?'

Neither man spoke.

Unperturbed by their silence, Grace picked up the conversation, suggesting that they appropriate the wires for their own use. She seemed oblivious to Ryan, who had come to a standstill, his mouth dropping open . . .

'The house was set up as a satellite incident room,' she said. 'This was years ago, when the Murder Investigation Team were under pressure with five similar incidents happening simultaneously, some of them linked, all of which the Assistant Chief Constable at the time was keen to resolve. Nothing whatsoever to do with his application to become Deputy to the Metropolitan Police Commander,' she told them. 'I was drafted in to lend a hand.'

'Go on,' Newman was on the edge of his seat.

'When the room was wound up, the wires were simply dropped beneath the floorboards for future use. Obviously they were forgotten about. Years later, when the house went up for sale, I bought it. The wires were still there when I tried to find the earth for a new boiler installation recently.' She looked at Ryan. 'Like you, I forgot to mention it. No, I did!' She pointed at the floor. 'Take a look for yourself.'

'I'd rather not,' he said. The pacing resumed. 'And what's this got to do with my old ID?'

Newman had already made the jump.

Ryan wasn't far behind. The idea was as preposterous as it was ingenious, but he didn't like the sound of it. The spook, on the other hand, seemed to be considering her ludicrous idea as a goer.

He was smiling at her. 'You are an amazing woman, Grace Ellis.'

Ryan swung round to face them. 'Have you completely lost your minds?' He was almost yelling. 'I've pulled some strokes in my time, but that has to be the craziest idea I ever heard. For Christ's sake, I'm a serving police officer! Count me out. I can't, I *won't* be involved in whatever it is you have in mind.'

Newman was enjoying himself. 'Call it recycling.'

Ryan reacted with an emphatic: 'No.'

'Got any better ideas?' Grace didn't wait for an answer. Her focus was on Newman. 'You think it can be done, Frank?'

'If we use a pro.'

'Ah, now I understand,' Ryan rounded on Newman. 'I might have known it was your idea. You're barking mad, the two of you.'

The quarrel lasted a while. Newman didn't enter into it. He sat there watching the other two go into battle, knowing they would work it out eventually. Every argument Grace put forward, Ryan countered, re-emphasizing the point that he stood to lose the most if he involved himself in her bizarre plan – until the phone rang and they were blindsided by a call from Hilary.

29

Ryan slammed open the door to A & E and raced to the reception desk. A young blonde woman looked up, a question in the eyes beneath her gold-rimmed specs. She was attractive, not pretty, sensibly dressed, with skin the colour of porcelain. No make-up. She didn't need it.

Misreading the visible stress on Ryan's face, she asked if he needed to see a doctor.

'No, I'm not ill,' he said. 'Where will I find Jack Fenwick? He's a policeman, emergency admission, brought in by ambulance about an hour ago.'

'Are you family?'

'No, we work together.'

'I'm going to need ID.'

Ryan flashed his old warrant card in front of her face. Accepting it without further examination, she consulted her admissions log and told him that Jack had been treated and transferred to the high-dependency unit, next floor up.

That didn't sound good.

'I'm not sure what room,' she added. 'You'll have to ask when—'

But Ryan was already gone . . .

Racing down the corridor, he dodged patients, medical

staff and visitors in a department stretched to the limit, following signs that would take him to the second floor. He arrived at the lifts. There was no queue for either one, but both were stuck several floors up.

He didn't wait.

Bolting through a double door, he took the stairs two at a time, then through more double doors into an identical corridor to the one he'd just left. There was a sign for High Dependency on the wall facing the stairwell. He was out of breath and sweating like a pig when he finally reached the ward.

Pushing open the door, he entered a four-bedded room, three of which were occupied by elderly patients, one of whom was giving cause for concern, so much so that she'd drawn the attention of the full intensive care team, who were so busy they didn't see him standing in the doorway.

Ryan didn't bother them. Instead he slipped silently through gaudy curtains into Jack's sickbay, surprised to find him alone. When Hilary called she was heading straight there. Maybe she'd taken the kids out to give him some rest. Then it occurred to him that she'd been asked to leave because of the emergency going on in the ward. Having seen the old lady a moment ago, he was firmly of the opinion that she wouldn't need her bedpan later.

There were two chairs stacked beside Jack's bed. Lifting one from the other, Ryan placed it down quietly, the wrong way round. Taking his leather jacket off, he straddled the chair, his forearms leaning on the backrest. The heat in the room was unbearable.

What were they trying to do, fry him better?

Jack's lips were dry and split, his skin so pale it made his facial injuries stand out all the more. His arms were outside of the covers, chest and shoulder heavily bandaged, hands resting by his sides, knuckles bruised and bloodied, fingernails almost ripped off. There were no bones in plaster, drips or beeping heart monitor, unlike the other poor patients in the room. Then again, they were geriatrics and he was as strong as an ox, always had been. There was evidence that he'd been hooked up at some point, a pulse-monitor on the bedcover. The cheeky bastard probably pulled it off so he could get some kip. That was so like him. Pity the staff hadn't got round to giving him a wash and manicure too.

Ryan smiled to himself.

'You look like shit, boss.' His relief at finally being reunited with his DI soon turned to anger. 'You should have told me. I might've saved you some grief. Look at the state of you. You wanted to play the hero, is that it? Hilary's not impressed, mate – and neither am I. You're a selfish git sometimes.'

Jack didn't stir.

Ryan could understand him not wanting to get into it. He was probably exhausted. Well, tough. He wasn't going to be let off the hook that easily. Ryan had questions and wasn't leaving until he got some answers. He was about to deliver that lecture when the curtains behind him whipped open. He turned, expecting to see Hilary and the kids. Instead, he came face to face with a male nurse ready to throw his weight around.

'Sir, are you related to Mr Fenwick?'

'No, but I explained downstairs—'

'Then I must ask you to leave. Patients on this ward are allowed next of kin only. You can't be in here—'

'So, pretend I'm his brother,' Ryan said.

The nurse wasn't smiling. 'If you don't leave now, I'll have to call security.'

'Go ahead, I'm interviewing a witness.' Ryan flashed ID again but the nurse stood his ground. He didn't look like the type to make allowances. Put a uniform on some people and suddenly they're a dictator. 'I won't be long,' Ryan stressed forcefully. 'He's more than a colleague, understand?'

'I'm sorry, we have rules.'

'And I'm asking you to break them.'

'Sorry.' The nurse swept his hand to one side, inviting him to leave the bay. 'If you don't mind.'

'I do mind. You listen to me,' Ryan whispered. 'I've spent three days looking for him. I'm entitled to ask him a few questions, so piss off and leave us be. You want to make a complaint, ring the Chief Constable. You want the number? While you're at it you can tell him DS Matthew Ryan sent you.'

The nurse stood his ground. 'DI Fenwick can't tell you anything, sir.'

'I'll be the judge of that!' But even as he said it, Ryan realized what he meant. He looked at Jack, taking in his insipid complexion, the pulse monitor lying idle on the bedcover, no chest movement. No Hilary . . .

He hadn't seen the obvious because he couldn't bear to. He dropped his head as the nurse covered his best friend with a sheet.

30

Officer down. Officer down! Ryan didn't make it far from the ward before breaking down completely. He found himself in the corridor, fighting for breath, the stuffing knocked out of him. Jack couldn't be dead. He couldn't. Ryan stood outside the door, his forehead leaning against the wall, his broad back turned on hospital staff as they went about their business, every part of his being screaming in agony. He'd been angry with his DI before, but never like this. If only the stupid bastard had said something.

Anything.

Ryan sobbed openly, tried to push the hurt away. He didn't want to deal with the possibility of a new boss – not now, not ever – or consider who'd take care of Hilary and the children, who'd discuss tactics at the match or listen to him talk about his dad. He wanted Jack.

The man was irreplaceable.

No one else would do.

This cannot be happening.

A hand on his shoulder made him spin around. The intensive care nurse who'd asked him to leave was standing there, less strait-laced than before. For a moment, Ryan thought that he had somehow managed to resuscitate Jack and had come to tell him that there had been a terrible mistake and that he was breathing again. Instead he gave his condolences, offering to buy him a cup of coffee, or call someone on his behalf. Ryan declined. Thanked him, or tried to. His mouth was moving but his expression of gratitude was drowned out by the ear-splitting din inside his head.

The nurse pointed at a seat in the corridor.

On autopilot, Ryan made his way towards it and sat down. Shivering as a ghost walked over his skin, not for the first time in his life he heard his father's voice telling him to be a brave boy and do the right thing, be sure to look after your sister. Thoughts of Caroline made him wail all over again. He couldn't face telling her that the one person she cared about, after him, was dead. Jack had become her confidante, her go-to person for everything, even more so than Ryan himself since their mother passed away. The two men had laughed about it. The sad fact was, she knew Ryan was dealing with his own grief, had sought and found solace elsewhere – with Roz.

And what a dog's bollocks that turned out to be.

Jack was more than happy to help Caroline through the bereavement. He loved her, almost as much as he loved his own family. Ryan had let them both down – and not only them – he'd failed Hilary too, her kids and his former colleagues in Special Branch. The red mist descended and his blood began to boil. As things stood, there would be no police hero's funeral for his DI. No Union Jack draped over his coffin. No guard of honour. No heartfelt speech from the Chief Constable.

As things stood . . .

Ryan swallowed hard.

He'd see about that.

Finding the truth and clearing Jack's name was even more important now than it was before. Top priority. However long it took – in or out of the Job – he made a promise to hunt the killers down and put them before a court of law. If it was the final thing he'd do, he'd make it count – for Hilary and the children's sake and, to a lesser extent, his own. Anything else would be unjust. By the time he'd finished, there would be some kind of memorial to show what a fine officer Jack Fenwick really was.

A noise made Ryan lift his head.

A porter was pushing a trolley along the corridor, his smile unreturned by Ryan. The guy was scruffy, acceptable for transporting bags of clinical waste to the incinerator perhaps, not so for accompanying Jack to the hospital mortuary. He didn't look like he gave a shit either. He could almost have been whistling. Ryan wanted to grab him by his crumpled bottle-green scrub-suit and knock some respect into him. As he got to his feet, a phone rang, startling him.

It took a second to realize it was his.

Pulling his mobile from his pocket, he saw that it was Grace. He ignored the call but the audible alert had jolted him into the present. He had to find and comfort Hilary. That was the only thing on his mind. Nothing else mattered. Not Grace or Newman, not even Caroline. Hauling himself to a standing position, he grabbed an elderly nurse, asking for the relatives' room. She gave him directions, offered to accompany him, but he was already on his way, a sense of dread eating away at his insides.

Hilary was sitting alone when he arrived. She'd had the foresight to leave Robbie with the young ones when she left for the hospital. She'd called her dad from her car, asking him to go round and look after them. Relieved that he didn't have to face all four at once, Ryan brushed away a tear and pushed open the door, trying to stem his emotions as he held her close. The rest of the night was a blur.

31

It was light when Ryan eventually got home. As drained and exhausted as he was, he hit the beach running, north towards Low Newton. He didn't stop until his legs would carry him no further, until he was gasping for breath. Then he slumped down on the sand close to the water's edge. Looking towards the horizon, he wept. Not quietly, but in huge, irrepressible sobs like the night his father died – *the worst day of his life* – something he knew he'd never get over.

The wind blew, icy and hard, throwing sand in his face; miniature spikes that stung his eyes and turned his skin red raw. The North Sea was grey and wild. Unremitting. It pounded the shore in great bursts of foaming energy, adding to the fury Ryan was feeling as he scrolled through distressing images of the past few gut-wrenching hours.

Leaving his own vehicle at the hospital, he'd driven Hilary home in hers. She hadn't said a word on the way there, her mind on the grim task facing her. He'd held her hand while she told the children that their father was never coming home, hung around after to offer support. But as close as he was to the family, he felt like in incomer, a stranger who didn't belong.

Ryan wiped his eyes with the palms of his hands,

unable to shake one image in particular: the accusatory expression on Robbie Fenwick's young face as he heard the news he suspected might come but didn't want to believe.

You promised us, it said.

The atmosphere between man and boy wasn't lost on Hilary's dad. He took over then, calling for a taxi to take Ryan away so that the family could grieve alone. It was for the best, he said. Ryan understood. He wasn't welcome. That painful truth made the journey back to the hospital even harder to bear. Having collected his car, he'd sat in it for a while, trying to get his head around what had happened. Unable to take it in, he'd driven to Fenham to break the news to Grace and Newman, then on to Alnwick to repeat the story one final time to his twin.

Caroline said nothing.

Like a shell-shocked soldier, she didn't cry. She seemed incapable. She listened in silence and then asked him to leave, saying she was going to bed. She wanted to deal with this one alone. She didn't need or want his help this time. He pleaded with her to let him stay. But she was having none of it.

Hours afterwards, it still worried him.

It wasn't like her to push him away.

Totally spent, he walked back along the beach, the remains of Dunstanburgh Castle in the distance. Crossing the golf course, he trundled up the road to his cottage, drank half a bottle of Scotch, then lay down on top of his bed fully clothed and fell into a deep and disturbed sleep.

Sad faces invaded his dreams: Hilary, Robbie, Jess and

Lucy holding hands beside an open casket, tears rolling down their cheeks and his. Jack looked so peaceful lying there. No bruises or bandages visible. Just the fit bloke he was, toned and strong, proud of the physique he worked so hard to maintain. Family onlookers faded from view as Ryan approached the coffin.

Jack opened his eyes and sat bolt upright, extending his hand. No hard feelings. As Ryan reached for it, the skin fell away like molten candle wax, exposing raw flesh. Jack's lips were moving. Ryan strained to hear what he was saying. Unable to make it out, he leaned forward, poised to receive a secret, so close their cheeks almost touched, but still he didn't understand.

Something touched his face, causing him to look up.

Pages and pages of handwritten text floated down from above. He grabbed a few but on contact with his hands the sheets melted away like snowflakes, rendering the words useless, the secrets unattainable.

The notebooks were gone . . .

'Ryan . . . can you hear me?'

The voice sounded odd and far away. Ryan fought for control, an overwhelming sense of panic rising in his chest, cutting off his air supply. The neckline of his jumper felt like a ligature. He tried pulling it away, blood vessels popping beneath his skin as he strained to take in vital oxygen. He was choking, the rattle in his throat growing louder and more desperate with every passing second.

Breathe . . .

Breathe.

Try as he might to force his eyelids open, they were

stuck fast. Jack's bloody hand touched his shoulder. He pushed it away, his body jerking and thrashing, as if he was fighting several people at once: Grace, Newman, Caroline and a long line of others, shadowy figures he failed to recognize.

The hand was back, shaking him.

The voice too . . .

'Ryan, wake up. It's OK. It's me, O'Neil.'

The name alone was enough to jolt him awake. Groggy with sleep, Ryan sat up. Swinging his legs over the side of his bed, he stood up, drenched in sweat, hair wringing wet and stuck to his forehead. His mouth was dry. He reeked of booze. When he spoke, he was almost hoarse.

'What the hell do you want?'

'The door was wide open,' she said, stepping back on to the threshold of the tiny room. 'I was worried about you.'

'It's a bit late for that, wouldn't you say?' He pointed at her, something he'd never have done in his right mind. It was offensive and confrontational, but he was hurting . . . and way beyond caring. 'This is *your* fault. Jack's dead because *you* wouldn't listen, because *you* came to the enquiry from the wrong standpoint. You screwed up and never gave him a chance.'

She looked wounded. 'That's not fair.'

'Isn't it? Maguire isn't exactly into finding the truth, is he? He's too busy scoring points against me. Well, I'll tell you something, shall I? My DI was a top bloke. His wife and kids deserve much more than his pension. You were wrong, guv. And I'm on a mission to ensure you pay for it.'

O'Neil just stood there looking at him, a pained expression on her face, visibly shaken by an accusation she didn't think she deserved. 'I do understand—'

'No, you fucking don't!'

She flinched when he yelled at her. Ryan raised an index finger, then withdrew it, clenching his fist so hard his nails dug into his palms. He stuck both hands in his pockets to stop himself from scaring her. He apologized. 'I didn't mean to frighten you. Just don't tell me you understand!'

'I don't scare easily. I follow the evidence. What more can I say?'

'You can tell me how you're treating his death. You know now that he wasn't a fugitive. Did you see the state of him, what they did to him? He took quite a beating—'

'He was hit by a car.'

'What?' The revelation stunned him.

'Whether it was accidental or deliberate is under investigation . . .' O'Neil paused, giving him time to digest information she knew he didn't have. As unpleasant as it was, he took it better than she expected. 'There are, however, some things that give me cause for concern—'

'Like what?' he asked. 'He was innocent!'

She thumbed over her shoulder. 'Could we sit down?'

Ryan brushed past her, moving through the hallway and into the living room. As always it was tidy, apart from an empty bottle of Scotch that lay abandoned on the tartan sofa, along with his leather jacket, his wallet sticking out of the side pocket. Picking it up so she could sit down, he wondered if she'd looked at it while he was sleeping. If she had she'd have seen his old warrant card, his passport into a covert murder room.

Maybe Grace's idea wasn't as crazy as he'd first thought.

O'Neil sat down where the jacket had been, her eyes drawn first to the sea view through the recessed window, then across the room to the patio door that overlooked his outside space, a sheltered yard where, in other circumstances and a different season, he might have invited her to sit and share a bottle of wine. Her focus switched to the wood-burning stove laid ready in the hearth.

'You cold?' he asked. 'I'll light the fire.'

'No, it's cosy.'

He could see she loved the room. Bizarrely, that pleased him. He'd taken such care to make it his own. He adored it: the sea-grass rug, an old chest for a coffee table, especially the sea urchin footrest Caroline had bought him as a housewarming gift – and books – lots and lots of reading material, his secret passion. This cottage was his sanctuary, the only place he felt at peace.

Roz hated everything about it.

'You were saying,' Ryan asked.

O'Neil drew in a breath. 'Jack wasn't wearing anything on his feet when they found him.'

'And that's not suspicious?'

'It needs investigating, yes.' She almost looked embarrassed. 'Initially I thought he'd lost his shoes as a result of the impact. But we've combed the scene and didn't find any. The search is ongoing. His shoes are still missing. He wasn't wearing any socks either and his feet were filthy. It would appear he was barefoot when struck.'

For a moment, the only sound in the room was the wind howling in the chimney, echoing the waves crashing on to the beach a few hundred metres away.

'Why are you finding it so difficult to accept that Jack was held against his will?' Ryan asked.

'I'm not ruling it out—'

'For Christ's sake, listen to yourself! If he'd gone dark he'd have been living the high life in the Mediterranean, wouldn't he? Running about the countryside unshod is hardly the action of someone in cahoots with gunrunners, is it?'

'No, it isn't . . .'

There was more. Ryan sensed it.

'Look,' she said. 'The only information I have at the moment is that he was run over.'

'Mown down, more like.'

O'Neil didn't react.

'Eyewitnesses?' he asked.

A nod. 'One female travelling in the opposite direction . . . she called it in—'

'And?'

'Evidently, the driver had no chance to take avoiding action. Jack ran into the middle of the road and was struck. The car that hit him stopped, so our witness didn't. She was very shaken up. We're trying to trace other witnesses. It's possible that Jack was trying to flag a vehicle down.'

'Because he needed help.' It was a statement, not a question.

'Maybe.'

Ryan searched her face. 'What is it you're not telling me?'

O'Neil hesitated. 'The collision vehicle didn't hang around.'

'You're not suggesting he was the victim of a hit-and-run?'

'The post-mortem will tell us more.'

'His death is being treated as murder, though? Please tell me it is.'

'Not at this stage.'

Ryan felt his temper rise. He didn't even try keeping it in check. 'Why not wash over the whole bloody business? Maybe Jack just came into some bad luck while he was escaping the police. Hey, anything's possible. No murder equals no expense to HQ, physical or financial. That'll be a win-win – a tick in the target box. Give yourself a pat on the back, why don't you?'

'Ryan, you're not helping.'

'No, you're the one not helping.' Ryan paused, white noise filling his head. 'Jack was out of it when he reached the hospital. He flatlined before Hilary got a chance to speak to him . . . did he say *anything* to paramedics at the scene?'

O'Neil recoiled as if he'd hit her.

'What?' he barked.

A shadow crossed her face. 'He asked for you.'

Ryan stood up and turned his back on her. He was fighting for breath, only this time for real. Resisting the urge to bawl in front of her made his sore throat worse.

He stood stock-still, memories of Jack occupying all con-scious thought.

Back in control, he swung round to face her. 'Mind tell-ing me where it happened?'

She gave him a pointed look. 'You know how this works.'

He stared her down until she answered.

'Remote,' she said. 'Durham – I can't say where.' He was about to interrupt but she got in first. 'Before you bite my head off, I want you to know that the scene is being foren-sically examined as we speak.' She glanced at the wooden floor, avoiding his gaze. When she raised her head, he knew she had something to say he wouldn't want to hear – *but first the preamble*. 'I know you don't think so, but I've been straight with you all along—'

'Your point being?'

'Before I came here, I had a word with the duty SIO on the Murder Investigation Team. Although no murder enquiry has been launched yet, I'm treating Jack's death as suspicious. I managed to persuade them to link it with my abduction and uploaded the case on to HOLMES.' That was a big deal. The acronym referred to the Home Office Large Major Enquiry System, a computerized tool for dealing with only the most serious incidents. 'You know as well as I do, mowing someone down, as you put, it is an easy kill. You also know how difficult it is to prove intent.'

'And where do I stand in all this?'

'In what respect?'

'Am I on board? Can I work with you on it?'

She seemed to be considering his request. But then

something happened to change her mind. She was preoccupied all of a sudden, looking anywhere but at him,
her colour rising. Maybe she'd seen his warrant card after
all.

'Guv? What's up?'

'You tell me.'

'Well, it's gone cold in here and it's not coming through
the double-glazing.'

O'Neil pointed at a pile of stuff in the corner of his tiny
living room. On top was Express Quest packaging. 'What
was in the parcel, Ryan?'

'Nowt.' Ryan felt hot. He knew his explanation would
be met with a level of scepticism. 'I know you'll find it
hard to believe – and I'm in no position to prove otherwise – but apart from a load of shredded paper, it was
empty. Why? Has someone sent you one?'

'What do you mean?'

'Come on, guv. It must be relevant for you to ask.'

'The same courier was used to send a video of the
hijack to Nick Barratt at the BBC.'

'Take it,' he said. 'Search the house. It'll only take you
ten minutes. It came yesterday. Delivered to a neighbour
in my absence. I have no idea who sent it. The shredded
stuff is in the recycling bin if you want it for Forensics.
Now, are you lifting my suspension or not?'

'No. I'll review the position when the PM results are in.'

'You're making a mistake.'

'I'm sorry,' O'Neil said. 'I've made my decision. That's
the way it is.'

'Did I say anything?'

'You didn't have to.'

Ryan shook his head. 'If you had no news for me, why the hell come here?'

'Because Jack Fenwick was a police officer and so am I.' Her eyes misted ever so slightly. She recovered quickly. 'And because you worked with him and I know you two were very close. I've been upfront with you, now it's your turn. If there is any information you're withholding, you need to hand it over. There's no longer any reason to hold back.'

'Jesus! How many more times?'

'OK.' She raised her hands in defence. 'Don't say I didn't give you every opportunity.'

'I don't believe this.' Ryan's frustration was mounting. 'I know nothing that can help you. Ask your mates in the Organized Crime Unit, why don't you?'

A flash of incredulity crossed her face before she could hide it. She was genuinely staggered by the allegation that the unit had taken an interest in her case. He said nothing as she stood up to leave. It was time to go to work, for both of them. Frozen out of the enquiry, Ryan made up his mind to go along with Grace's suggestion.

Covert murder room coming right up.

32

'Are you in or out?' Newman asked.

Ryan hesitated. He knew the risk he was taking but was full of hell after his showdown with O'Neil. Although Grace's plan to resurrect an incident room from old wires under the floor didn't inspire him with confidence, Newman assured him it could be done. He nodded his consent. 'I can't see any other way. O'Neil's not listening. She's suspicious of me and she's holding the best hand. She has the law on her side: manpower, equipment and HOLMES at her disposal. It's hardly a level playing field, is it?'

'Yet,' Newman said.

'You sure, Ryan?' Grace was staring at him. In bits, having spent her morning with Jack's widow and children, she'd returned home so drained she'd gone straight to her room, preferring her own company, a situation that was as worrying as it was out of character. She'd always been a team player. Retreating into her own world and blocking them out wasn't her style. She'd only just emerged and even Newman looked troubled.

'Positive,' Ryan said.

As they discussed the way forward, he lost all concentration. The news on the radio was almost as depressing as the task of hunting Jack's killers. A case in Greece had made the headlines after DNA testing proved that a little girl was not the biological daughter of a Roma couple. In similar circumstances, a second child had since been taken into care by child-trafficking officers in Ireland, reminding Ryan that he wasn't the only one searching for the truth.

Grace had gone quiet.

Newman too.

It was obvious to Ryan that the spook felt their sadness, even though he'd never show it and had never met Jack personally. The two men would've got on. Undoubtedly. They had similar personalities. Both played their cards close to their chest, a characteristic Ryan was convinced had contributed to the death of his DI.

'Ryan?' Grace's voice jolted him from his thoughts, prompting him to look at her. 'I'm unhappy about the Organized Crime Unit creeping around the investigation.'

'Me too,' Newman said. 'Are you certain you weren't followed?'

'We're clean,' Ryan said.

'Good.' It was the first expression of faith from Newman.

Ryan understood his reluctance to confide in others.

In their line of work it was dangerous to share intelligence or shoot your mouth off to the wrong kind. The less said, the better. It was second nature to keep your own counsel. They had both learned to rely on their wits to see them through. As Grace had already pointed out, Newman's scepticism had probably saved his life more than once. But like all games, when the stakes were high you had to up the ante. In this particular instance, it meant enlisting specialist expertise.

Newman wanted to bring in a trusted wires man. A highly qualified technician who'd worked for a government-led top secret computer project team, an underground unit only high-level officials knew about. No longer employed by the Home Office, he was up for hire, a consultant and private contractor.

'They come no better,' he said finally.

'We've decided it's your call,' Grace said.

'Do it!' Ryan said.

Newman took out his mobile, scrolled through his address book and pressed the call button. While the number rang out, he put the phone on speaker. A woman came on the line, answering with the number.

'Suzy, it's me. Is Garry in?' Newman asked.

'For you? Always. You want him to call you?'

'Sure . . . the usual number, ASAP. Cheers, hon.'

Newman hung up. Taking another mobile from his pocket, he held it up like a US marshal holds up a badge. He smiled as it rang in his hand. 'Now that's what I call service,' he said, answering.

This time he kept the call private.

'I need a favour.' The smile was gone. 'The way I roll, mate, you know that. Usual place . . .' He didn't specify where, just glanced at his watch. 'An hour,' he said and pocketed the phone.

33

O'Neil burst through the door of the Regional Organized Crime Unit looking for a fight and found one. DC David King stopped chewing, swept the rest of his mid-morning snack into a wastepaper bin and stood up as she entered, introducing herself with an ID card and a look that could kill from a mile away. Her intent was clear. This was no social visit.

'I want all you've got on Jack Fenwick,' she said.

King met her gaze. 'We haven't got much—'

'You obviously knew he was under investigation, correct?' She took in a weak nod. 'Did it not occur to you to contact me or one of my officers?'

The DC blushed. 'We didn't know who he was initially.'

'That I can accept. But subsequently?'

'We knew . . .' King paused, playing for time. 'We'd been following a target for weeks, guv. One day this guy walks in and we didn't know who the hell he was. Only when he was arrested did we realize—'

'Then I'll ask again. Why wasn't I told?'

'It was thought to be inappropriate at the time. We didn't know for sure why Fenwick was there or how involved he was with the people we had under observation. Our guv'nor took the view that you had him sewn up and that we should keep quiet in case it jeopardized our operation.'

'Well, you can tell your guv'nor I don't "sew up" fellow officers.'

'Sorry,' King said. 'Bad choice of words.'

'No shit! Surveillance not your thing, Detective?'

'Pardon?'

'Who sanctioned the tail on DS Ryan?'

O'Neil felt sorry for Ryan. He was devastated by the death of his colleague. Maguire was out to shaft them both. She'd had to rein her number two in, tell him to lay off, at least curb his enthusiasm. She was beginning to think that it had been wrong to suspend the Special Branch officer. If the same was true of Jack Fenwick, she couldn't live with that.

'DC King? I asked you a question.'

'My DCI.'

'Why?'

'For the same reasons you suspended him. We suspected he might be involved with Fenwick somewhere along the line. It seemed worth pursuing. Fenwick and Ryan were close and we were scratching for information. It seemed like the logical thing to do.'

'Involved in what?'

King didn't answer. He was cornered and knew it.

'I see. So, with bugger all evidence you have enough resources to follow policemen around because you think it's a good idea? What the hell did you think you were doing? If you had nothing on Ryan, you had no business mounting such an operation. And by the way, whoever was on that duty wasn't very good at it, because he clocked them.'

'Says who?'

'Says Ryan. He thought I was following him, so he pulled me about it. I assured him I wasn't. It seems he lost your Mickey Mouse team and then followed them here. He thinks I knew all about you. But I didn't, did I? I want answers, Detective. What were you working on?'

'I can't tell you that.'

'You can and you will, or you'll face a disciplinary.'

'Sorry, you're going to have to take it up with my guv'nor.'

The DC was getting more and more nervous as O'Neil persisted. She wanted information and she wasn't leaving without it. In the end he felt compelled to fill the silence by trotting out the party line: 'I have nothing for you, guv. You'll have to go over my head.'

'That's bullshit!' O'Neil glared at him, held her ground. If it wouldn't land her in it and bring on a visit from her own department, she'd rip his head off. 'Has it passed you by that your targets might be the same people my team have been looking for? I may be investigating a miscarriage of justice here and I need answers, so you'd better start talking.'

King was sweating. 'We caught Fenwick bang to rights, associating with guys knee-deep in illegal firearms. So if you think he's innocent, think again, guv. After you arrested him there was no need to tell you we had him in the frame for our job. That's all I'm prepared to say.'

His words made O'Neil feel slightly better.

Slightly.

Maybe Ryan was wrong. Maybe he'd allowed a personal relationship with Fenwick to cloud his judgement. It wouldn't be the first time, or the last. For her own sanity, O'Neil needed to be sure. She pressed on, telling King that what he'd told her so far wasn't good enough.

The DC let out a big sigh, his eyes finding the window, an action that angered her.

'Will you please look at me when I'm talking to you?' she said. 'I have already established that the shotguns found in DI Fenwick's house were recently sawn off, stolen in a series of burglaries on farms in Cumbria. Hardly international arms dealing, is it? It happens almost every week.'

'He was seen, guv! Our targets were in a boozer in the arse-end of South Shields when your man Fenwick wandered in and shared a pint with them at the bar.'

'And . . . ?'

'And nothing.'

'Guilt by association, eh? How long have you been in this unit?'

'Six months.'

'Six months,' O'Neil said. 'Impressive. And where were you before that?'

'Foot patrol in Byker—'

'Well, get ready to go back there. Let me put you straight on a few things. The very nature of being a detective – particularly in Special Branch – means that you associate with prigs on a daily basis, in pubs, at the match, anywhere you can. Most times it's a mutual piss-taking exercise. But even so, it's how you find things out. Is that clear?'

The DC said nothing.

'If I had a quid for every time I'd spoken to an offender in a bar I'd be minted,' O'Neil said. 'It's called intelligence gathering, you idiot. The fact that Fenwick spoke to your target means nothing. It proves nothing. If you'd bothered to read his record you'd know that he was way too clever to shit in his own nest. Even you must've heard of the cliché "keep your friends close".' She paused for breath. 'Where are you in your investigation?'

'Nowhere. We lost them. We shut it down.'

Her expression held a message: *That's a downright lie.* 'You were tailing Ryan yesterday.'

'Maybe you should ask *him* then, guv. Or Fenwick. I heard you picked him up.'

'He's dead, you prick!'

O'Neil walked out. Organized Crime hadn't heard the last of this. Not by a long chalk.

34

The Centurion pub was one of Ryan's favourite haunts in the city centre. Built as a first-class waiting room for Victorian passengers at Newcastle Central Station, the Grade I property was once used as cells by British Transport Police, much of its interior design covered up by unsympathetic decoration. As someone once said, it was tantamount to slapping a fresh coat of paint over Leonardo da Vinci's *Mona Lisa*. Fortunately, the building had since been restored to its former glory.

Newman entered first, Ryan close behind.

The idea of bringing someone else into the mix was less palatable now than when first proposed, Ryan thought, as he approached the long bar. But Jack's death had changed everything. Considering Northumbria's Murder Investigation Team weren't yet treating it as homicide, what other choice was there but to work under the radar and resurrect a murder room so he could investigate the matter himself? Still, he felt his nerve going slightly as he scanned the tables, unable to ID anyone who might be waiting for them.

His agreement to meet with Newman's wires man now felt like a bad move. Try as he might to push that worrying thought to the back of his mind, it continued to niggle him, reminding him that such a devious plan might end his career as swiftly as a knife had ended his father's a quarter of a century ago. Garry Snaith, whoever he was, had asked no questions before agreeing to meet. His keenness to get involved, without due consideration of what Newman was planning, bordered on the suicidal. That, or he had more faith in the spook than Ryan could presently muster.

Ordering a pint for himself and one for Newman, Ryan turned his back to the counter, his eyes once more scanning the busy room, the buzz of conversation drowning out his anxieties.

'No show, eh?' He almost relaxed.

'He'll be here,' Newman said.

Ryan didn't doubt the spook's ability to assess a tricky situation and pick an associate to sort it out, but he felt compelled to point out the seriousness of what they were about to embark upon. 'Setting up a satellite station is one thing. Hacking into HOLMES and the PNC is something else.' On the off chance that he'd forgotten, he reminded Newman that breaching Data Protection and Telecommunications Acts – and that was just for starters – could send them both down for a very long time.

'Grace, too,' he added. 'If your man squeals, we're done for.'

'He won't.' Newman was the epitome of cool.

'You trust him with something this big?' Ryan asked.

'There's only one person in the world I trust,' Newman answered drily. 'Garry comes a close second.'

'OK, he's as good as gold. So where is he? Is Garry even his real name?'

Newman glanced sideways. 'Drink your beer.'

Ryan took a mouthful. 'And if he can't do the job?'

'It can't be done.' Newman just looked at him. 'Relax. He's the best in the business. I've used him many times. What he doesn't know about wires and what goes down them isn't worth knowing. O'Neil left you dead in the water. What alternative do you have but to accept my word for it? You promised Jack's widow you'd hunt his killers down—'

'And that's exactly what I plan to do.'

'But?'

'It's the rules that differentiate us from the shite we're hunting, Frank.'

'Ordinarily, I'd agree. But without my man you don't have a hope in hell of finding them.'

Ryan took another long pull on his pint. He was changing, not necessarily for the better. Newman was right, though. This was no time to lose his nerve.

The pub door opened.

A man walked in and made a beeline towards them, extending a hand to Newman, a big smile on his face. Garry Snaith was a friendly fifty-four-year-old with a dry sense of humour and a twinkle in his eye; a quiet, self-effacing man.

Ryan didn't stand on ceremony. 'Mind telling me why you're no longer working for the government?' he asked.

Snaith grinned. 'I didn't run away with the Crown Jewels, if that's what you mean.'

Ryan's eyes found Newman's.

The spook had a smile on his face. 'My description of Garry as a wires man was accurate but understated. He knows his wires but he's really a genius.'

'Get out of here.' Snaith was almost blushing.

Newman looked at him. 'Credit where it's due, mate. Don't be shy.' He nodded towards Ryan. 'You can tell him. He's Special Branch. An old friend has vouched for him. He's trustworthy.'

Ryan bristled. *Just who was being assessed here?*

'Then he'll know all about the Security Service's need to be able to crack encryption to keep us safe in our beds.' Snaith lowered his voice a touch. 'Let's say that part of my role went up for grabs to a private company who reckoned they could do it a damned sight cheaper than me. They could – only not as well. Contractors have a habit of shaving off corners in order to undercut the competition. How secure do you think that is? I couldn't live with it and said so.'

'Loudly,' Newman added.

'When I wouldn't keep my mouth shut, I was fired,' Snaith explained. 'These days I'm a free agent. I work for people who rate quality and are prepared to pay the going rate for my expertise.' He thumbed in Newman's direction. 'Except when he calls. Then my services are complimentary.'

Ryan looked at him, his reservations melting away.

There would be a story there somewhere.

Snaith turned to Newman. 'What's the deal?'

Newman pulled his chair closer. 'We have an old police

house hardwired to run a major incident. When it was sold, the gubbins were never disconnected. It's not been used for years. We need you to rig it up again . . . like yesterday.'

Ryan was half-hoping Snaith would say no.

'Can you handle it?' he asked.

'Child's play.'

'Will you?' Newman asked.

Snaith couldn't wait to get started.

Ryan relaxed. *No wonder the spook liked him.*

35

Within minutes of arriving at the house, Newman's new best friend was dressed in full forensic suit, including mask and gloves, ready to resurrect what Grace was calling the 'silent room' from under the floorboards, protective equipment his safeguard against shedding DNA. He wanted to help but had no wish to implicate himself should the police discover their treachery further down the line.

Ryan shuddered at the thought.

According to Snaith, technology had moved on at a rate of knots since the original hardware had been installed. He was kneeling on the floor assessing the equipment required to run a major incident from the comfort of the dining table in Grace's living room. The woman herself was uncharacteristically quiet, standing by, watching events unfold. Although severely shaken by Jack's death and incapable of hiding her sorrow, her tough persona hadn't deserted her entirely. Determined to find his killer – unruffled by the engagement of a third party – at Snaith's behest she was noting down a list of paraphernalia required to finish the job. Following an inspection of what lay beneath the floorboards, he took the list from her and left the house.

*

Snaith was back within the hour carrying a large cardboard box full of electrical equipment. Grace couldn't wait to get started. Like a nurse in an operating theatre, she laid the items out on the floor while the surgeon gowned up to make the patient well. The manual labour was a cinch, a question of using the right gear to splice old wires to their more up-to-date counterparts. Working with lightning speed and forensic attention to detail, it took him less than three hours to get the electrics sorted. He then turned his attention to the more difficult task of bringing the incident room to life: setting up a proxy and routing traffic through it, the idea being that it would mask Grace's IP address, hiding the trail of Internet activity so any searches undertaken didn't lead the authorities to her – and ultimately to Newman.

Ryan had the distinct impression that *he* was way down the list of people to protect. Even so, he couldn't fail to be impressed. On the face of it, Snaith was nothing more than a glorified electrician. However, it soon became apparent that he was a computer mastermind with the knowledge to hack his way into the most secure systems at will. Ryan's warrant card would give them access to police systems, but he was in no doubt that Newman's man could infiltrate HOLMES without it.

Snaith picked up his tools. 'Any final questions before I leave?'

'I have one,' Ryan said. 'How will we know if we're being monitored?'

'If it all goes blank, you've been rumbled. I've set up a series of safeguards. If anyone tries to find you, the system will crash and you need to get rid of the evidence. Loosen up, man. That won't happen.' Snaith held out his hand. 'Nice meeting you, Ryan. You too, Grace.' He gave them each a firm handshake, high-fived Newman and let himself out.

36

Ryan nipped home, took a quick shower and packed a bag of clean clothes. He put his computer in the back of the car so he could link it up to Grace's, arriving back at her place after dark. She'd worked wonders while he was out.

The silent room was almost ready.

At the forefront of HOLMES 2 when it was first introduced, Grace knew how the system worked and how to get the best from it. Hell, she'd helped design some of its key features back in the day. As qualified as anyone who currently worked on Northumbria's Murder Investigation Team, the strategy was that she would monitor the computers and feed any progress to the other two. From now on, they were off the grid.

Newman had been busy too. Producing from his pockets three clean smartphones programmed with each other's numbers, he handed them out.

Ryan took one and turned to Grace. 'O'Neil told me that Jack's death will be a linked incident with the abduction. Will all the information we're likely to need be there?'

Grace was nodding. 'Be warned, though: your warrant card doesn't yet have MIR security clearance. I'll have to update your authorization. So don't go putting it in there until I'm done or we'll be sunk before we start.'

Ryan understood. He'd never had Major Incident Room status. The system was password-protected, an authorized warrant card the only way in. In the future he expected it to be fingerprint recognition, but the force was way behind the private sector with a specification well below that required of the average iPhone. Once his approval was activated, his administrator status would give them full access. Bearing in mind the fact that he'd never had a HOLMES course, that was pretty impressive. *They were ready to rock 'n' roll.*

Grace put Ryan in one of three guest bedrooms, the room next to hers at the front of the house. Newman took one at the rear. Ryan figured she couldn't bear the thought of sleeping in the same house as her former lover with just a few inches of plasterboard separating them. While the two men unpacked, she went downstairs to test the computer.

A few minutes later, Ryan followed her down, a lingering doubt in his mind that they could pull off her daring plan without getting caught red-handed and slung in jail. 'Tell me the system is working perfectly,' he said as he walked up behind her.

'Seems to be.' Grace didn't look up from her monitor. 'Everything appears to be responding exactly as it should. No glitches I can identify.'

'Outstanding!' Newman had arrived by their side. He glanced at Ryan. 'Told you Garry knew his stuff. What's up? Still not convinced?'

'I'm on board, aren't I?'

'So why the face?'

'I was thinking about the last-minute change of judge

at Jack's bail hearing. You think it was a deliberate ploy to keep him in custody?'

Newman shrugged. 'It would be difficult to prove.'

'And could equally have been just one of those things,' Ryan said. 'Grace? Any thoughts?'

'For what it's worth, I reckon it was the latter. To believe anything else is taking a conspiracy theory too far.'

On that worrying note, they broke off for a drink and something to eat.

When Ryan returned to the living room, Grace was already hard at work on the computer, engrossed in the system, scrolling through recorded actions for the night of Jack's arrest. He lingered a moment, peering over her shoulder at the monitor. Under the heading 'Scene Searches' he noted that only one date and time was registered.

A knot began to form in his stomach.

Something was wrong.

'Hang on!' he said. 'What about the second search?'

'Second search?' Taking her fingers from the keyboard, Grace looked up, waiting for an explanation. On his instruction, she hit the keys again, accessing a different screen, one that would show which police officers attended Jack's home on the day he was arrested, a category specific within the system. 'There's no mention of it here. All I have is a firearms team and a dog handler. No second search.'

'That's inaccurate,' Ryan insisted.

Alerted by the sharp tone of his voice, Newman wandered across the room to join them. Sure enough, there were only seven names listed: six firearms officers – one inspector, one sergeant, four PCs – and a K9 officer.

The absence of a second search on a system designed to eliminate error worried Ryan. 'Hilary definitely said that two detectives arrived shortly after Jack's arrest and carried out a thorough search. So why isn't it there?'

Grace shrugged. 'According to this, there was no CID search.'

'Maybe she's mistaken,' Newman suggested. 'Let's face it, the woman's in hell right now.'

'She is,' Grace said. 'But she's not stupid.'

'No, she's not,' Ryan agreed. 'And she doesn't make things up. The second search involved two detectives, both male.' He looked at Grace. 'What's the delay in an MIR? Is it possible that the information is with O'Neil's team awaiting input?'

'No, this isn't a rape case, an abduction, or a murder with thousands of messages and statements queuing up awaiting a response. Although it's high-priority, with renewed impetus now Jack is dead, it was a low-key job then. Indexers would be bang up to date. All the information must be there. This was weeks ago, remember. You need to talk to Hilary.'

Ryan sat down in Hilary's kitchen. He'd called ahead to tell her he was on his way, explaining why he wanted to see her. He hated intruding on her grief so early after Jack's death, but the missing details needed investigating and he couldn't afford to hang around 'til morning. Unable to tell her how he'd come by the discrepancy –

grateful that she'd been a copper's wife for long enough not to ask – he repeated his question: 'Who exactly came to see you?'

Her face was blank. 'They were detectives, Ryan. That's all I know. I was in no mood for social graces. I was still trying to calm the kids.'

Ryan had been trying to work out what was wrong since he'd arrived in the house. Mention of the kids gave him the answer. If music wasn't playing, then the television was usually on, the youngest two kids fighting or giggling like a couple of lunatics at some secret they were keeping from their parents, the thunder of feet running up and down stairs. Hilary was always on the go too, forever laughing, cooking something or other. But today the house was deathly quiet, no sounds, smells or warmth. It was cold and uninviting – unheard of in the Fenwick household.

He tried again. 'Do you remember what department they were from?'

'You want the truth?' She glared at him. 'I haven't got a clue. They had warrant cards, that's all I know. I let them in . . . Jack had been arrested. What else was I supposed to do? What does it matter now, anyhow?'

'I'm not criticizing you—'

'Aren't you?'

'No.' Ryan changed direction, coming at the problem from a different angle. In order to jog her memory, he began walking her through the exact sequence of events during and after Jack's arrest. 'I need you to go back to the very beginning. How many officers were in the firearms team?' he asked.

'Five, six—'

'And a dog man, yes?'

'Yes.' She scratched the side of her face, frustrated by his questions. She wanted to be left alone. 'Why are you asking me if you know already?'

'And the detectives came later?'

'Yes—'

'How many?'

'Only two . . . why?'

'Did they have a warrant?'

'They didn't need one. Ryan, I saw the guns with my own eyes.' Her expression shifted from frustration to fear as she put the pieces together. 'Oh my God! Are you saying what I think you're saying? You're not seriously suggesting they *weren't* police?'

'I don't know who they were.' It was a truthful answer. Ryan didn't. But he wouldn't rest until he found out. The possibilities were endless. They could've been Professional Standards. But, if he was reading her right, he didn't think O'Neil would be that devious. Newman's suggestion that they might be part of the Security Service made no sense to him.

'Ryan?' Hilary was way ahead of him.

'They could've been police.'

'Or the men who took Jack?'

'That too.'

'They wouldn't dare, would they? No . . .' She was shaking her head and sobbing at the same time. 'That's not possible. They were the real deal. They had ID. I saw it with my own eyes. I'll tell you this much: if their warrant cards weren't genuine, they were very good forgeries.'

Ryan felt like a total shit doing this to her before Jack was even in the ground. She was inconsolable, unable to bear the thought that the men who'd killed him might have walked around her house within a few feet of her children. He felt much the same, but tried not to let it show. Putting a hand on her arm, he let her bawl. When she was calm, he decided to level with her.

'You cannot share what I'm about to tell you, OK?' He took in her nod. 'The facts and what is officially recorded don't match. I can't go into detail. You'll have to take my word for it. I need you to concentrate, Hil. Forget about the team who arrested Jack. I'm interested only in the two that came after. Can you do that for me?'

Her nod was almost indiscernible.

'Can you remember when it was? What time, I mean?'

'No. It wasn't long after they took Jack away. Ten minutes, fifteen maybe, no more than that. I was still clearing up after the firearms team.'

'And you didn't recognize them?'

'No, but I would if I saw them again. Their faces are etched in here.' She tapped the side of her head.

'What did they look like?'

'Smart suits. Mid thirties, early forties, both dark – hair I mean, not skin. The one who spoke to me had brown eyes. He was in need of a shave. Looked like a bit of a spiv. The other one never approached me so I didn't get such a close look at him. I did notice he had a pronounced dimple in his chin, bit like Aaron Eckhart.'

'That's good to know. Did they give names?'

'No, and I didn't ask.'

'Did they say what they were looking for?'

'That much was obvious.' Hilary's eyes found the floor. There were tears in her eyes when she lifted her head. 'I was trying to calm the kids down, Ryan. Lucy was in hysterics. You know how sensitive she is, how much she idolizes . . . idolized her dad. She screamed and screamed when they took him away. she'd gone into shock. I had to call the doctor out. He arrived shortly after the two men left.'

'How is she?' When she didn't answer, Ryan didn't push it. He knew perfectly well how Lucy would be. Unable to bear the image of her tear-stained face when she was told her daddy wasn't coming home, he quickly changed the subject. 'Did these men offer any information as to why they were here?'

Hilary shook her head.

'They must've said something.' Ryan hung fire, giving her time to reflect, hoping she'd remember something of significance, however small; difficult for anyone at the best of times. More so, given the level of stress she was under.

She looked up, tucked her hair behind her ear. 'I can't remember his words exactly, something about ammunition and other items and articles in connection with Jack's arrest. Only one of them spoke. The other one got on with the search. He didn't say a word.'

'You sure?'

Ryan seized on that tiny snippet of information, his mind working overtime. *Only one of them spoke.* They were the very same words the security guard, Irwin, had used. That thought triggered panic in his chest. He had to get hold of Caroline *fast!*

37

Ryan ran to his car, got in and drove away. Pulling out his mobile phone, he keyed in Caroline's number. His heart was in his mouth as it rang out for what seemed like an age before she finally answered. He told her to lock all her doors and not open up to anyone. 'Not anyone, you hear me?'

'What for?'

'Do it!' he said. 'Put the phone down and put the deadlocks on, bolts and all.'

'Matt, you're freaking me out.'

'Just do it. I'll wait.'

The phone went down. Ryan drove on, imagining her, vulnerable, walking through the house, checking front and rear doors, ramming bolts home, wondering what on earth was going on. He pictured Bob, registering her mood change. Anxious to keep her safe, he'd be there with her, every step of the way.

'Matt?' She sounded alarmed.

'Is it done?' he asked.

'Yes. What's going on?'

'Trust me, it's a precaution. The surveillance team I told you about? It may be that they weren't police after all. Yes, I'll be careful.'

Satisfied that she was safe, he rang off and called Hilary.

'It's me again. Are you absolutely sure only one of the detectives spoke when they were with you?'

'Yes. Are you OK? You sound weird.'

'I'm fine.' Traffic lights changed and Ryan put his foot down. 'I had to call Caroline in case the men we discussed earlier were the same two who've been following me round, trailing me to Alnwick. Although I'm certain I lost them on the way, I'm taking no chances.'

'Is she OK?' Hilary's fear was almost palpable. 'Are you going there now?'

'I can't yet,' he said. 'Don't worry about her. She's very security-conscious. That house is like the Bank of England vault. I need you to concentrate a moment longer. This could be very important. The detective who spoke to you: was he British or foreign?'

'British, English . . . Are you sure you shouldn't be with her?'

'Relax,' Ryan said. 'Caroline has locked all the doors. She'll be absolutely fine. I'll call her later. This Englishman, did he have an accent of any kind?'

'He wasn't local, that's for sure.'

'OK. So, out of area. Can you be any more specific?'

'He had no identifiable dialect. Cosmopolitan is the best way to describe his accent. Southern, but not regional, if you know what I mean.'

'You're doing well. This is helping.' Ryan slowed as a car changed lanes, pulling into his path without indicating. He swore under his breath.

'What? I didn't catch that.'

'It wasn't intended for you. Some prat who needs to take another driving test nearly put me off the road. How long did these so-called detectives stay with you?'

'An hour, no more.'

'When they left, did they take anything away?'

'Nothing.'

'Don't suppose you remember what vehicle they were driving?'

'A dark saloon, I'm not sure what kind. This is all my fault—'

'No, it's not. I don't see what else you could've done.'

'It was blue . . . or maybe grey.' Hilary was weeping. 'I didn't think to get the registration number. Pretty hopeless for a copper's wife, aren't I?'

More lights. Ryan brought the car to a stop. For a copper's wife she was pretty bloody perfect. Jack's luck had been in when he met and married her. They were a winning combination. A couple made for one another. He wanted to tell her that, but now was not the time. Instead, he wished her goodnight and rang off.

At the silent room, he grabbed a coffee and sat down to discuss Hilary's evidence with Grace and Newman. Had there been no personal connection to the victim, the buzz of working on a murder case would have been intoxicating. As it was, it was a deeply depressing, energy-sapping exercise, made worse by working round the clock under constant threat of discovery. Jack was a big miss – *a one-off* – Ryan still couldn't believe he'd gone, but dwelling on his death was counter-productive.

Focus!

'I can see two scenarios here,' he said. 'Only one detective spoke to Hilary. Only one offender spoke in the course of the hijack. Assuming that these might be the same two guys, we're looking for one foreigner, possibly Scandinavian, and one heavy from out of town, in all probability from the south of England. With me so far?'

The others were nodding.

'The way I figure it, these guys were watching the house, waiting for the arrest. They see the firearms team go in and come out with Jack, guns 'n' all. They wait until the coast is clear and then breeze in there pretending to be the mop-up squad. I'm surprised they didn't make believe they were there on behalf of the Federation, cheeky bastards.'

'I don't buy it,' Newman said. 'Guys like that don't hang around. They want Jack gone, they would've taken him out. End of. I mean with a bullet, not by framing him for possession.'

'I'm with Frank,' Grace said.

'That's my point,' Ryan countered. 'They didn't, did they? They could've walked up his garden path at any time and blown him away on the doorstep. Instead they planted guns. Jack is hauled out to face the music. Maybe these guys miscalculated. Didn't figure on the remand in custody. I didn't say I had all the answers. They get another chance to kill him when they hijack the van. They don't. My guess is, they know he has incriminating evidence hidden away, so serious it must be found. They went to the house on a mission to find it, pretending to look for ammo when they were after something else.'

'The notebooks?' Newman said.

Ryan nodded, his eyes flitting from the spook to Grace and back again.

'And the second scenario?' Grace asked.

'The fact that only one of them spoke might be coincidental,' Ryan continued. 'Or, they weren't the hijackers at all. They could be detectives from our own force. Either way, we need to find them. I questioned Hilary about their search method. It was systematic and methodical, exactly as you or I would approach it. From what she told me, they had all the patter. They were professional investigators, or maybe private security personnel, not two organized thugs pulling drawers out willy-nilly. My money is on the police. But in case I'm wrong, I want Caroline here.'

38

Caroline resisted the move on the grounds that it would disrupt Bob and hamper her brother's covert investigation. But Ryan wouldn't hear of her staying home alone. In the end, after some gentle persuasion, he got his way. He packed her a bag, substituted his mother's Honda Jazz for his Discovery, loaded up the car, dog and all, and drove back to town.

It was late, almost ten thirty, by the time they arrived in Fenham. Before she'd even taken her coat off, Newman introduced himself, making her feel at home. The man was charm personified. Conveying his condolences – he knew she was very close to Jack – he sounded more like a parish priest than a former MI5 operative. There was no song and dance, no bullshit, only heartfelt sympathy for her loss.

Ryan appreciated that.

They were all too wired to go to bed so they made small talk, avoiding any further mention of what had brought them all together. Newman said more to Caroline in the first ten minutes of their meeting than he'd said to the others in three days. There was a tenderness in him Ryan had never seen before, a quality that seemed to bond him to his sister. Caroline took to him instantly, laughing at his wit, appreciating his politeness and intellect. To be able to get that reaction when she'd lost her best friend was nothing short of a miracle.

Newman was captivated by her too, transfixed by her likeness to her brother – the reaction most people had when first they saw them together. His eyes flitted constantly between the two, comparing them. It all made sense when she told him they were twins, born a few minutes apart, either side of midnight, Ryan being the younger of the two.

'He must have had a hard paper round,' Newman joked.

'Aw, don't you be mean to my baby brother.' And so it went on.

Grace had wandered off. She was standing alone with her back to them, staring at a bookshelf, only not seeing it. Something about her body language made Ryan's misery over the death of their mutual friend deepen. Her head and shoulders were down. He wandered over to join her, flicking his eyes in Newman's direction.

'Maybe if I'd worn a skirt,' he joked. 'He's so obviously a ladies' man.'

Grace followed his gaze. 'Yes, he seems quite taken with her.'

'If ever there was an understatement, that was it.' Ryan's tone was friendly, jocular. He hated seeing her distressed. 'He's taken with you too, I noticed.' He regretted the words as soon as they had passed his lips.

Her mouth was smiling but her eyes were not.

She'd gone to a darker place, somewhere upsetting –

Heartbreak Hotel – perhaps a moment in time when she'd split with Newman, her true love. Ryan knew her well, but hadn't asked how come she'd never married. Although, he had to admit, the thought had occurred to him from time to time. Now he had his answer. At least she had experienced that level of feeling. He'd had his fair share of relationships, but not like that.

Not even close.

A giggle from Caroline reached them from across the room. Grace didn't look round. She was on the brink of tears. Emotionally spent. Ryan wasn't sure what to do. He wanted to reach out to her but wouldn't risk humiliating her with Newman in the room. There had been enough tears in this house in recent days. Looking at her now, he could tell how much it had cost her to involve her former lover in the search for Jack. She was breaking down, her past and present torment bubbling to the surface. It wasn't Ryan's place to pry. He felt sure that if he said anything – *anything* – the floodgates would open.

He mimed, *I'm sorry.*

Grace managed a smile and then turned her head away.

Newman excused himself from the room and disappeared upstairs. Whether he'd seen her anguish was anyone's guess. When she wandered off into the kitchen, Ryan didn't follow. He joined Caroline, who had just sat down in an easy chair by the fire.

'You OK?' He stroked her shoulder.

'Is Grace?' She'd picked up on the atmosphere.

'She's fine.'

'Not according to Frank.'

So, Newman had noticed the exchange.

'Don't worry,' Ryan said. 'She's tough. She'll handle it. Mind if I leave you for a moment? I want to run through the crime scene video one last time before I turn in.'

'Go,' she said. 'I've got Bob to keep me company, haven't I, boy?'

The dog's tail began to wag.

Ryan ruffled his fur, then sat down at the dining table. He'd examined the scene video several times and yet it told him nothing. Obscured by the prison van, there was no footage of Jack physically getting into the Audi before it sped away. Ryan had watched it twice more by the time Grace emerged from the kitchen with a light supper on a tray. Setting it down on the coffee table, she made a head gesture for him to join her. He stood up as she began pouring the tea, her distress well buried and invisible. She pointed at a plate of thick-cut toast and jar of Marmite, telling him to help himself.

Ryan shuddered inwardly. He hated the stuff.

'Any joy?' Grace was getting stuck in.

'None.' He tried to keep the frustration from his voice. 'We're no further forward than we were at the beginning. There's no verbal exchange whatsoever between Jack and the hijackers that I can see. If there was any dialogue, it must've happened inside the prison van after the comms were smashed, although Irwin was adamant no words were spoken.'

Newman was back, already munching toast, speaking with his mouth full. 'It's possible that he was too far away to hear it. Remember, he was lying on the deck, the rain tanking down, his co-driver in tears, car engines running.'

'That's true,' Grace said. 'And the hijackers would've kept it short.'

'I agree,' Ryan said. 'You can hear them, can't you? *Walk or the security guard gets it*. Or: *Come quietly or we'll kill your family*. Either one would guarantee compliance. So Jack walks calmly from the van to the car, making it look like he's in cahoots. They pile into the Audi and drive away.'

'What about the other car?' Caroline asked.

The question stunned the others into silence. All three looked around, none with any idea what she was on about. Sitting very still, head cocked to one side, Caroline was facing away from the computer, her back to the dining table. Ryan hadn't realized she'd been listening to the running tape. He moved towards her, the others tagging along behind. His sister's face was a picture of concentration, a sight that made his heart leap. He'd seen that expression before and could tell instantly that she'd heard something that might prove vital.

'What other car?' he asked.

'The one that starts up after the Audi takes off. It heads in the opposite direction. I heard it on the tape just now.'

For as long as he could remember, Ryan had known that she possessed extrasensory perception. Neuroscientists had clinically proven that those born blind used other parts of their brains to refine their sensation of sound to a level that surpassed that of sighted people. Was it too much to hope that she was right?

He willed it to be true.

Getting up, Caroline joined him at the table, asking him to run the tape from the beginning. After he'd done so, Ryan glanced at the others. Their blank expressions told him that nothing had registered. Newman edged ever closer, straining to listen as the tape was replayed one more time. At the end of it, they were still as mystified.

Ryan's enthusiasm died.

Grace was shaking her head behind Caroline's back.

'I feel your doubt,' Caroline said. 'Grace, stop it!'

'That's you told.' Ryan grinned. Shuffling forward in his seat, he extended an arm towards the track pad.

Sensitive to the movement, Caroline grabbed it before he could stop the video. 'Let it run on a few seconds after the Audi pulls away.'

Taking his hand away, Ryan did as she asked. Still he couldn't hear anything. In the end, he turned the volume up as high as it would go and, sure enough, he heard a very faint purring sound. Indistinct. Nothing he could identify or use in evidence. He certainly didn't hear what his clever twin was insisting was a second vehicle. He'd have to wait and hope that the enhancement he'd commissioned privately would throw light on her theory, one way or the other.

Even without it, Caroline was adamant. 'It sounds like an old diesel to me,' she said.

39

Eloise O'Neil hadn't slept well. With no food in her apartment, she'd breakfasted at a cafe on her way to work, a simple poached egg on toast and coffee. The news headlines were depressing: more bushfires in the Blue Mountains in New South Wales. Strong winds making matters worse. A state of emergency declared.

With problems closer to home occupying her thoughts, she tuned out the radio. All night, she'd stewed over her angry encounter with DC King and his refusal to share information vital to her case. She'd emailed his guv'nor a formal request for full disclosure of files relating to the surveillance operation on Jack Fenwick, including the names of individuals he was accused of associating with. Ryan too. She wanted the lot.

So far Organized Crime hadn't responded.

The Express Quest packaging she'd retrieved from Ryan's cottage had also kept her awake. She didn't want to believe there was anything sinister in it. Despite the trouble he was in, she rather liked Ryan. Felt sorry for him even. Everyone in the force knew that his father had died a hero, fallen in the line of duty, a memorial stone erected in his name at force HQ. Although Ryan didn't know it, she'd seen him paying his respects on more than one occasion. Now he was in disgrace, suspended without charge, the case against him as weak as any she'd handled since she'd joined Professional Standards almost three years ago – and all because of Maguire. Ryan had lost both parents, his best friend, his sister was blind and, according to O'Neil's source, he wasn't having any luck in the love department either.

The guy deserved a break.

Secretly, she wanted to clear him of any wrongdoing – taking time off mid-shift was hardly a hanging offence – but first she had to be sure that he was telling the truth. She'd collected every scrap of shredded paper from Ryan's bin, raising an action to have it weighed in the box to see if the postage was correct. As soon as she got to work, she sent the package off for forensic examination, hoping that scientists might prove whether or not it had ever contained anything, other than the shredded paper Ryan had insisted was in it when it arrived. Someone's idea of a joke, he suggested, as they said their goodbyes – an attempt to frame him and throw doubt on his credibility.

Well, it had certainly done that.

Drawing her eyes away from a rain-lashed window, O'Neil scanned the room, finding Maguire. She hadn't shared her recent find with him. He'd be sure to twist it to suit his particular point of view, spreading malicious gossip around the station about Ryan. What, she wondered, was behind their mutual dislike? She hadn't given either officer the satisfaction of knowing that she was interested in the reason behind it. She couldn't deny she was. The issue had bugged her during the small hours. No one in her immediate team seemed any the wiser. If she had to take a punt on it, she'd bet on Maguire being the one at fault.

He had his feet up as usual, his head in the back pages of the *Sun*. Thoroughly sick of his underhand methods, she was anxious to write his next appraisal. When she marked him down, he'd be shifted from her department. If by chance he wasn't, she intended to request a sideways move, perhaps to the Murder Investigation Team. Two SIOs were retiring in the next few months and she had her eye on a transfer.

Sensing her gaze, Maguire lifted his head from his crossword puzzle. Taking in the clock above the door, he ignored her in favour of the paper.

God forbid that he'd do any work before nine.

Wind and rain rattled the windows. O'Neil shivered. Drawing her cardigan around her shoulders, she sat up straight. Time to do some meaningful work. 'Any news on Nicholas Wardle?' she asked.

'Some.'

The rude bugger didn't even look up. All O'Neil could see of him were hands gripping the newspaper and the front-page headline, a revelation she assumed had come from Alex Ferguson: *I GAVE BECKS PUSH OVER POSH.*

Lucky him – she was desperate to do the same to Maguire.

'Would you mind sharing it?' she asked.

'I got his employment details from the Tax Office. The neighbours were spot on. He is an oilman working out of Aberdeen.' The rest of his response came out through a gaping yawn. 'I spoke to some arsey cow in HR. She insisted on ringing me back to verify who I was before she'd put me through to his PA.'

'And that surprises you? It shouldn't. Nigeria is a lucrative but perilous place to work. That means tight security in anyone's book.'

'Yeah, s'pose.'

'And did she?'

'Guv?' He lowered the newspaper.

'Did she call you back?' O'Neil was beginning to lose her temper. 'In your own time, John. Don't let me hurry you.'

'Eventually she did.' Another glance at the clock. The long hand clicked forward a notch and was pointing straight up. Taking his feet off his desk, Maguire made a meal of folding his newspaper. Opening his desk drawer, he stuffed it inside and took a notepad out, reeling off the details. 'Wardle caught a British Airways flight on the sixteenth of October.' Another yawn. 'Departed London Heathrow at 11.45, arrived Lagos at 18.15.'

'Did you verify that he was actually on the plane?'

He gave her a hacky look.

'When's he back?' she asked.

'Whenever his work is done, so his office reckons. Despite the fact that he's from Blunderland, I gather he's management. Which means a fat salary and large expense account, hence the high-end Audi. He only ever travels business class. Those tickets don't come cheap but it means he can swap flights whenever the mood takes him. Sorry I can't be more specific.'

His put-down of Sunderland was designed to annoy her.

That's where her folks were from.

O'Neil didn't bite. 'You have no idea when he's due to return?'

'No, but he won't hang around any longer than he needs to. According to his assistant, he's in and out in a week, ten days tops.'

So . . . potentially four more days.

O'Neil sighed. She'd have to wait.

40

Ryan lucked out chasing up his enhancement job on the video shot at the scene. Roz's memory stick was faulty. Accessing its data was proving more difficult than he'd hoped. He swore under his breath. 'Please tell me by faulty you don't mean irretrievable.'

'No,' his contact said. 'We'll get there.'

'When?'

Ryan rolled his eyes at Grace as she looked up from her computer, hands hovering over the keyboard. He could see from the monitor that she was searching the HOLMES database, trying to match their unofficial investigation with the official one. In his ear, Ryan's contact was apologizing, offering no assurances whatsoever. The guy was being noncommittal rather than evasive.

'C'mon,' Ryan pushed. 'You must have some idea.'

'It's difficult to say. I can't give you a timescale.'

Ryan sighed: a further delay was not what he needed. Six days in and he was nowhere. Urging his contact to do his best, he hung up, swearing as he threw his mobile on the table.

'Problem?' Grace asked.

'You could say that.'

'It's not going too well this end either.' She pointed at

her monitor. 'I can't be certain that what is in here corresponds with the original statements and house-to-house forms.' She pushed a few keys, her eyes on the screen. 'The only way to be absolutely sure is to look at one and read the other.'

Ryan groaned.

Grace sat back, her face set in a scowl. 'Indexers are fallible, Ryan. They may be skilled at inputting data but they're human. We can't afford to take it as read. There's a shedload of difference between "he didn't hit him" and "he didn't hit him very hard". All it takes is for someone to be interrupted, miss a couple of words, and you end up with something else entirely.'

'Reminds me of the Derek Bentley case.'

'Yeah, although that was an argument about the meaning of the spoken word rather than a simple typo.' She paused. 'Aren't you a bit young to know about that?'

Ryan didn't answer. He could see from her expression that she'd realized how daft the question was. From a very young age, he'd held a deep – some would say, unhealthy – fascination with the murder of British police officers. It was an old case that had received massive media attention. The interpretation of 'Let him have it' as in, *Let him have it with both barrels* or, as Bentley's defence argued, *Hand over the gun*, were fought over for decades. Bentley received a posthumous pardon in 1998.

'Aren't statements scanned in nowadays?' Ryan asked, changing the subject.

'Not according to my source at MIT. It's manual input only, I'm afraid.'

Ryan made a derogatory comment about the police force moving at a snail's pace. 'On the plus side,' he said, 'there are very few witnesses to the abduction. It's a tight scene, the offence carried out in broad daylight. Minimal house-to-house, given its location—'

'What we need is access to O'Neil's data,' Grace interrupted.

Ryan pulled a face. 'You want to ask her for that? Because I don't.'

'There *is* another way.'

'Oh yeah?'

Grace was grinning.

The penny dropped: *she meant Roz.*

'I don't want to involve her,' Ryan said. 'It's unfair to ask just because we were once an item.'

'You're history?'

'Yes, nosy.'

'Since when?'

'Does it matter?'

'It might if we need her.'

'No, Grace. She has too much to lose. She may only be a DC but that doesn't mean she's not going places.'

'True . . .' Grace paused. 'Her looks will help.'

'What?'

'C'mon, she won't think twice about flashing her eyelashes if it means she'll rise through the ranks before the officer standing next to her. She'll stand on their necks if she has to.'

'That's a bit harsh.'

'But true, sadly.' Grace looked up. 'Her charm certainly worked on you. I never liked her.'

'You never said—'

'What on earth do you take me for? I may be plain-speaking but I'm not callous. Besides, you can't believe in that old fairy tale, otherwise known as a meritocracy. Ugly birds like me don't count, but looks like hers mean stripes on sleeves and pips on shoulders. She'll outrank you in a couple of years, matey. Mark my words.'

'She sat and passed her sergeant's exam.'

'Mentored by you, as I recall.'

'That's what partners are for.'

'Pity she didn't see offering support as a two-way street. I wonder who marked her paper.'

Ryan laughed. He couldn't argue with a thing she'd said. If only she'd warned him earlier. The sad thing was, Roz didn't need to abuse her femininity. She was intuitive and clever, even though she'd acted like a spoilt child, stamping her feet over his refusal to put his parents' home up for sale, prepared to turf Caroline out on her ear without a second thought. It was time she thought about someone other than herself: Jack's wife, his kids, would do for starters.

To hell with it!

Grace's point was valid. Without access to the right data, they were screwed, forced to rely on the accuracy of unchecked information. That really wouldn't do. HOLMES was a wonderful invention if left alone by humans. He needed to get his hands on those house-to-house forms, and tapping Roz was the only way.

41

Ryan chose a rendezvous point far from the city. The Rat Inn was tucked away in the tiny hamlet of Anick, high above the Tyne Valley. It was busy when he arrived, the smell of lunch hitting his senses as he walked in out of the cold, closing the door quietly behind him. It was like stepping into the thirteenth century. The room had low-beamed ceilings and stone walls a metre thick. Karen Errington – landlady and friend of a friend he'd known for years – was serving behind a bar fashioned from a great oak sideboard. Taking an order for food from a regular, a family man Ryan thought lived along the road, she acknowledged him with a nod as he formed his hand round an imaginary beer glass and waggled it in front of his face.

She already knew his poison.

As she pulled his pint, Ryan scanned the room. Roz was nowhere to be seen. He poked his head into the conservatory – she wasn't there either – so he wandered back to the bar and took a seat beside the fire blazing away in the cast-iron range. With his back to the deep-sill window, he'd spot her the moment she stepped through the door.

If she stepped through the door.

It was twelve forty-five when he glanced at his watch,

fearing she might have bottled it. As he sat waiting, he wondered how his enhancement job was coming along, whether those working on the memory stick had managed to extract any data from it. If anyone could, they could. He'd worked with the firm before. Assuming there had been another vehicle at the scene, as Caroline suggested, they were sure to reveal it. It would explain so much. He already knew the Clio had been stolen and that the driver wouldn't be coming forward. If he was involved, it was likely that the mystery vehicle had been parked up in the woods ready for him to make good his escape. It needed tracing.

Ryan lifted his left arm – another check on the time.

Roz was selfish, but never late. He worried that she might have changed her mind. Maybe, like him, she was dreading the encounter, their first in a while. When they first got together, things had been so good between them. He'd thought she was a keeper. Someone he'd settle down with. Sadly, that wasn't the case.

The words 'familiarity' and 'contempt' sprung to mind. At first he hadn't noticed her making demands, messing with his head. It crept up on him gradually, taking him by surprise, until nothing he said or did was to her liking. Their final row had gone on and on. He'd waited patiently for the noise to die down, but she kept on pushing, winding him up until he snapped. Not a pretty sight.

'You look like you need this.' Karen was standing beside him, his pint in her hand. Setting it down on the table, she asked how he was doing. 'Want anything solid to go with it?'

Ryan declined, even though he was hungry.

'Let me know if you change your mind.'

The pub door opened as she moved away.

Roz had nothing with her, Ryan noticed. No sign of the file he hoped she might be carrying. At the bar, she ordered a large glass of Pinot, telling Karen to put it on his tab, bringing a wry smile to his face – *same old Roz*.

Turning away from the bar, she approached his table and sat down beside him. For a moment there was an awkward silence. They were both tense. Uncommunicative. Neither knowing what to say or even where to begin. They had hardly spoken since he'd packed her in – a decision he didn't regret.

When her drink came, she waited for Karen to return to the bar before shifting her attention to him. 'How are you?' she asked.

'I've been better. You?'

'So-so.'

She examined him closely, her eyes reaching deep inside him. She had that knack of putting him on edge, making him feel both nervous and excited at the same time. He'd never tell her, but he missed those lips on his when he woke in the mornings, her soft skin and incredible smell. It took a lot of resolve on his part to fend off the overture he was sure she was about to make.

It didn't take long to arrive . . .

'I laughed when they told me you were dodgy,' she said. 'You're probably the most decent man I know.'

Ryan forced a smile. He didn't want or need her endorsement.

'I've been daft,' she said. 'Behaved badly.'

Sure had. He wasn't about to rub it in.

At least she had the decency to look repentant.

'I don't suppose there's any chance—'

'No.' Ryan got in quick. 'I know the risks you're taking and I appreciate that, but I'll be straight with you, there's no reconciliation on the cards. This is purely business for Jack's sake. No strings. I thought I'd made that clear on the phone. You and I are history—'

'Do you always have to be so damned honest?' She glared at him, revealing her true personality, the one he'd learned to live without.

'You know me, Roz. I can't operate in any other way.'

'Except where Jack Fenwick is concerned?'

He didn't rise to her unkind remark.

'O'Neil's all over it,' she said. 'Why not leave her to it?'

'Because she's not listening.' Ryan lowered his voice. 'Even if she was, she's not moving fast enough. I'm not doing this for me. I promised Hilary and the kids I'd find . . .' He choked on the words, recovered quickly. 'I told her I'd find the bastards who killed Jack, and that's exactly what I intend to do. You do know he wasn't the victim of a hit-and-run?'

'You sure we're finished, you and I?' She couldn't help herself.

She always did this. Twisted everything to her advantage, putting herself first, turning the screw when she had the upper hand. He'd finally found the courage to tell her he'd drawn a line under their relationship and yet she still wasn't listening. Unbelievable. Her expression was more angry than upset. Leaving her drink untouched, she stood up and walked away. Ryan's head went down. As she reached the door, she turned, looked at him one last time and disappeared.

Ryan head-checked the small car park at the rear of the pub. Roz was long gone. His own vehicle was parked on the top road in Anick. The view from there was stunning, the snaking River Tyne in the distance, nothing but fresh air and countryside. It was a sight that would normally lift his spirits.

Not today.

Walking towards his car with a heavy heart, a cold wind stinging his face, he had no wish to return to the claustrophobia of the silent room. He was tempted to keep on walking, spend the day outside now the rain had stopped, to clear his head and focus, before he drowned in his own misery. He missed his home, the big sky, the crashing waves, the peace and tranquillity of a stroll on an empty beach. Most of all, he missed Jack.

Even from this distance, he noticed that the nearside door of his car wasn't properly closed. He broke into a run. A blank file was lying on the passenger seat, a set of keys beside it. He scanned the line of cars along the narrow road before getting in.

No Roz.

The file contained everything he was after: photocopies of house-to-house forms and witness statements relating to the hijack as well as incidental notes. There weren't that many – a couple of dozen at most – but they were all there as far as he could tell. At first glance, there was nothing he could identify that was wildly different from the results Grace had gathered during her under-the-radar enquiries at the scene. Attached to the front cover was a brief, hand-written, pink Post-it note.

> *For what it's worth, I'm sorry.*
> *I hope this helps. Left*
> *the keys, seeing as I won't be*
> *needing them.*
> *Love you. Roz x*

Ryan blew out his cheeks. His ex had come through for him. He thought about calling her. Instead, he reread the note. *Love you.* No, he couldn't go there. Not now. Maybe never. He turned the engine over and headed for town.

He never saw it coming, not until it cleared the brow of a hill, a Traffic car, blue lights strobing across the dual car-riageway about a mile behind him, travelling like a bullet in the same direction. His eyes shifted to the file on the passenger seat. As an officer suspended from duty, it was evidence he had no excuse for.

If caught in possession, his career was over.

Hiding the file beneath the seat seemed futile. He did it anyway. He couldn't think straight. Couldn't turn around. Couldn't get off the A69. He could do bugger all except wait for the Traffic car to catch up with him. That wouldn't be difficult. His old Discovery was a lumbering beast. It would run all day but not very fast. It did nothing in a hurry.

A million thoughts rushed through his head. Maybe he was being paranoid. Maybe the car wasn't after him at all. Any minute now, it would scream right by en route to an incident he wasn't aware of. A decisive person by nature, all of a sudden he didn't trust his own judgement. What was that about? For days he'd felt like he'd had a target on his back. He couldn't explain why, but he just knew the Traffic car was after him. It would stop *him*. What a 'mare.

But how the hell did they know where he'd be?

Ryan's thoughts were all over the place. They swung wildly, this way and that. Roz had played a blinder and betrayed him. He'd been so distracted by Jack's death, he'd walked into a trap. No, that couldn't be it. She was devious, yes, but he'd have seen the deceit on her face if that had been the case. Besides, that theory made no sense. By informing on him, she'd be dropping herself in it too.

Unless . . .

He didn't want to believe it. The only plausible explanation was that she was in cahoots with O'Neil and Maguire. In all probability, they had found out about his request for information. They might have tapped her phone or caught her photocopying stuff for him. Maybe they had questioned her, turned her, and put her to work – ensnaring him her only way of escaping a disciplinary and keeping her job. Or maybe Grace's opinion that his ex would stoop low to climb the slippery slope to the top was more realistic than his. In which case, Roz might have gone to them, proffering her services in exchange for a promotion – payback for dumping her.

And still the Traffic car kept coming.

Ryan palmed his brow. Roz had motive – her position afforded her the means – and Maguire would jump at the chance to shaft him good and proper. What had the slick-talking arse offered her, he wondered – a job on Complaints? Whatever the inducement, he hoped it would make her happy – make them both happy.

They deserved each other.

Momentarily, the Traffic car was lost behind a slow-moving lorry that couldn't change lanes because the inside carriageway was chock-a-block. It bought Ryan a little time. He floored the accelerator, panic rising in his chest. Taking the slip road, he quickly called Grace.

'I'm in trouble,' he said.

'Kind of trouble?'

'In possession of house-to-house with a Traffic car up my chuff.'

'An accident maybe?'

Ryan glanced in the rear-view. 'Yeah, and maybe I'm sixteen.'

'You sure?'

'Positive. If I get locked up, you'll take care of Caroline?'

'It won't come to that.'

A siren reached him. 'It just has.'

Lucky for Grace, Ryan hadn't made it to Newcastle or he might have led them to the silent room. The car slowed, the STOP – STOP – STOP sign illuminated, instructing him to pull over. The Traffic car did likewise. It was triple-crewed. The officer who got out was someone he knew,

PC Jimmy Smith – aka Jinky Jim, after a Scottish international/Newcastle United football player from way back, his father's idea of a joke.

'Jinky! Long time no see.' Ryan got out of the car for two reasons: to put himself on a level with Smith and to distance himself from the incriminating material beneath his seat. He stuck out a hand. Played it cool. 'You're not going to accuse me of speeding in this old thing, are you? I could walk quicker. Need to get myself a new set of wheels.'

The PC seemed embarrassed as they shook hands. Apologetic even. 'I don't quite know how to put this, Ryan. We got a call on the blower to stop and make an arrest.'

'Yeah, pull the other one.'

'I'm not kidding, mate. Wish I was.'

'I'm intrigued. How come you knew where to look? I'm not often out this way.'

'I didn't.' The PC thumbed over his shoulder. 'Clocked you crossing the Styford roundabout minutes after the call came in.'

'Do I look dumb to you?' Ryan gave him a dirty look. 'Mind telling me who instigated the stop?'

'Professional Standards. Our orders are to take you to the West End nick.'

'Not until you tell me why, you don't.'

'You're not going to like it.'

'Get on with it.'

'It's in connection with the death of your DI. I'm sorry.'

The accusation felt like a knife to the heart. 'You're having a laugh!'

The PC's reddening face said he wasn't. Administering the full caution, he told Ryan he was under arrest and put him in the rear of the Traffic car, next to another officer he knew. There was a discussion between the three cops, a toss up between waiting for a low-loader to transport the Discovery to the station or for one of them to drive it. The cop in the rear got out and the Traffic car sped off.

Ryan stared out at the countryside as it rushed by. He was confused. What would Roz have done if he'd told her at the Rat that they were reconciled? In his head, he saw her walk calmly out of the pub, pull out her phone, giving some cock and bull story that he'd had second thoughts, changed his mind, been under a lot of stress lately and had already apologized for asking her to provide information he had no business to. But that hadn't happened. With his fingerprints all over that file, Ryan could almost see O'Neil or Maguire unearthing it from beneath the seat of his four-by-four, hear a judge passing sentence, a cell door slamming on his life.

42

Maguire was behind the arrest. O'Neil was nowhere to be seen. Ryan was processed by the custody sergeant and put in a windowless cell to wait and wait – almost two hours in total – surrounded by the constant racket of a busy cellblock. If he stayed there a month, he'd never get used to the foot traffic toing and froing beyond his cell door. There was clanging and crying, some aggro too. A fellow prisoner screamed to be let out the whole time he was there. Ryan didn't know what bothered him the most: that din, losing face in front of his colleagues or disgracing his father's memory. Ordinarily, he'd have declined a brief. Not this time. *He needed one.*

When she arrived in the interview room at four thirty in the afternoon, Ryan's twin looked pale but in control. There were no visible signs of distress and – because she couldn't see Maguire's ugly face – he was unable to intimidate her with hard eyes or the smirk he was currently sporting. He was having a ball.

Ryan's gaze shifted to Caroline.

The more he looked at her, the more he noticed the transformation. Gone was the fragile young woman he'd cosseted since their mother passed away. If that was what

Maguire was expecting, he was in for a nasty surprise. No, Ryan could see that the woman taking the seat was strong and confident, ready to fight tooth and nail for his livelihood. It almost brought tears to his eyes.

'Shall we get started,' Caroline said.

Her guide dog became agitated as Maguire switched on the tape, introduced himself and went through the motions, giving the time, date and names of those present, even mentioning Bob. Ryan had spent a lot of time with the animal. Never before had he seen it react negatively to anyone – but it didn't like Maguire.

Excellent judge of character.

Ryan studied his fellow DS across the table, anticipating a fair fight, with Caroline emerging victorious at the end of it. The feeling of euphoria was fleeting. It melted away as the 'hot' file in his car pushed its way into his head. Any second now it would be discovered, if it hadn't already been. Was that why Maguire looked so pleased with himself? Any hope Ryan had of wriggling out of his predicament quickly vanished.

A woman's voice reached them through the door.

O'Neil.

She sounded less than happy. Maguire had hardly got started when the door opened and his guv'nor walked in. She stood on the threshold, holding open the door. Her voice was calm. Her eyes flashed a warning. She was as mad as hell.

'DS Maguire, may I have a word?'

'Guv, I'm in the middle—'

'Please.'

When he didn't move, O'Neil marched forward, identifying herself for the benefit of the tape, checking her watch at the same time. 'It is 16.42 on Wednesday, October twenty-third 2013. I am Detective Superintendent Eloise O'Neil. This interview is terminated.' She switched off the tape, her face showing no emotion whatsoever as she walked out.

Maguire got to his feet, his chair scraping across the floor as he pushed it away from the table without a word to either prisoner or advocate. He followed O'Neil out, slamming the door behind him. In the interview room, Caroline's hand found Ryan's.

Seething, Maguire stood to attention while O'Neil paced up and down the corridor, hands clenched by her sides, trying to keep her temper in check. It wasn't working. She rounded on him. 'What in God's name do you think you're doing?'

'I arrested him.'

'I can see that. Why?'

'Because the post-mortem results are in.'

'And?' She'd been out for most of the afternoon.

'Fenwick was beaten to a pulp before he was hit by the car.'

'You think Ryan did that?'

'There's more. It appears that the car not only hit Fenwick, it reversed over him. Someone wanted to make bloody sure he didn't get up again. Who better than someone he could identify? The pathologist found extensive leg injuries consistent with impact from a large vehicle, probably a four-by-four. The measurements coincide with that of a Land Rover Discovery 2, which is what Ryan drives.'

'I'm well aware of what he drives.' O'Neil looked at him pointedly. '*Only* a Discovery 2?'

'Well, no . . .' Caught out, Maguire blushed. 'But I still have grounds for detention and arrest. Accident investigators have conclusive proof that the offending vehicle was fitted with Goodrich All-Terrain tyres—'

'Which you're going to tell me he uses.'

Maguire nodded. 'Yes, guv.'

'Is that right?' O'Neil almost laughed, even though he had planted a tiny seed of doubt in her mind. 'Well, while you were arresting Ryan, I was comforting Hilary Fenwick. Her house was burgled by a couple of heavies she saw legging it over her garden fence when she returned home at one o'clock. Broad daylight. Does that ring any bells?' She didn't wait for an answer. 'Trashed *this time*, she tells me. No finesse whatsoever. Two men. Possibly the same two' – she used her index fingers as inverted commas – '*detectives* who knocked on her door after her husband's arrest.'

'What detectives?'

'Bogus ones, I should imagine.' O'Neil paused, allowing time for the information to sink in. 'No one from CID went anywhere near that house after Fenwick's arrest. I checked. The search unit had done a thorough sweep, the team leader entirely satisfied that they had everything covered. So, it looks like you may have to reconsider. If Ryan's vehicle is clean, you're going to have to bail him.'

'I don't see why—'

'Are you mad? You think he's going to use his own vehicle to run over and kill a police colleague that half the force are looking for? You really think he's that daft?'

'The evidence—'

'Is circumstantial and uncorroborated.' O'Neil shut her eyes, took a long deep breath, then opened them again. 'Fenwick and Ryan were a dream team, John. You haven't the first idea how close they were.'

'Bit like us, eh, guv?'

'Don't backchat me. Your treatment of Ryan has bordered on persecution. He knows it and so do I. It stops here. Now. He was shattered when Fenwick was found dead and, if I am any judge of character, he wasn't faking it.'

O'Neil stopped talking and stepped away.

Two officers had come down the stairs and were ear-wigging the confrontation. Waiting for them to disappear into another interview room, a flashback of Ryan came into her head: twitching and writhing on his bed; the smell of whisky permeating every room in his tiny cottage; the Express Quest packaging – the tortured-soul expression on his face when he woke and found her leaning over him. She hoped it was distress, not guilt, she'd witnessed.

Forensics had done an urgent job on the packaging and found jack shit. No conclusive proof that Ryan had done anything wrong or lied to her. The postage weight confirmed that view. There was nothing Maguire could pin on him, much as he might like to. O'Neil rubbed at her temples, her thoughts all over the place. She couldn't afford to rule Ryan out totally. Nor would she rule him in without evidence. Had she been seduced by his charisma, the tenderness he'd shown towards women he valued? He cared. That much was obvious. About his sister, Hilary Fenwick, even *her*.

You cold? I'll light the fire.

'Ryan is a reasonable man,' she said, a niggling doubt, a little less conviction. 'We've never seen eye-to-eye, but is it any wonder? You've done your utmost to alienate the guy since day one.' She paused to take a breath, lowering her voice. 'You could have talked to him, John. Asked to examine his car without arresting him. For crying out loud, have I taught you nothing?'

'Guv, that's not fair—'

'No,' she insisted. 'What's not fair is your gung-ho approach to your sodding job. You pull a stunt like that again and I'll have *your* warrant card.'

About to say something, Maguire stopped himself.

O'Neil dared him to kick off, to give her an excuse to bollock him for insubordination. In every relationship there was a tipping point. This was theirs. Even he must recognize that. He backed off, dropped the attitude. Just when she thought they were done, he hung himself, telling her he stood by his decision, adamant that he was right and that Ryan was guilty.

'Wait in my office,' O'Neil said. 'No, better still, get your arse over to Fenwick's house and investigate that burglary. In future, you steer clear of DS Ryan, you hear me? You and he obviously have history and it's not helping this enquiry. I'll deal with him myself. Step out of line again and you'll live to regret it.'

O'Neil re-entered the interview room at 16.55, sat down in the seat Maguire had vacated and restarted the tape. Apologizing for the interruption, she introduced herself properly to Caroline, stating her name and rank.

The two women shook hands.

Bob wagged his tail.

Ryan covered his mouth to stop himself from laughing. He didn't want O'Neil misreading him, thinking he wasn't taking the interview seriously. Hell, his career was at stake here. The next hour or so would decide his fate.

It was Caroline who spoke first. 'Superintendent, I don't want to make things awkward here but, not to put too fine a point on it, your DS is a bit of an arse. He seems to have a downer on my brother . . . sorry, my client. We'd like to know precisely why he's been arrested.'

'We need to examine his car,' O'Neil said.

'On what grounds?'

Pushing the accident investigation report across the table, O'Neil explained what she was doing for Caroline's benefit, asking Ryan to read it out so his twin would be party to what it contained, including details pertaining to the crime scene and the post-mortem.

Ryan did as she asked, leaving out the more gory details he didn't want Caroline to hear. 'It appears that a vehicle very like mine was responsible for Jack's death. It had similar physical characteristics, distance off the ground, et cetera.' He pushed the report back towards

O'Neil and spoke to her directly. 'I'm sorry to disappoint you. It wasn't mine.'

'You left out the part about the tyres,' O'Neil reminded him. 'For the tape and your legal counsel, please.'

Leaning forward, Ryan picked up the report, playing for time. Glancing at the document a second time, he began to relax.

There was a God.

'The vehicle was sporting Goodrich All-Terrain tyres,' he said for Caroline's benefit.

Stumped by their significance, she turned towards him, inviting further comment.

The only thing he did was to reiterate his contention that it wasn't his car.

O'Neil took her time. 'Ms Ryan, whether your client likes it or not, his vehicle will have to be retained for forensic examination. This will be done as soon as humanly possible. It shouldn't take too long to clear this matter up.' She switched her focus to Ryan. 'I take it you have no objection?'

Ryan was struggling to remain cool. Logic told him he was about to be found out. He felt sick – for him and his twin. He was so wound up his hands had formed into tight fists in his lap. Fortunately, they were hidden beneath the interview room table. He fixed on O'Neil. She was nobody's fool. When no answer was forthcoming, she pushed him on it . . .

'It seems clear to me that you're unhappy with the idea,' she said. 'Is there any particular reason why you don't want me to examine the vehicle?'

Her eyes shifted to Caroline, no doubt taking in her anxiety, waiting for a response from one or both of them. Ryan looked beyond her through the window. It had begun to get dark and was raining hard, torrents of water splashing down on to the windowsill from a blocked gutter above. Maguire was walking across the car park, looking decidedly dejected. The fact that O'Neil had sent him packing was cold comfort to Ryan.

Caroline's voice took his attention. 'Matt, Superintendent O'Neil asked you a question. Have you anything further to say?'

'No, nothing.'

'DS Ryan, I shall ask you one more time,' O'Neil said. 'Why don't you want the vehicle examined?'

'Why do you think?'

O'Neil snapped. 'That's not an answer.'

'Jesus! Isn't it obvious?'

'Not to me. I must be dim.'

'Because you'll keep it for days,' Ryan barked. 'It's pissing down. My sister and I will have to make our way to Alnwick on public transport with a wet dog. Happy now?'

Caroline apologized, tried her best to take the heat out of the situation. 'My brother has answered your question. He has nothing more to say on the matter.'

'With respect,' O'Neil said. 'I think he does.'

'Guv, how many more times have I got to say it? It wasn't my car, I swear. And before you go to the expense and bother of forensic examination –' Ryan pointed out the window – 'I'd get your boy out there to check his facts.

Because from where I'm sitting, he hasn't done you any favours so far.'

Glancing over her shoulder, O'Neil head-checked Maguire, who was getting into his car. When she turned to face Ryan, she was far from happy. His bravado had bordered on insolence. No doubt she was making all sorts of judgements. Let her. He was cornered. Up against it. He needed her to reconsider. To release his vehicle before anyone got inside.

'I'm not sure I understand,' she said.

'No,' Ryan said. 'I don't suppose you do. I don't use all-terrain tyres at this time of year. I use winter slalom because of where I live. You've seen for yourself how remote my place is. That is easily checked. Is it too much to ask that Maguire might do his job properly, just once? He's made you look like an amateur.'

O'Neil was ready to kill. 'When did you have the winter tyres put on?'

'A fortnight ago.'

'You can prove that?'

'Absolutely.' Ryan was angry and it showed. 'Ring Simon at Bridge End Motors if you don't believe me; he puts them on every October and stores the others for me. If you . . . if Maguire had given me the courtesy of a call, I could've told him that. I'd have brought the car in myself. Instead, I had to go through the humiliation of being arrested by an officer I know. How the fuck do you think that makes me feel?'

Caroline put a hand on her brother's shoulder, the voice of reason, telling him to calm down. Trying to placate O'Neil, she apologized again for his outburst. He was incensed, justifiably so if he'd been wrongly accused. It was salt in the wound of a friend of a dead man.

Ryan didn't dare look at O'Neil because she sensed he was nervous with something to hide. Ending the interview, she bailed him, said she'd let him know when she'd finished with his car.

43

It was getting dark as Ryan led Caroline from the station. Exiting the car park, he pulled out his phone and called a cab, a firm he used on a regular basis. He told the cab office he wanted to go into town without stating exactly where he wanted dropping off. When under suspicion, it paid not to be specific.

'Aren't we going to Fenham?' Caroline asked.

'Not yet.'

'Why not?'

They turned right, heading east along the West Road, huddling together under her umbrella. 'We've got a slight problem,' Ryan said.

'We?'

'Me, I meant me.'

Stopping at the lights, Caroline's Labrador waited patiently at the kerb to guide her across the road, doing his job as if Ryan wasn't there. He was a fantastic dog, the best so far, keeping her mobile, providing companionship – her lifeline – and yet he'd retire in a few years' time, to be replaced by another, equally amazing animal.

A coach pulled away from a bus stop, oblivious to a passing motorcyclist, almost wiping him out. Ryan kept his eyes on the busy road. When he was a rookie cop, he'd been called to a horrific accident further along this same stretch. A girl had been knocked down on a pelican crossing by an uninsured driver. She'd suffer catastrophic head injuries and almost died. The event had stuck with him, made him wonder how his sister coped without coming to grief with more traffic on the roads than ever before. He wondered if Jack had felt the impact, if he'd known his time was up as he lay dying in that awful hospital bed.

The cab pulled up, the driver waiting patiently for them all to get in. 'Where we off to, folks?' he asked.

'City centre,' Ryan said. 'Let you know when we get there.'

Caroline pulled on her seat belt. 'Matt, what aren't you telling me?'

Ryan did likewise, took hold of her hand. 'Not here.'

He kept quiet as the taxi sped down the West Road, passing the Blue Lamp – a local landmark – and down the hill to the heart of the city. Caroline was chatty, reassuring him that everything would be fine. Ryan knew different. O'Neil would find the file and crucify him. Then it would be game over . . .

In every sense.

He pictured his vehicle up on a ramp, paint scrapings being taken, the chassis under forensic scrutiny, every single dint being painstakingly examined for traces of Jack's blood and skin. The image made him cringe. With a bit of luck, forensic examiners might have been so intent on the exterior of the vehicle, they wouldn't have looked inside.

Yet.

City traffic slowed them up, clogged nose to tail in a bottleneck at St James' Boulevard. It was getting on for six as the cab slowed outside Eldon Square, the driver checking his rear-view mirror for instructions.

'Grey's Monument,' Ryan said.

On the corner of Emerson Chambers and Ellison Place, the cab turned left, pulling up outside a branch of Waterstones, a good source of Braille books for Caroline. Ryan had been in recently to buy her a John Grisham novel: *The Associate*.

'This'll do perfectly,' she said.

The driver gave her an odd look, amazed that she had a clue where she was.

'Inbuilt radar,' Ryan said proudly. 'She has a better sense of direction than you and I do, mate. Thank your lucky stars she doesn't drive!'

Getting Caroline and Bob out and settled on the pavement, he paid the driver, telling him to keep the change. As the cab drove off, they crossed the road into Grey Street, the focal point of Grainger Town, the historic heart of Newcastle. It was Ryan's favourite city destination, a street he'd never been able to adequately describe for his twin's benefit, however much he tried. Today, its fine Georgian architecture was ignored. He was preoccupied, beginning to regret not having come clean with O'Neil. Maybe if he'd put his hands up, she'd have seen her way clear to putting in a good word for him. In return for cooperation, prigs got off lightly – why not him?

Yeah, right . . .

He was a copper . . .

She'd be looking to lock him up and throw away the key.

Ryan didn't fancy coffee. He was wired enough without it. In dire need of alcohol, he considered the Theatre Royal bar, discounting it when he saw the sign outside. The RSC was performing tonight. The place would be heaving. Instead, he chose Brown's bar across the road. Ordering wine, he steered Caroline to a table with a view of the door.

'Now are you going to tell me what's worrying you?' she asked.

'Trust me,' he said. 'You don't want to know.'

'There's something. You can't hide it. I can hear it in your voice. O'Neil bailed you too quickly, in my opinion. Is that why we can't go to Fenham? You think she's having you followed?'

'It's a possibility.'

Ryan picked up her wine glass, considering. 'There's something incriminating in my car.'

'I knew it,' she said. 'You promised to be straight with me.'

'I'm sorry.' He put the glass in her hand, making sure she was holding on before letting go. 'I'd rather not say what it is. If I tell you and they question you, well, I'm sure I don't have to draw you any . . .' He stopped himself using a cliché that made no sense in her particular circumstance.

Excited voices reached them from the next table. Two middle-aged women were poring over pictures in the *Evening Chronicle*: the christening of Prince George.

They were discussing how cute he was in the royal christening robe.

'Matt, don't shut me out.'

'OK,' Ryan relented. 'Don't get angry.'

'Over what? What is it that's so incriminating?'

'A file I'm not supposed to have. I'm in the shit, Caroline. I've done stuff I'm not proud of. I wanted justice for Jack so badly that I asked a serving officer to photocopy evidence I couldn't get my hands on any other way. And before you ask what and who, it's not important. What is important is, I could lose my job over it.'

'I can't believe that.' Caroline took a sip of her wine. 'The Superintendent sounded like a reasonable woman. Bob thought so too, didn't you, boy?' She put a hand out to stroke her guide dog, a big smile on her face. 'O'Neil likes you, Matt. I can tell.'

'Think again,' Ryan huffed. 'Ever since she met me, I've been a pain in the neck. She's no slouch. She's knows I'm up to my eyes in something. I haven't been lying through my back teeth exactly, but she won't rest until she finds out what it is. My guts are telling me it won't take her long.'

'She still likes you.'

'You like chocolate, but it's not good for you.'

Caroline laughed. 'Go on! Confession time. You like her too, yes?'

'What's with the questions?'

'Is she a looker?'

'A looker?' It was Ryan's turn to laugh. 'Where d'you learn that?'

'Is she?'

'Sure is.' He pictured O'Neil in the interview room: red wavy hair, stunning grey eyes, great mouth. 'And she loves my cottage. You'd approve. Shame she's looking to bust my balls.' He looked around, certain they hadn't picked up a tail. 'Drink up. We'll catch a bus to Fenham and walk the rest of the way.'

44

As soon as they got in, Caroline went off to feed Bob, leaving Ryan in the living room with Grace. Despite the afternoon's events, she seemed to be on a high. Her greeting was not returned. Ryan took off his leather jacket and slung it on the sofa, so shattered he didn't know what the hell to do, what to think, much less what would happen to him in the next few hours.

'Where's Newman?' he asked.

'Out. What's up with you?' Grace handed him a shot of Jack Daniels.

'I want my life back.' He downed the drink in one gulp.

'O'Neil let you go, that's a start—'

'She kept the car.'

'We'll get you a new one,' Grace said, tongue in cheek.

Ryan couldn't fathom what was so amusing. He studied her as she walked to the dining room table, picked up a file and returned with it. When she waved it in the air, he noticed Roz's pink Post-it note still attached to the front cover. For a moment, he stared at it, unable to get his head around how it had come into her possession.

'Panic over, my man.' Grace raised her glass. 'Roz came up trumps.'

'But I thought she dropped me in the—'

'You thought wrong. As soon as you phoned me, I phoned her. When I told her the tale, she almost had a heart attack, so I asked her nicely to get her arse in gear and save the two of you. There wasn't any need for negotiation. She knew if you went down, so did she. She raced over there and did the business as soon as your car arrived at the nick. Pretty nifty, eh?'

Ryan wanted to believe it, but: 'She had no keys.'

'Didn't need any. It was in the secure lock-up. Guess what was dangling from the ignition?'

'They hadn't locked it?' His face lit up. 'Oh, that is class!' His joy was short-lived as his eyes shifted to the screen saver behind her showing the floating logo of Northumbria Police, something his eagle-eyed ex wouldn't have missed. He pointed at it. 'I hope *that* wasn't on when she was here.'

'Relax, I met her in town. Took possession. You're in the clear. You can thank me later.'

Breathing a sigh of relief, Ryan stepped forward, put his arms around Grace and gave her a great big hug. She pushed him away, telling him there was no time to get fresh. 'We're not out of the woods yet. Hilary was burgled. The house is totally trashed. O'Neil knows about the two guys, the second search.'

'Good,' he said. 'I honestly think she's on our side. That might have less to do with our sunny personalities and more to do with the dick she works with. Is Hilary OK?'

Grace nodded. 'She and the kids have moved in with her father for the time being. So, where do we go from here? Do you think it's time to come clean with O'Neil and close the silent room down?'

'Hell, no! She thinks I'm a waste of space.'

'The woman doesn't know what she's missing,' Grace said.

Ryan allowed himself a half-smile, reminded of Caroline's comments in the bar.

O'Neil liked him?

In his dreams, perhaps.

His phone rang, jolting him from his reverie. It was the woman herself. The conversation was short and sweet. She told him he could collect his car and apologized for any inconvenience.

Grace pulled up close – but not too close – to the station and switched the engine off. As Ryan opened the car door, she grabbed his arm to stop him from getting out. Letting go of the door, but leaving it open, he turned to face her. He was suddenly attentive, a question in his eyes: *you found something?*

Grace was quick to answer. 'While you were out getting arrested, I was busy checking HOLMES – specifically the vehicle index. The R1 motorcycle Storey mentioned at the scene was captured on CCTV a mile or two north of Durham.'

'Stolen?' It was an easy guess.

'From a Consett lock-up—'

'When?'

'Day before the hijack. Don't get too excited. It was dumped and torched. Found by a foot patrol in Scotswood earlier today—'

Ryan's shoulders went down. 'Which effectively closes down that line of enquiry.'

'Pretty much . . .' She watched him reach for the door handle. 'Not all the news is depressing, though.'

He shut the door, eager for more.

'When four-wheel drives – Discoveries in particular – were mentioned as potentially responsible for Jack's death, I put two and two together and began researching old diesel cars that might fit the one Caroline described on the tape to see if any were recorded in the system.'

'And were there?'

'Not at the scene, no.'

'I'm hearing a "but".'

'There were three in total. Yours, which Maguire seized on like a bird of prey because he likes you so much.' She made a crazy face. 'Another I think we can safely discount – it belongs to the firearms team – and a third, also seen on a CCTV camera five miles away. No one was looking at it because it was just another car driving on that road, quite a long way from the scene.'

'They will be, now they've ruled me out.'

'No actions have been raised to trace the owner so far. It belongs to a company trading as Claesson Logistics.'

Registering the foreign name, Ryan looked at her. 'Son of Claes? You reckon it's Dutch or maybe German?'

'According to my searches, the name is Swedish but the company itself is registered here. Irwin's co-driver mentioned Scandinavia.'

'He did.'

They locked eyes.

It was a definite link. Two pieces of evidence coming together. Tenuous, Ryan had to concede, but nevertheless exciting. He didn't dare believe that they might lead anywhere – not at this stage. Grace suggested she'd do some more digging and speak to Hilary. They agreed to rendezvous at her house later. Despite the hour – almost nine thirty – Ryan had an errand to run he didn't want to leave 'til morning. He wanted to thank Roz personally. He owed her that much.

Her quirky loft-style apartment was located in the suburb of Sandyford, within walking distance of leafier Jesmond – the centre of her universe – with its high-end bistros, bars and cafes. Plenty of scope to find a replacement partner or just get laid.

Ryan didn't intend staying long. Roz deserved his thanks but past experience had taught him that she might try to capitalize on her strong position, lay a guilt trip on him and seek gratitude for services rendered, a last shot at making their relationship work. As it turned out, she was in chunks when he arrived, fearful of repercussions and ready to punch someone.

Him, most likely.

Her shouty mouth was in full working order.

'What if I'm caught?' She didn't invite him to sit down. 'I'll lose my career, my pension. You used me. I knew I shouldn't have listened to you.'

'Roz, calm down.' He noticed she didn't mention his job or pension. 'That's not going to happen—'

'How could you possibly know that?' Her eyes flashed

in anger. 'There's CCTV in the lock-up. What if I was seen taking the file from your car?'

'Relax.' He sounded more like Newman every day. 'I didn't ask you—'

'No, you sent your pit bull, Grace Ellis, to do it for you.'

Ryan almost laughed out loud. How could he possibly have missed the animosity between the two women? He tried for reassurance. 'You have nothing to worry about. If anyone had seen you, they'd have reported it. Maguire would've broken your door down by now. Mine too. Think about it—'

'I've thought about nothing else!' She glared at him. 'I want no more to do with your hare-brained schemes. In fact, I want no more to do with you. Period.'

He reached for her.

She shoved him away. 'Don't touch me!'

'Roz, listen—'

'No, you listen. In fact, don't bother, just clear off!'

Ryan stepped back. On the one hand, he was sad to leave her this way. On the other, his relief was profound. She'd let him off the hook. Without saying anything more, he let himself out, dropping his key in the fruit bowl on his way to the door. One less problem for him to worry about.

Roz was weeping as she watched him walk away, shoulders hunched, head down. He'd been such a good catch, even her mother thought so, the only one of her boyfriends the crazy cow approved of. Roz was kicking herself for blowing her chances with him, more angry about that than the mess he'd created for her. She wanted to call him back, tell him she didn't mean what she'd said and beg for forgiveness. She wanted him in her life. She wanted to make up, make love, at least stay friends.

He was almost at his car when she saw movement off to his right. She froze as a big man stepped from the shadows into the orange glow of streetlights, his focus on Ryan's back. He was a stranger, not local, someone she'd never seen before. With evil intent written all over him, he moved more swiftly than she gave him credit for, his arm drawn back, some kind of elongated weapon in his hand.

Roz banged on the window.

Ryan turned. Looked up. Too late. He fell to the ground like he'd been shot. The big guy leaned over, grabbed him by the arms and dragged him along the pavement towards a waiting vehicle. Grabbing a can of pepper spray, Roz sprinted from the apartment, thundering down the stairs and out into the street, heart banging in her chest, no time to fear for her own safety. It seemed to take forever to get there.

'Hey, you!' she yelled. 'Police!'

As she ran towards the car, the attacker looked up. He smiled when he saw the size of her – five-six, slightly built, no more than eight and a half stones wet through. He carried on manhandling Ryan. Before he reached his own vehicle – lights on, engine running – Roz charged at the big man. He glanced up. Lifting her arm, she squirted him full in the face. Incapacitated, he screamed in pain, dropping Ryan's limp body as he tried to rub the chemical from his eyes, staggering to the passenger side of his vehicle. As she called the law, the waiting car sped away.

'Ryan!' she sobbed, dropping to her knees.

She'd seen enough serious assaults in her years in the force to know that he was in a very bad way. Blood seeped from a head wound, oozing through her fingers as she raised his head, trying to lift him up and get help, but it was useless. He was a dead weight.

'Ryan, please wake up . . .'

The next thing Ryan knew, he was coming to in the Royal Victoria Infirmary with a banging headache and O'Neil standing over his bed, arms crossed, a puzzled – or was it worried – look on her face. It was odd, seeing her in jeans, a sloppy sweater. The scarf round her neck matched her eye colour exactly.

'We've got to stop meeting like this,' she said.

'What?' he joked. 'I'm not looking my best?'

She smiled. 'How you feeling?'

'Like I've been run over by a juggernaut.' Ryan put his left hand on his head, feeling the thick bandage wrapped around his skull, wincing at the lightest touch. 'Just don't play any heavy rock.'

'What's going on, Ryan?' The smile had gone.

'Maybe you should ask Maguire. I hope he's got an alibi better than his sister. The guy hates my guts. The feeling is mutual, by the way.'

'I'd never have guessed.'

A phone beeped.

'It's not mine.' O'Neil's eyes shifted to the small cabinet

beside his bed. 'Want me to get that?' She looked on as he hauled himself up on his pillows with great effort. 'Lie still, you've got seventeen stitches in there.' She made a move for the drawer, took his mobile out and handed it to him. 'At close to midnight, I'd say that's probably a girlfriend.'

'That would be hard. I don't have one.'

'Not the way DC Roz Cornell tells it.'

'She's having trouble letting go,' Ryan said.

O'Neil took a seat. 'She was the one saved your ass, by the way.'

'I don't remember a thing.'

'You never made it to your car, apparently. The blow to the back of your head knocked you out cold. Roz pepper-sprayed the ape trying to bundle you into a four-by-four. Had it not been for her rapid action, I dread to think what might have happened. You be sure to thank her when you get out.'

Ryan couldn't tell her that was why he was there in the first place. Roz must have watched him leave her flat. Intervened. Then, forced to explain why he was there, she'd made out that they were still an item when they really weren't. Good ploy to keep Professional Standards from delving any deeper. The text message was from her: Let me know you're okay.

The voice message was from an unregistered mobile. Newman's.

It's me. As soon as Hilary's place got done, I installed a covert camera at yours. Your cottage has also been screwed. I'm en route to get rid of the evidence. Get the hell out of there! End of message.

45

With no car at his disposal, Ryan called a taxi, asking the driver to take him the short distance to Roz's place, ringing ahead to let her know he was coming. Although he was taking a risk, he felt fairly sure that the offenders who'd assaulted him would be long gone in case the law was on the lookout for them. He'd been strongly advised by hospital staff not to discharge himself and instructed not to drive under any circumstances. Fortunately, his car keys were still in his jacket pocket. Memory loss was common after a whack on the head. That was his excuse anyhow.

The minute the taxi pulled up, Roz rushed outside and flung her arms around his neck.

'OMG, look at you. Why aren't you in hospital?'

'It may not be safe there—'

'What?' Roz looked around her. 'You think they'll come back?'

'They might.' There was no sign of either police or offender, but he warned her to be on her guard and managed to persuade her to stay with a friend for a few days. 'There are things you don't know about the guys who assaulted me. I want to keep it that way. You can't afford to stay here until they're caught.'

'I'm too bloody terrified to go to bed anyhow.' Her wide eyes locked on to him. 'I hate living alone. And before you say anything, I'm perfectly well aware that it's my own doing.'

'It never crossed my mind,' he lied.

'I've been such a fool.'

'We don't have time for that now, Roz. I've got to go.'

'Go where?'

'Trust me. It's better you don't know.'

'Can I drive you?'

'No, you've done more than enough. I'm grateful. I owe you one.'

Kissing her on the forehead, he left her on the doorstep, reminding her to pack a bag and bunk in with a mate until it was safe to go home. Similarly spooked by the events of the evening, he decided not to return to Fenham. He couldn't risk leading anyone there. Instead, he drove to Alnwick, intending to spend what was left of the night at Caroline's.

Fairly sure that Frank wouldn't yet be asleep, Ryan called him from the car, thanking him for the tip-off, asking what damage had been done at his cottage. The news was mixed. The closed-circuit device Newman's text alluded to had registered two men ransacking the place. Then came the bad news. Gloved up and balaclava-clad, there was no way he was able to identify them.

The real deal, these guys didn't make mistakes.

Depressed by this revelation, but grateful to discover that his home was now secure, Ryan was about to ring off when he heard Caroline's voice in the background. After the evening's drama, it seemed that the whole wide world was still awake. He spoke briefly to her, reassuring her that he'd take it easy, then started up the engine and headed off into the night.

It was two in the morning when he finally pulled into the driveway, killed the engine, and stepped out of his four-by-four. Putting his key in the lock, he pushed the front door open, taking a moment to listen for intruders before turning on the light. Nothing unusual; only the letter box rattling behind him and a low howling sound, the result of a downdraught from open chimneys in the three-storey house.

He reached up and dropped the switch, squinting as the light came on. Making his way to the kitchen, he took a bottle of water from the fridge, then went straight upstairs and sat down on his bed. There were fresh blood spots on the outside of his leather jacket to accompany those on the inside, a weird and creepy connection to his father that made him feel like a child.

Be strong, son. Never let the bullies win.

This in response to the black eye he'd received at school from the son of a local thug, arrested several times by *his* old man. In bed that night, a young Ryan had asked his dad why he had to be a policeman. Why not get a proper job like other kids' dads? His father had laughed, ruffled his hair, and told him that without people like him there would be anarchy. Seeing the puzzled response, his dad explained that coppers were needed to keep the peace.

'And that's what I need right now,' his dad said, tucking him in. 'It's high time you were asleep.'

Exhausted, Ryan lay on the bed. Sadly, the world was full of aggressors who'd do anything to get their own way, their violence cloaked in the name of a good cause – religion, often as not. *Terrorists.* Was that what was worrying Jack? The reason for his silence would suggest so. What was it Jack's solicitor had said?

Scores of innocent people would be affected if he went about it the wrong way . . .

Those words repeated over and over in Ryan's head, but still he didn't understand their significance. What people was Jack on about? And who in hell's name would eliminate witnesses and destroy evidence? This was heavy shit. The most burning question of all: what had he done with his notebooks? If Jack had mailed them, to his wife, to Grace, to *him*, they would have arrived by now. Hilary had no idea where they might be and, according to Grace, there was no mention on HOLMES of their existence.

Ryan was beginning to think he'd never find them.

The weight of his old man's eyes bore down on him from his photograph. Except, he never would be an old man. He'd remain forever young, strong and genial, a hero to a small boy who needed his wisdom more than ever now. Pulling the duvet over him, Ryan could almost feel him sitting there, willing him to fall sleep. Seconds later, he was gone.

46

He woke almost five hours later, soaked to the skin from having slept in his clothes. Hauling himself upright, he stripped off and walked naked to the bathroom. It was still dark outside. He hadn't bothered checking his watch and had no conception of time. He just needed to be up and at it. He showered quickly, feeling instantly refreshed, but as he stepped from the shower, the stairs beyond the bathroom door creaked.

Pulling the towel around him, Ryan froze, dripping wet and defenceless, O'Neil's soft-spoken voice arriving in his head, pleading with him not to leave the hospital. 'You're concussed. If you were to fall, get another bang on the head, it could have dire consequences. It may even be fatal. What do I have to do, tie you down?'

The stairs again.

Whoever was there was a third of the way up. As a teenager, sneaking in late at night, those creaky stairs had always caught him out. No matter where he stepped, they always gave him away and woke his mother, lying half-asleep in the room above. Someone unfamiliar with the house was trying to be quiet and failing miserably . . .

Closer now . . .

Clenching his fist, Ryan drew his arm back ready to

defend himself against attack. His eyes flew to the window. Even if he'd been stupid enough to climb through in his condition, locks had been fitted limiting the sash travel, a security precaution. There was no way out. More noise on the stairs brought his focus to the door. Slowly, it began to swing open.

'Jesus! You scared me!' Caroline's neighbour, Luke, was fifty-five years old. A keen rugby player, he had a lot more go in him on the field than men half his age, but little bottle off it. For a have-a-go hero, he was sheet-white and looking pretty relieved to find Ryan and not some thug burglar in a balaclava, tooled up, with a baseball bat in his hand. 'I saw the light on,' he said. 'Caroline texted to say you were both away, I—' With the sentence half-formed, he pointed at Ryan's head. 'What happened there?'

Relaxing his fist, Ryan let his arm drop by his side. 'I wish I knew.'

'You look like shit, man.'

'You don't look too good yourself. Maybe you should call the police next time you suspect a burglary.'

Luke jumped, startled by the sound of a mobile ringing in the bedroom behind him. Chuckling to himself, Ryan tightened his towel and moved past him to answer it, his boyhood neighbour tagging along behind. Caroline seemed delighted to hear the sound of his voice as he answered the phone.

'I've not slept a wink,' she said. 'How about you?'

'Like a log.' Ryan pointed at the phone, miming *Caroline* to Luke.

'No symptoms during the night that sent you hotfoot-ing back to A & E?'

'No.'

'You sure?'

'Bit of a headache is all.' She knew him so well. He was fine, apart from a dose of intermittent nausea she didn't need to know about. 'Luke couldn't sleep either. He's here looking after me. We're about to share a pot of coffee and talk about you while you're not around to interrupt.' It felt really good to hear her laugh.

Luke mimed a *thank you* for saving his blushes.

Ryan gave a nod, kept his focus on the phone. 'You need anything while I'm here?'

'Bob is almost out of dry food.' Caroline's guide dog was uppermost in her mind, her first priority, day and night. It was a mutual arrangement.

'Last time I looked, the bin in the kitchen was running low,' Ryan said. 'I'll pick some up in Alnwick before head-ing off.'

'No need,' she said. 'There's plenty in the utility room.'

'You sure? I haven't bought any in a long while.'

'Just bring what's in the plastic bin. We'll shop for Bob later. I don't want you lifting and carrying heavy loads in your condition. Besides, Jack brought twelve kilos last time he came round.'

That final short sentence hit Ryan like a brick.

Jack's visit had been over a month ago.

'Was he in the habit of bringing you dog food?'

Caroline was puzzled. 'What?'

'Had he ever done it before?'

'No, it was the first time. Wouldn't let me pay for it either. Told me to consider it a gift. You know how generous he was . . .'

A gift?

Of dog food?

Unlikely.

'He said that you were tied up. That you'd asked him to drop it in.'

'Oh yeah, I forgot.' *It was only a white one.*

Caroline didn't know about the notebooks so, unlike him, she had no reason to be suspicious. She was still talking, but he'd tuned her out. Jack had lied to her and Ryan had an idea why. Aware that he was in imminent danger, had he hidden a note where it would be found? Had he taped a clue to the underside of the storage bin, knowing *she* wouldn't see it but Ryan would?

Ryan's mind raced back in time. He'd been so preoccupied with sorting out their mother's financial affairs and helping Caroline through her grief, it had been weeks since he'd cleaned and refilled it for her.

Pumped up by a sudden rush of adrenalin, he couldn't wait to get rid of his uninvited guest.

'Ryan, you still there?'

'Yeah. Sorry. Anything else you need?'

'No, that's it. Say hi to Luke for me.'

'Will do. I'll be with you in an hour or so.'

'No rush,' she said. 'Enjoy your coffee.'

He rang off. 'Sorry, Luke, she needs me urgently.'

'Is everything OK?'

'Yes, she just ran out of dog food. At least, that's what

she said. For once I think it's me she's more concerned about. The sooner I get over there, the sooner she'll relax.'

Luke never made a fuss. Given that Ryan didn't need rescuing, there was no longer any need for him to stay. Almost frogmarched to the door, he continued to apologize for using his key and entering the house without an attempt to ring the bell first. Ryan told him not to worry, but still he lingered on the doorstep . . .

'You sure you're OK?' Luke asked.

'You mean this?' Ryan pointed to his head. 'I've had worse.'

'No, I didn't mean your head. You're not pissed with me, are you?'

'Eh?' Ryan was losing the will to live.

'Caroline said that you—'

'Luke, I'm really pleased you live next door and look out for my twin, but—'

'Margie would love it if you'd join us for breakfast.'

'I'd love it too, but I can't hang around. Not today. Some other time?'

'It's no trouble.'

'Look, I'm freezing my balls off here.' Ryan began to close the door. 'Have a nice day, Luke.' *At last, he was gone.*

Sprinting along the hallway, Ryan made his way to the utility room, a blast of icy air hitting his bare skin as he opened the door. Flipping the switch failed to bring the light on. He looked up. Tried again. The bulb was spent. With no need for illumination, Caroline had always referred to such useless items as her 'extra-special energy-saving light bulbs' and called him a wimp for needing them. At the moment he was living up to that description. He was the one who was blind. He couldn't see a thing.

Opening the door wider, allowing light to flood in from the hallway, he peered inside. A transparent food storage container was under the window by the back door. He wheeled it out into the hallway, spun it round three hundred and sixty degrees. No note visible. Nothing taped to the rear or underside. There was a covering of almost ten inches of food inside the bin, enough to hide a small notebook or two. He pulled off the lid and tipped the food out, his hopes plummeting as dry pellets spilled out over the slate-tiled floor.

No notebooks.

Gutted, he sat back on his heels, the smell of lamb and rice fit only for dogs filling his nostrils. Disgusting. His eyes shifted once more to the utility room. Above the washing machine and tumble drier, boxes of soap powder, dishwasher powder and cleaning materials were lined up in precise order so that Caroline wouldn't get them mixed up. To the right of the washing machine was a large cupboard. Scrambling across the floor, Ryan pulled open the door and found two more bags of dog food, both unopened.

More supplies than the Battersea Dog's Home.

Ryan got to his feet and dragged the bags out by their handles. He examined them carefully, finding nothing to suggest they had ever been slit open and resealed, until he upended them and felt along the bottom seams.

Bingo!

One of them had been tampered with.

Taking the stairs two at a time, he grabbed the unregistered mobile Newman had given him and retraced his steps, photographing the bag in situ. Only then did he peel away the seal – marginally, halfway and then fully – taking pictures of each stage of the process. Keeping his fingers firmly crossed, he then tipped the whole thing upside down, scattering the food pellets in all directions.

As the last of the contents spilled across the floor, the notebooks fell out with a solid thump. Taking yet more photographs, he knelt down on the floor, examining them before picking them up and turning them over in his hands. Wrapped together in cling film and covered in smelly food, they were unremarkable but identical reporter's notepads with blue plastic covers, the like of which you'd find in any bookshop or supermarket for just a few pounds.

Ignoring the mess he'd created, Ryan placed the bag in a clean refuse sack he found in the utility room. Sealing it with gaffer tape, he grabbed a ballpoint pen from the hall table and signed over the seal so it couldn't be tampered with before it reached the hands of forensic examiners. Moving to the breakfast room, he laid the lot out on the kitchen table. He took yet more photographs, then scrolled through the images, making sure he had enough. Satisfied, he removed the cling film, bagged it, washed his hands and opened up the books.

The first was full of stuff he didn't understand. It was obvious that the notes contained therein had been made contemporaneously: the entries were in different ink, some in script, others in capital letters. They included references to times and dates going back months and details of people or organizations whose names were merely initials: AF being mentioned several times.

His frustration grew . . .

AF meant nothing to him.

He speed-read the notes, trying to decipher Jack's shorthand. He'd used many acronyms – RFCC, LUN, FAT, CAT, ITR, MCCR, TRF – but they failed to generate a single connection to the work the two men were normally involved in. One thing was clear. Whatever Jack had kept to himself, it was outside of the territory of Special Branch.

Undeterred, Ryan put on the kettle, then ran upstairs again and pulled on a pair of jeans and a warm sweater. Collecting his old laptop and his watch, he returned to the kitchen and made himself a strong coffee. His computer was slow to boot. Switching on the radio, he caught the news headlines at eight o'clock and then set to work, hoping the notebooks would reveal something – anything – that might spark him into action.

Nothing did.

The second notebook was only half full. AF was mentioned several times, along with a new set of initials – VP – which stymied Ryan all over again. He was beginning to give up hope when, on the inside back cover, he noticed among the doodles a small flag with an uneven cross sketched in black ink, the horizontal line in the centre, the vertical off to one side. Logging on to Google, a quick search brought up the CIA's Flags of the World database.

That particular flag configuration yielded only six possible countries, all Scandinavian: Denmark, Finland, Faroe Islands, Iceland, Norway and Sweden. That detail picked at the edges of his brain as he made a list. Unable to get a handle on why, he searched other sites too and came up with three more possible places he'd never even heard of: Åland Islands (Finnish), Bouvet Island and Svalbard (both Norwegian); conclusive proof, if he needed any, that he was looking in one direction only – northeast of Newcastle, across the North Sea. The last entry was dated a week prior to Jack's arrest and detention on firearms charges. *RIP 1960–2013.* It made him weep.

Ryan stared at the dates.

Was Jack hinting at his impending death, referring to his own lifespan, or had someone else died in the course of his enquiries that happened to be the same age? Dashing upstairs to his mother's study, he turned on her printer. Fortunately it was still in working order with plenty of ink. He made three copies of the notebooks for himself, Newman and Grace. Bagging the originals, he left the house, placing the evidence in his car. There was no doubt in his mind that he was closing in on those responsible for Jack's death. Too late to save him, sadly, but not too late to prove what an exceptional person he was.

Before driving away, Ryan pulled out his mobile and made a call.

In the silent room, the phone rang. Grace picked up. There was no greeting, no friendly *Hi, it's me* or *how you doing?* Ryan didn't even bother with hello.

'Is Frank there?' he asked.

'Affirmative. Will I not do?'

'You're far too young for me.'

'Ha!' She smiled. 'If only that were true.'

Grace felt her spirits rise. She didn't need to see his face to know that he had something important to say. Ryan had always been like a kid with a new toy when in possession of breaking news. It wasn't just his jokey tone that led her to that assumption. There was a serious undertone to his voice she recognized from the days when they were colleagues.

'You want the phone on speaker?' she asked. 'Then I can listen in. You know how nosy I am.' She was only half-joking. She hated being left out of anything.

'Good plan. This concerns all of us.'

'OK, shoot, we're all ears.'

'I'm on my way in. Is now a good time to have that extraordinary general meeting?'

'I'm free.' Grace winked at Newman.

The spook had received Ryan's cue.

By the look of her, Caroline was curious too.

Even Bob's tail was wagging.

'Copy that,' Newman said.

'I'll bring my notebook and take the minutes.' Ryan said.

Although Jack's body was lying in the morgue, Ryan still couldn't help but feel aggrieved that he'd gone off-piste without telling anyone. Trying not to dwell on that, he imagined Grace and Newman's impatience. They would be clearing the decks, readying themselves for his arrival with vital evidence, something tangible they could work on. Without being specific, Ryan had said enough to ensure that his cryptic message hit the target. He'd spoken in code, unable to trust the phones.

Only a fool would do so these days.

As he got ready for the drive south to Newcastle, that fact was reinforced on the radio. Presenters were full of outrage because of a tap on Angela Merkel's mobile. The German chancellor was demanding an explanation from Barack Obama as to why the US National Security Agency was monitoring her calls. The practice was commonplace. What chance for anyone else?

Newman and Grace were thrilled to see him when he arrived shortly after nine thirty. Ryan took off his coat, gave his sister a kiss, handing over the dog food. He put the evidence he'd collected in Grace's safe, along with his unregistered mobile, the food bags, the wrapping and notebooks. The plan was to use the photocopies only, preserving the originals for forensic examination when he eventually presented them to O'Neil.

When the others had read through both notebooks, Ryan stood up. 'You got a whiteboard we can use?' he asked.

Grace shook her head. 'No, sorry.'

'You want me to go out and buy one?' Newman asked.

'No, I'll improvise.' Ryan turned to Grace. 'You got a roll of lining paper or wallpaper?'

'In the garage.' She handed him the key.

Minutes later, he was back with it under his arm. Cutting off a long piece, he asked Grace if she minded him covering the patio doors leading to the garden, utilizing the space as a makeshift murder wall.

'Ready?' Grace asked when he was finished.

Ryan put down the Blu-tack, nodding.

'OK, let's have a look at these acronyms,' she said. 'I'll act as Receiver and search HOLMES. You two research the Internet.'

Caroline disappeared into the kitchen to make a pot of tea and the room went quiet as they got to work. Grace was first to hit on one of the acronyms, finding a reference to RFCC on the system: Regional Flood & Coastal Committee. When no one round the table got excited, she wrote it down and continued, the guys ploughing on with their Google search.

'Jesus!' Ryan said, a few minutes later.

'Found something?' Newman didn't look up.

'TRF is the code for Sandefjord Airport, Torp.'

'Never heard of it,' Grace said.

'I have.' Newman took his hands away from his keyboard, eyebrows knitting together. 'From memory it's about a hundred clicks south of Oslo, a low-budget airstrip serving the east of the country—'

'Yeah, but even more interesting,' Ryan interrupted, 'is the fact that Jack flew in there in June.'

'You sure?' Newman asked.

'I remember that.' Grace was nodding in agreement.

'Can you remember why?' Newman again.

'A weekend away from the kids,' she said. 'Late anniversary present, as I recall.'

'A surprise he kept from Hilary until the very last minute,' Ryan added. 'Such a secret, he didn't even tell me.' *Another thing he didn't share.* 'I don't think she was too happy either—'

Newman cut him off. 'You think he had another agenda?'

'No,' Ryan shook his head. 'He'd never put Hilary at risk.'

'Under normal circumstances,' Grace said. 'But these weren't normal, were they?'

Ryan's thoughts were all over the place. Everything they had learned so far had led them to the conclusion that Jack had been desperate to right a wrong. Maybe he'd also been reckless, just this once. Had he used a romantic weekend away as cover for something altogether more sinister? He looked at Grace. 'O'Neil would have interviewed him about the months leading up to his arrest, yes?'

'Of course.'

'Is Norway flagged up anywhere on the system?'

The two men looked on as her fingers flew over the keys, eyes glued to her computer screen. Her search flashed up a positive result. 'Yes, it is . . .' she said. 'There's a mobile telephone number in Jack's phone history with a +47 prefix. According to the data here, that's the international dialling code for Norway.'

For a moment, no one spoke.

'It's a link,' Grace said.

'It's a damned sight more than that!' Ryan was getting excited.

'Did O'Neil raise an action on it?' Newman asked.

'She did.' Grace pushed a few more keys. 'It was traced to a man called Anders Freberg. There's no record after that. Looks like she hasn't yet allocated a follow-up.'

'She will when she sees these.' Ryan pointed at the notebooks. 'There's a lot of contact here between Jack and someone with the initials AF. That must be Anders Freberg. It's too much of a coincidence not to be.'

Grace was still reading from the computer screen. 'Jack didn't try to hide his holiday in Norway. He claimed the Norwegian number belonged to a mate. Anders Freberg is apparently someone he's known for years – or that's what he told O'Neil. I've known *him* for years and yet that's the first I've heard of him.' She glanced at Ryan.

He shook his head. 'The name means nothing to me. We're on to something here.'

Picking up a pen, he walked to the do-it-yourself murder wall and scribbled a number of points down in chronological order of discovery. If his memory was correct, a definite pattern was emerging:

1. *Foreign voice at the hijack scene – Scandinavian?*
2. *Claesson Logistics 4x4 – near the scene (Swedish name)*
3. *The flag in Jack's notebook – definitely Scandi*
4. *Sandefjord Airport, Torp (Norway)*
5. *Jack/Hilary Norwegian holiday*
6. *+47 mobile – Anders Freberg (Norwegian prefix)*

Ryan stood back, admiring his handiwork. It was all coming together. Grace reeled off Anders Freberg's number and he wrote that on too. Newman immediately made the call. The line was unobtainable.

He shook his head. 'Sounds like it's on the blink.'

Ryan hoped it was nothing more ominous.

47

Eloise O'Neil linked her hands together and stared at her computer screen. Until recently, she'd been running a very closed enquiry, keeping everything tight, believing Jack Fenwick to be a perpetrator, rather than a victim. She'd been looking at the hijack scene, the security van and Jack. Nothing more. Then things had spun off in a different direction – a post-mortem ruling out accidental death. After being hit by a car, Jack Fenwick was run over.

He was murdered.

O'Neil looked across the room at Maguire. He'd fingered Ryan as a likely suspect. She'd since ruled him out. His vehicle was not involved. Thank God. The Job had enough bad press without adding to it. She'd instructed Maguire to widen the search to include all similar vehicles within a five-mile radius of the scene. A few minutes ago, he'd come up with a contender: a four-by-four belonging to a firm called Claesson Logistics.

'Find out who they are and where they operate from,' she said. 'And while you're at it, chase up that Norwegian guy, Anders Freberg. I feel so sorry for Jack Fenwick and his family, but I'm not sure he was telling me the whole truth about him. Do it now and let me know how you get on.'

Maguire picked up the phone. She could feel his resentment from across the room. He'd hardly said a word since she'd bollocked him over his sloppiness and bad attitude to a fellow officer. Given the GBH on Ryan yesterday, Maguire had to concede that he'd been wrong to point the finger at him. Just as well he didn't know what she'd found on her computer or he'd start his vendetta all over again.

Before she'd left the hospital last night, Ryan had accused her of being behind the curve. He wasn't wrong. Not only had the Organized Crime Unit been tailing him without her knowledge, they'd lied about it and failed to respond to her request for full disclosure. A keystroke check on the PNC for the vehicle they used produced surprising results when she followed it through with a systems background check. The Police National Computer had been accessed via HOLMES.

Someone had gone into the system using Ryan's ID.

Another glance at Maguire.

How was that possible when he'd taken possession of Ryan's warrant card? Given the bad blood between the two men, O'Neil wouldn't put it past him to set up his rival, a man he hated with a passion. She knew what was eating him up. Why he was so spiteful when it came to this particular officer. As she suspected, it involved a woman. DC Roz Cornell had dumped Maguire and taken up with Ryan, a relationship that had since blown off course.

Men!

Eyes back on the screen. Pushing a few more keys, she noticed something odd, something she could so easily have overlooked. Her eyes grew big as she stared at the computer, hoping she was wrong, knowing she wasn't. She'd been too quick to judge Maguire. Ryan's warrant card was an old one, upgraded days ago by none other than retiree Grace Ellis. *What the hell were those two up to?*

48

Grace picked up her ringing landline and checked the display: *O'Neil*. Ignoring the call, she continued to search the HOLMES database, leaving the answering service to kick in.

'Grace, it's Eloise. We need to talk.'

Four angst-ridden eyes turned in her direction. Passing a worried look to the others, Grace was about to say something when Ryan's mobile began to vibrate on the dining room table. He picked it up, examined the screen, the hairs on the back of his neck rising when he recognized the caller.

'Is it her?' Grace asked.

Nodding, he let it switch to voicemail, waiting to see if O'Neil would leave a message, worrying when he noticed a red dot pop up on the tiny screen to indicate that she had. 'I think we've been rumbled,' he said.

Newman disagreed. 'If that were the case, she'd be on the doorstep with a backup squad.'

Dialling his voicemail, Ryan lifted the phone to his ear: *Call me the minute you receive this.* He deleted the message. 'She's on to us.' He pointed at the computers on the dining room table. 'We've got to shut this lot down.'

'Relax,' Newman said. 'She'd hardly ring first and tip

us off. She probably wants to invite you out for dinner.'

Ryan glanced at Caroline, who in turn dropped her head. It was obvious she'd told Newman that O'Neil had taken a shine to him. Since he'd come clean about Roz, she'd been keen to hitch him up with the Superintendent, who she seemed to think sounded so nice at the station.

Was that only yesterday?

As far as Ryan was concerned, his twin was way off target and in for a shock. All he'd done for days was mislead O'Neil, something he hated doing to anyone. Not the way he liked to impress a lady. It was time to pool resources, he suggested. The others disagreed. They wanted to get a handle on the notebooks before sharing their findings with Professional Standards. Grace was begging for twenty-four hours more, her focus on Ryan. Avoiding her gaze, he watched his twin stick her earphones in and return to her music. It was safe to talk without worrying her.

'It's too risky,' he said.

Newman wasn't happy. 'C'mon, where's your bottle? Garry said we'd know the minute we were discovered. I trust him and so should you. He installed a failsafe. It won't let us down. I vote we work on it today and review the situation in the morning. I'm owed a few favours from people who can track down Freberg quicker than you or I could blink.'

'You in?' Grace pushed. 'Ryan?'

Ryan had always been a believer that, when approaching a crossroads, you didn't stop until you reached the white line. The question he was asking himself was: had he overshot it? If he had, then the only thing he could see on his horizon was a long stretch in prison if Maguire got wise to the silent room. The prick would like nothing better than to humiliate him in the worst way possible and O'Neil would be forced to support him. Ryan wanted to push on through. Of course he did. They were close to a breakthrough.

So close he could almost taste it.

'We take it to O'Neil tomorrow?'

Newman and Grace were both nodding.

'OK,' he said. 'I'm in.'

49

While Newman went off to do his thing, Ryan and Grace carried on with their electronic legwork on the computers, batting ideas back and forth across the dining room table, putting stuff in, taking it out, cross-checking each other's work. The acronyms in Jack's notebooks were driving them both insane.

Grace looked up from her computer. 'Does the River Forest Country Club mean anything to you?' she asked.

'No, should it?'

'Other than the Regional Flood & Coastal Committee, it's the only reference I found in HOLMES with the initials RFCC. Someone who works there once gave a statement on a low-profile enquiry, nothing that rings any bells. It's not local either.'

'Where is it?'

'Hampshire force.'

Ryan was none the wiser.

Grace pointed to the notes in front of him. 'You faring any better?'

'A load of care clinics and country clubs like the one you mentioned.' He kept his eyes on the screen. 'There are so many it's hard to know where to start. Research Flight Control Computer worries me, as does Residual Fluid

Catalytic Cracking,' he said. 'I had to look that one up. It's something to do with the petroleum refining process. I also found a reference to a Ready For Commissioning Certificate too – whatever that means.'

With Newman off the grid, the hour hand on the clock flew round several times and they ended the day collating information to share with him when he got in. It made interesting reading, a definite theme emerging, pointing to the inspection and testing of electronic equipment and electrical power distribution, much of it used within the oil industry.

'All very worrying if we're talking terrorists,' Ryan said.

Grace pushed a few keys. 'Hmm . . . that's interesting.'

'What is?'

'The Audi used in the hijack belongs to an oil employee. Could be a coincidence, I suppose.'

'From this region?' Ryan queried.

'He's presently in Nigeria – estimated time of arrival in the UK is the twenty-seventh.'

'Another link,' Ryan said. 'Norway is one of the richest nations because of oil.'

'I'll take your word for it,' Grace said. 'World economics was never my strong point.'

He laughed. 'The industry is worth in excess of five hundred billion to them. I read somewhere that the lucky buggers only work two weeks in every six. They also earn three times more than you and I ever could grafting full-time. Jack's sister-in-law told me that. As young as he was, Oliver left her with a hell of a pension.'

'I met him once or twice. He was a great lad, the double

of Jack in looks and personality. You didn't meet him, did you?'

'No, sadly. He'd been dead about a year when I joined Special Branch. Jack never got over it, you know, not really. I recognized his loss the first day I met him. For me, it was like looking in a mirror.'

'You two had a lot in common.'

Ryan cleared his throat. 'Some of it was toxic, Grace.'

Her gaze was intense but supportive. 'Did he discuss the accident much?'

'Occasionally . . .' Ryan palmed both eyelids, wiping a thin film of sweat away. 'He talked about Oliver, of course, but not the other stuff. It was too painful – for both of us. We tended to avoid the subject of his brother and my old man unless we were stone-cold sober. Drink had a melancholy effect on us sometimes. We were a couple of saddos whenever we got into it. It seemed easier not to.'

'He didn't share it with me. Every time I brought it up, he changed the subject. I didn't push it. I figured he'd talk when he was ready. He never did.'

Ryan could see she looked hurt. 'That surprises me.'

'Does it?'

'He used to call you his second mum.'

'Never to my face.' She almost choked on that.

'He loved you to bits, Grace.'

'And me him.' She quickly guided the subject away from Jack. 'I was going to say you'd be better off on the rigs, but money isn't everything, is it? Anyway, you're too much like me. There's nothing quite like police work, no other job I'd rather be doing anyway. I knew the day I walked away that I'd made the wrong choice. Wish I'd stayed on.'

'I'm not so sure,' Ryan said. 'Maybe it's time for a change.'

'Yeah, right! They'll have to prise you out kicking and screaming.'

'I dunno, I quite fancy myself as Red Adair.' He was only half joking. He really was wondering what else he might be good for, other than policing. He had to face facts: he'd gone from hero to zero in a matter of days. 'Maybe a change of direction is exactly what I need. Think I'll buy a Stetson and move to Texas. Every cowboy needs a good woman. Wanna come for the ride?'

Their laughter cancelled out the sound of the front door opening and closing behind them. With her earphones in, Caroline hadn't heard it either. It was only when Bob sat up, wagged his tail and looked at the door that Ryan turned round to see what had alerted him. Newman was standing in the doorway, soaking wet. Responding to Bob's movement, moreover his interest, Caroline paused her music and got up to check on their meal.

Newman greeted her as she walked by flashing a smile in his direction, welcoming him back to the fold. 'I missed you,' she said. 'These two haven't said a word to me all afternoon. Is it raining?'

'How did you know?'

She threw him a smile. 'I can smell it.'

Newman waited for her to disappear. It was obvious to Ryan that he had something on his mind. Grace stopped what she was doing and swivelled her chair to face him.

The spook moved closer to the dining room table. 'Freberg is an electrical engineer,' he said. 'An expert in his field working for a company called QiOil . . . or should I say, he *was*. He's dead. He went missing four months ago.'

Newman had their undivided attention.

'You know how he died?' Ryan asked.

'Went out to meet a man and never came back.'

'Last seen when exactly?'

'Sunday, June sixteenth. His fully clothed body washed up a few days later. Verdict misadventure. My source tells me he was happily married with two kids and a wife he adored. He'd been suffering from depression. No suicide note. He was found at a place called Verdens Ende. Translated, that means the end of the world. Well, it was for him. Geographically, it's around an hour's drive from Sandefjord Airport, Torp. So, did he fall or was he pushed?'

50

Ryan's mouth dropped open. Turning away from Newman, he dashed off another Google search and sat back, speechless, when it confirmed his suspicions. 'Jack was in Norway then. Sixteenth of June was Father's Day.' Ryan shut his eyes. It was all coming back to him. 'It was an impulse buy. Not unusual. Jack was always surprising Hilary. She didn't want to go if it meant leaving the kids but she had no choice, he'd already booked. Insisted he hadn't realized. I never thought anything of it at the time.'

Grace looked at him. 'You sure it was that weekend?'

'Positive. He roped me in to take the kids out. I seem to recall you weren't available.'

Grace blushed.

It was no secret that she was awkward in the company of children and would do all she could to avoid them. Ryan was beginning to understand why. Falling in love with an MI5 operative was hardly conducive to bringing up a family. She'd poured herself into work, mothering her team as an alternative to the real thing. No wonder her retirement had left a gaping hole in her life.

'Looks like we're on to something.' Newman drew up a chair and sat down. 'We know who Freberg was. Hilary will confirm if Jack was the person he went to meet that day. This is big. Very big.'

'We've got to be careful here,' Ryan said. 'Jack has been accused before, don't forget.'

'You're not suggesting—'

'I'm suggesting nothing,' he snapped. 'I'm advocating caution, that's all.'

'Matt, calm down . . .' Caroline was in the doorway. 'Sounds like you guys need to eat. Dinner's ready.'

As she told them what they were getting to eat, Ryan stopped listening. He was thinking about Jack, a methodical and meticulous gatherer of intelligence. The best. And yet the notes in his diary were sketchy. Was Freberg the man he hoped would make sense of them? Ryan felt hot as well as bothered. Approaching the mirror above the fireplace, he tore off the plaster holding his dressing in place and unwrapped the bandage.

Grace giggled. 'Bruce Willis eat your heart out.'

Ryan grinned, glad to be rid of the tension between them.

'What's going on?' Caroline was smiling, wanting in on the joke. 'C'mon, paint me a picture, someone . . . please.'

Ryan moved towards her. Taking hold of her hand, he placed it gently on the top of his warm, shaven head. Caroline stroked it, wincing when she felt the uneven line of stitches and elongated scar beneath her fingertips.

Grace cocked her head on one side. 'Actually, it suits him.'

They adjourned to the kitchen. It was time to take that break.

Caroline had prepared a banquet. Just how she'd managed to do that in a strange house was a mystery to all but Ryan. Grace had fallen over herself earlier with offers of help. She'd been shooed away and told not to fuss. All Caroline needed was the ingredients, the relevant utensils and cooking pots, someone to turn the oven to the correct temperature and she was good to go.

They all sat down, a happier and more relaxed atmosphere around the table tonight. Bearing in mind their collective decision to pull the plug on the silent room, the meeting would be their last as an undercover team. For Caroline's benefit, they engaged in small talk for a while. But their conversation inevitably turned to the case that had occupied every waking moment since Jack's disappearance less than a week ago.

Ryan shared his theory that Jack had been putting things together. 'Given the state of his notebooks, I'm not sure he had all the answers. It seems pretty clear to me that Freberg had agreed to help him join the dots. I think they were both killed investigating something bigger than either of them could possibly imagine.'

Grace looked up, a forkful of vegetable curry in her hand. 'We don't have much to go on, but too many people have been hurt. We need to turn the whole thing over to O'Neil in the morning.'

'First you need to talk to Hilary,' Newman suggested.

'You took the words out of my mouth,' Caroline said. 'Before any more accusations are levelled at Jack, I think you should warn Hilary and ask her about that trip. She's had such a rough time of it lately. She could do without another interrogation from Eloise O'Neil, no matter how pleasant the woman is. It'll be better coming from you, Matt.'

'I'll go round later,' Ryan said.

'I can do that . . .' Grace was searching for the right words.

'No, I will.' Ryan overruled her, swallowing his grief. 'I may not be her favourite person in the world, but I wouldn't want her thinking that I don't care. I have to face her some time. May as well be now.'

Hearing the sadness in his voice, Caroline reached for his hand. 'She's hurting, Matt. She'll come round, in time. She thinks the world of you.'

Ryan wasn't too sure. He'd made promises he'd not kept, to Hilary and the children. He'd have to live with that for the rest of his days. The way he saw it, his relationship with the family would never be the same.

51

When they had finished eating, Ryan picked up the phone, arranging to meet Hilary at a neutral location, a place where they could talk freely away from the kids. At this time of night the young 'uns would be in bed, but he couldn't face Robbie.

Not yet.

Feeling like a coward, he set off straight away.

Hilary's dad lived in Tynemouth – a house overlooking Longsands beach – so he'd chosen the Grand, a hotel nearby. Grand by name and by nature, the Drawing Room Bar was a warm and comfortable place to sit and have a quiet drink. Perfect for their needs. She was already there when he arrived, tucked away in a corner of the room, to the left of the bar. Sitting with her back to him, she'd selected a table for two so that none of the hotel guests would be tempted to join them.

Stopping at the bar to order drinks, Ryan hovered for a moment and then forced himself forward, a lump in his throat the size of a football.

He was dreading the encounter.

Pale and haggard, Hilary looked up as he sat down.

Ryan took the opportunity to ask after the children, then explained why it was so important to see her, why it couldn't wait 'til morning. He told her about O'Neil's calls too, and his hunch that she'd be knocking on his door sooner rather than later.

When Hilary was ready, he placed a small recording device on the table between them and got straight down to business. Reminding himself that this was his friend and not a witness he'd never met before, he began gently by asking whose idea it had been to go on a trip to Norway, even though he was pretty sure of what her answer would be.

'It was Jack's,' she said. 'You know it was.'

Ryan registered the resentment. 'I just needed to be sure. The timing is very important. If this blows up in my face, as I suspect it might, I won't be the only one asking you these questions. O'Neil will. That's what the tape is for. I'm hoping it'll suffice, that no one else will bother you.'

'Thank you,' she said. 'I appreciate you're in no position to offer guarantees.'

'Your trip was a rather special weekend. A surprise, wasn't it?'

Hilary nodded, her eyes misting slightly.

He pointed at the tape. He needed a verbal response.

'Yes,' she said.

He tried not to lead her. 'Can you tell me about it?'

'It was the weekend of Father's Day.'

'Which was Friday the fourteenth to Sunday the sixteenth of June?'

'If you say so. Sorry, yes, it was that weekend.'

'I understand Jack sprang it on you.'

'In more ways than one . . .' Hilary frowned. 'I couldn't believe he wanted to spend the day without the kids. He'd had his head in the clouds for weeks and was gutted when he realized what weekend it was. That's why we asked you to—' She stopped abruptly, glanced at the recorder on the table. Ryan nodded his permission for her to continue. He had absolutely nothing to hide. She understood and carried on. 'That's why I suggested you deputize for him. If Jack had known it would be his last Father's Day, he never would have gone.'

'I'm sure that's true.' Ryan took hold of her hand, squeezed it gently, giving her a moment to compose herself. 'Had anything happened beforehand to spark the idea? Had he received a phone call, a letter, anything out of the ordinary you might have noticed?'

'No.' She cleared her throat. 'But he was a bit stressy.'

'In what way?'

'In every way.' Her tone was bitter. 'I . . . I could tell he needed a break.'

'So you weren't too surprised when he gave you less than two days' notice?'

'Not really.' She'd not touched her drink. The conversation was killing her. Ryan felt like a shit walking her through it so soon after Jack's death. It had to be done. There was no way round it. 'For someone so cautious, he was an impulsive man when it came to me. He was always buying gifts and hiding them around the house for me to find: tickets to concerts, that sort of thing. He'd made a mistake with the dates, that's all.'

Or so you thought.

Ryan pressed on. 'Which airport did you fly from?'

'Liverpool.'

'To?'

'Sandefjord, Torp.'

'Were you met off the plane?'

'No, we took a taxi straight to the hotel.' She rubbed at her forehead, exhausted with all the questions. 'Ryan, I think I know where all this is heading.'

'Stick with me a second. Where did you stay?'

'The Thon Hotel Brygge in Tønsberg.'

'For how long?'

'A couple of nights. It was wonderful, right on the quayside. Jack must've booked it beforehand. They were certainly expecting us.' She paused, the light leaving her eyes. 'I was in a bit of a strop when we left. I noticed he didn't pay the bill . . . I assume he'd prepaid.'

Unless Freberg had organized the trip at the other end.

Ryan made a mental note to check that out later. 'Tell me about it. Did you go sightseeing?'

She was nodding. 'In the immediate area; there was no need to go further afield. It was the perfect location for a weekend away.' Her voice grew cold. 'Except it wasn't a weekend away, was it? It was a fishing trip.'

Ryan didn't quite know what to say. 'Did you visit Verdens Ende, by any chance?'

Another nod. 'It was the first place on our list. We went straight there after breakfast on the Saturday morning. Jack said he'd heard it was amazing. He wasn't wrong. It was beautiful.' The memory brought forth a smile. 'He told you about it?'

Ryan felt his stomach tighten. He took a sip of beer, sidestepping the question with one of his own. 'Did you meet anyone, either there or at the hotel afterwards?'

'I didn't.' She met his eyes across the table. 'Jack was planning to do so on the Sunday morning. He dropped that bombshell when we got back to the hotel, said it would only take an hour or two.'

'At Verdens Ende?'

'So I gather.'

It was so like Jack to do a recce the day before.

'You said "planning to"?'

She looked away. Ryan allowed her some time to think. This was all beginning to fit and he didn't want to push her too far too soon. But after a few minutes, she seemed to have drifted away from him, as if she was in some other space and time. He needed to regain her attention and get her back on track.

'Hilary?' he said gently. 'Did Jack meet someone?'

She shook her head. 'We had an awful row when I found out what he was up to. I felt used, like I was there under false pretences. Jack . . .' She pressed her lips together, holding on to her emotions. 'I don't think I've ever seen him so stressed. I went off on one, which didn't help matters.'

Ryan felt sorry for her.

As a couple, they hardly ever argued.

'What *was* he up to?' he asked.

She acted as if she'd not heard.

'Hilary?'

'It was something to do with Oliver. At least, that's what

he said.' She could see Ryan wasn't convinced. 'Don't look at me like that. You know as well as I do that it was an obsession with him.' Her comment drew the stares of an elderly couple arriving at a nearby table. Hilary looked at them, apologetic. They changed their minds and moved away.

'I had no idea it was that bad,' Ryan said. 'I promise you.'

'Do you seriously expect me to believe that?'

'It's true. I knew how upset he was but—'

'Upset?' She was close to tears. 'It haunted him every single day. He was convinced that the accident was preventable. Nothing I said made any difference. I told him to stop torturing himself.' She paused. When she spoke again, her voice was harder than before. 'You two were so alike. Friends, yes, but couldn't you see that it was an unhealthy alliance? You never got over the loss of loved ones because you didn't want to. You allowed those tragedies to define your whole lives. Take my advice, Ryan. Get on with yours before it destroys you too.'

Ryan stared into his beer glass.

There was no arguing with anything she'd said. In fact, she was spot on in one respect. He'd had been drawn to Jack before they had even been introduced, having found out through idle chatter in the police canteen that he'd lost a brother. Grief did that to people sometimes. It was a strong foundation for friendship Ryan wasn't about to apologize for. Hilary was wrong about one thing: they shared so much more than she gave them credit for.

Didn't they?

Seeing that she'd hurt him, she apologized.

He changed the subject. 'Do you know who he was meeting?'

'Some guy he tracked down on the Internet shortly after Oliver died, someone he thought might be able to answer his questions. The man wasn't interested in talking to him then – and who could blame him? Jack was in a hell of a state. I guess the bloke changed his mind.' She glared at Ryan as if he was partly responsible. 'Is that what all this is about? Jack threw his life away trying to work out who or what killed his brother?'

'I'm sure there's more to it than that.' Ryan didn't go into it. She'd hear the full story the minute he made sense of it himself. He wanted to put her out of her misery. She deserved the truth. 'Did Jack take anything with him when he went to meet this man, or bring anything back when he returned?'

Hilary shook her head. 'He wasn't away that long. The guy didn't show.'

'He told you that?'

'He didn't have to. It was written all over his face. We weren't really talking on the Sunday. He was jumpy from then on, constantly making calls and checking his watch right up until the flight left on the Monday morning. As soon as we were in the air he apologized, said he'd make it up to me.'

'And did he?'

Hilary nodded. 'And some. He'd called my old man from Norway, asking if he could keep the kids a bit longer. We stayed at the Hard Days Night in Liverpool – quite apt, under the circumstances. Jack had read a review in the *Guardian* when it first opened. We'd been planning to go for ages. He joked it was a second honeymoon.'

Ryan smiled. 'Sounds like a great way to kiss and make up.'

A tear rolled silently down Hilary's cheek. 'I haven't been very fair on you, have I? I'm sorry for being mean.'

'Forget it. I have.' That was a lie. What she'd said couldn't be unsaid. Worst of all, she was right. He and Jack had allowed their past to shape the present – and now her husband had no future. Ryan wouldn't let that happen to him. Armed with her account of what went on in Norway, times, dates, et cetera, he ended the interview and walked her back to her father's house. Giving her a hug, he told her he'd be in touch and left to tell the others.

52

By the time he reached Fenham, Grace and Newman had taken down the silent room. The living room was back to normal, not a computer in sight, all equipment and murder wall disposed of, a bottle of red breathing on the coffee table, surrounded by five glasses, a few crisps in a bowl. They were ready to knock the enquiry into touch. Ryan felt a surge of fear.

Something had happened in his absence.

'Why the rush to get rid?' he asked.

'While you were out, Eloise rang, three times,' Grace explained. 'She was polite – too polite, in my opinion. I gather she's been trying to get hold of you too. Frank and I were forced to make an executive decision. We were running out of time before she knocked on the door with a battering ram.'

That didn't sound good.

Ryan felt for his pocket. He'd switched his phone to silent while he was with Hilary and had missed a series of calls. O'Neil was annoyed that he'd not returned them. She didn't mince her words. She wanted to meet at his place first thing in the morning. She was losing patience: 'If you two don't show,' she said. 'I'll come looking.'

'She sounds pissed.' He pocketed his phone. 'She wants to see me tomorrow.'

He'd only told them half the story. He omitted telling Grace that she was invited too and deliberately missed out the part that O'Neil had chosen a rendezvous away from her office. That was one trip he intended to make alone. Instead, he congratulated them on a job well done before focusing his attention on the spook.

'We're clean?'

'Forensically so,' a familiar voice said from behind.

Ryan turned. Their wires man had just walked in through the back door fully kitted up and with a big smile on his face. He pointed to the floorboards. 'I've stripped the lot out. Any evidence of recent activity has been taken care of.' He took in Ryan's cynicism even though he tried to hide it. 'Trust me, I've done this before.'

'Good to see you, Garry.' Ryan stuck out a hand, received a firm shake in return. 'There's nowt left under there?'

'Not a damn thing.'

So, Ryan thought, he had until morning.

Breathing a sigh of relief, he thanked the others for taking the initiative, accepted a drink and toasted everyone for helping him. Holding up the digital voice recorder containing Hilary Fenwick's statement, he turned to Grace. 'You need to disappear,' he said. 'I don't know how O'Neil is going to take this.'

Grace wasn't having any. Making a string of excuses as to why she should stay home, she told him to chill, insisting that he was seeing complications where they didn't exist. 'There's no need to keep my head down. You heard Garry: we're all tidied away. Anyway, where the hell would I go? Besides, I can't leave Hilary before Jack's funeral.'

Ryan urged her to listen to reason. 'You know how this works. This is a murder enquiry. O'Neil will hang on to Jack in case the bastards that killed him are caught and want a second post-mortem. They have rights too, re-member. It could be weeks or even months before they release his body for burial.'

'He's right.' Newman was looking at Grace. 'You can't afford to take chances. We don't know what O'Neil has up her sleeve. If she has any proof of your involvement, she could come after you.'

'Jack's family need me,' Grace insisted.

Ryan wasn't taking no for an answer. If O'Neil wanted to meet tomorrow at his place, the clock was most defi-nitely ticking. Maybe she had information she was duty-bound to disclose. Keeping it to herself would com-promise her position as a senior investigating officer in Professional Standards. Was she trying to protect them, or tricking them into thinking she was?

A worrying thought.

'Go and pack,' Ryan said. 'Caroline and I will take care of Hilary and the kids. Besides, Hilary is staying put at her dad's for the time being. She'll have all the support she needs. I promise to make contact as soon as the funeral is arranged or the heat dies down, whichever is the soonest.'

'I'm not running off leaving you to face the music alone,' Grace said. 'It's not fair. The silent room was my idea.'

'Yes,' Ryan argued. 'And I went along with it.'

Crossing her arms was Grace's answer. 'I'm going nowhere.'

Ryan sighed, frustrated with her, but understanding where she was coming from. Back in the days before he got to know her better, he'd shared Roz's assessment of Grace as a pit bull. It was a facade. She was so much more than argumentative. Like Jack, Ryan had grown to love, respect and value her. He'd witnessed first-hand how fiercely she defended her own in return for their loyalty and commitment. Just as she couldn't countenance leaving O'Neil to search for Jack, it would kill her to leave *him* with all the explaining to do.

He was scratching to find a way of persuading her.

Sensitive to the impasse, Caroline joined in. 'Please don't worry about Ryan going it alone, Grace. He's more than capable of handling Superintendent O'Neil. If I'm any judge of character, she'll play nice.'

'With all due respect,' Grace interrupted, 'you don't know her as well as I do. She's a great cop, but the only way she plays is straight. I was more of a renegade myself, but life would be boring if we were all the same. Believe me when I tell you she could go either way.'

'You just made my point,' Ryan said.

'You really did.' Caroline stood her ground. 'Matt will be fine. I think you should take his advice.'

'Sounds like a plan to me, Grace.' Ignoring a black look from his former lover, Newman smiled at her, a flash of possibility in his eyes. 'I'm stir crazy. You are too. We've been cooped up here for far too long. I feel a road trip coming on. Fancy joining me, in case I get lonely?'

'I'll drink to that.' Garry obviously knew of their history.

It was news to Grace. She looked at him as if to say: *Frank talked about me?*

Ryan held up his glass. 'Me too,' he said.

'Looks like you've been outvoted.' Newman was still smiling, the prospect of spending quality time with her pushing away his habitual detachment. 'C'mon, make an old soldier happy.'

For once, Grace had no words. Pocketing his voice recorder, Ryan slipped his free hand into Caroline's. Her face was the picture of delight. The two women had obviously been sharing secrets. In spite of herself, Grace was finding it impossible to hide her joy. Despite her misgivings, she'd already packed her bags.

53

Ryan spotted O'Neil's car the minute he pulled into the courtyard behind his seaside cottage. She was alone – *one less problem to contend with* – but her body language, even from this distance, didn't bode well. A face-off with her was not something he looked forward to.

He checked his watch: 9 a.m.

Right on schedule.

His heart rate increased as he got out of his car and approached hers, his mouth devoid of saliva. O'Neil didn't immediately acknowledge him, so he knocked on her window.

'About time,' she said as she climbed from the vehicle, locking the door behind her. She glanced at his car as they moved towards his property. 'Where's Grace?'

'She won't be joining us.'

'Oh?' She stopped walking, turned to face him. 'Why's that?'

'I didn't tell her she was invited.' Ryan held the gate open.

As a storm rolled in off the North Sea, he led the way across his paved rear yard. He was never there long enough to mow a lawn. Opening the back door, he stood aside to let her in. Even though he'd been anticipating the fallout from a burglary, he was shocked by the state of the place.

Not as shocked as she was, though.

Swearing under her breath, she caught his eye.

'I was expecting it,' he said.

Closing the door quietly behind him, he held out a hand, inviting her into his tiny living room. She hesitated, surveying the damage, before making a move. Stepping over a pile of books and ruined photographs on the way in, her feet crunching on broken glass, she turned towards him, her face pained with regret. The place was trashed.

'When did it happen?' she asked.

'Wednesday night. This is the first time I've seen it. I've been busy getting assaulted, remember?'

'Did you report it?'

'What's with all the questions? I'm the victim here.'

'Did you?'

'Not yet.'

'Who boarded up the window?'

'A friend.'

She didn't push it.

Relieved that he didn't have to lie, Ryan viewed the devastation. The few personal belongings he had were strewn across the floor, his small piece of Northumberland no longer a safe haven, the place he couldn't wait to return to. Quite the opposite: it was totally destroyed, violated, not to mention filthy. O'Neil stooped to pick up a framed photograph that lay face down on the floor, ripped off the wall near the patio doors. She turned it over. There were deep scratches across his father's face where the glass had smashed and been trampled on.

'Bastards!' She handed it to him. 'I'm so sorry.'

Not as sorry as he was. That photograph was taken long before the move to digital photography. He doubted his mother had kept any of the negatives. That particular moment in time was lost forever.

'Careful where you walk,' she said. 'I'll get a Forensics team out here.'

He couldn't tell her she'd be wasting their time, that Newman had found nothing of use on his surveillance camera. The 'burglars' were far too clever to leave incriminating evidence. Despite his undeserved misfortune, Ryan stood, almost to attention, waiting for the dressing-down he felt sure was on the cards. He knew a little break-in wouldn't blow O'Neil off course.

He deserved what was coming.

She suggested they move back into the hallway-cum-dining room, where there was less mess, the only place where they could possibly park themselves. Pulling out two chairs, Ryan dumped his haversack, brushed some papers on to the floor and sat down.

She followed suit, hands in pockets.

The atmosphere was heavy with anticipation as they locked eyes. A strand of hair fell loosely around her face. She was twisting it through her fingers nervously. He wished she'd stop. He couldn't afford to let his guard down. Wilting under the intensity of her gaze, he cast his mind back to the first time he'd seen her, that figure-hugging dress and red suede shoes, long hair cascading over her shoulders like a river of blood. She looked like an entirely different woman with it pinned into an untidy mess – but not enough to hide the potential.

'I know what you've done.' She was studying him closely. 'But not how you did it. Do you have any idea the trouble you are in?'

Her opener could've been so much worse, Ryan thought. Like, *You are not obliged to say anything . . .* 'With the greatest respect to you, guv, my DI is dead. I don't give a monkey's what happens to me. I've got some intelligence for you, if you're interested. I intend to save you the trouble of throwing the book at me. As soon as I find out who's responsible for this travesty, I'm jacking it all in.'

'Why?' She looked genuinely sorry to hear it.

'Because all you've done throughout your enquiry is focus on the wrong people for the wrong reasons.' He paused, feeling the need to clarify his criticism, to leave her with a modicum of self-respect. 'I don't dispute that you had good cause to suspect Jack. The initial evidence was compelling. It was your follow-up that was flawed. The way you went about it. That's why you hit a brick wall.'

O'Neil cut him dead. 'You've made your point, DS Ryan.'

The formality was back – not a good sign.

She was off again. 'I specifically told you to stay the hell away from my enquiry. It seems you didn't listen. Is that why you commandeered the help of Grace Ellis?' She didn't wait for an answer and Ryan didn't give one. 'An exceptional detective, I must say. You chose well. I not only rate her, I like her too. What exactly is her involvement in all this?'

'I'm not prepared to discuss it. I'll never discuss it.'

'You're not making this easy for me.'

Ryan looked at her, inscrutable, neither admitting nor denying that he or Grace had been involved in anything underhand. His eyes found first one coat pocket, then the other.

'Relax,' she said. 'I'm not wearing a wire. Are you?'

He shook his head.

'You sure about that?'

They were both being cagey. It was like a game of poker – and she was winning.

Those eyes.

'So,' she said. 'What do you suggest? Do we strip off to our underwear and have this discussion on the beach?'

'I will if you will,' he said.

'I'm in no mood for your jokes, much less your paranoia.'

Ryan shrugged. He'd been trained not to trust a soul, but then so had she.

'You want me to admit that Maguire was too quick to suspend you, is that it?' She sighed. 'OK, consider it done. I'm meeting you halfway here, Ryan. It's high time we started trusting each other and pooling resources. Please tell me you've stopped your covert enquiries.'

She knew . . .

But could he trust her?

'OK,' she said. 'You've had your say. Now it's my turn. I did an audit trail yesterday. I found a young detective

Ryan in the system. Are you going to tell me how you have administrator status in HOLMES without ever having taken an official course? On its own it's grounds for dismissal.'

He remained silent.

O'Neil knew more than he'd given her credit for. Her hackles were up and it showed. 'Answer me. This is a serious matter and I'm sick of you playing ring-a-ring o' roses with Grace Ellis. I have a lot of respect for her—'

'So do I – more than you might think – which is why I want her kept out of this.'

'That could be arranged . . . if you talk to me.'

What did he have to lose? Grace and Newman were long gone. They had left before seven. With no idea where they were heading, Ryan hoped they would stay away long enough for him to talk some sense into O'Neil. Opening his haversack, he took out a few items and placed them on the table between them: two small ring binders containing photocopies of Jack's notes in one easy-to-read format, chronological volumes that replicated the originals, a transcript of his interview with Hilary at the Grand Hotel and his digital recorder.

He pointed at the binders. 'They're photocopies of Jack's notebooks.'

'Notebooks?' O'Neil opened one up, flicked through a few pages. 'Is this the reason they trashed your home?'

'And Jack's,' he reminded her.

'How long have you had them?'

'That's not important.'

'It is to me!' Her eyes flashed a warning. She was an

SIO in Professional Standards and he'd do well to remember that. 'I'm sorry, I didn't mean to yell. But I want the whole story, not half. If you play your cards right, who knows? It might even make a difference to the outcome of this discussion.'

Ryan backed off. 'I found them yesterday. I have the originals in a safe place.'

'You knew of their existence and didn't tell me?'

'You know what your trouble is, guv? You knew nothing about the man beyond the crap Maguire was feeding you. If you'd asked me about Jack, I'd have told you he was a systematic and scrupulous gatherer of intelligence. If he were choosing bloody breakfast cereal he'd make a list. He wrote everything down. Might I remind you that I offered my assistance and was turned down.'

She tapped the binder. 'Where did you find these notes?'

'Concealed at my sister's home in a place he knew I'd find them eventually. Sadly, not quick enough for either of us to save his life.'

O'Neil listened carefully as he explained exactly where they were hidden, giving a brief summary of what they contained – not that the information made much sense – including the fact that he had physical and photographic evidence to back up his claim.

She was impressed.

'You need me on board, guv. Believe me, I'm a lot further down the road than you are. I'm not asking for any favours. I know I'm well out of order. No doubt I'll pay the price for that. But know this: I was only ever interested in finding the truth, not saving Jack's reputation. You have my word on that.'

Ryan held his breath.

O'Neil looked away, her eyes travelling across what was left of his home, digesting his proposal. It seemed to take forever for her to come to a decision.

54

The kettle was lying on its side. Ryan picked it up and put it on, hoping it still worked. O'Neil had followed him into the narrow kitchen, was standing behind him, so close he could smell her perfume. She had her back against the wall, contemplating. He'd already decided to hand over the evidence he'd gathered – no matter what punishment she had in mind.

It was the only option available.

With the silent room decommissioned, Newman and Grace gone, there was no point carrying on his private crusade. More than anything, he wanted to bring about a prosecution, get justice for his friend and mentor. If the case were weak when it got to court, a good defence barrister would demolish it in seconds. With O'Neil on board, he could build a solid argument. Right now it was full of holes. Going it alone might jeopardize the outcome. Evidence gathered illegally would be inadmissible. Jack's killers could get bail, flee the country and disappear. Ryan couldn't bear the thought of that.

'We need to put these people behind bars,' he said.

'What?' O'Neil was confused.

He blushed. She had no clue what he was on about.

'Sorry,' he mumbled. 'Thinking out loud, guv.'

'OK,' she said finally. 'If you can stand the sight of me, you're in.' Her head was in the file again. She turned the pages, taking her time.

'By the way . . .' He met her gaze as she looked up. 'I'm not working with Maguire. Just so you know, that's non-negotiable.'

'Don't push it.'

'I mean it, I won't work with him.'

'Are you always this difficult, or are you trying extra hard? Loosen up, Ryan. Maguire is on other duties until I say different.' O'Neil pointed at the kettle. 'You're wasting your time with that,' she said. 'C'mon, I'll buy you breakfast at the golf club.'

It was dark and stormy outside but it had stopped raining, so they walked towards the beach and golf course. O'Neil was quiet on the way down the lane, her attention drawn to the ruins of Dunstanburgh Castle. Ryan's focus was altogether different. It was on her. More specifically on wisps of red hair escaping the clasp at the back of her head, brushing the delicate contours of her face. He wished they had got off on a different footing and were off duty walking Caroline's dog. Instinctively, he knew O'Neil loved the coast.

At the edge of the fairway, he opened the gate. A sign warned of the danger from flying golf balls. Resisting a growing desire to show her the magnificent stretch of shoreline, he guided her left, taking the footpath that ran alongside the course, rather than crossing to the beach. They would catch a glimpse of the sea through the dunes as they walked on, or maybe on the way home if the rain stayed off.

'Are you keeping the case, even though it's gone beyond your remit?' Ryan asked.

'It seems sensible. The Chief thinks so too. It'll avoid a time-consuming handover to the Murder Investigation Team. Manpower is stretched, apparently. Anyway, I might be joining them soon. Or not. There's something even more exciting on the horizon.'

He looked at her, a question in his eyes.

'I've done my stint in Complaints,' she said. 'I'm ready to move on.'

In spite of their differences, Ryan thought she'd make an excellent SIO on the murder squad. He thought she'd make an excellent anything once she got rid of the bagman from hell. Maguire was a liability an officer of her calibre could well do without. He suspected that was the reason for a sideways move.

They turned left across the car park. He pulled open the clubhouse door. She entered first. Ryan was well known there, it being the nearest watering hole to his home, a place to grab a bite to eat if he couldn't bother cooking or fancied company. They served good coffee and a fabulous breakfast. Noticing a few odd stares as they walked in, he assumed it was because he had a different woman in tow, until he remembered his shaven head, the row of neat stitches that had been pinching and itching as the skin began to knit together.

Shit! He checked his watch.

'Am I keeping you from something?' O'Neil asked.

'I was supposed to be at the hospital for ten thirty. Check-up. I forgot.'

'Don't worry about it. If you keel over, I'm a first-aider.'

Ryan grinned. *It was almost worth a try.*

Ordering coffees and bacon rolls, he took a seat with his back to the bar, hoping no one would disturb them. Away from her office and the chaos of his home, she relaxed. The neutral territory seemed to have done the trick. Gone was the awkwardness between them. They were on the same side now – a tour de force.

Slipping a hand into her pocket, O'Neil pulled out his warrant card and handed it to him. Torn by mixed emotions, he stared at it for a long time. She'd made him sweat, yes. She'd also come prepared to give him a chance to prove himself. Providing Maguire didn't look too hard, Ryan hoped he might get away with his short secondment to the silent room.

'Thanks,' he said.

'Don't make me regret it. We'll eat, then talk.'

A lingering doubt over his tenuous position was quickly dispelled as their breakfast arrived. The rolls went down well. When they had finished eating, the waitress came over and replenished their coffee free of charge.

'That was great.' O'Neil licked her fingers. 'Who's going first then, you or me?'

Ryan hesitated.

'What? You don't have all the answers.' She was teasing him. 'Then I suggest you start at the very beginning and give me what you do have. I mean the lot, no keepy-backs.

In return for taking you under my wing, I require your full cooperation.'

Ryan told her she had it. 'Jack's solicitor, Godfrey, did he call you?'

'Yes.'

'Then you'll know that Jack was desperate to speak to me when his bail was refused and that he had no clue he wouldn't make it back to jail. He thought he was on to something big, guv. I now have reason to believe that it might involve Norway, which is, in all probability, our first link to the hijackers.'

'You've lost me already.'

'I thought I might have. One of them had a Scandinavian accent.'

'What? Maguire said it was Eastern European.'

'He was wrong.' Ryan felt sorry for her. This case could blow up in her face. She was staking her reputation on him. The last thing he wanted was to row with her. But she deserved the truth. 'Maguire's an incompetent moron. He questioned Irwin about the hijacker's foreign accent but not his co-driver, Storey. Fortunately, I did. The kid was so much more switched on. He said Irwin was mistaken. The shooter was Scandinavian, not European.'

'Jack went to Norway,' O'Neil remembered. 'We talked about it.'

'He did.'

'And?'

'Bear with me, guv.' Ryan stroked his eyebrow. 'At the time, I thought it was odd that he arranged to visit the country in the middle of summer when Hilary had begged him for years to take her in the wintertime, a chance to catch the Northern Lights. I thought they must've changed their minds. But I now have reason to believe that he had an ulterior motive for going there.'

Her shoulders dropped.

He could tell she was seething. 'What's up?'

'I'm wondering what else Maguire got wrong. He's made me look like a complete idiot.' Her face was flushed at the thought. 'You know as well as I do where the buck stops—'

'No one will think badly of you.'

'You do.'

'Jack used to say, "You're only as good as your subordinates."'

'Yeah, well, that won't count for much when the Chief gets wind of this. It's not Maguire with his head on the block.'

Ryan's mobile rang.

She nodded that he should answer. His private video enhancement commission had come back positive. There was a second car driving away from the scene just as Caroline had intimated, a heavy diesel engine. *Spot on.* A report was on its way to his private email address, the tape itself would arrive by private courier. Hanging up, he shared the intelligence with O'Neil. Her reaction wasn't what he expected. She was already looking for the second car. If they could get a handle on that, they might stand a chance of progressing the enquiry.

'Without it, we're screwed,' Ryan said. 'Have you re-interviewed the witnesses?'

'Maguire has.'

'And?'

'In view of the cock-up you just outlined, I'm not sure I can trust anything he told me.'

'Even he can't get everything wrong.'

'Hmm . . . coming from you, that's pretty generous.'

'I'm a nice guy.' Ryan smiled at her. 'I've been trying to tell you that for a week.'

Her eyes narrowed. 'Are you flirting with me, DS Ryan?'

'Just stating the truth.'

Amused by the exchange, she moved on. 'There were only two witnesses from the three terraced properties at the scene. Maguire said one guy had taken the day off. Don't get too excited. He's a family man. His two eldest were at school. His youngest was off with earache – a frequent occurrence, since borne out by their doctor.'

'They saw nothing?'

O'Neil shook her head. 'The old man in the next house down doesn't count. He's as deaf as a post. Didn't hear a thing. Doesn't like wearing his hearing aid. He has a kip on the sofa every afternoon.' She chuckled. 'Sleeps well too, I gather. The uniforms saw him through the window and couldn't raise him. They practically broke his door down thinking he was dead. Suffice to say, he noticed nothing untoward.'

Maguire was doing OK so far.

Everything O'Neil fed back replicated Grace's fleeting house-to-house and matched the information contained in the official files that Roz had risked copying for them, a fact that he failed to mention because doing so would drop them both in it. He wondered where Grace was, what Newman's intentions were. He hoped they had a future together.

'What about the third property on the block?' he asked.

'A couple of female students live there. One is a friend of the young woman who took the video at the scene. I have no idea who took the other, by the way. Do you?' Ryan shook his head and she continued. 'Our witness is young and loving the media attention. According to her mates, she's still full of it. She's the one whose parents called the Control Room. To hear her tell it, you'd think she'd saved those prison guards single-handedly. She took a video. Big deal. She wouldn't have been so up herself if the hijackers had shot her, would she? Silly bitch could have got herself killed.'

'Did she see a second vehicle?'

'If she did, Maguire never mentioned it.'

'What about the Audi? You spoken to the owner yet?'

'No. He's due in from Nigeria any day.'

'You think he might be involved?'

'Who knows? I don't think so.' She paused. 'It's more likely that someone got wind of the fact that he's out of the country so they could play with his vehicle for a few days without raising suspicion. A professional could've entered his premises and stolen the keys, I suppose.'

'Why bother when they could nick one? They were planning to dump it anyway.'

'Search me.' She shrugged her bemusement. 'It does

seem nonsense to steal from someone they were acquainted with, however slightly.'

'The Audi is probably in the drink where they know we'll never find it.'

O'Neil sighed. 'These guys seem to have no fear. They fit Jack up. They visit Hilary minutes after he's lifted. They attack a prison van in broad daylight, kill and torture him. They have the gall to whack you in a busy Newcastle suburb. They're ruthless, Ryan. Willing to go to any lengths to get what they want. The question is, what do they want?'

55

Convinced that the answer lay within the pages of Jack's notebooks, Ryan suggested they head off, pick up a car and return to work to examine them in closer detail.

A fifteen-minute stroll along the windswept beach saw them back at his cottage. Had it not been for the urgency of the case they were dealing with, he could so easily have kept on walking all the way to Craster under a vast Northumberland sky, maybe treated O'Neil to a pub lunch at the Jolly Fisherman, his all-time favourite pub and restaurant. Instead, they were ensconced in her office within the hour, tossing around ideas, generally getting up to speed on what their dead colleague had been up to.

Ryan studied her closely: her nails were neatly trimmed – no varnish – no rings either, nor an indentation where one used to be. Like him, she kept her personal and private lives separate. There was nothing in her office that was superfluous to her job, no clue to who she really was.

This woman intrigued him.

After a quarter of an hour, she looked up, flipping the notebook closed. She'd given up trying to decipher Jack's shorthand. Ryan suspected that she was no further forward now than on the opening page. He had felt much the same on the first run-through. Defeat was written all over her.

'It may as well be written in Chinese for all the sense it makes,' she said. 'What does it all mean?'

'Some of the acronyms relate to electrical procedures and safety tests,' Ryan told her. 'They concern voltage, pressure, blast loads and switchgear. We need to talk to an expert. I've put feelers out.'

'Good.' She sat back in her chair, an uncomfortable silence opening up between them. 'Can we talk about Jack's death for a moment?'

'What about it?'

'I can't get my head around it. A witness swears he ran on to the carriageway without looking, that the car that struck him had no opportunity to take avoiding action. But you seem to think the hijackers' brief was to rough him up and get hold of these –' She pointed at the note-books. 'This is pure guesswork, but I think he was being pursued when it happened. I reckon he was running for his life, probably being chased across country by someone on foot while the other hijacker tried to head him off in the four-by-four. Jack ran into the road and bang. They hit him.'

A shiver ran down Ryan's spine.

Seeing his reaction, O'Neil apologized for her insensitivity.

Angry that he'd not been able to hide his revulsion, Ryan nodded when she asked if he was OK to continue. He was a copper. Whether he liked it or not, he had no alternative but to keep going, even if it was killing him. What could be worse than seeing his best friend's lifeless body on that hospital bed?

Don't get mad, get even.

'You won't want to hear this,' O'Neil said. 'But I'm going to say it anyway. I'll be honest with you, Ryan. I think whoever was driving that vehicle hit Jack by accident, then panicked, a split-second decision with fatal consequences.'

'You're saying this was death by reckless? Motor manslaughter? I don't give a shit what you call it. For Christ's sake! That report you showed me says they reversed over him!'

'Yes, after they struck him the first time—'

'Same difference,' Ryan bit back. 'Spur-of-the-moment it might've been, but it was a deliberate act. Once they'd hit him, those bastards had a decision to make: drive on, help him or kill him. Tough if they made the wrong one. They were saving their own arses. Making certain he didn't get up to tell the tale. However you dress it up, it was murder, plain and simple. You'll never convince me otherwise.'

'I'm not trying to,' she said.

'Aren't you?'

'No. What I'm suggesting – in a ham-fisted way, by the sounds of it – is that Jack had something they wanted. Why kill him?'

'Because he was too badly hurt to keep hold of him, that's why.'

'But alive enough to shop them?'

'Exactly, so they finished him off.' Ryan paused, hard eyes on O'Neil. 'Jack gave them nothing, guv. He remained silent until the very end. Once he was dead, they went after me. These guys are professionals. They will have worked out that you, us, the police, have nothing on them. If we did, we'd be kicking their door in. That's why they're still looking for the notebooks and not legging it to wherever it is they came from.'

O'Neil was forced to concede that he was making a lot of sense. It was in the hijackers' best interests to keep Jack breathing, to torture him until he gave them what they wanted – the notebooks. Thanks to Ryan – and Grace Ellis too, although he'd never admit it – the information they contained was now in her possession. All she needed to do was make sense of it.

Ryan looked at her. 'Use me as bait, guv.'

'What? Are you crazy?'

'No, I'm deadly serious.' He'd never been more certain of anything in his life. 'Let them think I'm still suspended from duty. You think I'm a tosser, let me act like one. If I start shooting my mouth off that I found incriminating evidence, they might come out of the woodwork and show their hand.'

'Absolutely not.'

'Why not?'

'Because I say so.' She glared at him. 'I mean it, Ryan. You'd be better off helping me understand what this lot means.' She was holding up the notebooks. 'I presume you did some digging before handing them over. What conclusions have you drawn?'

Ryan let his big idea go.

For now.

'Well,' she said. 'Are you going to tell me or not?'

He was still wary.

'Look, Ryan, I understand your reluctance. I do. But you have to trust me now. For the record, I don't think you're a tosser. Quite the opposite; you're a good man, a clever detective. The force needs guys like you. Whatever you think of the job I do, I'm not out to shaft you. I'll blow the whistle on any bent copper, that's what I'm paid for, but I'll also put myself out to prove innocence where I see fit. In fact, I've forgotten my audit trail already.'

'And if someone else finds it?'

'Then I'm afraid you're on your own.' O'Neil looked deep into his eyes. 'Get rid of your old warrant card.'

That was such good advice. If the powers that be couldn't find it, they had no hope of proving he'd used it. *Right now it was burning a hole in his pocket.*

56

Ryan told O'Neil that Jack's notes went back almost a year, inviting her to look at the second notebook, back page. The moment she saw the flag Jack had scribbled there, her reaction was immediate, a sharp intake of breath that raised his expectations. It was clear from the expression on her face that he'd hit on stuff she knew – but he didn't – something vitally important to the case.

Pooling resources was the right way to go.

'Tactical Support found a crime scene late last night,' O'Neil said. 'There's no doubt it was where Jack was held and beaten up. We found his watch nearby.'

'Go on.'

'It's an old icehouse on an abandoned country estate, not far from the road where he came a cropper. A team of CSIs are in the process of examining the place. Two different blood groups were found.' She glanced at Jack's doodled cross. 'A similar uneven cross was marked out roughly on the dirt floor in one corner. They, we, didn't know what it meant at the time, whether or not it was relevant.'

'Well, now you do.'

Ryan fell silent, his eyes finding the window. A group of new recruits walked by, full of hope and expectation, the promise of a long police career stretching out in front of them. He remembered what it felt like. What *he* felt like when he first joined the force. Young. Invincible. Proud to be wearing a uniform, keen to get his training over with and hit the streets.

Hauling himself back to the present, he met O'Neil's eyes across the desk. He wasn't altogether sure how to proceed. It was shit or bust time. He had to level with her now. 'You already know about Anders Freberg, but not who he is, right?'

'You found him?'

'Yes, he's an electrical engineer, a safety expert in oil and petrochemical installation. The guy has worked for some big multinational players – Royal Dutch Shell, ConocoPhillips, Statoil, who incidentally are Norwegian owned and have their headquarters in Stavanger. Freberg has more letters after his name than the alphabet. Jack talked to him years ago after his younger brother Oliver died in an oil-rig disaster off the Ukrainian coast.'

Ryan hesitated.

'Go on.'

'Although this appears to be something to do with his death, I think there's more to it than that. If it had been that simple, I'm sure he would have said. Instead, he went under the radar, scribbling away in his bloody notebooks like a kid hiding an exam paper.' Ryan stopped talking. He was convinced that Jack hadn't confided in him in case it would set him off thinking about his own tragic loss. Not in an idolizing his hero way, but in a violent and unnecessary death way that would destroy him eventually if he didn't get a grip. Hilary had said as much when he'd last seen her.

'Ryan?'

He looked up, still mulling over Hilary's words, wondering if she'd ever get over Jack and live a normal life – wondering if he would. 'Sorry, I was miles away.'

'You had no clue about Jack's covert investigation?'

'None. He locked me out.' Ryan brushed a hand over his head where already the hair was starting to grow back. 'The point is, Freberg is dead.'

O'Neil was all ears. 'How the hell do you know that?'

'Don't ask.'

'OK, then how did he die?'

'He went walking near a Norwegian fjord and never came back. No exit note. No witnesses to see if he was helped into the water. His body washed up a few days later.'

'You think the two deaths are connected?'

'I think it's safe to assume that, don't you? Hilary claims that Jack got very depressed when Oliver died. By the time I met him a year or so later, he seemed to have come to terms with it, but apparently not. At home, he couldn't let it go. It had become an obsession with him. He was always talking about it, convinced that . . . well, put it this way: he didn't think his brother's death was accidental.'

'Murder?'

'Negligence. He thought it was preventable, brushed under the carpet, covered up to avoid a big lawsuit, a massive compensation claim. Five men died along with

Oliver, a catastrophic systems failure. I don't understand the technicalities.'

'And you think he'd found out what it was and who was responsible?'

'Not entirely. The notebooks would have made more sense if he had.'

'He didn't discuss it with you?'

'Only in passing.' Ryan wiped his face with his hand. 'I knew it bothered him, of course I did, but not the full extent of how it affected him. You know what the job's like. Bringing your problems into work is frowned upon. Jack recognized . . .' Ryan choked on his words, let out a big breath. 'Let's just say he knew I was dealing with my own shit. There are some things you never get over.'

'I understand,' O'Neil said.

Ryan doubted that. 'What I don't get is why Freberg got in touch with Jack, having refused to speak to him seven years ago. Whatever it was, it prompted him to take that trip to Norway.' He paused. 'I haven't told you the best yet . . . or should I say the worst. They were supposed to meet on the day Freberg disappeared. I reckon the minute Jack stepped on to the tarmac at Torp airport the engineer was a goner. Someone didn't want that meeting to take place. And, before you say anything, I know it looks bad for Jack.'

'Is Freberg's death being investigated?'

'No. The coroner's verdict was misadventure. Then again, the Norwegian authorities don't know what we know.'

'We need to pack a bag and get over there.'

'I agree. Before that, I need a favour.'

'Name it.'

'Hilary and the kids are staying with her father. He's getting on. If the hijackers were to pay them a visit, he'd be about as useful as a wet lettuce leaf.' Ryan stopped talking and looked at her. 'It's a lot to ask.'

'So ask.'

'I want you to organize close protection for Hilary and the kids until this is all over. Whatever way you view his covert enquiries, Jack died in the line of duty, chasing the bad guys. He deserves that much.'

'What about your twin?'

'She'll be there too.'

'Two birds, one stone – makes sense.'

'On so many levels: Caroline and Hilary are close, the kids love her dog, I just think it might help them, the younger two especially. Animals are very therapeutic. Caroline's guide dog Bob was trained to be that way. He's as good as they get.'

O'Neil didn't argue or hang around. She picked up the phone and made the arrangements. Ryan was relieved. He could get used to working with her.

57

Ryan promised that the original notebooks would be on her desk within a couple of hours. Without telling her where he was going, he left her office to fetch them. She was relieved to see the back of him. She needed time to deal with the issues he'd raised about Maguire. Her DS's ineptitude had to be addressed and she relished the opportunity to give the sloppy git a piece of her mind.

When Maguire failed to answer his mobile, she carried on without him, briefing the rest of her team, ensuring that notes were taken to pass on to him, should he ever elect to put in an appearance. And as the meeting came to an end, he materialized, in a foul mood and angling for a fight.

'You wanted to see me, guv?' He bit his lip.

'Yes.' Her tone was unfriendly. 'Sit down.'

Peeling off his jacket, Maguire walked to his desk, kicked his chair out from under it and sat down. He loosened his tie, undid the top button of his shirt. Opening his desk drawer, he tossed in a Bounty bar, testing her patience. 'Where's the fire?' he said. 'Front desk told me it was urgent.'

'It was, half an hour ago.' O'Neil wondered how to play her hand. Either way, Maguire wasn't going to like it.

She'd been on the verge of asking where he'd been, but held her tongue. What did it matter? He was here now, bracing himself for a bombshell, despite an attempt at cool. 'A lot of new information has come to light this morning. Some of it concerns you.' She pointed at the in-tray on his desk. 'There's a list of actions there I want you to get on with. Things are about to change around here.'

'Oh yeah? In what way?'

'In every way.'

Although Maguire didn't mention it directly, O'Neil could tell by looking at him that he'd either seen her enter the building with his nemesis in tow and kept his head down, or been told about it subsequently. A lot of detectives rated Ryan. More than one would jump at the opportunity to get one over on Maguire. Underneath the nonchalance, her useless bagman was seething.

He wasn't the only one.

'Ryan's on board,' she said. 'He'll be taking an active part in our investigation from this point on.' The words were delivered casually. The impact they were having was obvious. Maguire's hands were clenched involuntary. When he realized, he spread his fingers, laying them flat on the surface of his desk. Not quick enough. O'Neil had already clocked his anxiety. And now his left eye was twitching.

'How come you lifted his suspension?' he asked.

'He's been very helpful. That's all you need to know. I briefed the team. They're up to speed. Make sure you are too. Briefing notes are attached to the action sheet – also on your desk. I'll deal with specific concerns next week during your evaluation.'

'Specific concerns?' Maguire stalled. He glanced at the documents, then at her. After what seemed like an age, he asked her to enlighten him. 'Sounds like I'm in trouble, guv.' He didn't even have the decency to sound like it bothered him.

'You are,' O'Neil said. 'But now's not the time. We have enough to do.'

'What is the new information and where did it come from?'

'You can read, can't you? Familiarize yourself with the notes. If you can't answer your bloody mobile, I have no intention of repeating myself. Is that clear?'

'Crystal.'

O'Neil was aware that a chasm had opened up between them. From this point on, there would be no going back. 'As soon as Nicholas Wardle steps off the plane from Nigeria or arrives in the region by car, I want him interviewed, without asking direct questions. I assume you can manage that?'

'Reckon I can.'

'Bravo. I'm particularly interested in whether or not he has any responsibility for offshore electrical installation.'

'Why?' Maguire asked.

She flicked her eyes to the papers on his desk. 'Read!'

Maguire picked up the briefing sheets, his facial colour rising as his eyes scanned the pages. And still he continued to make light of it. 'Wardle is employed in the oil industry – so what? You think there's some connection between him and the hijackers? You're not suggesting he lent his Audi to them, are you, guv?'

'No, John! But I suspect that they, whoever they are, may know him or know of him and that they might even have taken advantage of his being out of the country. You said yourself that it was common knowledge. They could be trying to muddy the waters, make it look like Wardle is our man in order to throw us off the scent. As far as I can tell, that's the only plausible explanation for using his car.'

'Coincidence? They do happen.'

'That's also a possibility,' she conceded. 'Which is why we need to rule him in or out. In the meantime, I want you to chase up Claesson Logistics.'

'And what's Ryan going to do while I'm working my arse off?'

'He'll be accompanying me to Norway.'

'You are joking!' Maguire didn't try to hide his anger.

'I couldn't be more serious.'

He shook his head, a smirk almost. 'So this tosser manages to wheedle his way in and gets a trip abroad as your wing man while I'm stuck here investigating shit lines of enquiry. And you expect me to take that on the chin? I don't think so!'

'That's about the size of it.' O'Neil was almost enjoying this.

'Expect a complaint,' Maguire said.

O'Neil chuckled. 'Try your damnedest.'

'I mean it, guv. It's not on.'

'I'll tell you exactly what's not on, what's happening here and why, shall I? I've had about as much as I can take of your incompetence. You, John, are taking a back seat.

In the last few months, you've dropped more balls than Ronnie O'Sullivan.'

Maguire opened his mouth to speak.

O'Neil got in first. 'I'm not impressed with your work or how you've handled yourself. You'd better start pulling your weight or you're out of here. With his hands tied and no warrant card, Ryan has come up with more information in his bait time than you have all week. So suck it up and keep your mouth shut. If you decide to go over my head, I warn you it'll be you who'll end up looking like a tit. I want to see an improvement. Consider yourself on a final.'

'Don't hold back, guv, whatever you do.'

O'Neil was done. Conversation over.

Incensed, Maguire stood up, his face turning beetroot. He seemed in two minds whether he dared challenge her authority any further. Shaking his head, he grabbed his jacket and made for the door.

'John,' she said before he reached it.

He turned, looking daggers at her.

'If I arrange a briefing in the future, be there!'

'Or what . . . guv?'

'I might let it slip that you've been buggering about, letting the side down, trying to shaft Ryan over a woman. That won't do your reputation as a ladies' man any good whatsoever. By the way, she's available, so take your *Sun* newspaper and shove your complaint up your arse.'

58

Ryan and O'Neil had just missed a flight to Torp. He'd managed to get them on to a Ryanair flight out of Liverpool the following day, a two thirty departure that would get them to Norway by five twenty local time. Fortunately, by the time he arrived at her office with the notebooks, Maguire had slung his hook and was nowhere to be seen. The heavy atmosphere and O'Neil's face said it all. The 'word' she'd promised to have with her DS hadn't gone well.

'Thrown his dolly out the pram, has he?' Ryan handed over the evidence, feeling sorry for her. There was enough conflict in her job without it coming from within her own team.

'What did you expect?' She took the notebooks, hardly glancing at them. 'Maybe now he'll put in a decent shift.' A big sigh. 'Think I might be off his Christmas card list.'

'He'll get over it,' Ryan said. 'Eventually.'

'You reckon? It looked terminal to me.'

Ryan tried not to smile. It was only two thirty and she looked done in. There was nothing worse than not being able to rely on a colleague.

He'd been so lucky with Jack.

Casting his eyes around the room, he noticed that the

only chair available was behind Maguire's empty desk. He thought better of using it, for her sake, not his. There was no point aggravating an already difficult situation should Maguire return. Ryan couldn't give a damn either way but, with nowhere to park himself, he left her alone for a second. A moment later, he returned with a swivel chair from the office next door, sliding it across the floor so that they were facing one another over her desk.

'Did you manage to talk to Freberg's widow?' he asked.

O'Neil shook her head. 'I was going to but changed my mind. For all we know, she doesn't speak English.'

'Depends what age she is. Anyone under sixty probably will; those above, I'm not convinced. Depends where they live too. City folk are more likely to speak a foreign language than someone yodelling from a wooden hut in the back end of beyond.' He took in a raised eyebrow and laughed. 'I'm kidding!'

'Either way, we'd better find out before we get in touch. What age was her husband?'

'I'm not sure.' That was the truthful answer. Ryan was certain that Newman hadn't said. Or maybe he had and Ryan had been so shattered by news of Freberg's death that he hadn't listened. *Rest In Peace: 1960–2013.* 'Unless those dates in Jack's notebook relate to him, in which case he was fifty-three when he died. You want me to liaise with Norwegian police and ask them to approach his missus on our behalf? There's one thing for sure, they and she will speak our language a damned sight better than we can speak theirs.'

'Even if she does speak English, she may not be fluent.'

'Yeah, we might still need an interpreter. Just as well you'll have me.'

'You speak Norwegian?' O'Neil was seriously impressed.

'*Gä ut, gä hjem.*' Ryan kept a straight face. 'Gan oot, gan yhem – they're practically Geordies, guv.'

The tension left O'Neil's face, a wide smile replacing the frown she'd been wearing when he first walked in. 'You had me going there,' she laughed. 'Talk to the police by all means; tell them we're on our way and what time we'll arrive. Maybe leave out the exact details until we're face to face. I don't want them jumping the gun until we've gathered our thoughts.'

'Sounds like a plan.'

It felt good to be on the same side, even better shafting Maguire, who was last seen sulking in the station canteen, dishing the dirt on O'Neil, according to Ryan's source. If she found out, there would be hell to pay. Some pricks never learn.

59

They left early on Saturday morning, meeting at head-quarters and taking her car. Traffic was heavy as they drove west over the A69, much of it a single carriageway. It was a beautiful day, bright sunshine and very little breeze. Ryan drove, O'Neil content to let him, leaving her free to drink in the stunning view of the surrounding countryside.

For the first part of the journey, Ryan allowed the miles to roll by without much conversation. On the M6 south, he picked up speed. He was thinking of the times he'd been double-crewed with Jack on this very road, the laughs they'd had, the fights over who'd drive, whose shout it was for breakfast, whose choice of cuisine for dinner.

'You're thinking about him, aren't you?' O'Neil turned her head to face him. 'Sorry, that was a silly question, Ryan. I don't expect an answer but I want you to know that I'm a good listener, when you're ready. You can talk to me.'

'Thanks, guv. I think about him all the time.' Ryan glanced at her. 'We were like brothers, one I never had, an absent one he was gutted to lose. I can't get used to the fact that he's gone.'

O'Neil looked away, regretting what she'd started.

Ryan went quiet, hit by another wave of grief he hadn't

even begun to process, much less deal with. Maybe he never would. Jack's murder had made him realize that he'd not come to terms with losing his father twenty-five years after the event. He envied those who had faith. For him, whatever form it took, death was a bloody black hole, a dark and empty space that sucked people up and never gave them back. Another funeral was his worst nightmare, an event he'd avoid, if only it wouldn't be viewed as disrespectful. There were times he'd have preferred to have been a woman with a licence to cry – no stiff-upper-lip macho bollocks that made your throat sore and your head pound so hard it felt like it would explode. He was drowning in sorrow, slipping under the surface, and had forgotten how to swim.

The flight from Liverpool was full. It touched down in Sandefjord, Torp a quarter of an hour ahead of schedule. Fifty minutes later, a Mercedes taxi dropped O'Neil and Ryan off in Tønsberg, immediately opposite the police station in Baglergaten. By quarter past six, they were ensconced in an office, being treated like royalty by two officers from the local constabulary keen to impress their important English visitors.

The most senior, Politioverbetjent Eva Nystrom – a superintendent – was a woman with striking features and thick, almost white hair, worn short, and blue-grey eyes that cut right through you. She listened carefully as O'Neil outlined why they had made the long journey to Norway, rather than picking up the phone. She was testing the water, without going into much detail.

'There was no criminal investigation into Freberg's death?' she asked. 'Even in the initial stages?'

'As far as I can tell, it was an unfortunate accident,' Nystrom said. 'It happens more regularly than we would like in our country. People don't take care near water. It can be hazardous. Occasionally they slip and drown; if alcohol is taken, even more so. It creates many problems for us.'

'Freberg was intoxicated?' O'Neil asked.

'A little . . . in Norway, we enjoy a glass of wine or beer in summer. Then we all think we can walk on water, no?' She smiled, showing perfect teeth – clearly not a woman who took life or death too seriously. 'An accidental drowning for sure,' she continued. 'I wouldn't normally deal with a case like that. British Special Branch interest has sent you up the stairs to me. Your arrival has caused a lot of interest.'

'We won't take up much of your time,' Ryan said. 'We understand that the coroner pronounced death by misadventure. There was no doubt at all when his body was found?'

'You know different?' Nystrom's second-in-command, Knut Svendsen, was mid-thirties, a sergeant, tall and fit. He'd been hanging on every word of the conversation, taking it all in. He'd seized upon the inference that all was not as it appeared to be. His concern and that of Nystrom was quickly gravitating towards suspicion.

Ryan was still waiting for a response.

'We are less sure of what happened than you appear to be.' O'Neil chose her words carefully. 'All we know is that, had he still been alive, we would've liked to interview him in connection with a very serious matter at home. We are hoping to speak to his wife to see if she can help us with our enquiries.'

'The officers who dealt with the case noted that Freberg was depressed,' Nystrom said.

'We were aware of that.' Ryan knew what it meant, too. No sweat, folks: just another saddo who couldn't hack a high-pressure job taking the easy way out. No need to spend too much time looking for clues that aren't there. Freberg could've been pushed. If there had been any suggestion in the background that he was a suicide risk, it wouldn't exactly be written off, but the police wouldn't look very far or tie up resources trying to find out. 'We're not suggesting he took his own life.'

Nystrom held his gaze for a moment and then glanced at Svendsen. '*Hent dokumentene, Knut. Jeg antar at våre gjester ikke har kommet hele denne veien for ingenting . . . ta med kaffe og kaker . . . ser ut til at de blir en stund.*' As he got up and left the room, she turned to the others. 'I asked him to bring the documents for us and some coffee and cake. You have me intrigued.'

'Thank you,' O'Neil said. 'That's very kind.'

A few minutes later Svendsen walked back in. No sign of coffee, but he had a blue folder under his arm. Opening it up, he laid it out on the desk for Nystrom's attention. She studied the contents for a moment or two. The file was paper-thin, not enough inside to take her any longer.

'No one saw him go into the water,' she said.

'Any injuries on him?' O'Neil asked.

Eva Nystrom scanned the file. 'Nothing that he couldn't have done going in: a nasty head injury here, where he struck the rocks.' She pointed at the side of her head to indicate where.

'Which could equally have come from a weapon,' Ryan said.

Nystrom shook her head. 'Not according to our pathologist.' She spoke to Svendsen, in her native tongue. '*Vis dem webfilmen fra Verdens Ende.*'

Svendsen immediately logged on to his computer and hit the keys, bringing up an image from the Helgerød webcam. The screen showed the deep blue Skagerrak, vast waters that stretched from Norway to Sweden and the Denmark peninsula. Whitewashed rocks in the foreground were like a lunar landscape. The area was desolate. Ethereal. Very, very beautiful.

Jack's voice entered Ryan's head: *According to the UN, Norway has the highest standard of living in the world.* Looking at the webcam picture and thinking about the crystal-clear waters and boats filled with smiling Norwegians he'd seen from the taxi on the way from the airport, he could see why.

'According to this report,' Nystrom tapped the file, 'Freberg wasn't any more drunk than you or I would be if we took a test now. No drugs in his system. No one saw anything. The only reason we searched at Verdens Ende was because his car was parked there. It's quite a distance from his home, approximately half an hour by road.'

'The car was locked when found?' Ryan asked.

'And unattended, yes.'

'There was nothing in the vehicle to suggest he'd done away with himself?' Ryan queried. 'He didn't leave his wallet, house keys, that kind of thing?'

Nystrom smiled and raised an eyebrow to O'Neil. 'We are lucky, you and I. We both have colleagues with quick brains.'

Ryan blushed at the compliment.

Nystrom was an experienced detective. It would not have passed her by that people who topped themselves did the oddest things. Suicide was a monumental gesture. Even so, those contemplating it often made things easier for loved ones left behind: putting car and house keys under the seat, leaving credit cards, mobiles, money and such. These were the clues that switched-on coppers looked for.

She moved on. 'The attending officers reported nothing of a personal nature in the car, no indication that he did not intend to return to the vehicle. His jacket was there. It was a hot day. His keys and a few kroner were still in his trouser pocket when the body was recovered.'

O'Neil had heard enough. Thanking Eva Nystrom for her help, she checked the dead man's address was current – a simple search by Svendsen on his computer – and stood up to leave. The door opened and coffee arrived. 'It would be discourteous not to,' Nystrom said, and they all sat down again. 'Cake first, then Knut will take you to your hotel.'

60

It was dark, too late in the day to be visiting Anders Freberg's widow unannounced. Ryan suggested they wait until morning. Before leaving the police station, Svendsen had bent over backwards to assist him, supplying stills of Freberg's car parked at Verdens Ende, along with pictures of his body at the discovery site and on the slab at the morgue. There was so little written information available, he'd offered to translate for them and email it by morning, a level of cooperation the British detectives knew wouldn't necessarily have been reciprocated had the roles been reversed.

Ryan stifled a grin.

Hospitality appeared to be Svendsen's watchword. Absolutely nothing was too much trouble. Clearly, he had his eye on O'Neil. His tongue was practically hanging out.

Good luck with that, mate.

Still, who could blame him?

Ryan glanced at her. That smile could melt ice. O'Neil – who could probably give the Norwegian ten years and some – was trying her level best to fend off the offer of transportation for as long as she needed it. She was out of luck. This virile young man thought he was in with a chance and wasn't letting go. Neither was he taking no for an answer. He insisted on dropping them at their digs, despite being told that they would rather walk.

It seemed churlish not to indulge him.

The Thon Hotel Brygge was a mustard-coloured, traditional wooden structure, built on the harbourside, overlooking the sea. Ryan was in love, his tiredness melting away as he took in the fresh sea breeze, the sound of gulls overhead and the chatter of tourists and locals sitting outside having a drink.

Home from home.

'Fancy a pint?' he said, watching Svendsen's car drive away.

'Better check in first.' O'Neil looked at him. 'Actually, no, I'll do that. Have a seat in the lounge. Didn't you want to call Caroline?'

'If I can get a signal around here.' He needn't have worried, made a quick call and hung up.

He waited, people-watching through the window for a while. When O'Neil didn't show, he went looking and found her in reception. She was facing him, her back to the counter, one foot crossed over the other, head bowed, eyes on the floor. Deep in conversation, she had her mobile stuck to her ear, a wry smile on her face. He couldn't help wondering who was on the other end, making her blush. He was about to back away when she looked up and saw him standing there.

Now they were both red-faced.

'I've got to go.' She ended the call abruptly.

She smiled at Ryan, an alluring expression on her face.

Whoever she'd been talking to had altered her mood considerably. Unlike him, she seemed more relaxed, playful even. He tried not to let his resentment show.

What was wrong with him?

He'd only known her five minutes.

'How's things at home?' She handed him a room key.

'So-so.' He couldn't look her in the eye. 'It's going to take time, guv. Hilary's holding up but, until she can bury Jack, she'll never rest.'

'And Caroline?'

'She's fine . . . making herself useful. The kids love having her there.'

Before she could respond, the receptionist appeared with an A4 sheet in her hand. She gave the document to O'Neil. She scanned it and passed it on. Ryan read it carefully. It was a copy of an itemized hotel bill in Jack's name. At the bottom of page there was a signature: *Anders Freberg.*

Ryan raised his head. 'Links don't come any better than this,' he said.

'It certainly ties Jack to Freberg. C'mon, I need some air. Let's walk before we get that beer and a bite to eat.'

'You're talking my language. That cake was great, but I could do with something more substantial.'

'Unless you'd rather eat first and walk later,' O'Neil said.

'No, guv, I'm happy either way. I've been sitting so long my bones are creaking.'

Roz would've been in the bar by now.

They turned left out of the hotel with the sea on their right and walked along to the marina. An occasional sailor himself, Ryan loved the sound of the rigging slapping against the masts as boats bobbed up and down in choppy water. 'When I booked the hotel, the receptionist told me that Tønsberg is the oldest city in Norway,' Ryan said, for no other reason than to make conversation with his temporary guv'nor. He pointed at the pontoon in front of them. 'Locals call this the *Båthavn*.'

'Boat haven?' O'Neil said. 'How lovely. Have you always been drawn to the sea?'

'Always.'

'Maybe you have some Nordic blood in your veins.'

Ryan smiled. 'Don't worry, guv. I'll keep my plundering to the bare minimum. You're safe with me.'

O'Neil made a chopping gesture with both hands in front of her face à la Bruce Lee. 'I'll have you know I'm a black belt in several martial arts, so watch yourself.'

Ryan feigned relief. In the few hours since he'd joined her team, he'd felt only good vibes. They had a chemistry that was hard to come by, one you couldn't force. Bond was perhaps a more appropriate word to describe what was developing between them. Whatever it was or wasn't, he'd experienced it with Jack from the get-go, a connection that turned into a deep and meaningful alliance.

The magic was broken as O'Neil's phone rang.

'Maguire,' she said.

You'd think he'd been watching.

'Maybe he has news of the four-by-four.' O'Neil pressed to receive the call, checking over her shoulder at the same time. There were very few people around, none of them standing still. She put the phone on speaker so she wouldn't have to repeat the conversation. 'Yes, John.'

'Claesson Logistics are an absolute waste of space. According to the guy I spoke to, the four-by-four we're interested in can't be traced—'

'Does the registration belong to them or not?'

'The vehicle is theirs, but they can't find it . . . allegedly.'

O'Neil rolled her eyes at Ryan. 'They're suggesting it was nicked?'

'Yes and no.'

'Go on . . .'

'They have a fleet of identical vehicles. It wasn't missed right away. They assumed it was lost in the system; that someone parked it up and forgot about it. Their admin is sloppy, guv. The logbooks for the day of the hijack aren't available. When I pressed them on it, they said they must be in the car, along with the keys. To be honest—'

'Did they report the vehicle stolen or not?'

'Eventually.' Maguire was dragging his heels.

O'Neil could tell he was holding on to something, making them sweat. 'What's the date on the FWIN?' she asked, her tone impatient. A Force Wide Incident Number was issued as soon as any offence was reported to the police and uploaded on to the police computer. 'John, you still there?'

'Where else would I be? You've got Golden Boy with you while I do the donkey work.'

'Oh, for God's sake! Stop whingeing.'

'You're not going to like it, guv.'

'Why?'

'It's dated Tuesday twenty-second.'

'The day after Jack died?' Ryan exploded. 'How

convenient. They kill him and suddenly the vehicle is hot. Don't take their bullshit, Maguire. Go back and put the pressure on.'

'Fuck off!'

'Oi! Cut it out, both of you.' O'Neil threw Ryan a black look. 'I issue the orders round here.' She turned her attention to the phone. 'Ryan has a point, John. Find out who reported it and bring them in for a formal interview. Are the team any further forward researching the notebooks?'

'No, guv.'

'OK, if there's any news, call me.'

As soon as she hung up, Ryan apologized for overstepping the mark, feeling guilty – *but only slightly* – for having laid into Maguire when it was her call to make. He was more bothered that the exchange had interrupted a perfectly amiable conversation between the two of them.

'Forget it,' she said. 'C'mon, I need that drink.'

They walked back along the quayside, the *brygge*. They took a seat outside the hotel, ordering a large glass of Ringnes – local beer. It was getting chilly but they were in no hurry to rush off and check out their rooms.

Ryan held up his beer.

'*Skål*,' he said.

'*Skål*,' she replied.

They clinked glasses.

Ryan opened the menu, his appetite for local cuisine not as high on his agenda as it was for her. The menu was wholly in Norwegian. He looked at her, a wry smile on his face. 'Can't make head nor tail of it. It's written in reindeer blood.'

61

The Freberg family home was in Åresund, a typical wooden dwelling, painted in duck-egg blue with a wide wraparound balcony and a large garden that ran all the way down to the water's edge. Ryan couldn't imagine a place more tranquil. It was heavenly. An old Volvo was parked in the driveway with a small boat, or *snekke*, hooked on to the back. Despite the early hour for a Sunday morning – still only seven forty-five – the woman who lived there came out to greet them as they walked towards the front door, a curious look on her face.

Hilde Freberg was fit, if tired-looking. Late forties, Ryan guessed, with a tanned and slightly weather-beaten face, a complexion not dissimilar to many of his neighbours who lived by the coast across the North Sea. Even if he hadn't spotted her boat on his way in, this woman looked every bit a sailor.

Svendsen took off his cap and spoke to her in Norwegian. Ryan caught a few words of the language he understood, something about the Englishman not speaking Norske. A firm handshake later and they were seated in a large living room in front of an enormous wood-burning stove.

Introductions dispensed with, O'Neil took the lead.

'Mrs Freberg, we are sorry for your loss. We appreciate how upsetting it is for you to discuss your husband's death with strangers, but we have reason to believe that on the day Anders died he was going to meet an Englishman, a Special Branch colleague of ours. Does that make any sense to you?'

Svendsen explained that Special Branch was like state security. The woman was shaking her head, a look of understandable panic crossing her face.

'This officer's name was Jack Fenwick.' Ryan stepped forward, showing her a picture of Jack, watching for a reaction. This close to her, there was no escaping the effects of being widowed at a relatively early age. The wrinkles round her eyes told a tale of sleepless nights and having to fend for herself for the first time since she was in her twenties.

No response was forthcoming, verbal or otherwise.

'His brother died in an industrial accident on an oil rig in January 2006,' Ryan added. 'Detective Fenwick approached your husband around that time hoping he might help him to understand what had gone wrong. Did he ever mention him to you?'

Mrs Freberg shifted her gaze to Svendsen, whether for guidance or reassurance, Ryan couldn't tell. With a sympathetic nudge, the Norwegian officer told her, in English, that the British detectives were involved in an important case in their country and urged her to answer the question.

'No . . .' She looked at Jack's photograph and said: 'I don't know him. I never heard of him.'

345

Ryan was disappointed. Although he had no proof, he suspected that it was Anders Freberg who'd initiated contact recently. At the outset, it had been the other way round. Jack had been told to sling his hook, Freberg accusing him of talking rubbish. Safety was of paramount importance, blah blah . . . billions of dollars were spent every year recruiting the world's best engineers to construct oil platforms that kept the workforce safe. Their expertise was highly prized and lucrative. It was laughable to accuse them, or the companies employing them, of a cover-up.

'Are you absolutely sure?' O'Neil said. 'Perhaps Anders mentioned officer Fenwick to you at the time?'

'If he did, I don't recall it.'

Ryan thought this odd. He didn't think the woman was being deliberately evasive but, if there was no cover-up, then why not mention such an unusual event to his wife? Some nut-job Brit with a score to settle would be something he'd share, surely. It isn't every day that a member of Special Branch contacts you, or any other foreign police officer for that matter.

'Mrs Freberg?' Ryan could see cogs turning.

'Please,' she said. 'Call me Hilde.'

'You have something you'd like to tell me?'

'My husband had become unhappy in the months leading up to his death.' She wiped her face with her hand. 'I didn't tell the police this at the time – I was too ashamed because I didn't get help for him – the depression was so acute he didn't want to leave the house.'

O'Neil and Ryan exchanged a look.

'And that was unusual behaviour?' O'Neil asked.

Mrs Freberg nodded. 'Before that, he was always outside, sailing, gardening, playing tennis. He lost all interest. I was worried for him, of course, but he refused to see a doctor. What could I do?'

'Did your husband keep his work papers at home?' Ryan asked.

'Yes, he often worked remotely.'

'May we see his office?' O'Neil asked.

'Through that door.' Hilde pointed off to the side. 'But there's very little in there.'

Ryan led the way into a light and airy south-facing room, O'Neil, Hilde and Svendsen following him in. There were many textbooks on the shelves. The desk, however, was bare apart from a few pens and pencils stuffed into a glass tankard, some personal photographs of Hilde and two grown lads he assumed were her sons.

'No computer?' O'Neil asked.

'A laptop,' Hilde said. 'But it belonged to his employer, QiOil.'

Ryan's head went down. 'They took it away?'

'Yes.' Mrs Freberg opened the desk drawer, took out one of her husband's business cards and handed it to O'Neil. 'In case you want to talk to them.'

'Thanks,' she said. 'What about a diary? Did he keep one?'

'No. He used the calendar in his phone and made notes there too—'

O'Neil turned to face Knut. 'Was there a mobile in Anders' possession when they found him?'

347

'They don't have it,' Hilde interrupted. 'The police told me it was probably lost in the water.'

Ryan had an idea. 'This is important, Hilde. Have you ever been burgled?'

It was a straightforward question. He registered the doubt on her face.

The woman gave a shrug of apology. 'I'm not sure how to answer that. It's possible.' Seeing their bewilderment, she offered clarification. 'Anders and I took a trip, just for a few days. My sister was very ill at the time. When we returned, he was convinced that someone had been in, that things had been moved.'

'In this office?'

'And the rest of the house. I was equally sure he was imagining it. He was always losing things. My husband was a brilliant engineer but a very untidy man.' She managed a half-smile. 'I was always telling him off.'

'Was this before he started to get depressed?' O'Neil asked. 'When he stopped wanting to go out?'

'Yes, he worked at home a lot more after that. He seemed very agitated. I thought it was stress. He'd been under a lot of pressure. A few weeks before he . . .' She tripped on her words. 'Before he died, he told me not to concern myself any more. He said he knew . . .' She stopped talking and closed her eyes, fighting to keep her emotions in check.

Svendsen asked if she was OK to continue.

She nodded tearfully.

'Hilde, my colleague and I are grateful for any information.' Ryan was trying to build trust. 'And we can see how distressing it is for you to share these memories, but what we are doing is vitally important and may even save lives. We can't tell you how. We don't yet know the full extent of what we're dealing with.'

'I'm sorry. You'll have to ask the detective Anders was meeting. I can't help you.'

O'Neil stepped in. 'Jack Fenwick is dead, Hilde. And I have conclusive proof that your husband paid for his stay at the Thon Hotel on his credit card. They were planning to meet on the day Anders died.'

You could cut the atmosphere with a knife.

Ryan fully expected Hilde to ask how Jack died, but she remained silent. Maybe she couldn't bring herself to speak because the implication was too hard to take. He gave her every opportunity and then pressed on. They had covered a lot of ground and he couldn't afford to lose momentum.

'You said your husband told you not to worry. That he knew something. What was it he knew, Hilde?'

'He said he knew it would soon be over. The day he went missing I had a horrible feeling that he'd done something stupid. And when they pulled his body from the water, I thought that's what he meant. I thought he'd jumped in. Except . . . I couldn't believe that.' She glanced at her countryman, the stress making her lapse into her own language once more. '*Jeg følte meg så skyldig. Det var en lettelse når dommeren avsa dommen. Jeg vet ingenting om et møte med en engelskmann.*'

When O'Neil looked at Svendsen he began to translate. 'She was feeling guilty,' he said. 'She was relieved also to learn that his death was not a suicide. She insists she had no knowledge of the meeting with Jack Fenwick.'

'OK, thank you.' O'Neil decided to leave it there. 'I may come back at some point to ask more questions and to carry out a more thorough search of the house, if you'll permit us to. Is that OK? DS Ryan and I need time to gather our thoughts.'

Freberg's widow spoke Norwegian to Svendsen one more time, her tone urgent, as if she had something to add and was worried it wouldn't be heard. Sergeant Svendsen had an intent look on his face. Thoughtful. Whatever she'd said, it was important.

'Knut?' Ryan waited.

O'Neil was equally rapt, her focus on Freberg's widow. 'Hilde? Can you repeat that for me – in English?'

The woman hesitated.

'Please?'

'I said if it wasn't an accident, it definitely wasn't suicide. I was at my sister's when Anders left the house. He knew I wouldn't be home until very late. If he was going to kill himself, he'd have let the dog out into the garden.'

62

'Even if she agrees to let us search the rest of the house, I don't think we'll find anything,' Ryan said as they made their way down the garden path. 'I think Anders Freberg's evidence was either taken from him on the day he died by persons unknown, or it was going to be verbal. If I were a betting man, I'd say the latter is true.'

They had reached the police car.

'Where next?' Svendsen asked.

'Good question.' Ryan climbed in the rear next to O'Neil.

'Your place will be fine,' O'Neil said. 'I'd like to use a computer at the station, if you have one free, then make some calls and find out if our incident room has come up with anything we need to know about.'

'I wonder how far-reaching or serious this is,' Ryan said, as Svendsen pulled away, turning left on to a main road. 'For all we know, we could be looking at a potential Piper Alpha. No wonder Jack was so worried.'

It was a sobering thought.

In 1988, the same year Ryan's father was murdered, almost two hundred kilometres northeast of Aberdeen, one hundred and sixty-seven men – including two who were part of the rescue effort – had perished in the worst offshore oil disaster in history, a catastrophe from any-one's point of view. Thirty bodies were never found. As Svendsen drove them back to town, Ryan pushed both tragedies from his mind.

He had to stay focused.

O'Neil was quiet. Probably dwelling on what he'd just said, contemplating where to go next as she stared blankly out of the window, her mood as dark as the sky overhead. On the way there, she'd vented her frustration at always being one step behind the action. Ryan knew she wanted a result as much as he did. Right now, it seemed a world away. There was still much to do, so many unanswered questions.

As the landscape rushed by, something niggled him – almost, but not quite, in reach. They were crossing Kanalbroa into Tønsberg centre, approaching the *båthavn*, when it bubbled to the surface.

'The boat!' he muttered under his breath.

O'Neil turned her head. 'What?'

'The boat in Freberg's driveway.'

'What about it?'

'Knut, turn the car around. We need to go back.' Ryan looked at O'Neil, adrenalin pumping through his veins. He took a moment to gather his thoughts. 'Last night, here at the marina, I noticed that most of the smaller craft were gone, uplifted for the winter. That normally takes place around September/October time. It looks like Hilde has just done the same. Why else would the boat still be attached to her car?'

Svendsen pulled over.

He twisted in his seat, eyes on O'Neil. 'Ryan is correct. Unless it's a particularly good summer, they are mostly out by now. I took mine out three weeks ago to store at home. It's to stop ice or algae forming that might damage the hull. I do all the maintenance over the winter.'

O'Neil was making connections but Ryan shared his own thoughts anyway. 'If Anders Freberg *was* murdered, it's reasonable to assume that the hijackers went after Jack because they thought the information had already been passed on, otherwise they would have shut up shop long ago. But we know it wasn't. Where better to hide something than on board a vessel moored in a locked pontoon?'

'Drive, Knut!' O'Neil said.

Svendsen turned the car around and sped off the way they had come. Engaging his blue light to aid their passage, he spoke into the service radio clipped to his uniform, letting Control know what was happening so they could pass it on to Nystrom. O'Neil was hoping that Ryan's keen observation would be the key that would unlock the case. They were running out of options otherwise.

She smiled at him. 'I knew we'd make a good team.'

Ryan caught the eyes of Svendsen in the rear-view. *Oops! His Norwegian helper didn't like that.* 'Won't this roller-skate go any faster?' he asked. 'We need to get a wriggle on.'

O'Neil nudged him with her elbow. 'Stop teasing,' she whispered.

Twenty minutes later, they came full circle, arriving back at Freberg's home. As they entered the driveway,

Ryan caught a glimpse of Hilde as she walked into the house from the side garden with a neighbour.

The police officers jumped out.

At O'Neil's request, Svendsen stood guard by the boat while she and Ryan went inside to ask a few pertinent questions. When the neighbour, a young woman, realized that Ryan and O'Neil were British detectives who'd prefer the conversation to remain confidential, common sense kicked in. She shook hands with them and then excused herself, telling Hilde she'd catch up with her later.

As she hurried off, Ryan explained that they had not come to search the house, that the boat was the reason they had returned so quickly. He felt sorry for Hilde. Like Hilary, she was a woman who deserved to know the truth – for herself and her children – except in her case an accidental death verdict was about to be revoked and replaced with murder, if his suspicions were confirmed. He had an inkling she'd already worked that out.

'Your boat?' he asked. 'When did you lift it from the water?'

'On Friday. I'm giving it to Krystian, my son. I don't use it any more. I haven't since Anders died. We spent many hours aboard. It's too painful for me to be there without him. Why is it important?'

'We need to search it,' Ryan said. 'We think Anders left something there.'

'I don't think so.'

'Please, Hilde. Let us check and we'll be on our way.'

'As you wish.' Clearly, Hilde didn't share their optimism.

Explaining the urgency, O'Neil led the way to the front door. Nodding to Svendsen as they descended the wooden steps on to the driveway, she stood by and watched him drag the heavy-duty blue tarpaulin from the boat. Then Ryan took a deep breath and climbed aboard . . .

63

Ryan found something, but not quite what he'd hoped for: a few old maps, some boating equipment, Anders Freberg's deck shoes, an oily sweater, sunglasses. The list of items said a lot about the man and even more about a wife who couldn't bring herself to part with the personal stuff. With such a love of the sea, Ryan knew that, if things had been different, he and Anders Freberg would have got along.

After a few minutes searching, he struck lucky. Slipped in between a sheaf of nautical charts Hilde had left on the boat for her son, secured by dirty Blu-tack to a well-thumbed page, the note was short. It was addressed to Freberg's eldest son. Lifting it by the corner, Ryan climbed down, bagged it in a transparent plastic envelope and gave it to Svendsen to translate.

Krystian
   If you find this, then I'm already gone. I've been investigating a potential offshore disaster for many months. The motive is greed, corporate greed. It must be stopped. Not my company QiOil, I hasten to add. For several months, I've been troubled by it. I have a feeling – no, a premonition – that something bad will happen

*to me. Your mother may also be in great danger. I have
arranged to meet a politibetjent from UK Special
Branch intelligence soon. If I don't get there, you may
hear from him. Trust him. Jack Fenwick is a good man.
He will be able to help you. Look after your mother and
brother. I love you all.*

Your loving father, Anders

Ryan nearly lost it when Hilde began weeping. The
note contained only the briefest details, an idea where *not*
to look that fell woefully short of his expectations, failing
to point him in the direction of those responsible for
Jack's death. Anders Freberg was a highly paid professional who'd been scornful of Jack's approach all those
years ago. Something critical had led him to change his
mind. Ryan was convinced that they were innocent men
caught up in a situation they couldn't live with. One thing
was clear: Anders wasn't about to blow the whistle on
QiOil.

There was another company involved.

Ryan allowed Hilde to handle the note, to read it in her
husband's handwriting. The woman's hands shook as she
did so, followed by her shoulders and the rest of her body.
So distraught was she, and so concerned was he that
she'd collapse in a heap on the driveway, he put his arms
around her and held her close, a show of compassion for
a total stranger.

'Anders' references to Jack's character are a blessing for
us all,' he said gently. 'His widow and his children will
draw comfort from that note. You should too, Hilde. Your

husband loved you. I really wish things could have been different. You should be proud of him. Even after his death he has helped us a lot.'

Still weeping, Hilde stepped away from his embrace. She thanked him for his kind words and Svendsen took her inside. It was disappointing that Anders Freberg hadn't written down something more substantial that Ryan and O'Neil could use in evidence. The lack of specifics was a bitter blow. But it wasn't all bad news . . .

At the police station in Tønsberg, the contents of Anders' note and the hotel receipt that linked him directly to Jack galvanized an international team into action. With reason to believe that there was more to Freberg's death than previously thought, a murder enquiry was launched by Nystrom, British and Norwegians keen to join forces.

'Before we get started,' O'Neil said, 'I need to step out and make a call . . .'

Ryan watched her wander away from Nystrom's office, out of earshot of the others, envious of her attention, wishing it were him she was so keen to talk to. He knew one thing. Whoever had her arm was a lucky man.

Finding a number on her mobile, O'Neil pressed the call button and lifted the phone to her ear, urging Maguire to pick up. He did so on the second ring. 'John, did you revisit Claesson Logistics yet?'

'Giz a chance, guv. I've only just had my bait. I'm knackered. Clocks went back last night,' he yawned.

O'Neil shook her head, confused. 'That means you

gained an hour's sleep, not the other way round, so pay attention. Take it on the chin that the Claesson vehicle is missing. Hold on it for now. And that goes for the rest of the team too. I don't want anyone near them. Understood? Spread the word. I don't know how, but they're up to their necks in this and we don't want to tip them off that we're suspicious. In the meantime, get one of the team to check them out at Companies House. I want the full low-down on their operation, including the names of their board of directors so we can cross check with QiOil, although I'm pretty certain we won't find anything.'

'Key Oil?'

'Q I.'

'As in the TV show?'

'Yes. Google them. They're Freberg's employers. With the Norwegian's help, Ryan and I have them covered. You concentrate your efforts on stuff over there.'

'OK, call you later.'

'John, wait!' O'Neil managed to say before he put down the phone. 'Any sign of Wardle yet?'

'No, tomorrow.'

'Good. Keep on it.'

She hung up. With his track record, O'Neil didn't trust Maguire enough to let him handle something as important as Claesson Logistics. She needed all her ducks in a row before she started firing, otherwise it might frighten them off. She'd seen it happen before: documents tampered with or missing, logbooks mysteriously destroyed. Fortunately for her, some offenders didn't have the sense they were born with. Many failed to get rid of the evidence quick enough. Her plan was to give herself the element of surprise.

By late afternoon, the full capacity of the Norwegian police was at O'Neil's disposal. Nystrom had made contact with senior management at QiOil and sent a team over to retrieve Freberg's laptop for examination, another to establish whether or not the company server held any information relevant to their investigation. Company staff were 100 per cent in agreement. They had nothing to hide and gave their cooperation freely.

It turned out that Freberg's laptop had been left in storage, unused since the day he died. It contained information on a Russian-owned exploration and prodution syndicate trading under the name AMKL-Exploration Inc. Ryan quickly established that the company had nothing whatsoever to do with his work. It was pretty clear that Freberg had been mirroring Jack, investigating under the radar, a fact that led Ryan to the conclusion that – at long last – he was on to something big.

O'Neil felt it too. 'Is there any link between QiOil and AMKL?' She was looking at Nystrom. 'Any crossover of staff recently, any correspondence?'

Nystrom shook her head. 'Not that we have been able to establish.'

'What about QiOil and Claesson Logistics?'

'Negative,' Nystrom said. 'Hans Claesson, the man who started the company, is in fact Swedish, not Norwegian.'

O'Neil didn't argue. Norwegians were a proud race and very patriotic.

'That's right, guv.' Ryan looked up from a borrowed laptop. 'Claesson used to work offshore out of Aberdeen. When he made enough money, he began his own company, a logistics operation – very lucrative it is too.'

'You knew this?'

'No, I found it just now on the Internet. There's a feature on him in *Living North* magazine. He sounds like another mega-rich entrepreneur who probably doesn't pay his taxes in the UK.'

'Ha!' Svendsen's eyes were wide. 'You should try living here. Our taxes are much higher than yours.'

'Does Claesson have an office here in Tønsberg?' Ryan asked.

'Not here or anywhere else in Norway.' Svendsen seemed relieved by that fact. 'I'll check if there is any connection between AMKL and Claesson. Let's hope we come up with something.' With that, they parted.

64

Ryan and O'Neil had planned to sit down in the hotel bar to discuss the day's events, but the room was decked out with streamers and balloons, ready for a party. A covered buffet was set out on a long table on one wall. No free drinks, Ryan noticed. The price of them here, that didn't surprise him. Daylight robbery wouldn't be too strong a description. Consequently, people tended to buy their own – in Norway there was no such thing as getting a big round in.

On the other side of the bar, above the table, a banner read: *Lykke til og gratulere med ny jobb.* Someone obviously had a new job.

Even he could work that one out.

As his eyes took in the sign, Ryan found himself back in the police club in Newcastle surrounded by colleagues as a fractured memory played out in his head. The words morphed into: *Good riddance, Pete!* Police humour to see a mate on his way. The image brought a lump to his throat. That particular banner had been hanging from the ceiling at a retirement bash for a much-loved colleague in Special Branch, a DCI who'd decided to cut and run while he was young enough to enjoy a newly acquired holiday home in Greece. It was the very last night Ryan had spent in Jack's company and they'd both required a helping hand into a taxi afterwards.

'Penny for them,' O'Neil said.

Ryan looked at her. 'Just thinking about a party Jack and I went to.'

'He'll be a hard act to follow, assuming you intend to stay in the job.'

'Yeah.' Ryan's eyes found the floor.

'Will you . . . stay?'

'Depends if I'm demoted after my misdemeanour.'

'It hasn't taken you long to give up giving up. I'm glad, by the way.' She held his gaze as he looked up. 'A reduction in rank isn't on the cards, Ryan. Not if I have anything to do with it. Please don't worry about that.'

Something close and meaningful passed between them. Ryan suddenly felt awkward in her company – but also stimulated at the prospect of . . . he didn't know what. For a detective super, Eloise O'Neil was easy to rub along with, except this was no teacher/pupil relationship. Despite her rank, there was no discernible demarcation line, no formality. They had an obvious rapport. They might be two strangers at someone else's party but it felt good.

Would you care to dance, guv?

An electric guitar kicked off the celebrations, killing the moment. Revellers began popping streamers. As music blasted out, a local girl jumped on to a chair, grabbed a bottle for a microphone and began singing with a voice that reminded Ryan of chalk scraping on a blackboard. Partygoers didn't appear to notice the lack of talent. In seconds, the place erupted, everyone on the floor, dancing and having fun.

'Outside?' O'Neil suggested. 'I can't hear myself think.'

They sat as close as they could to the water's edge. For the time of year, it was a very mild night. No wind. Not a ripple on the surface as they took in the view. The moon reflected on still water drew a shard of sparkly light across the bay, a sight so atmospheric Ryan found it hard to draw his eyes away. The few people arriving were heading inside, leaving them free to talk openly about the case.

'So,' O'Neil asked. 'Shall we recap?'

Ryan nodded, his mind still on romantic possibilities. Her mouth was moving but he was finding it difficult to concentrate on the words. Something about Nystrom and QiOil. Then he remembered Roz and his vow never to get involved with a colleague. Relationships were tricky enough without the added complication of working for the same employer. O'Neil probably held the same view. What *was* he thinking?

'Hello!' She waved a hand in front of his face.

'Sorry, guv.'

'I said that QiOil seem to be in the clear.'

'According to Nystrom, they have a great safety record.'

'Yeah, she told me. Mostly down to Freberg.'

They watched two gulls fly down and settle on the *brygge* where fishermen hauled their catch off trawlers to sell on locally. There was nothing to see, but still the birds pecked at the edges of the jetty, scavenging for the remains of shellfish that had been tossed away by diners earlier in the day.

They knew a good restaurant when they saw one.

'I think Freberg was party to information he just couldn't keep to himself,' O'Neil said, interrupting the magic. 'But if he felt compelled to act, why not blow the whistle without involving Jack? You said yourself he was the foremost authority on safety.'

'That's why Jack approached him in the first place.'

'Precisely my point – it wasn't as if he wouldn't be listened to, is it?'

'I can't answer your question, guv. Whistle-blowers are often castigated. Maybe Freberg thought he'd be cutting his options down if he were ever to move on. You know how these things work: damned if you do, damned if you don't. I'm hoping our own expert will be able to help us out on that score.'

Ryan was referring to Alan Matthews, a safety engineer who'd agreed in principle to help make sense of correspondence found on Freberg's computer. Of particular interest was a Russian guy he'd been emailing before his death. Given that Oliver had died on a Russian-owned oil rig, both O'Neil and Ryan were convinced that those emails were pivotal to the enquiry.

'Did you get hold of him?' O'Neil asked.

'Matthews? Yeah, he'll hop on a plane in the morning.'

O'Neil shivered, rubbing her arms.

'You want my jacket, guv?'

She was shaking her head, scraping hair away from her face and tying it up. 'I'm going to turn in soon, but thanks for the offer.' She gave him a big smile. 'You're spoiling me, Ryan. I'm not sure Maguire would've been so gallant – not since our chat.'

Ryan suppressed a grin, not wanting to appear smug. 'I wonder if he's still sulking.'

'Actually, he didn't seem to be when we spoke earlier. Maybe he's seen sense. He's not a bad detective when he puts his mind to it.'

Ryan raised a surprised eyebrow. 'You said that out loud, guv.'

O'Neil laughed. 'I mean it. Yes, he needs direction *and* I need to rein him in occasionally, but it was this thing with you and Roz Cornell he couldn't take. It wouldn't surprise me in the least if she broke his heart running off with you.'

'He'd shaft anyone in order to make himself look good. He's known for it.'

'Nice sidestep. I didn't say he was perfect.' Seeing that Ryan didn't want to go over old ground, especially if it involved his former lover, O'Neil picked up her drink and promptly changed the subject. 'What you said about Jack seeking out the best? I think I would have too in his shoes.'

'No-brainer,' Ryan said. 'Oliver was his kid brother. He idolized him. But his death on that oil rig had no connection whatsoever to Freberg or QiOil. We already determined that. Let's hope Svendsen can link it with Claesson and AMKL. He said he'd work on it tonight and report back by morning.'

O'Neil noticed the melancholy expression on his face. 'Ryan? Something bothering you?'

'Not exactly, but it wouldn't surprise me if Freberg put the shutters up initially because of Jack's approach.'

O'Neil took her drink away from her lips. 'What do you mean?'

'Don't get me wrong, he was a great guy and a wonderful mate and I'd never have a word said against him—'

'But . . . ?'

'He wasn't the most diplomatic of souls. He could go in too hard sometimes. Frighten people off. We often talked about it. Freberg was a senior project engineer. It stands to reason he'd have had concerns talking to strangers on such a sensitive subject. He'd have to be careful, wouldn't he? I mean, a loose tongue in this litigious climate can get you into a whole lot of bother, especially if you're pointing the finger at a global organization, a multibillion-dollar player with first-class lawyers.'

'That makes sense.'

'He probably thought Jack was off his trolley. Hilary said he was so racked with grief he couldn't see straight. Don't forget, Freberg wasn't made aware of what was going on until much later. The first reference to anything in his notes is six months prior to his death, years after Jack first made contact.'

'Well, if we're reading it right, the information came from Moscow,' O'Neil said. 'Let's leave it there. We'll find out tomorrow.'

Seeing off her drink, she said goodnight, telling him she needed to soak her aching body in a hot bath. Ryan would've liked nothing better than to have climbed in next to her, then taken her to bed to explore a little of that amazing landscape – and he didn't mean Norway.

65

Dawn was breaking over Tønsberg. Matthews' flight had already touched down and he'd set to work examining Freberg's laptop. While they waited for results, O'Neil called a mini case conference in Nystrom's office. Overnight it had been converted into a makeshift incident room. Coffee and pastries had arrived. O'Neil, Ryan, Svendsen and Nystrom had just sat down to discuss progress when the internal phone rang. An alert staff member of QiOil asking to speak with the English detective who'd visited her company HQ yesterday. She was adamant it couldn't wait.

'It's for you,' Nystrom was looking at Ryan. Explaining the nature of the call, she held out the phone. 'You want to take it, or shall I tell her to wait?'

'I'll be brief.' Ryan put down his breakfast and took the handset. 'DS Ryan.'

'My name is Karin Ullman.' She sounded local, young. Her English was impeccable. 'I work in human resources at QiOil.'

'How can I help you, Ms Ullman?'

'I have information you need to hear.'

'Then I'd better put the phone down and call you back.' Hanging up, explaining to the others what was going on, Ryan apologized for holding up proceedings. Dialling the number of QiOil, he put the phone on speaker so they could listen in. When the call was answered, he asked for Ullman.

'A moment please.' The phone went down on a hard surface and words were exchanged.

Karen Ullman identified herself.

'Ms Ullmann, you'll understand the need to be careful when talking to witnesses.'

'Of course,' she said matter-of-factly. 'My work is also confidential, DS Ryan.'

'You said you have urgent information?'

'Yes, I don't work on Sundays so I only just heard about you and the local police carrying out investigations into my company at the weekend.' Ullmann paused. When Ryan didn't admit or deny it, she carried on. 'In the course of those enquiries, you will have been told that there was no contact between QiOil and a company called Claesson Logistics. Is that correct?'

'That's a subject I'm not prepared to discuss on the tele-phone,' Ryan said. 'Can I swing by later and chat face to face?'

O'Neil was waving at him, shaking her head.

'Hold on, please.' Ryan muted the speaker. 'Guv?'

'I'm detecting a little nervousness,' O'Neil said. 'I know it's not how things are normally done, but run with it, Ryan. We don't have time to mess about. Matthews will be done soon. We need to confer with him and head back to the UK. We're cutting it fine as it is. This woman sounds well informed. What she has to say might concern Fre-berg's correspondence.'

'Knut can take a formal statement later,' Nystrom said.

'It makes sense,' Svendsen added.

Ryan pressed the speaker button, returning to his call. 'On second thoughts, why don't you tell me what you have and we'll take it from there.'

'I'm not sure if it's relevant—'

'I'll tell you if it's not.'

'I thought you should know that a Claesson Logistics employee tried for a job in our company and was unsuccessful. It's our policy to destroy all applications once a prospective worker is turned down, so you wouldn't have found any mention of it in our records. This same man applied no less than three times, on each occasion to Anders Freberg's department. He was even interviewed one time. I remember it because Anders wasn't very keen on him.'

'I'm listening . . .' Ryan was doing more than that. He was becoming increasingly intrigued, as were the others as the exchange continued. 'Do you have a name for this man?'

'Michael James Foxton.'

'He's English?'

'Yes. Many British engineers work in the oil industry here in Norway. They are very good at what they do, highly trained and efficient.'

'Go on.'

'Anders Freberg's team are dedicated professionals, all of them handpicked by him. He was very suspicious of Foxton. He didn't believe the man had the qualifications he professed to. I was given the job of checking him out.

In the course of my enquiries, I found that much of his background and qualifications were false. That's why I remember him. Our security is tight here at QiOil. Even if he'd got the job, we would've discovered he was a fraud before he started work.'

Nystrom took over the conversation, thanking Karin Ullman, advising that Politibetjent Svendsen would visit her place of work and take a statement, warning her not to repeat what she'd said to anyone. Then she hung up.

'That sounds highly suspicious,' O'Neil said.

'A mole?' Ryan suggested.

'Sounds like it,' Svendsen said.

'I reckon Foxton was trying to get close to Freberg to find out what he knew or destroy evidence,' O'Neil added.

'I agree,' Nystrom said. 'That one needs to be found and interviewed as soon as possible.'

She picked up the phone, called QiOil and asked for Karin Ullman again. Speaking in Norwegian, in a tone that sounded like she meant business, she asked the woman outright if any evidence existed on his application to join Freberg's team. She listened for a while, scribbled down a note, and then put down the phone.

'It's amazing what you find out if you ask *politely*,' she said. 'Despite company policy to destroy all records, Ullman kept some hard copy information in case the fraudster applied again.'

'That explains her nervousness,' O'Neil said.

'This is the email address he gave on his application.' Ullman handed Ryan the note.

He checked it out but, as they all suspected, it was

dodgy. The best they could hope for was to trace the IP address when they returned to the UK. O'Neil led the discussion that followed, tying up loose ends, putting forward suggestions on how to divide up responsibility, what parts of the enquiry the Norwegians would handle, what to retain for action by British police. Nystrom was a breath of fresh air: no squabbling over finances, no trying to score points, an ideal situation all round. It was unusual to find such unconditional cooperation – even on matters this serious. By the time the meeting drew to a close, word had come in that Matthews had news and was ready to reveal his findings.

'I'll get him.' O'Neil stood up. 'I could do with stretching my legs. Is there another office I can use to interview him, Eva?'

'The one next door is free,' Nystrom replied.

O'Neil looked at Ryan. 'Can you move our stuff? I'll see you in there.'

He nodded and she left the room.

Scooping their belongings off Nystrom's desk, O'Neil's mobile rang in Ryan's hand as he picked it up. He walked to the door and stuck his head out. She was already halfway down the corridor, so he took the call on her behalf.

Maguire didn't bother to introduce himself. He started talking the second the connection was made. 'I have good news and bad, guv. Which do you want first?'

'I don't care,' Ryan said drily. 'Knock yourself out.'

'Is that all you're good for, answering her phone?' Maguire chuckled. 'Put her on.'

'She's indisposed. It's me or no one.'

The line went quiet.

Nystrom and Svendsen got up and left him to it. A fag break, Ryan assumed. With Mouth Almighty on the other end, he could do with one himself. Either that or the Norwegians had picked up on the animosity in his voice and were being discreet.

Ryan waited for them to close the door. 'C'mon, Maguire, stop buggering about and start acting like a grown-up. Give me what you've got.'

For once, Maguire acquiesced without a fight. 'Trace evidence from the Clio has been matched to a little scrote from Kenton Bar – Brian Platt. I made an arrest and he's been in custody overnight.'

The name wasn't familiar to Ryan. 'Is he talking?'

'Not at first, he wasn't—'

'And now?' Ryan sat down.

'He started to cough when he realized the trouble he was in. Claims he met two guys in a pub. They offered him money to nick a motor and follow Irwin's security van when it left the Crown Court – a bit risky, bearing in mind the idiot isn't surveillance savvy. Swears he had no idea what was going down, not until they pulled out the shooters, and by then it was too late—'

'Bollocks!'

'That's what I said. He's dim, but not stupid, if you get my drift. He obviously thinks I am, though. Alleges these men were strangers. That much I was prepared to accept until I searched his fleapit and found a letterhead from Claesson offering him casual work as a driver. He nearly pissed himself when I showed it to him. He's got more to tell us. I've applied for an extension to keep him in until you get here.'

That was the correct move until O'Neil decided what substantive offences might be on the charge sheet. The way the enquiry was going it could conceivably be multiple murder – and that was just for starters. In his early career, Platt might have been a lowly twoccer – car thief – but he'd since joined the big league, aiding and abetting a very serious hijack, assisting offenders who later killed Jack. Further enquiries would have to be made. This was not something the police would rush. And no judge in his right mind would refuse a request for a lengthy remand in custody.

'Result!' Ryan said. 'I'd buy you a pint if I was in the UK.'

'I'm choosy who I drink with, pal.'

'Don't be like that. You deserve a pint. Two even. What you told me should earn you some brownie points with your guv'nor when I tell her. What's the bad news?'

Maguire climbed down. 'It ain't good.'

'It doesn't concern Wardle by any chance?'

'It does. I met him off the plane. Drove him home, interviewing him on the way. He seems kosher to me, totally upfront and honest. Anyway, his flight was delayed and I'm dying for a piss, so I go and use the bathroom as soon as we get to his place and what do I find? A fucking hole in the window, that's what. Professional job. Glass cutter.'

'Seriously?'

''Fraid so.'

'The guv'nor said his place was locked and secure.'

'It was, on the ground floor. The numpty we sent round obviously didn't look up. Actually, to be fair to him, you could hardly see the small circle of glass missing from street level. Wardle was really hoping that his car had been cloned and would still be in his garage. I was with him when he unlocked the door expecting to find the keys to his vehicle on the hall table. He wasn't faking it when he saw they were gone. He was genuinely shocked when I told him that the Audi had been used in a hijack. Unless you know different, I figure that rules him out.'

'Does he have any connection with Claesson Logistics?'

'Yes and no.'

'Meaning?'

'Knows of them, doesn't rate them.'

'How come?'

'They approached him some time ago. Wardle's a bit like me, a first impressions man. He didn't like Claesson from the off. Claims he's a smooth operator with no morals and even less finesse. A bully, he called him. Suffice to say, they didn't hit it off. Their paths cross at conferences and so on. I gather they've had some lively exchanges of views on more than one occasion.'

'Sounds familiar.'

Maguire wasn't laughing. 'If you ask me, Claesson knew Wardle was out of the country and tried being clever by getting one over on him, making it look like he might be involved in Jack's abduction. As I said, there's no love lost between them.'

'It might be his downfall,' Ryan said. 'You did good,

Maguire. I'll pass it on. Things are hotting up this end. The guv'nor and I have one more person to see. After that, we're on the next plane home. In the meantime we need everything you can muster on Michael James Foxton. I'll email the details. I gotta go. If you find him, lock him up too.'

'On what charge?'

'Think of one.' Smiling, Ryan put the phone down and went to find O'Neil.

66

Alan Matthews had been working on the documents for three hours. He was a British OIM – offshore installation manager – former project manager and multi-linguist, working and living near Rotterdam, a man who came highly recommended. On Ryan's suggestion, O'Neil had flown him in with the sole purpose of consulting on what they had found on Anders Freberg's computer.

Taking off his reading glasses, rubbing his eyes, Matthews stifled a yawn as he sat back in his chair and looked at them. 'Apologies, I had an early start,' he said, placing his specs on the desk.

'Ready to rock 'n' roll?' Ryan asked.

Matthews nodded.

'Can I get you anything while we talk?' O'Neil asked. 'Coffee? Water? Cake? This station seems to run on cake.'

'No, I'm good, thanks.' Matthews looked at his watch. 'My return flight leaves in just over three hours. I'll give you the feedback, then I'm on my way. Svendsen has kindly offered me a lift to the airport. I'll eat there and get some shut-eye on my way home.'

Ryan picked up a pen. 'Take it slowly. We're coppers. That means we have trouble understanding technical terms. We may no longer be in uniform but don't let that fool you.'

'Speak for yourself,' O'Neil said.

'Well, it's all here –' Matthews pointed at Freberg's computer. 'Email correspondence and notes relating to safety concerns raised by a third party, a Russian engineer, Vladimir Pirotsky, who worked out of Moscow for AMKL. Apparently, he broached the matter with his company, who weren't interested. When he did so a second time, they demoted him and brought in someone less experienced and with a bad safety record. Pirotsky was too scared to go to the law and terrified to blow the whistle to the Russian press.'

'Which is why he turned to Freberg?' Ryan said.

'Yes. Reading the correspondence, it wouldn't be too big a jump to intuit that they were friends. At great risk to his livelihood, Pirotsky cited a specific case to demonstrate the extent of the problem. The correspondence between the two men relates to a purchase order for eleven-thousand-volt switchgear from a sub-supplier and what happened from that point on. Normally, a subcontractor would send all the relevant drawings to the purchaser along with what we call a type test certificate.'

'The purchaser being AMKL?' Ryan asked.

'No, that would be a subcontractor,' Matthews corrected him. 'There's nothing sinister there. That's perfectly normal procedure.'

'Go on.' O'Neil invited him to continue.

'When equipment is built, a factory acceptance test is requested by the supplier on the Bus Bars—'

'Whoa!' Lifting his pen from the paper, Ryan looked up. 'And they are?'

'They're copper bars that transfer voltages between different sections of switchgear. If all is satisfactory, the test is then accepted by the purchaser and end user.'

'In this case, the Russians – AMKL?'

The engineer's confirmation came as a nod. 'The switchgear is then taken apart so it can be shipped to the final location, where it's reassembled on site ready for installation. Other checks are carried out before a mechanical completion check record can be issued.' He paused. 'Still with me?'

Ryan nodded, even though he suspected that he'd have to read his notes to the engineer half a dozen times before they were done.

Matthews told him he'd go over it again if they were in any doubt and answer any question at the end of his verbal report. 'I'll write it up at the airport,' he said. 'You'll have it via email before I board for the Netherlands. The important thing to remember here is this: whatever the project, you can always guarantee that senior management want the switchgear energized ASAP. It supplies pumps that are needed to get production up to maximum.'

'Time is money,' O'Neil said.

'In *my* industry?' Matthews said. 'Always.'

'I imagine production stoppages cost billions,' Ryan said.

Matthews was nodding. 'The Russian economy is heavily dependent on natural resources. Anyway, an RFCC,' Matthews lifted his hand, a gesture of apology.

'Ready for commissioning certificate?' Ryan suggested.

'He's catching on.' The engineer grinned at O'Neil. 'I'm beginning to think you guys don't need me at all.'

'Yes, we do,' O'Neil said.

As Matthews had been talking, the acronyms contained in Jack's notebooks were finally beginning to make sense to her too. FAT, meaning factory acceptance test. MCCR, meaning mechanical completion check record.

Hindsight was a wonderful thing.

She was keen to move on. 'You were saying?'

'This is the important bit,' Matthews said. 'The case Pirotsky highlighted was similar to the one where Jack Fenwick's brother lost his life, exactly the same in fact. An RFCC was issued so that powering up could proceed without a high-voltage test being carried out – a test that you should know would take three hours max. In ideal conditions, if results are acceptable, there's no problem. You issue the certificate and away you go. If there is a problem, investigations are required until it is resolved and retested. If everything is hunky-dory, what we call a livening up notice is issued.'

'And if the problems aren't resolved as they should be?' Ryan asked.

'Power is put on the switchgear and it explodes, killing anyone in the vicinity.' Matthew's expression was sympathetic. 'This is exactly the area where Oliver was working seven years ago. I checked the accident report. It's a matter of public record. The case Pirotsky cited, not so. There were twenty deaths in that one. It could have been an awful lot worse. Anyway, the Russian couldn't live with it – and you know the rest.'

The room went quiet.

'Why would the switchgear explode?' O'Neil asked.

'Because non-visible dust had accumulated on the bus bars over many months of being in storage,' Matthews said. 'The same can happen if equipment is left in the construction area for an extended length of time.' He paused, took a sip of water from a bottle, allowing them time to process this before continuing. 'When eleven thousand volts is applied to bus bars in that condition, the voltage jumps, or flashes over from one phase to the other, causing ultra-high temperatures and ultimately an explosion. Arc flash temperatures can reach in excess of thirty-five thousand degrees Fahrenheit, nineteen and a half thousand Centigrade.'

'Jesus!' Ryan bit down on his teeth so hard his jaw set like a vice. 'So you're saying both of these industrial accidents were preventable.' It wasn't a question.

'Entirely.'

A dark shadow crossed Matthews' face. No wonder. The man had spent the last twenty years of his working life dealing with safety issues. Bad housekeeping was inexcusable, tragic for all concerned. Men had died unnecessarily, leaving behind distraught relatives. Hilary and the kids were minor ripples on the edge of a pool of sorrow that resulted from an oil-rig explosion in the Ukraine before Lucy Fenwick was even born.

It was a shocking revelation, one that angered Ryan, reminding him of his conversation with Garry Snaith. In any line of business, contractors tried cutting corners. Sometimes that put security at risk. Like Freberg, Garry

382

couldn't live with it. And when he challenged those who should know better, he found himself out on his ear with nowhere to go.

Glancing at his notes, Ryan sought clarification from Matthews. 'And it was the arbitrary issuing of ready for commissioning certificates that the Russians were trying to cover up in order to avoid any blame being apportioned to them?' he asked.

'Precisely,' Matthews said with conviction.

'How can you tell the switchgear wasn't tampered with en route?'

'Sabotage?' Matthews took in Ryan's nod. 'Switchgear is always transported in secure containers. Even if that were possible – which it's not – if the correct testing protocols were followed, it would've shown up. There is no excuse for what happened to those men. None. That's why we have such stringent regulations.'

O'Neil and Ryan exchanged a look.

'You thinking what I'm thinking, guv?'

O'Neil was way ahead of him. 'Possible link to Claesson Logistics?'

'It would make sense of their involvement. Security is a big part of their business.'

'Vladimir Pirotsky is our next port of call, then.' O'Neil turned to the engineer. 'You've been remarkably helpful, Mr Matthews. It all makes perfect sense. You may be called as an expert witness in due course. For now, thanks for talking us through it.'

67

Ryan held up his phone. 'Email from Nystrom,' he said. 'She tried contacting the Russian engineer and guess what? Pirotsky is no longer with AMKL. They say he was an alcoholic and didn't show for work so they terminated his contract. Local police say he's not at his address. Hasn't been seen for months. If you want my opinion, we'll never find him. If we do, he'll be zipped inside a body bag and no doubt it'll look like an accident.'

They had arrived at Torp airport with minutes to spare, Nystrom paving the way for them to walk straight on to the aircraft. *Would that the Brits could be so efficient where the law was concerned.* The Ryanair flight took off on time and they were due to touch down in a little over ten minutes. In the seat beside him, O'Neil yawned. Like him, she was exhausted, the dryness in the pressurized cabin getting to her.

'You think Vladimir Pirotsky has gone the same way as Jack and Anders Freberg?' she asked.

'Don't you?' The thought depressed them both, Ryan in particular. 'How many more have to die before this case is finally resolved?' he said. 'I bloody hope Maguire has had more luck tracing Foxton than Nystrom did Pirotsky – I'm looking forward to having a conversation with him.'

They disembarked at ten to five. By the time they had cleared Immigration and found O'Neil's car, rush hour was in full swing. Slow-moving traffic was yet another drag on their time as they left Liverpool; more energy-sapping, mind-numbing sitting doing nothing. They found that hard to stomach after the shifts they had put in recently in order to crack the case. Then suddenly things got even worse. They were stationary, with no police escort to smooth their way. Ryan found himself wishing they were still in Norway.

'Mind if I call Caroline, guv? She worries if I'm flying.'

'Go ahead. Just don't get caught.'

There was no answer, so he left a message and rang off.

'I think it's lovely how you consider her all the time,' O'Neil said.

'She's my twin, my only family. Why wouldn't I?'

'Just an observation. Not everyone would.'

'What about you?' he asked.

'No ties,' is all she said.

Ryan felt like he'd stepped in something sensitive. He didn't push it. O'Neil was staring straight ahead. It was her composure he found irresistible. He was tired, undoubtedly, and so was she. But sitting in the car with her, even after a long shift and an even longer journey, he still felt relaxed and hassle-free, totally calm, like he used to with Jack. No easy achievement in the short space of time they had worked together.

Two and a half hours later, Ryan depressed the accelerator, moved forward a few metres and stopped, a line of taillights stretching as far as the eye could see in front of them. O'Neil's phone beeped. Taking it out of her pocket, she checked the display. Feeling her spirits lift, he glanced in her direction. She had a wry smile on her face.

'Good news, guv?'

'Some.' She didn't lift her head. 'Organized Crime have coughed the names of the arms dealers they were after. They're nowt to do with our case. They were wrong about Jack and have said as much. I reckon they were inept rather than dodgy. Although if I never see DC King again, it'll suit me down to the ground.'

'Anything else?'

She was flicking through emails.

'Maguire hasn't found Foxton?'

'No, but he's managed to break down our friend, Brian Platt. Sounds like he's giving him bloody good intelligence too. John reckons he has still more to tell. I told you he'd come up trumps if pushed—'

'And work miracles if threatened.' Ryan couldn't help himself.

'Yeah, well, I won't have to put up with him for much longer.'

Ryan looked sideways. 'Did your transfer come through for the Murder Investigation Team?'

A flash of excitement crossed her face. 'Something even better.'

He waited. When she didn't elaborate, he asked her outright what she meant.

'I can't talk about it yet.'

'I'm intrigued.' The logjam eased and Ryan picked up speed, pulling into the outside lane. He didn't get far as everyone ahead of his vehicle did the same, frustrating the hell out of him. 'C'mon,' he said. 'I didn't figure you as a tease. I had enough of that with Roz. I'm done with begging.'

'I need to select a colleague I can trust,' she said playfully. 'Only she or he and I can know about it. I'd like to tell you, but it's *Eyes Only* stuff.'

He didn't need to see the excitement in her eyes. He could hear it in her voice. Ryan bit his bottom lip. She was tantalizing him. If only she knew what he and Grace and Newman had been up to in the silent room. He checked his left-hand wing mirror in order to pull over, catching her eye. Impenetrable.

Bet she was skilled at poker.

'So, what's the criteria?' he asked.

She shifted in her seat to face him. 'That's fishing, DS Ryan.'

'You can't blame me for wondering if I'd qualify.'

'It wouldn't suit your lifestyle.' She was still grinning. 'Anyway, ten minutes ago you were jacking it all in. I need someone whose commitment I can count on.'

'Now I know you're taking the piss.'

Whatever it was, it must be good.

'You have Caroline,' she said. 'I couldn't possibly impose.'

Ryan was laughing out loud and so was she, a real belly laugh she couldn't control. It felt good to release the tension. 'Will you stop talking in riddles and tell me. Scout's honour, I won't spill, not if my life depends on it.'

What she told him would remain on his mind for the rest of the journey home.

68

It was getting on for eight forty-five by the time they finally reached Newcastle city centre. On the way to Interview Room 1 at Market Street police station, they decided that Ryan would take the lead, for no other reason than that was how things were normally done. 'No point in keeping a dog and barking yourself,' he joked.

The leg-pulling continued, this time from O'Neil. 'You don't mind me sitting in . . . in an advisory capacity? I want to see how you handle yourself with the opposition.'

'Oh yeah?' Ryan grinned. 'In case there's a dearth of worthy candidates to work alongside you in your swish new job?'

She didn't look at him. 'I hate scraping the barrel, but needs must when the Devil drives.'

Since she'd confided what the position entailed, Ryan had thought of nothing else. Before he could muster a witty retort, she opened the door, leaving him with no option but to park his humour and concentrate on the task in hand.

Brian Platt tapped the table nervously as they entered. The detainee and his brief, Tomas Marek, seemed surprised and somewhat disturbed to see a change in personnel. The detectives sat down, switched on the recording device and dispensed with the introductions quickly, keen to get the interrogation over and call time on a very long day. They were dead on their feet.

Forcing the notion of a permanent partnership with O'Neil away, Ryan fixed his eyes on the prisoner. 'Mr Platt, you've already admitted that you stole a Clio from the Shell garage at the top of Shields Road in Byker on Friday the eighteenth of October. Is that correct?'

The prisoner nodded, chewing the inside of his cheek.

'For the tape, I need a verbal response.'

'Yes,' Platt said. *If looks could kill.*

'Good start.' Ryan gave a half-smile. 'In fact, we have CCTV of you doing it.'

'Bully for you.'

'You further admit that you were asked by Michael James Foxton to follow a security van from Newcastle Crown Court to a prearranged position on that same date,' Ryan said. 'And that your role was to pull up behind the van and put your handbrake on hard when Foxton arrived at the scene in an Audi. Is that correct?'

'If you say so.'

'It's what you say that's important.' Ryan pointed at the recording device. 'For the—'

'Tape . . . yeah, I get it.'

'So answer the question.'

'Yeah, it's all I done.'

'That's not true though, is it?' Ryan glanced at O'Neil.

Rolling her eyes, she exhaled loudly, a gesture designed to show the prisoner that they didn't believe a word of it. She crossed her arms, eyes on Platt. He looked away and then at his solicitor with an expression that said: *Do what the fuck you're paid for.* In turn, Marek looked at Ryan.

The stalemate lasted for a while.

'There's no hurry,' Ryan said. 'If you two need a moment in private, my guv'nor and I can step outside.'

Marek was having none of it. 'If it's all the same to you, I'd rather not sit here all night. If you have evidence against my client, please disclose it. It's late and we've already been through all this with your colleague, DS Maguire.'

'All in good time,' Ryan said. 'My guv'nor and I are here to tell Mr Platt that extensive enquiries into very serious matters are ongoing and that he will remain exactly where he is until he answers our questions truthfully.'

'I have!' Platt blurted out. 'Ask the other tosser.'

Ryan eyeballed him. 'You and I both know that's not the case though, don't we? I can see you need time to think on it.' Pulling up his sleeve, he checked his watch. 'It's late. Maybe we should adjourn 'til morning—'

'Fuck that! My lass'll be going crackers. She's pregnant! Ready to drop, if you must know.'

'Aren't we all.' O'Neil spread her hands, looked at Ryan, a question in her eyes. 'Up to you, DS Ryan. I'm happy to sleep on it.'

'No!' Platt yelled. 'I want out of here. I nicked a car, so what? I've done it before and you haven't kept us in overnight.'

'I'm going to ask you one more time,' Ryan said. 'And if you don't come up with the truth, you will be charged with very serious offences. Is that clear? So tell me what you know before I lock up your mate Foxton. There's another team doing that, by the way, so you'll soon have company. I'm here to establish the truth and I know you haven't got there yet, so try harder. What exactly was your part in the hijacking?'

Pushing away from the table, Platt stood up suddenly, knocking his chair flying. 'I told you! I nicked a car, drove it to where they said and legged it. End of—'

'Sit down and stop wasting my time.' Ryan watched him right the chair and retake his seat. 'You denied theft of a vehicle initially. You denied any knowledge or association with Claesson Logistics until DS Maguire went to your home and found documents that proved you work for them occasionally—'

'That's proof of a falsehood,' Marek interrupted. 'Nothing more.'

Ryan ignored him. 'This is the final countdown, Brian. Tell us or we'll have to assume that you are more involved than you say you are *and* that you are protecting others. Instead of being charged with TWOC of a vehicle and assisting offenders, you'll be charged with much more serious offences – conspiracy, for starters. It could make the difference between a four-year term of imprisonment, fourteen years, or life. You have a decision to make. If you want to see your child outside of a prison visits room before it reaches its teens, speak now. By the way, I know exactly what you did, but I want to hear it from you.'

Platt was sweating. 'I told you everything.'

'That was said without conviction.'

'Eh? What does that mean?'

'It means it's bollocks! We know about the video.'

It took a while for Platt to speak. His bottle was going, his non-verbal communication giving him away. He blew out a long breath, painfully aware that Ryan was playing it straight and that he was facing a lengthy stretch in jail.

Time to push his buttons.

'I hope they paid you well if you're willing to take the rap for them.'

'They paid me nowt! They said I wasn't getting any more work unless I went along with it. I've got a kid and one on the way. They need to eat. What was I supposed to do? I was told to take a video to show the copper walking away with the others like he was part of the hijack. That's all, I swear.'

'And?'

'Nothing! I legged it to the four-by-four and drove away.'

'The one you'd left in the woods earlier?'

He nodded. 'Yes.'

'That proves premeditation and planning.'

'So what? Can I go now?'

'No, I'm afraid not. That vehicle was later used to kill a police officer.'

'Nothing to do with me!' Platt was exposed and on the back foot. He looked at Marek. 'I'm not havin' that. Tell the bastard!'

Marek's facial expression confirmed only that his client was in deep trouble, more than he could possibly handle, and far more serious than any of his previous convictions. Ryan had him cornered. They both knew it. There was nowhere to go. As the prisoner was informed that numerous enquiries were being carried out – and that he'd be kept in custody until the conclusion of those investigations – a tear ran down his cheek.

Ryan looked at O'Neil. 'What do you say, guv?'

'I'd say we're done here.' She looked at Platt. 'Unless you have anything else to tell us?'

'No,' he said, defeated. 'That's it, I swear.'

With that, the interview concluded. After the prisoner and his brief were led away by a member of uniformed staff, the detectives high-fived. Next stop Claesson Logistics, but first a drink to celebrate and then some well-earned rest.

69

The raid on Claesson Logistics was swift and carried out at seven a.m., the minute they opened up for business. Timing was important. O'Neil wanted a result. Collaring Claesson and Foxton would be ideal. Failing that, one or the other would do. Platt was small fry, already in the bag. The important thing was to seize evidence. Arrests would come later.

Foxton made a run for it the minute the detectives entered the premises. He got as far as the door and was brought down by Maguire in a rugby tackle worthy of Welsh international George North. As he was led away in handcuffs and put into a panda car, O'Neil and Ryan were told by the receptionist that Hans Claesson wasn't expected in.

'No matter,' Ryan said. 'We have a search warrant.'

Showing the document they'd managed to secure from a magistrate overnight, O'Neil asked to be taken straight to where the company stored their mainframe computer hardware. Excitement radiated from her. Ryan felt the adrenalin pumping too. They were after a link between Claesson and the Russian oil company AMKL-Exploration Inc., preferably one that involved Vladimir Pirotsky.

His family were anxiously waiting for news in Moscow.

The receptionist handed back the warrant, stood up and asked them to follow her to the second floor. They were about to pass through double doors at the top of the stairs when Ryan's mobile rang. O'Neil stopped walking, turned to face him, nodding her permission for him to take the call.

He listened for a moment and then hung up. 'Technical support, guv. They'll be at reception in five. They're asking to be met and allowed in. You want to go down and wait or shall I handle it?'

'Go ahead,' she said. 'Bring them up. I need them to examine the servers.'

Turning on his heels, Ryan retraced his steps and disappeared. O'Neil noticed a maintenance man arriving in the corridor ahead. The receptionist ordered him to take her to the room where the servers were kept and left them to it.

O'Neil was shown into a windowless, air-conditioned room with a bank of electrical equipment along one wall and not a lot else. The server racks were extensive, about the size of a large fridge freezer. Inside were thick metal trays – each with its own hard-drive slot. On some of the equipment, lights flashed as data was transferred. Knowing little about technology beyond what she'd learned at school, she assumed the apparatus worked much like her hub at home, albeit a giant version.

She looked around for a place to sit.

'I'll need four chairs and another table I can shove together with that one if you can manage it.' She flicked her eyes to a table in the centre of the room, before switching her attention to the electronics. 'Given that we can't take this lot away, we might be here a while.'

'You look like you mean business,' her escort said.

A foreign voice.

O'Neil was suddenly wary, eager to get rid of her escort. As he moved away, she ran her eyes over him. He was a big bugger with a dimple in his chin, brown eyes and hair in a style that was close to an American crew cut. A bit of a thug. Not someone she'd care to meet on a dark night. She observed him lean over the desk in order to lift extra chairs from a stack in the corner. As he reached out, his shirtsleeves rode up, revealing a Swedish flag tattoo on his right forearm and bruises to his knuckles.

Claesson.

An attempt to hide her growing anxiety was met with a hostile glare. He looked like he could kill with one punch and she had no backup.

'I'll get you that table,' he grunted.

'Thanks.' She tried for cool, urging Ryan to hurry.

O'Neil shut her eyes, exhaling in relief as he disappeared, trying to quell her fears. She needed to warn Ryan that the man who'd just left the room could well be Jack's killer. Fumbling to find her phone, she had second thoughts. What if he returned and caught her in the act? Ryan and others would be along any second.

Better to wait and stay calm . . .

Maybe she was imagining what wasn't there . . .

Maybe . . .

The lights dimmed and went out. Fearing the worst, O'Neil began to panic, inching her way to the door as the fire alarm kicked in. The noise was deafening but it would alert Ryan and he'd come looking for her. Using her phone, she lit her way to the door and tried the handle. It wouldn't budge.

What the fuck?!?

The Swede wouldn't need to punch her. Her hands shook as she scrolled through her address book for Ryan's number, using her free hand to cover one ear. *Thank God! It was ringing.*

The explosion blew out the windows in reception. Along with everyone else, Ryan had been marshalled through the front door to an assembly point at the side of the building. The phone in his hand stopped ringing: *O'Neil.* He looked around, expecting to see her waving her hand above the walking wounded, hoping she'd been led out another way.

He scanned shocked faces.

She was nowhere in sight.

When he heard another loud bang, he froze, heart banging in his chest. He stepped back, helping a woman in distress. And still he couldn't see O'Neil. A ceiling inside the building collapsed in a thunderous crash, sending plumes of dust high into the air. From his position in the street, he could feel the intense heat burning his skin. Suddenly, the alarm stopped and there was a deathly hush.

The explosion had thrown O'Neil across the room with such force that it knocked her out cold. When she came to she was groggy and choking, small pockets of fire all around her. More worrying was the fact that one of the server monitors had caught fire and was popping and sparking, ready to blow. The flame from the fires gave her light – the wrong sort – and her mobile was nowhere to be seen in the debris.

'Ryan!'

She listened, relaxing as she heard the sound of running feet. In her head, she saw him charging at the door, taking it off its hinges, but then realized that the footsteps were moving away and not approaching. Stunned from being blown off her feet, she tried to get up. Pain shot up her right leg and hip. Her ankle was broken. The sight of bone sticking through the skin made her vomit.

Terror gripped Ryan by the throat, sending him into a spin, recurring nightmares jockeying for space in his head: his father lying on a filthy carpet of a drug dealer's den, bleeding from a knife wound; Jack on his deathbed; the torment on his kids' faces when they heard he was dead.

What was that?

Had he imagined it?

No, there it was again . . .

O'Neil's voice, faint and far away . . .

She was calling his name.

A male voice pulled Ryan from the abyss. He turned to find the TSG team leader, a horrified look on his face and that of his crew. The building was well alight.

'Two seats of fire,' one of them noticed. 'Top and bottom floors.'

'Deliberate,' someone else said. 'No doubt about it.'

'Jesus Christ!' Ryan's voice sounded muffled. His ears hadn't yet recovered from the blast. 'We need to get in there!'

The heat was intense. No one could get near the entrance without flameproof clothing for protection. Ryan raced round the side of the building, hoping to find another way in. 'Eloise!' he yelled up at the second floor. 'Guv, can you hear me?'

Nothing.

A fire engine screeched to a halt in the lane running alongside. As firefighters piled out and got to work, their crew manager emerged with his distinctive yellow helmet, advising him to move away.

'I'm police.' Ryan held up ID. 'You have one tender?'

'Stand back!' The crew manager yelled. 'Our lads are stowed off. I sent for reinforcements; ETA five minutes. There's a massive fire at a paint manufacturer on the Team Valley.'

'What? You must have contingency plans.'

The fireman's eyes were hard. 'Move it and let my lads do their jobs—'

'My boss is frying in there.'

They both ducked as part of the roof fell in, sending tiles crashing to the floor just metres away.

'I need a torch,' Ryan said.

The fireman shook his head. 'No way.'

'Hand me a fucking torch or I'm going in without one.'

*

Stay close to the floor. Deep in the interior, O'Neil could hardly see. Covering her mouth with a fragment of her blouse she found on the floor next to her, she tried calling out but her voice was gone. She'd never be heard. Even if she'd been able to stand, she knew she couldn't open the door. There was a small gap under it, smoke creeping in and curling up the walls. She could see a fire raging in the corridor beyond. *Stay close to the floor.* The problem was, the wooden floor beneath her was getting hot. Downstairs must be well alight.

A couple of ambulances arrived. Ryan looked up as the vibration and sound of rotor blades caught his attention. India 99, the police helicopter, had arrived, its down-draught whipping smoke around, sending debris flying everywhere. It hovered for several seconds, surveying the damage before touching down on a playing field a couple of hundred metres upwind of the burning building, a much safer distance with aviation fuel on board. Ryan was scared but knew he couldn't wait any longer. Despite a natural desire to get the hell out of there before the whole lot went up, he knew he had to run towards the fire and not away from it. He couldn't leave Eloise.

He won't leave me. Not Ryan. I'll be fine. Stay awake and breathe. O'Neil coughed, the smoke searing the back of her throat. She thought she heard him calling out to her, then the sound faded away like in a nightmare. Out of reach. Unattainable. One panel of equipment in the corner of the room was like a giant torch, flames belching out the top, reaching the height of the room. Then she saw it. Smoke drifting through a crack in the ceiling. The plaster was sagging and stretching, the crack elongating until a gaping hole appeared. Her eyes widened as the gap opened up and the beam began to fall, down and down, almost in slow motion. *Please, Ryan, don't leave me. I'm here . . . right here.* And then everything faded to black like a movie screen.

Dousing his clothing with water, Ryan somehow made his way to where he'd left O'Neil at the top of the stairwell. Fortunately for him, water was pouring into the building through a hole in the roof. Wrapping his hand in a wet cardigan he'd pulled from a chair on the ground floor, he opened doors, yelling for O'Neil as he made his way down the corridor. He found one that was locked. On it, a partially melted sign he could just make it out: **NOTICE**: NO ADMITTANCE TO SERVER ROOM WITHOUT AUTHORIZATION.

Ryan kicked it in. 'Eloise!'

O'Neil was lying on the ground, not moving. A beam had fallen, missing her by inches. It was smouldering and near enough to set alight her hair and clothing. Her motionless body reminded him of Newman lying in the road a few days ago outside a grotty pub on the edge of an industrial estate – a near disaster. Difference was, he'd got up. She wasn't moving.

'Eloise!' He pleaded with her to do the same.

No response.

The debris in front of him was too hot to touch. He

took a step backwards and vaulted over it, picking his way across the blackened room towards her. He managed, with great difficulty, to lift her off the floor, yanking her up by the arms.

'Watch out!' A fireman yelled from behind him.

There was a whooshing sound as a huge piece of the ceiling rushed past Ryan's ear, smashing into pieces as it hit the ground, right where O'Neil had been lying. She coughed once, her eyes rolling back in her head. He heard himself telling her she'd be fine – he was getting her out of there – his voice cracking as he spoke the words. Tears rolled down his face, partly caused by the smoke, mostly from sorrow. He couldn't stomach losing another colleague. Not so soon after Jack. Not ever. O'Neil was choking in his arms. She seemed to draw one last breath, a huge gulp of poisonous gas, then she was gone again, her whole body limp and lifeless.

70

Three people lost their lives at Claesson Logistics. Fortunately, Ryan and O'Neil were not among them. The site had been secured and was being treated as a crime scene: murder and arson with intent to endanger life just two more crimes to add to a growing list of offences on the charge sheet.

Ryan sat ashen-faced in the conference room, the Northumbria Police logo at his back, a hastily prepared press release lying on the table before him. Glancing at his watch, he wondered how Eloise was doing. He'd totally lost it yesterday as a paramedic resuscitated her on the ground before she was flown by police helicopter to hospital in a race to save her life. Later, he'd rushed to her side – as she had his a week ago – remaining at the hospital until she was out of surgery and no longer in danger, only leaving when he was sure she was going to make a full recovery. In time, her leg would heal. The rest? Nothing a good night's sleep wouldn't fix, according to the doctor treating her.

Sitting with Ryan was his Chief Constable, in full dress uniform, as well as representatives of the emergency teams: fire, ambulance, air support. Also Northumbria's HR manager, less switched on than Karin Ullman, the alert member of QiOil staff who'd helped the investigation more than she would ever know.

Her commendation would come later.

Out front, members of the press were squashed like sardines, pens at the ready, in competition to submit their copy before the next deadline. Someone called for order and the conference got underway. Ryan dropped his head as the Chief hailed him a hero, infuriating him by referencing his father's death on duty, for no other reason than to drive home the risks all policemen and women face every day of their working lives, and make himself look good.

His showboating soundbites were ignored when someone had the effrontery to open the door, interrupting him mid-flow. Heads turned to see who was arriving. Ryan lifted his and smiled as O'Neil was brought in by wheelchair. Behind her, Maguire pushed out his chest, like the real hero of the hour. It was *his* picture that would appear in every newspaper and on every TV screen for the foreseeable future. Ryan stifled a grin, locking eyes with Eloise, that special something passing between them.

Thank you, she mimed.

Corporate manslaughter charges against AMKL were ongoing. Litigation would run and run, possibly for years yet. A fine of billions was on the cards following huge compensation claims from relatives who'd lost loved ones: Oliver's wife for sure, as well as the parents, partners and next of kin of the other twenty-five oil workers who'd lost their lives in two avoidable disasters brought about by greed. Thankfully, because of Jack's obsession with his brother's death and the bravery and integrity of Norwegian and Russian engineers, a third would be prevented. The very least that would happen was that safety for oil employees would be revisited and tightened up.

Jack's solicitor, Paul Godfrey, had demanded financial recompense for Hilary and the children, as had lawyers acting for Hilde Freberg in Norway. They were already making progress with claims in the pipeline. Sadly, the situation relating to Vladimir Pirotsky's wife in Moscow was unclear. The engineer was the subject of a missing-persons file. In Ryan's mind, there was little doubt that he was dead. Hopefully, one day, his body would be found.

The Norway trip had been so much more than a police investigation. More too than amazing open spaces, pretty houses surrounded by water and lush green forests. It had cemented a relationship between two coppers Ryan felt sure would stand the test of time. Certain that Anders Freberg had been murdered to shut him up, Politioverbetjent Eva Nystrom had vowed to do all she could to prove it. It's always difficult to establish if someone fell or was pushed, but a close-up CCTV image from Torp airport proved that Hans Claesson was in the country at the time. Besides, Knut Svendsen was still keen to impress Eloise O'Neil.

May the best man win.

Hans Claesson and Michael James Foxton's Not Guilty pleas were laughable. They had managed to destroy much evidence, but Hilary had picked them out in an ID parade. She'd always said she'd recognize them if she saw them again, and that proved to be the case. Added to the testimony of Brian Platt, Claesson's DNA from the ice-house and the intelligence-gathering from Russian police who'd raided AMKL-Exploration Inc., there was enough to convict. The life sentences handed down meant little to Ryan; Claesson and Foxton had taken away the best friend he ever had. Nothing could make up for that.

Jack Fenwick was buried with full police honours with a Union Jack draped over his coffin, his old uniform hat on top of a discreet, simple white wreath. Stoical, proud, and close to tears, Hilary held Ryan's hand at the graveside. Behind them, Grace clasped Newman's arm, weeping openly. Jack was the son she'd never had, but her life as a spinster was about to come to an end. Newman had finally proposed. On one condition, he told Ryan: that she agreed a move to Scotland's east coast to live by the sea. Ryan approved. He looked forward to visiting them there.

He glanced along the beach near his home, where a young man was skimming stones on the water. The scene reminded him of the start to that Indian summer. Three days after the fire and explosion at Claesson Logistics, he'd driven O'Neil to his place, her broken ankle still in a cage. As they travelled north, he'd talked about the one un-answered question that had been bothering him: the blanket fibres found in Jack's car.

He hated loose ends.

Turning into the courtyard behind his tiny cottage, the sight of the vehicle kicked him in the guts, taking his breath away. It was heartbreaking to see it parked there, the tailgate up, Caroline's guide dog asleep in the rear.

The answer came to him in a flash.

With O'Neil sitting next to him, Ryan tried hard to stem his reaction but it was impossible. His eyes had filled with tears he'd held on to for far too long. It was the moment he finally realized the case was over.

He shut his eyes, feeling the winter sun on his face, O'Neil's voice pushing its way into his head . . .

'*So* obvious,' she'd said under her breath. Keeping her eyes fixed on Jack's car, affording Ryan time to get his shit together, she waited. He got out, walked round the car and opened her door. She wasn't about to let him get maudlin. 'So Jack was in the habit of airing his car after taking Caroline and Bob out. Simple really. Anyone passing could've deposited those fibres.' She lifted her good leg out. 'Call yourself a detective? No wonder Roz went back to Maguire.'

'Ouch!' Ryan didn't dare look at her.

'Now will you stop going on about how the bloody fibres got there? It's a compelling explanation. How come you didn't think of it?'

'I have no idea.' Helping her from the car, he narrowed his eyes as he handed over her crutches. 'Like you'd have believed me if I had.'

''Fess up, DS Ryan.' She hooked the crutches under her arms. 'You're not firing on all cylinders. Admit it. You don't have the know-how.' She was trying not to laugh. 'I may have to reconsider that job offer after all.'

'You giving me the brush-off?'

'Might be.'

He locked the car. 'If I'm in the doghouse, don't bother, I'll bail.'

'Don't you dare!'

She'd stopped hobbling by the time Caroline, Hilary and her two youngest came out of the yard to greet them, Lucy running ahead and leaping into Ryan's arms. They had tidied up the mess from the burglary and lunch was already in a picnic basket, ready for the off. They walked down the road together.

Opening his eyes, Ryan glanced along the beach, the memory receding. It was time to let go. He'd never forget Jack while he was looking out for his son. They were so alike. As great white waves pounded the shore, Robbie Fenwick looked up and smiled. They continued skimming stones . . .

Acknowledgements

I'm thrilled to be celebrating my first standalone, *The Silent Room*. From the outset, my agent Oli Munson (AM Heath) and publisher Wayne Brookes (Pan Macmillan) were passionate about publishing this thriller. Collaborating with them is always a pleasure. Their love of crime fiction is what drives me to raise the bar with every book.

I have many others to thank: an ace editorial team; my wonderful publicist, Philippa McEwan; a talented art department; sales and marketing staff too numerous to mention individually. As always, I'm enormously grateful to my editor, Anne O'Brien, who manages to make it all look so easy.

I'd also like to acknowledge friends and followers on social media and the army of booksellers and readers who have helped and supported me along the way. Your positivity is infectious. It makes the hard yards seem less onerous somehow.

This book is dedicated to two special people. My brother Rob, who shared technical expertise and insight into a world I knew very little about. I can't tell you what it is. It would be a major spoiler! And Marit, my sister-in-law, whose patience and help with all things Norwegian, linguistically and geographically, brought parts of this book alive for me. Returning to Norway (even in my head) reminded me of why I love the country so much.

To the best family a writer could ever have: my mum, Marie; Paul and Kate; Chris and Jodie; Max, Frances and Mo. During the writing of this book there were times when I missed you all so much. Thanks for putting up with my imaginings. It's safe to unlock the door now.